# REMNANT

### Katie Sweeting

RESOURCE Publications · Eugene, Oregon

REMNANT

Copyright © 2024 Katie Sweeting. All rights reserved. Except for brief quotations in critical publications or reviews, no part of this book may be reproduced in any manner without prior written permission from the publisher. Write: Permissions, Wipf and Stock Publishers, 199 W. 8th Ave., Suite 3, Eugene, OR 97401.

Resource Publications
An Imprint of Wipf and Stock Publishers
199 W. 8th Ave., Suite 3
Eugene, OR 97401

www.wipfandstock.com

PAPERBACK ISBN: 979-8-3852-0371-0
HARDCOVER ISBN: 979-8-3852-0372-7
EBOOK ISBN: 979-8-3852-0373-4

Library of Congress Control Number: 2024900906

01/23/24

"Since She Whom I Loved," Holy Sonnet XVII, by John Dunne
Romans 5:1 KJV
Plaque dedicated to Anna Maria Vassa at Saint Andrew's Church, Chesterton, England, UK.
"I Saw Three Ships" https://en.wikipedia.org/wiki/I_Saw_Three_Ships

Any references to historical events, real people, or real places are used fictitiously. Names, characters, and places are products of the author's imagination.

www.katiesweeting.com

To
Mom and Dad
Bill
Caroline

# Contents

| | |
|---|---|
| Olu's storyline | ix |
| Joanna's storyline | x |
| Prologue—Olu's story | 1 |
| Chapter One: Olu | 3 |
| Prologue—Joanna's story | 17 |
| Chapter Two: Joanna | 19 |
| Chapter Three: Olu | 32 |
| Chapter Four: Joanna | 40 |
| Chapter Five: Olu | 52 |
| Chapter Six: Joanna | 61 |
| Chapter Seven: Olu | 69 |
| Chapter Eight: Joanna | 76 |
| Chapter Nine: Olu | 84 |
| Chapter Ten: Joanna | 95 |
| Chapter Eleven: Olu | 103 |
| Chapter Twelve: Joanna | 112 |
| Chapter Thirteen: Olu | 125 |
| Chapter Fourteen: Joanna | 139 |
| Chapter Fifteen: Olu | 153 |
| Chapter Sixteen: Joanna | 165 |
| Chapter Seventeen: Olu | 177 |
| Chapter Eighteen: Joanna | 189 |
| Chapter Nineteen: Olu | 199 |

| | |
|---|---|
| Chapter Twenty: Joanna | 216 |
| Chapter Twenty-One: Olu | 231 |
| Chapter Twenty-Two: Joanna | 244 |
| Epilogue: Joanna | 262 |
| *Fact or Fiction?* | 263 |
| *Author's Note* | 265 |
| *Acknowledgments* | 267 |
| *Helpful Books* | 269 |
| *Book Club Questions* | 271 |

# Olu's storyline

*Oluchukwu (Olu) Equiano\** (Olivia)
*Olaudah (Ledu) Equiano*—1745-1797*
Teddy Cross
Theodosia (Sadie) Cross
Samuel Cross—plantation owner
Beth Cross—Samuel's wife
Susannah Cross—Samuel's daughter
Noah—tutor to Susannah
Lydia and Thaddeus Cross

*Enslaved people on Cross Plantation*:
Suraya (Sarah)
Martha –cook
Mary –maid
Geoffrey –butler
Samson and Maybell
Capt'n Thomas—pilot
Jones—driver in charge of rice fields
Nathaniel—boat pilot
Will, Ambrose, Letty

*Escape to the British side*:
Chogun & Etchemin—Native Americans
*Lord Dunmore - governor of Virginia**
Sue and June- freed slaves on ship
Captain Williams—on Dunmore's ship
Daniel—freed slave

# Joanna's storyline

*Joanna Vassa Bromley*—1795–1757*
*Rev. Henry Bromley*—1798–1878*
*Anne Cullen*—Joanna's grandmother*
*Catherine Bromley*—Henry's sister*
Fredrik—African barber
*John Audley*—guardian*
Jane Audley—John Audley's sister
Simon Farmer—butler to Mr. Audley
Annie Farmer—cook to Mr. Audley
Richard Blake–manservant to Mr. Audley
Deirdre—Irish assistant cook/hairdresser
*William Wilberforce and his wife Barbara, and children: William, Barbara, Lizzy, Robert, Samuel, Henry*
*Zachary and Selina Macaulay*
Mrs. Limebear—school headmistress
Mr. Harding—teacher at the school
Maisie—maid of all work at the school
Girls at Mrs. Limebear's: Miranda, Anne Knight*, Candace, Rose, Violet, and Samantha
Bridgett—maid/cook
Sushila & Captain Welbourne—Clavering
Mrs. O'Neil—son Abner—Clavering

*Historical characters

# Prologue—Olu's story

AFRICAN GIRLS ARE PRODUCTIVE. We trade goods and manage households. We grow cassava and nurture palm fruit kernels. We share our men and teach our boys. African girls are fearless. We climb trees and scale walls. We start fires and train as warriors. Nothing phases us . . . except kidnappers. This is my story, one more African girl snatched from home, carted across a continent, thrown on a slave ship, and deposited on the shores of America. My story is unique, yet universal; distinctive, yet representative; mine alone, and belonging to all the other African girls who due to terror, illiteracy, or death, cannot tell their own stories.

My husband urged me to write this memoir based on my journals. I am neither the most virtuous or educated, nor have I suffered more than most of my fellow Africans. I tell it so others will know what we suffered—a warning and a plea. I'm Oluchukwu—call me Olu.

Looking back over the years, I remember the little kindnesses and the monumental sacrifices. Miss Martha making my favorite dish, and Teddy teaching me to read. The years I spent at the Cross Plantation seemed endless, yet when they ended it was almost as though I went from Africa to New York with nothing in between.

I wasn't inclined to pick up my pen, but my husband can be very persuasive. For the past three years I have pieced together memories, journals, lists, and letters. I will attempt to do justice to those who helped me along the way, and not eviscerate those who abused or stymied me.

I can picture my mama and papa, and my brothers; Suraya; Susannah, Mrs. Beth and Mr. Cross; Samson, Ambrose, and Thomas; Daniel; Teddy. All of them impacted my life and in some ways, made me who I am today. I don't know what happened to most of them, and I don't know what will happen to me tomorrow. I have my memories, my story, and today.

Bear with me as I relate some of the incidents of my life. I never thought of myself as a slave, even when I was a slave. I'm just an African girl—a fearless (sometimes) African girl.
New York City, America, September 1781

# CHAPTER ONE

## Olu

### October 1753—Igboland

I AWOKE IN THE arms of my brother. The hard ground dug into my hip, and I snuggled closer to him, trying to block out the memory of our kidnapping many suns ago. I still missed my mama and papa, and even my bothersome older brothers. Even though I am eleven, older than Ledu, he has always been my protector—I have always looked up to him, but especially now.

This is how it happened. We were at home—Mama was down by the water hole and Papa out hunting. Our brothers were in the fields, and Ledu and I kept watch over the house.

"Ledu, let's play Ayo," I said.

"I'll beat you!" Ledu said.

"I don't think so."

Ledu found the small stones we used for the game and distributed them evenly in two parallel rows of eight dug-out holes on the ground. A nearby goat bleated loudly.

"Don't you need to milk the goat, Olu?"

"Not yet. You're trying to distract me. I'm first." I dropped my handful of stones in strategic holes. Ledu went next, and I couldn't tell what his strategy was. Three moves later, I was winning.

"Well, it looks like I'm winning THIS time," I said.

"A na-ekwu ekwu, a na-eme eme," Ledu said (talk the talk, walk the walk).

"I'm talking," I moved the last of his stones over to my side, "and your stones are walking!"

"You got lucky," Ledu said. I smiled at him, and my eyes drifted up . . . and stopped. Ledu swung around to see what I was looking at—a strange man and woman. Before we could cry out, the man clasped his calloused, dirty hands on our skinny arms as the woman tied a dirty gray rag across my mouth and around the back of my head, forcing my tongue to the back of my throat, and then did the same to Ledu. I inched my tongue up over the disgusting rag, breathing heavily through my nose. I closed my eyes, hoping it was just a bad dream, but when I opened them, I gagged on the rag in my mouth. As I choked, the woman snatched the rag off and slapped me across the face, initiating a bout of vomiting.

She snarled at me in a language I could barely decipher, her chin went up and lips puckered up to point to the man. She spoke in a different dialect, but I understood the meaning—don't be stupid; listen to him.

The woman wore a cloth with a hideous pattern in purple and red. Older than mama, every part of her sagged—her eyes, her breasts, her arms, her mouth. The man's face was slashed with scars, horizontal lines stretching from his nose to his ears. He had small lips and a big nose. His hairline started almost in the middle of his head, revealing a protruding, bumpy forehead. He grunted and said something in low, angry tones to the woman. He speared us with dull, angry eyes; in my terror I wet myself. I squeezed my legs together and gritted my teeth to keep from crying or screaming.

I looked at Ledu. His wide, unblinking eyes urged me to be calm. I gazed at him as tears slid down my cheeks. Ledu bowed his head in silent petition.

Once they tied my legs together with a dark, heavy rope, they did the same to Ledu and then fastened another rope around our waists and bound us together. I was content to be tied to my brother if it meant we would not be separated. Then the man pulled us up to our feet and yanked us to the path. He took us straight to the nearest opening in the compound wall, avoiding the only one of my father's wives nearby. I saw the smoke rising from the fire pit in front of her house, an unheeded warning signal—*Danger, Kidnapping in progress.* I wanted to scream, but didn't, and then it was too late. We were down the road . . . the road that led out of the village.

It was after midday when we were taken, and we walked until dark. Rocks and pebbles lay in a haphazard pattern across the path, impossible

## CHAPTER ONE: OLU

to avoid. My bare feet sprouted blisters, bubbling up and oozing. My stomach rumbled in hunger, but most of all I was thirsty. At first, we passed familiar landmarks—the path to the river, the road to the next compound, the tree where lookouts would perch to warn off trespassers. Our kidnappers didn't lead us near any of the other family compounds in our village but stayed close to the small river. The village spread out like a hand with six fingers. Our family compound was the biggest, as papa was the lead elder of the village. His three wives each had a house, and he lived in a house in the center. There were also separate houses for cooking and for animals. A wall of mud and dung surrounded the compound, protecting it from wild animals and unwelcome guests . . . usually. The six other families in the village each had their own compounds, with a similar layout, spread out surrounding our compound.

I guess no one saw us as we left, and soon we were beyond the village, in unfamiliar territory. The trees were taller, and the riverbed was dry. The path along the riverbed inclined and I saw other hills and valleys ahead. The sun's relentless heat, in a cloudless sky, triggered the perspiration that rolled down my forehead and back. My mouth felt as dry as the riverbed. The ugly pair knew the land, as they skirted flocks of cattle or goats, and avoided contact with people. They had likely scouted out our village before. Soon we were farther than Ledu or I had ever been. The path we were on widened. Shrubs and palm trees lined the path, and we could hear, and occasionally see, a stray hog or a pack of hyenas.

I stepped on a small rock and stumbled, bringing Ledu down on top of me. The man immediately jerked us upright, slapping me across the face as Ledu winced in sympathetic pain. My heart sped up and I tried to focus on the path—not my home, not my mama, not my brothers, not my rumbling stomach. Just one foot in front of the other. At least I had Ledu.

We stopped abruptly, long after the sun had set. The woman laid a thin cloth on the hard ground, underneath a fruitless udara tree, and shoved Ledu and me down. She thrust a dirty gourd at us, with only enough water to make me even thirstier, and then gave Ledu and me each half a yam. I could tell it was old and past ripe, like a dried-up, emaciated cow, but I ate it anyway, skin and all. Ledu shook his head and made a face, but I thrust my chin and lips out, motioning him to eat. Our first day ever away from our family ended with blistered feet, nearly empty stomachs, and pounding heads. A cool breeze blew through the trees, and Ledu and I held each other, laid out side by side on the thin blanket, on the hard ground, far from home. We looked up at the sky, the one familiar sight, and found the lion killer, the chief, the cooking pot, and the winning Ayo board sparkling in their starry patterns.

"Ledu?" I whispered.

"Olu, hush, they'll hear us."

"They're sleeping already. Let's run back."

"We're tied together, and our feet are tied together, Olu. How far could we get?"

"It's worth a try. Right?" I willed Ledu to agree with me.

"I don't think so. We don't even know which way is home." Ledu propped himself up on his elbows and looked around.

"Hmmm. Wasn't that yam awful?" I grimaced.

"The worst. My stomach hurts. I really miss Mama's stew."

"I really miss Mama." I reached out to hold Ledu's hand.

"Me, too."

Holding hands, side by side, hips pressed into the unyielding ground, we gazed at our favorite stars until sleep came.

Many days and nights followed that first day. We began to walk at night and sleep during the day. The water supplies increased as we passed lakes and rivers in a more fertile area. The trees were smaller, but greener, and the river was much wider than the one near our home. The water ran quickly and noisily over the rocks, calling to us—come and swim, come and play. As we walked, night after night, I forced myself to think pleasant thoughts. I had been a happy girl, and why not? My mama and papa were kind to me, especially as I was the only girl in the family. I didn't have many hard chores to do, and my brothers treated me like a queen. We always had plenty of food to eat, and I had friends to play with.

After we were kidnapped, I began to have nightmares. I relived our kidnapping every night, sensing the hard rope cutting into my wrists, feeling the urine wetting my leg, and seeing the man's slashed face. The images and impressions stayed with me when I awoke. I started wetting myself at night, something I had never done before. I dreamed of mama and papa but woke in the arms of my brother. I talked less and less and smiled not at all. I ate simply to relieve the stomach pains.

After many suns had risen and set, the ugly man and mean woman sold us to an African chief for a goat. The chief and his wives spoke a language like ours, and soon we felt a bit less frightened.

Our joy was brief.

One day a short, heavyset man came into the village. He approached the chief, and as we sat outside by the fire, we overheard their conversation.

"How much you pay for this pair?" the chief asked the short man.

"I don't want the girl. I'll give you this musket for the boy," he said, looking at Ledu.

"One musket? Make it two and we have a deal," the chief responded.

While they were bargaining, I said to Ledu, "He doesn't want both of us."

"We go together, Olu; he'll have to take us both."

"Where do you think we're going?" I asked.

"I don't know. But at night I've been keeping track. We've gone nine moons towards the lion killer in the sky. If we're separated, keep looking up. When you get a chance, make a run for it. Follow the lion killer."

"I wish a lion would kill him." I glared at the short man.

"Olu!" Ledu remonstrated.

"Quit talking," the chief said. "You're going with him. Get along." The chief pushed Ledu towards the short man. The short man grabbed him and started walking away.

"Take me, too!" I cried.

"I don't need a girl," the short man said, glancing back at me, then he kept walking.

"I'll be good. I promise," I called out.

But the short man kept on walking. Ledu looked back at me, and I fell on the ground, crying silently. Ledu. Ledu. What am I going to do without you??

The sun rose and set. I ticked off the days, and when I reached twenty-four, I gave up hope of ever seeing Ledu or the rest of my family again.

I was sold again, and this time I stayed in the new family compound for several days with my master's daughters. My new master was kinder than the chief and had three wives and more than ten children. His name was Ndungi and the wife who looked after me was called Uduo. I stayed in a simple house made of mud and branches, with Uduo's three daughters.

The chief's daughter Maliki and I communicated with some difficulty as our dialects were quite different. After a few tries, we were able to get our meaning across. She asked me where I was from and I told her the name of our village, Olututuopuok.

Maliki asked me how I ended up in her village. Neither of us had a word for *kidnapped* in our vocabulary, but I managed to express to her what had happened to us using words and gestures. When I explained how I had been separated from Ledu, Maliki assured me her father would help. She said he was a chief with power. I thought about my own father, also a kind of chief, but he couldn't prevent Ledu and I from being kidnapped. I also wondered how her father would use his power.

Maliki thought on that for a moment. She was a beautiful girl—short hair, a small, slightly flattened nose, expressive large brown eyes, and a full mouth. She wore a green and black cloth draped over one shoulder, tied in a knot under her left breast, barely beginning to swell. She spoke so confidently; at the time I was very reassured. I was treated almost like one of Ndungi's daughters, although my mat was smaller, I had no blanket, and the portions of food I received were sparse.

Maliki asked me who was there when we were taken. I told her it was just Ledu and me as Papa was hunting and Mama out washing. My mind went back to my last happy moment, beating Ledu at Ayo, laughing at him.

She told me her papa never allows the children to be alone. Maliki pointed to the other houses and the thorn branch fence. There were two houses for the chief's wives, a cooking house, and a hut where the chickens and goats stayed at night. The fifth house was the largest—the chief's own house. All the houses lay in a circle, surrounding the center area where the wives gathered with their babies, wove baskets, cooked over a fire pit, and talked.

Maliki told me, "Girls stay here or go to river with the women. Boys stay with men. Girls are never alone."

I began to wonder why Papa left Ledu and me alone. Papa always did the right thing. He was a wise man—all the men in the village came to him to settle disputes. Was it wrong for him to . . . no. Papa was right. Maliki didn't know everything. I was convinced her papa could not help me. He was not a good man like Papa. He gave those kidnappers a goat—and I was his. For a goat? Not even a cow? I smiled to myself, remembering something my mama used to say to me. "You are worth all the cattle in Igboland." Then tears began to flow, blurring the vision of mama.

Maliki frowned. "Why do you cry?"

"I miss Mama," I said, through my tears.

Still frowning, Maliki leaned over and hugged me—rocking me like a baby. "Don't worry. Don't cry. Papa will help."

Maliki was some comfort to me, but whenever I thought of Ledu or Mama, all I wanted to do was lie down, curl up, sleep, and dream of home.

Three days later Ndungi, Maliki's very helpful father, sold me to a traveling slaver for a calf. At least it was a calf. I didn't want to wake up in the morning. I was afraid, but more than that, I didn't care anymore what happened to me.

One afternoon I was taken to a house, and to my astonishment and great delight, Ledu was there.

"Ledu!! Oh, Ledu," I cried out, running to him.

Ledu hugged me and held me back to look at me.

"You okay, Olu? How're they treating you?"

"I'm okay. Thirty-two. I've been counting," I said.

When it was time to go to sleep, the man who *bought* me lay between us, but Ledu and I still managed to hold hands over his chest. I slept well for the first time since we had been separated. But in the morning I was taken away and Ledu left behind. No volume of tears swayed the slaveholder.

Months later, I had long since stopped counting the days, after being traded from one master to another, and walking farther and farther from home as I could tell by the changing night sky, I saw a body of water so vast I couldn't see the end of it, frightening, yet beautiful, and awe inspiring. I had never seen a body of water so blue, immense, and endless. I could throw a pebble clear across the watering hole and not cause a splash. This, this was like a lake with no shore, a river with no banks—it seemed to contain all the water in the world. I couldn't look away. It approached, and I briefly hoped it would swallow me up. I think now of all the bodies of water I have seen and traveled across, but nothing stopped my heart like that first glance at the ocean.

As I stood gazing at the limitless water, a pale man with stringy long brown hair came over and dragged me to a fenced-in area where other children were chained together in a line. He looked unnatural. The only light-skinned people I had seen were albinos, but their features were still African. This man had a long nose and thin lips—he looked sick. I couldn't stop staring at him, but I couldn't bear to look at him.

I was chained to another girl, who spoke an unknown dialect, so we couldn't communicate. The hard, stiff chain hurt my wrists, worse even than the ropes to which I had become accustomed.

Children were whimpering and crying, and women were wailing in a variety of tongues—none of which I understood. Some were wordless moans in the language of grief words cannot harness. I had never seen such a despairing group of Africans in my life. We hadn't been fed and didn't know what was coming next, so the girl to whom I was chained and I sat down on the ground together. Although we didn't speak the same language, I soon learned her name was Biba—the name was longer but too difficult to remember or pronounce—she was thirteen.

I searched the motley crowd looking for Ledu. I saw others looking, longing for their loved ones, but hopeless stares soon replaced hopeful searching gazes. At some point I fell asleep. I rested my head on Biba's shoulder and tried to forget where I was.

Night passed. I awoke with a pounding heart as I saw a large, floating house sitting atop the water near where we were kept. I had seen canoes, but never floating houses like this. How did it stay on top of the water when it was so big, I wondered? What kind of magical spirits did these ugly pale men employ?

Men were shouting and pushing us up a flimsy wooden board and onto the floating house.

"What's happening? Where are we going?" I tried to ask, but no one near me spoke my language. Biba, a few inches taller and much heavier than I, didn't seem alarmed—I gripped my new friend's hand harder.

Men hurried about pulling off the clothes or cloths covering us and throwing them in a pile on the deck. A tall, heavy man with a hairy, reddish face grabbed a long brown snake, and water came out of the end of it! He sprayed us with water that hit us like hail pellets. I was never more embarrassed or humiliated in my life—standing naked while the men stared dispassionately at me, a girl, not yet a woman, with no womanly features to cover. The hard water felt like pebbles thrown at me, hurting my skin, the reason I would give for my tears if anyone asked why I cried. Just thinking about it now makes me yearn to cover myself.

Given the chance to grab something to wear out of the pile, I ended up with a cloth that barely covered me—not my own. A man pushed us roughly down the broken ladder below decks where no natural light or fresh sea air reached us.

The accommodations below might befit a few gaunt goats, but not men and women, nor even boys and girls. The bunks were about two feet wide and five feet long, dozens of wooden planks side by side, with one layer stretching across one side of the hold, and one layer on the other side—like rows of Ayo boards with holes not big enough for stones. Then another layer stretched out on top. We were laid out side by side, with no room to move, squished up against strangers.

# CHAPTER ONE: OLU

Though we were surrounded by water, I was always thirsty. It was a kind of thirst I'd never experienced before—deep and unquenchable. Even when given a small amount to drink, it only made me want more. The drink only reminded me of what I was still missing, never enough to satisfy, only enough to enlarge my thirst. I soon looked forward to eating the inedible liquid that passed as soup, as it placated my dry mouth.

I watched as a mother gave all her soup to her son. She handed a cup of soup to her son and prodded him to eat it. He was younger than I, probably nine or ten years old. The mother was already thin, her arms like sugar cane stalks. She wore a faded black cloth wrapped around her head, a ripped tan cloth on her body, and a colorful bracelet, traded to a sailor early in the journey in exchange for, well, being left alone.

She coaxed him to take another sip. He pushed the cup back to her, urging her to eat, instead. She shook her head and pushed it back to him. I knew she hadn't eaten, but she insisted her son eat.

Above them was another mother, whose children looked to be five, eight, and eleven—all girls. I had witnessed a sailor pull the oldest girl away from her mother, and the mother shoved her daughter back down to the bunk and went with the sailor. I didn't understand what was happening at the time, I do now. Mothers would sacrifice their own bodies to prevent their daughters from being raped. For reasons I will never understand, I was not sexually assaulted on the slave ship. Was I too dark, too skinny, too undesirable? Good fortune or the providence of God? I'll never know, but I'm thankful.

The eight-year-old girl complained to her mom, and her mom pulled her against her breast. During the night I heard the girl vomit and the awful stench was nearly contagious. She died within days. The littlest girl then fell sick and died. The mother hung onto life. But the sickness, lack of food and water, and grief overcame her. She died one day before her oldest daughter also died.

For a sheltered girl who had never witnessed death before, near or far, other than an animal killed for food or ceremonial worship, death now surrounded me. I both wanted to postpone it and hoped for my own death. Some days the hope was stronger, and other days the fear won out, and I would continue to eat. When the boy's mother died, only two days before the ship reached shore, I saw anguish in her son's eyes. Whether one willed to live or die, it made no difference.

I reached over to the motherless boy across the small space separating our bunks and held his hand. Although we spoke different languages, I told him my name was Oluchukwu, and he said his name was Dsidsing.

I had been "up top" on the deck of the ship when Dsidsing's mother died.

A skinny pale man had pushed me down, making me sit on the deck. I looked around and saw some men climbing up the tall pole holding the sail, others washing the deck with a mop, and a few playing cards. There was even a fiddler. I saw about ten other Africans sitting on the deck.

A cheery-looking man with a thick red beard called out to us unintelligibly. When we didn't respond, another sailor grabbed each of us and raised us up to our feet. The fiddler began to play, and we understood we should follow the moves of the red-bearded man. So we danced. We couldn't follow his awkward moves. Instead, we danced our own dances, our African dances—feet moving, hips gyrating, bodies swinging up and down, back and up, down and around, faster and faster. We jumped, we danced, we swirled. As I swirled around, I saw two sailors unceremoniously throw Dsidsing's mother's body over the side of the ship. I slipped and fell, and the dancers around me stumbled. But the red-bearded man motioned us to get up, keep moving, so my body moved, but my heart stood still.

I began to believe these pale men were devils, content only when others were in pain—whether those others were Black or White made no difference. They seemed to hate everyone almost equally. By marks I made on the slab of wood I slept on, I counted the days from our departure to our arrival—fifty-three days. Biba did not reach the shore with us.

## April 1754—Barbados

When the floating house, the slave ship, stopped moving, we were brought up top. Having lost Biba, I was now chained to an African girl about my age named Suraya. We were shoved off the ship, and onto the waiting dock. After weeks of unchanging routine and endless hours of panic and boredom struggling for predominance, the hurried sailors, frightened Africans, and shouting captain jolted me into my new reality.

Leaving the ship, I saw the beach—beautiful white sand glittering like silver morning sun through the trees, holding the water back, stretching endlessly in both directions. As we stepped down onto the sand, it was hot beneath my bare feet, and at first I cringed, but soon I enjoyed the sensation of the sand squeezing between my toes, soft and pliant under my feet, massaging the remnants of my healed blisters. Trees reminded me of home—long, thick trunks and dark green fernlike branches fanning out on top, large fruit hanging below the branches.

Men herded us like goats into a large pen. Our numbers had shrunk since we left home, and I noticed even many of the pale men were no longer around. Suraya and I were taken into a large holding area, and we sat down together on the hard ground, watching the proceedings. Africans were lined up in two rows, glistening black with oil smeared all over their bodies.

At a small platform in the front a man yelled out instructions. He grabbed a tall, thin African man and held him by a chain attached to his wrists. The man in charge shouted and another man came forward and pulled the African's arms up, then ran his hands up and down his legs. He even opened his mouth and looked at his teeth—only a few were missing.

The man doing the prodding and pulling asked a question, and after some back and forth with the man in charge, money was exchanged. The two men shook hands, while the African being sold looked from one to the other in shock. The new "owner" pulled "Moses" by his chain. The proceedings continued.

A boy was brought forward, not more than ten or eleven years old, eyes wide and body trembling. He reminded me of Ledu. Two men came forward and touched and poked at the boy, even lifted him up to see how heavy he was. I couldn't look any more.

A few men avoided the buying and selling in the front, and simply rushed in and grabbed other Africans. Before they left, they were stopped by two men at the gate and money changed hands. We watched, trying to shrink so as not to be noticed. We waited.

Then two men pulled us up, Suraya and me. My ears filled with a swishing, roaring, thundering sound, and I couldn't hear the man speaking, but I saw his lips move. The next thing I knew, three men came up and began to touch me and Suraya. I dreamed I was back home sitting outside the cooking house, stirring a pot of stew. I could smell the stew, goat meat and yams, with peanuts and herbs. The men's hands on my body faded away as I inhaled the imaginary stew. I felt light, then heavy. The next thing I knew I was on the ground looking up at five men's faces, screwed up in derision and anger. The auctioneer was still selling Africans to the highest bidder.

I was sold, along with Suraya and about seven other women. We were pulled out of the pen and walked back down on the same lane we came in on. I looked back where men and women were being sold, and ahead to the ocean, swelling in all its glory. How could this world be so ugly yet so beautiful?

The sunset over the horizon momentarily stunned us with its beauty. The reds and yellows were shot through with purples, pinks, and oranges, painting the sky with uneven swaths of bright color. Our gazes were diverted by the sight of a new ship, smaller than the one we had sailed on, docked in the harbor. Two men lifted Suraya and I and took us to this new ship. I almost fainted again then and there.

The captain smiled at us—well almost a smile, at least it was not a frown, or a grimace. He spoke to us in a tongue we did not yet understand. We clung to each other and watched as a few other girls and women were brought up on the deck of the ship.

The space below-deck seemed luxurious compared to our previous ship. We each had our own mat, and I could almost stretch my legs all the way out. I would guess these bunks were about three feet wide and over five feet long.

I must have fallen asleep almost immediately, the strain of the journey and the unknown ahead taking their toll. I dreamed I was running from Ledu—he was the lion and I was the antelope. We had often played such games, and always, when Ledu was almost upon me, I would dodge his grasp and leap away laughing. He never caught me. But the dream did not mimic reality. In the dream Ledu became a real lion and as he reached for me his paws became human hands—white and hairy. I woke up screaming, to see above me an ugly White man, with long uncombed hair, and big, fat hands, shaking me and saying something in English. I gasped for air and began to shake.

Suraya and I were led, trembling, up top. Seeing the ocean dip and swell from the deck both fascinated and frightened us. The ship seemed so small in such a vast sea. But we were happy to breathe fresh air and soak up the sunlight. The White man pushed us down near a pole and we sat, content for the moment.

Over the next several days, we spent many daylight hours up on deck, rotating with the other girls and women. Occasionally a fight broke out between sailors, and we would scramble below, afraid of angry voices and the crunching sound of fist meeting bone. At times, the ship would stop, and remain in one place, bobbing up and down in the water. Our stomachs felt queasy then, and some of the women vomited, though I never did. The men held out long poles over the water, and sometimes when they pulled on them there would be fish on the end of a long string. No doubt these men were mean and ugly, but they did seem to have powers over the sea and the fish.

Suraya and I began to teach each other our languages and formed a hybrid which we used to communicate with each other. Suraya learned about Ledu, Mama and Papa, my favorite roasted potato and goat meat stew, and games I played with all my brothers. I learned about Suraya's four elder sisters and learned that not only boys went through the coming-of-age ritual, but also girls.

Suraya informed me not only boys get cut. Girls too. I didn't believe her. Girl cutting was more secretive, painful, and damaging, Suraya said. But without it, girls could not marry. I insisted that my people did not practice that ritual among girls, but Suraya said they probably did, and no one told me as I was too young and had no older sisters to warn me. Suraya was not yet old enough for the ritual.

We ate and drank what little was offered and looked longingly as the sailors ate fresh fruit brought on board in Barbados, and roasted fish. I will never forget the time a young sailor, not yet as hardened as the others, glanced around, and without looking at us, rolled over an orange. When we began to eat right through the rind, he came over and snatched it away. We thought he was only teasing us, and we would never see the ripe fruit again. But he only took it to peel it and gave it back to us fit to eat. I have never, before or since, enjoyed anything so much as that ripe, sweet, juicy orange. Even writing about it now, I can still taste the tangy sweetness, and the palpable feeling of juice dripping down my chin. We saved about half of it and took it down below to share with the other girls.

About a week into the trip, a furious storm overtook the ship, smothering us with rain and nearly burying the ship in massive waves. If I thought I was scared when we were kidnapped, or put on the first ship, or watched others being sold, that panic paled in comparison to this terror. Suraya and I both thought the waves would simply swallow the ship, and we would all die in the sea. When a wave came up over the bow of the ship, reaching its angry fingers toward us and pushing us aft, we moved to go below deck. But it seemed too scary down below, too close to the water, so we hovered between the top deck and below deck, on the second step of the ladder going down. The captain and crew were too preoccupied with keeping the ship afloat to even notice our whereabouts. Water sloshed on the deck in huge waves, running past us to the hold below. We yelled to the women to come up, but it was too late for some of them. Two of the girls and one of the women drowned below deck.

We squatted on the top of the ladder, perched on the precipice between life and death, hearts pounding as we viewed the deaths of our fellow Africans, and prayed to whatever gods would listen to help these White men keep the ship on top of the water.

As Africans drowned below unnoticed by the sailors and captain, a lone sailor fell overboard. Half the crew labored to rescue the sailor.

A fellow sailor yelled out to the man floundering in the water, Sam, and threw a round, white object to him which had a hole in the middle. Sam didn't catch it. One man cried out and another yelled words of direction or encouragement.

Finally, Sam reached out and caught the circular object, and he was pulled up to the deck. Their triumph at rescuing one of their own reflected on their faces, and we watched, absorbed as a sailor thumped the nearly drowned sailor on the chest, turned him over, and pounded him again for good measure on the back, until he gagged and threw up a bucketful of seawater, and his heavy lunch.

No such ministrations were given to the Africans drowning below decks, and when the storm abated, and the sailors discovered the dead bodies beneath, they were thrown overboard to a watery grave.

Suraya and I didn't speak of the incident. The words were impossible to translate.

# Prologue—Joanna's story

I'VE LIVED ALL MY life within a few English counties, have done nothing laudable, nothing noteworthy. Truly, any notice I might attract is due only to my name, my father's name, Gustavus Vassa. My papa was kidnapped with his sister when he was eight or nine and she was eleven. They were born and raised in the Igbo area of Nigeria and Papa ended up serving a Captain Pascal in the British Navy. He traveled to many places around the world, as far-flung as the West Indies, the Arctic Circle, and the Mediterranean Sea!

He wrote his memoir to aid the abolition movement in 1789, and several editions of his book were published. In fact, that's how my mama and papa met. She attended one of his book tours! Sadly, I have few memories of my papa as he died when I was but two years old. My mama and sister also died when I was a baby. I was an orphan by the time I was two years old.

Mama and Papa were not a traditional English couple. My mama was a White English lass, and my papa was African. That explains my pecan brown complexion and wide nose. Mixed marriages were not unheard of in England in the late 1700s, but they weren't common. There were about 20,000+ people of African descent living in England before 1800, and many of them were servants. But my papa was a recognized author and abolitionist, and the richest African living in London when he died in 1797. I reread Papa's memoir so many times, some of the pages are torn. Papa has no relatives in England, so I rely on the memories of some of his compatriots in the abolition movement to learn more about his life, what kind of man he was.

I learned about my mama from her mother, Grandmamma. She was an avid reader and gardener, but not a great cook or seamstress. She believed a person's faith was more important than his or her skin colour. While my grandparents were surprised at her choice of husband, they didn't disown her or forbid the marriage. They came to respect and admire my papa.

I will relate here some of the more noteworthy incidents of my life. My entrance onto the world stage, you must know I speak in hyperbole here, rather my brief acquaintance with recognition occurred when I was just 11, at the House of Commons, upon the successful passage of the abolition bill, on 23 February 1807. I was an impressionable girl of eleven and already quite overwhelmed with my unwarranted fame during the Parliament vote. What I needed was some time to digest all that had occurred—however, instead more new experiences and people were thrust before me pell-mell.

Joanna Vassa
Clavering, England 1829

# CHAPTER TWO

## Joanna

23 February 1807—London

THE BILL PASSED. AFTER more than twenty years of debates, votes, research, negotiations, bargains, defeats . . . the passing of the bill was almost anticlimactic. William Wilberforce got up to address the House of Commons one last time on the Abolition of the Slave Trade bill. His speech, printed in *The Times*, is copied here.

"Gentlemen, peers, fellow parliamentarians, esteemed guests, my lord—I have stood before you on many occasions over the past two decades. The debate over slavery continues unabated, however, as other debates have been resolved, to our benefit or detriment. The abhorrent institution of slavery remains an ugly stain on Great Britain and her leaders. You have heard me speak against the debasement of fellow humans, decry the foul practice of capturing and enslaving innocent African boys and girls, men and women, and implore the end to the slave trade.

"You have seen the evidence—inhumane muzzles intended to silence and starve, chains not fit for animals. Some of you have seen and smelled the berths in the belly of slave ships, fit for no living thing, spaces too small to turn around in, where Africans, fellow human beings, are plastered against other sick, hungry and dying Africans, with neither fresh air, adequate food, nor sunlight. If any of us were subjected to such conditions for a day, let alone the weeks and sometimes months it takes for a slave ship to make the voyage from the West Coast of Africa to the Indies, we would surely not survive.

"The cargo on these ships is not sugar or rum, but children, men and women—created by God to do His will and His work, not created for the pleasure and profit of slaveholders.

"Now is the time—a moment appointed by the creator—a Kairos moment—to stand for your convictions, to stand for justice, to stand against oppression, and end the ignominious barter in human lives known as the slave trade. I appeal not to your passion, but to reason. It is reasonable to end such a deleterious trade in human lives. It is reasonable for our great country to benefit from profitable trade with Africa, instead of stealing their youth for our own gain. It is reasonable to allow forms of moral and legal trade to compensate slave-owners for the insubstantial loss of money which the abolition of the slave trade will engender, thereby cleansing the foul stench of the slave trade from our country and allowing us to rise once again to our former glory."

Uncle John had brought me to the House of Commons to witness history, he said. He told me William Wilberforce had tried to pass this bill for over twenty years—almost twice my lifetime (at the time). Papa had worked hard for this cause, which explained my presence for the vote on the Abolition of the Slave Trade bill. William Wilberforce was not much taller than me, but when he rose out of his seat all the whispering and coughing and moving stopped. All eyes turned to his slight, frail frame, both supporters and detractors.

I had awaited this moment with a calm exterior, but my heart fluttered. With my maid Deirdre's help, I had dressed in a dove gray gown, with a high scoop neck and sleeves ending in an elegant V on my hands. My willful hair was restrained with several combs, and harnessed into a bun, from which a few strands were allowed to escape down my back. A simple pearl necklace and matching earrings, gifts from Grandmamma, completed the ensemble.

Mr. Wilberforce continued. "Among our esteemed guests today is the daughter of one of the abolition movement's most eloquent voices, most passionate defenders of human rights, the daughter of Gustavus Vassa. Miss Joanna Vassa, *would you rise.*"

I smoothed down my dress, lifted my head, and slowly rose, trying to hide my anxiety behind a tentative smile. To my chagrin, the hall erupted in cheers and clapping, "here, here" was heard from the majority of those present in the House of Commons, and all eyes were upon me. I sat down quickly.

Wilberforce continued . . .

"Her father was kidnapped from his home with his eleven-year-old sister Oluchukwu, torn from the bosom of his mother. Miss Vassa stands before you now, at eleven years old, a free British citizen.

"With the passage of this bill, you will ensure that no more eleven-year-old girls and boys will be snatched from their homes and subjected to the Middle Passage, forced labor, torture, and an early death. No more girls and boys will suffer the weeks-long journey in the hold of a slave ship, subjected to death and disease, allowed a space not fit for your hound dog. No more will young girls and boys suffer the pain of separation from families, forced to work long hours in abysmal conditions with no reward.

"With the passage of this bill, a collective sigh of gratitude and relief will emanate from the shores of Africa, and our beloved country will establish cordial and profitable and just trade—in commodities rich in Africa—not in their people.

"The passage of this bill is a step forward—a step toward ending a practice that degrades both the enslaved and the slaveholder. Slavery leaves no one unscathed in its insatiable path of destruction. All who associate with the practice are lessened; conversely, all who work together to end the slave trade are elevated. May we so work together to end this insidious trade, thus lifting our fellow man—slave and slaveholder. As we work together to end this detestable trade in human lives, God's mercies will be shed on us and our beloved country."

The House of Commons stood as one man and erupted in three loud cheers—huzzah, huzzah, huzzah. Wilberforce sat down, overcome by the moment. He acknowledged the cheering, while he probably remembered only too well how many of those who now cheered had once jeered him and his "lofty" ideas of abolition. I saw Mr. Wilberforce's face, at once exalted and exhausted. I know now, after our long acquaintance, how hard and long he fought. How the passage of this bill, the culmination of decades of work by hundreds of people, represented his most important life's work.

The night had already become morning by the time the bill passed, an overwhelming 283 to 16, and it neared 5:00 a.m. as members of the House began to depart. Uncle John, my guardian, took my hand, congratulating my poise, and we left the House of Commons. The Palace Yard thronged with supporters cheering the passage of the Slave Trade Abolition bill. I was amazed to see so many people, so exuberant, at such an hour.

The crowd of men, with a few women and even children scattered among them, pulsed as one. A young man with longish hair capped with a short bowler hat, waistcoat unbuttoned, and a nose set askew by one too many a fistfight, took a flask out of his coat and passed it round. My eyes widened to see a young, buxom woman, with her head uncovered, curly dark hair brushing her shoulders, reach out, lean back her head, and take a large swallow. The predominantly White crowd was freckled with a handful of Africans—their dark faces punctuated with wide grins.

I remembered that we almost avoided coming to the House of Commons altogether. Earlier that day, when Uncle John heard the news that three criminals, one of whom was a woman, had been hung at Newgate the morning of the vote, and over thirty spectators killed in the stampeding crush, he almost canceled our plans. Upon seeing the crowds outside the House of Commons, worried for my safety, he ushered me into the waiting carriage and we headed home.

Later that morning, as Uncle John and I broke our fast at the late hour of 11:00 a.m., an invitation arrived for Joanna Vassa (that's me) and Mr. John Audley (I call him Uncle John though we aren't related). Simon Farmer, the butler, brought it to Uncle John. He gazed at the unfamiliar wax seal of the letter *W* on the letter and sliced it open with a letter opener. His lips pursed and eyebrows dipped as he read the short invitation, and my curiosity was aroused.

"Mr. Wilberforce has requested the 'pleasure of our company' at his home tomorrow night for a celebration dinner. He asked me to bring 'young Miss Vassa.' What do you think, dear? Would you like to attend?"

"Oh, yes, Uncle John. I'd love to! But what shall I wear? I don't think I have the proper dress at all!"

"Well now . . . what a dilemma! What about that lovely deep blue gown made for you last fall? That would be the perfect dress."

"I forgot about that dress. Thanks, Uncle John." I fled the room to check on the said blue gown, leaving a plate of congealed egg and fried tomato half uneaten.

At precisely four the following afternoon, Richard Blake, who had served Uncle John for many years as both manservant and carriage driver, pulled the carriage around to the front door and escorted me out to its open door.

"Mr. Blake. You needn't make such a fuss over me. I'm only eleven," I reminded him.

"Yes, miss. But a very mature eleven-year-old young lady. And you have a fine affair to attend, so you must be properly escorted, ain't that right Mr. John?" Mr. Blake winked at me.

"By all means, Richard. Escort away." Uncle John waved his hand out to us.

Before Mr. Blake handed me up into the carriage, I went to greet the horses, whispering to each of them and petting their manes. They lifted their heads and whinnied in response. Uncle John laughed at me. "We have our own resident horse whisperer. She even speaks their language!"

Mr. Blake helped me up into the carriage and I sat facing the horses, drawing the curtain aside and peeking out at the darkening sky, wondering how long the trip would take, who would be at the Wilberforce home, and if any girls my age would be there. If so, would they be friendly, or standoffish?

After the late night at the House of Commons, I was tired, and soon lulled to sleep by the rocking motion of the carriage. As we approached Broomfield, the turn into the drive startled me awake, and I sat up, pulled the curtain aside, and looked at the grounds. It was so different from the close quarters of London, the bustling streets and tiny or non-existent gardens. Missing were the flower girls and milk maids, baked potato men, newspaper boys and muffin men—hawking their wares during all the daylight hours in London. Here was quiet—a pervasive, calming quiet.

I noticed the smell, or rather the lack of any foul smell. The smells of smoke and horse manure did not assault my nostrils, rather the soothing vanilla and honeyed fragrance of the newly blooming snowdrop flowers reached me, and I leaned out of the carriage window and breathed in deeply.

"Uncle John. Do you smell that? Snowdrops. Aren't they beautiful!"

"Yes, child. We're out of the city here, not far from London proper, but in a veritable countryside."

The carriage slowed and horses tapped their hooves as they stopped at the entrance to the modest mansion.

Mr. Blake opened the door and Uncle John, stepping down first, took my gloved hand in his own and assisted me out of the carriage. I looked up at the candles in the windows and thought I had never seen such a cheery, welcoming house. It was not tall, but quite wide and seemed to have dozens of windows in the front aspect. The house appeared to smile—and I grinned at it in return.

As Uncle John rapped on the front door, the door opened to a rotund, jovial servant, who escorted us into the main parlor. I had never seen such an assortment of people and animals in one place. I was accustomed to being the only person of colour in the room, but here there were men and women of various shades of white and brown, mingling among various animals littered about the large room. A brown-skinned woman with a voluminous cloth of bright orange wrapped artfully about her body, and a red dot on her forehead between her eyebrows, conversed with a young, brown-skinned woman who looked slightly familiar to me, and two white men, who from their uniform upright posture appeared to be military men. Two very dark-skinned men were talking animatedly, gesturing and grinning. The shorter of the two had three large scars on each cheek, slashes resembling rows of crops waiting to be planted.

The fireplace drew my eye, for it was not only large, flanked by stones of pink and beige hues of varying sizes, flecked with quartz, and blazing with flames shooting up from a small mountain of logs, but on either side sat large black retrievers. I avoided dogs, but when they remained motionless, my fears subsided. I glanced around the room, taking in the various seating arrangements, chairs and ottomans and sofas positioned to enhance small conversational groupings. Lamps and candles added a cheery glow to the drawing room.

Uncle John was likewise cautiously scanning the room before entering fully. He was almost the tallest man in the room, and at three and sixty some might consider him elderly, but his vigor and intellect made him seem much younger to me. He did not find gatherings of strangers at all pleasing, but he knew how I had anticipated the outing and agreed to attend to avoid disappointing me. He may not have admitted it to himself, but he was rather curious about Mr. Wilberforce and greatly admired his perseverance and dedication to many causes, primarily abolition.

I had wandered over to pet a fat and fluffy white house cat, which nuzzled my hand while loudly purring, and then I sat down in a wide, green, cushiony chair. Mr. Wilberforce freed himself from a group including Mr. Sharpe and Mr. Fox, and came over to greet Uncle John, drawing him into the room.

"Welcome to Broomfield, Mr. Audley. We are so pleased that you and Miss Vassa could join us." Mr. Wilberforce shook Uncle John's hand. I listened from my chair.

Uncle John thanked Mr. Wilberforce, smiling over at me, and Mr. Wilberforce admitted his fierce opposition tempted him to give up the fight, but he credited his faith in God with the resilience that kept him going. They both lamented that my papa did not live to see this day, and Mr. Wilberforce told Uncle John he carried out one of Papa's traditions last night—pouring out a bit of his drink in memory of Papa.

Mr. Wilberforce led Mr. Audley to a group of men who were laughing and talking loudly, warriors in the parliamentary battles. "Mr. John Audley, a barrister in London and the guardian of Miss Joanna Vassa, may I present Mr. Granville Sharp," Wilberforce said. "And this is James Stephens, a fellow barrister, and Mr. Thomas Clarkson. Here is Zachary Macaulay, a lifelong friend, and my neighbor, friend, and banker, Henry Thornton." Mr. Wilberforce put his hand out gesturing to each gentleman in order.

"Good evening gentlemen. I seem to have landed in the most auspicious group of abolitionists in England. I am honoured." Uncle John bowed.

They continued their greetings and spoke about the victory, Mr. Wilberforce, and his menagerie as Wilberforce himself wandered off to greet his other guests. I listened to their conversation.

"Have you ever seen such an assortment of wildlife indoors?" Mr. Clarkson asked.

"I must confess, I have hardly seen such an array even in nature," Uncle John replied.

"Yes, Wilberforce has many weaknesses—or strengths, depending on one's vantage point. He can't bear suffering—human or animal. Hence the fight against slavery and against animal cruelty. Do you see the tame hare over there?" Mr. Sharp asked.

Uncle John turned to see the hare, now resting on my lap, with the cat purring at my feet, and a crow perched on my right shoulder, and smiled at me and my new friends.

Mr. Wilberforce bent over to greet me and pat his favourite hare as he introduced himself. "And you must be the famous Miss Joanna Vassa I have heard so much about!" he said, bowing his head slightly.

"No, sir. I mean yes, sir. Yes, Mr. Wilberforce, I am Joanna, Miss Vassa, but no sir, I am not famous." I was so discomfited I couldn't get out one clear sentence!

"I hate to disagree with you upon our first meeting. But I must! As the daughter of my esteemed friend, Mr. Gustavus Vassa, your fame is well established," Mr. Wilberforce declared.

"I will admit to my father's fame, sir, but not my own."

"Well, my daughter, let us not disagree on first acquaintance. We'll save our debates for the future. I see you have met Pip and Miss Haversham. They are quite stimulating company, but I think you would enjoy the children's company even more."

A young African man stepped forward and said, "Mr. Wilberforce. I would be happy to escort your young guest upstairs to the nursery."

"Thank you, Fredrik, but I need a break from adult conversation and debate. I might just join the youngsters in a game of marbles!"

I was both impressed and surprised that Mr. Wilberforce declined Fredrik's offer to take me upstairs to the nursery.

Up two flights of stairs, Mr. Wilberforce led me down a hallway, and I heard the noise of the children before he opened the door to the nursery. Even in this room animals mingled happily with children—a small calico cat was nestled against a young boy intent on stacking up building blocks, and a black spaniel was romping about after flying marbles— barely restrained chaos! All the children appeared to be younger than me, the oldest a boy I judged to be about my age. Mr. Wilberforce smiled as the two girls hopped up from their places on the floor and hugged him. He introduced all the children to me: his eldest son William; a young lady with curls, Miss Barbara; a younger girl, Lizzy; and two boys, Robert and Samuel. I thought how nice it would be to have so many siblings.

Robert, his ears perking up at his name, shouted, "I'm five years old," holding up five fingers in proof. Robert stood up to his full height and lifted his chin in the air.

"What is it you're building there, young man?" Wilberforce asked his young son.

"The House of Cotton!" Robert exclaimed.

"Oho. The House of Cotton. A formidable replacement for the House of Commons no doubt," Mr. Wilberforce said to me. "Do you need a bit of help with those blocks?" he asked his young son.

"Yes, please Papa. The higher it gets, the more it wobbles."

"Funny that. Well now, we cannot have a wobbly House of Cotton."

After some time, Mr. Wilberforce had successfully shored up the House of Cotton and rose from his place on the floor. "Show Miss Joanna your playthings, and maybe one or two of your favourite books. I'm returning downstairs to the guests, children."

Right then I noticed a young woman sitting in the back of the nursery, with a baby boy on her lap. Mr. Wilberforce addressed himself to her as he prepared to leave and asked her to accompany me back downstairs after I was done playing with his children.

Barbara took me by the hand and led me to a bench along the back wall of the nursery which held an assortment of dolls. "Come see my dolls. My papa has bought me dolls from all over the world."

One of the dolls was black, with a yellow and blue cloth wound around her head and a matching dress. Several small silver bracelets circled her arms. I ran my fingers over the bracelets as I admired the doll.

"She's like a black princess, right?" Barbara asked.

"Or even a queen," I said.

"An African queen! Are you an African princess, Joanna?" Barbara asked.

I laughed. "Me? No! I've never been to Africa."

"Really? You look like African women Papa has over for dinner. Especially Sadie. You look a lot like Sadie." Barbara leaned forward and closely examined my face.

I wanted to meet these African women, especially Sadie, whoever she was. I held on to the African doll while Barbara picked up a white doll dressed in a gold silk dress.

We both heard a loud crash and turned to see Samuel knocking over Robert's tower of blocks.

"Hey! Why'd you do that? Blockhead!" Robert yelled.

William left his marble maze and tugged Robert back before he pummeled his brother Samuel with a block. Barbara set her doll aside and pulled Samuel into her lap. Miss Lindsay came over to me and said, "Miss Joanna, please hold Henry for a moment while I deal with these boys." I set the African queen doll on the floor as if she were a precious baby, and Miss Lindsay plopped Henry down in my lap. I had no idea how to hold a baby! I put my arms around him awkwardly, hoping he wouldn't wobble and fall, as Miss Lindsay dealt with Robert and Samuel.

Henry looked up at me, furrowed his feathery eyebrows, and started to whimper. He looked over at Miss Lindsay, and back at me, and started to cry in great hiccups. Miss Lindsay insisted Samuel apologize.

"Sorry, Robert," he said, more like an order than an apology.

I took Henry's tiny, chubby hands in my hands and gently clapped while softly singing "London Bridge is falling down, falling down, falling down. London Bridge is falling down, little Henry." Henry's cries turned to gurgles as he tried to sing along, and he started laughing when I pulled his arms out, then back together. I guess it wasn't so hard to entertain a baby!

Glancing over at the other boys, I saw William, Robert, and Samuel reconstructing the tower, and Barbara came back to sit next to me. Barbara smiled at her baby brother; "Henry likes you."

"He's so sweet! Aren't you sweet, little man?" I asked Henry. I leaned over and rubbed my nose on his—Henry scrunched up his nose and giggled.

Miss Lindsay said, "You're a natural with babies, Miss Joanna!"

"Not really. This is my first time holding a baby," I said.

"I never woulda guessed. You're so good with him. And Henry doesn't take to people easy," Miss Lindsay said.

"I just treated him like I treat my horse," I said, and then wished I hadn't.

"Like a horse! That's a good one," William laughed.

"I meant I like to sing to my horse and rub his nose. That's all." How could I get out of this one, I wondered?

"He does have a bit of a horsey smell sometimes," Barbara laughed.

Miss Lindsay came over and reached for Henry saying, "It's time for his bottle and bedtime." As soon as I handed Henry to Miss Lindsay, I felt the loss. His little, warm body and toothless smile reached a need in me to nurture I never knew I had.

I asked Barbara, "Isn't it nice to have brothers and sisters?"

"Nice? The boys can be pests, but I guess I like 'em well enough. Lizzy is sweet, but she's only six."

"How old are you?" I asked.

"I'm ten. Papa says I'm a big girl now," Barbara said, smiling.

"I'll be twelve in April."

"Don't you have brothers and sisters?" Barbara looked so expectant, I hated disappointing her.

"I did have one sister, but she died when I was two years old. I don't remember her at all. Anna Maria."

"You can be my sister. Right, Lizzy? We can be three sisters instead of two. How 'bout that?" Barbara asked.

"I'd love to be your honorary sister," I said, trying not to cry.

"What does honready mean?" Barbara asked.

"Well, it means I would like it above all things," I said.

The three of us decided a secret sign was imperative. After some debate, we decided to make a circle, with our backs together, holding pinkies and turning three times to the left and then three times to the right. So, the three of us, a reddish-haired six-year-old, a blond ten-year-old, and a pecan-brown eleven-year-old linked pinkies, standing solemnly in a circle with backs together, facing out, and vowed to be honorary, or honready, sisters, moving in a circles three times one way, then three times the other. I thought it was the closest I would have to a family for now, and I promptly fell in love with the Wilberforces.

Now that we were officially sisters, we returned to the dolls, Lizzy helping me and Barbara dress and undress the dolls, while the boys built and demolished several towers and buildings. Miss Lindsay put a sleeping Henry in a bassinet and suggested it was time I rejoin the adults downstairs. We three 'sisters' hugged, and Miss Lindsay brought me back downstairs.

I looked around the room—Uncle John was talking with the same group of men. I noticed the woman with the orange cloth wrapped around her (which I later learned was called a sari) conversing with the same woman whose complexion was like mine. I thought this must be one of the African women Barbara had mentioned.

I peered out the window and scanned the grounds. The garden, unlike traditional English gardens, appeared untamed, ignoring the borders, and threatening to overrun the footpath. Crocuses and statuesque daffodils reached toward the sun. Fragrant snowdrops showcased their fragile white bells, greeting garden dwellers with their perfume. Footpaths in the shape of a circular maze led to a central fountain, at which St. Francis was perpetually feeding a small flock of stone birds—swallows, nightingales, bluebirds, and nuthatches.

Startled by a voice behind me, I turned to see the young man who had offered to take me upstairs.

"Miss Vassa, would you enjoy a walk in the garden?" As he grinned down at me, my first thought was how white his teeth were against his dark skin. My second thought took in his height and pleasant demeanor. As I unselfconsciously stared up at him, Fredrik patiently awaited my response.

"Yes, sir. It's so pretty and unusual. May I ask you a question first?" I asked.

"By all means!" Fredrik replied.

"Who are those two pretty ladies talking over there?" I tried to point them out without being obvious.

"The Indian woman is Chitra, a friend of Mrs. Wilberforce, and the other young woman is Sadie, a midwife. Why do you ask?"

"Just curious. Miss Sadie looks familiar."

"I see a resemblance between you," Fredrik nodded.

Fredrik led me through the growing throng of folks in the drawing room. As we passed Uncle John, I informed him of our plan for a walk outdoors and Mr. Wilberforce encouraged Fredrik not to be remiss in showing me the swallows' nesting area. Fredrik promised not to neglect this important duty and we ventured outside.

"How do you find the gardens, Miss Joanna?"

"They are perfectly imperfect. Not so trimmed and cut up, like a proper English garden—but wild and untamed."

"Yes, just so. Mr. Wilberforce likes to allow free expression in his garden, as he does in other areas of his life." Fredrik waved his hand out at the garden.

"What do you mean?" I asked.

"Only that Mr. Wilberforce is always prepared to debate and listen to all sides of an issue, no matter how firmly held his own beliefs may be."

"Like abolition?"

"Yes, although after years—decades—of hearing the Tories' paltry excuses for continuing the trade, his patience had run dry."

"And sir . . ." I began.

"Please Miss Joanna, call me Fredrik. I'm not much older than you."

Flustered by my rudeness, I began again and mentioned his position with the Wilberforce family. Fredrik laughed. I blushed. "No, Miss. I'm not a servant. I live a few houses down, and Mr. Wilberforce often invites me to his gatherings. I'm his barber!"

"His barber?" I winced at my mistake.

"Mr. Wilberforce doesn't employ Africans as servants."

"I see."

"And as to my age, I am not yet one and twenty. Not so ancient as I may appear."

That still seemed a lot older than me, but I didn't say anything else about our ages.

"How long have you lived here in the neighborhood?"

"I've lived here for seven years."

As I looked at him questioningly, he continued.

"I came with thirty other African boys and girls. Mr. Macaulay started a school for us. But unfortunately, about half of the children did not adjust well; many of them died." Fredrik looked down.

"That's awful!" I gasped.

Fredrik proceeded to tell me that Mr. Macaulay and Mr. Wilberforce had good intentions and a good plan, but the cold climate and the food didn't agree with many of the African children. The plan was to bring sons of chiefs and African leaders to England, educate them, teach the gospel, then send them back to be leaders in Sierra Leone. They thought Africans reaching Africans was a better plan than English reaching Africans. It was an idealistic plan, but very few returned to Sierra Leone.

"Sierra Leone. I've heard of that place. My papa was involved in plans to resettle freed slaves there. And I'm told he wanted to go there himself."

"I heard that as well. I never met your father; I arrived in England in 1799. But I heard much about him, through Mr. Wilberforce, Thomas Clarkson, and others. Many good things. You must be proud to have such a father."

My eyes filled, as they often still did when Papa was mentioned. He was much more of an image than a memory, but every thought of him evoked pride and loss. I told Fredrik how my papa died before my second birthday. And my few memories included strong arms lifting me up and putting me in a crib; a deep voice singing a beautiful song in strange words; a certain smoky smell. I paused—remembering Papa's scent as clearly as if I caught it on the breeze.

Fredrik waited for me to compose myself, then suggested we go down to the end of the lane and check out the swallows' nesting area. I had recently begun birding with Uncle John and was prepared to be enthralled with the swallows. As we approached the barn, I saw dozens of very small, brown and black birds, with lovely V-shaped tails, swooping and swerving every which way in the air. Their flight seemed to follow no pattern whatsoever, and I was soon dizzy from trying to follow one at a time.

"They fly so fast and they're so unpredictable!" I exclaimed.

"I never thought of it that way. Yes, I love their crazy flight patterns. Don't try to follow one bird but take in the whole area. It's easier on the eyes," Fredrik suggested.

I gazed at the swallows and thought about what we just celebrated—the end of the slave trade. No more kidnappings. No more slave ships. I stepped off the path, threw my head back, extended my arms all the way out, fingers uplifted like a ballet move; and I mimicked the swallows, moving, flowing, dipping, stretching, running in circles and figure eights on the grass. I reveled in freedom.

Fredrik laughed. "I know how you feel, Joanna. I know just how you feel."

# CHAPTER THREE

## Olu

### April 1754—Atlantic Ocean and South Carolina

Suraya and I loved to watch the sky and name the birds we saw. Our favorite was the wulu wulu, Suraya's name for a small bird with white wings, a black *v* on its back, black wing tips, and long thin tail feathers. I loved the gulls best, envying their freedom of flight, grace, and speed.

The days blended into one another, until one day, a sailor yelled out and pointed to land. Sailors rushed to and fro, and amid all the commotion a small boy about our age climbed up the highest pole like a hyrax and looked through a long tube—he shouted with glee.

Within minutes we approached the shore and saw land for the first time in days. The prospect of land did not gladden our hearts as it did the sailors; we weren't going home to our families. However, we were happy to be getting off the ship.

Suraya and I clung to each other, watching as the sails were lowered and the anchor set. The surviving African girls and women below-decks were brought up slowly, blinded by the light and struggling to stand, limbs rendered limp after days of disuse. Suraya and I were healthier and stronger, having spent more time on deck and offered an occasional fruit.

Rowboats ferried us to the shore where we were prodded into a large, barn-like structure to wait. The next few hours brought new terrors and humiliations none of us had yet experienced. After a tall, detached White man had hosed us down, stuffed our anuses with cotton to disguise diarrhea, lathered us with oil to make our skin appear healthy and shiny, poked at our teeth, clipped our toenails, and inflicted myriad indignities on our tired black bodies, the remnants of our true selves were sold to the highest bidders.

With no regard for family ties or sisterly affection, the women and girls were sold and taken away to plantations. Suraya and I prayed in our own tongues not to be separated. Amazingly, our prayers were answered.

Money changed hands, and the seller spoke with the man who would take us—the buyer. What right did they have to sell or buy any of us? None, whatsoever! The buyer produced an iron implement, which the seller heated over a nearby fire. I was curious, wondering what use it had. I soon learned. The seller took the metal, which had some symbols on the end, came to Suraya and me, lowered our dresses, and seared the hot iron just where our breasts were beginning to swell. The pain, sudden, shocking, and severe, caused me to faint. When I opened my eyes, I lay in the back of a wagon. Suraya looked down at me, her own eyes filmed with pain. We were chained together. I could see Suraya's skin bubbling up in blisters and didn't look down at my own.

We sat in the back of a wagon, pulled by two large, rough horses controlled by the buyer, a short, fat, balding man with a whip, and sped off.

We shared our own words for 'horse,' and ended up with a hybrid, kete kumi. Exhaustion battled with curiosity, and curiosity briefly won out. We communicated succinctly in our own pidgin language.

"Wetin dat?" asked Suraya, pointing to fields upon fields of cotton.

I liked to have an answer for everything, and if I didn't know the answer, I would usually make one up. I tried to tell her the White man took the clouds from the sky and put them on the ground. Somehow, Suraya understood me. We stared with keen attention as we passed by fields of cotton. After a while, we were surprised to see Black men and women bent over the white clouds.

Suraya asked if the Africans were gathering clouds. Hmmm. Not clouds. I looked closer. I struggled to communicate the idea of a cocoon or a bird's nest. So, we agreed the Africans were touching fields of cocoons. I only learned much later that they were picking cotton, backbreaking work, for twelve hours a day, six or seven days a week.

Suraya and I looked at strange trees with white flowers, bright orange birds with black wings, and small cerulean blue birds. But we did not see any familiar animals. No jackals, cheetahs, or leopards. No pythons, antelopes, or baboons.

Eventually the heat of the day, the over-stimulation of the environment and the pain in our chests overtook our curiosity and we dozed off, sleeping fitfully in the rolling wagon until it came to a sudden stop before an enormous house.

Three stories high, tall, and proud like an Igbo warrior, the house boasted two staircases leading up to the front doors, with an opening in the middle where you could see straight through the house, a balcony, with pots of geraniums, marigolds, and camellias brightening the porch and scenting the air. We counted seventeen windows at the front of the house alone. Solid brick, with white frames on every window, the house was solid, forbidding, and odd to us—so used to mud and dung houses or grass thatched homes.

"Big!" Suraya exclaimed.

"Much ezi," I said, trying to explain my thought that many families must live in this house.

Our reverie was interrupted by the short, fat man who had tied up the horses and now approached us. As he came toward us, the large front doors opened and an African in a black suit and white frilly shirt emerged, followed by a tall White man in riding gear, with thin lips, a large, straight nose, rather large protruding ears, and short brown hair. His jacket seemed to have a tail, which we thought was funny, but not funny enough to laugh.

The tall, commanding White man strode out to the wagon as the short fat man took one of us in each arm and plopped us on the ground, like rotten sweet potatoes. We were still chained together. The White man seemed unhappy to see us and yelled "Clarence" and a lot of angry words at the man. They went back and forth, questioning, explaining, excusing. I tried to get the gist of the conversation by their tone and body language. The man in riding gear seemed unhappy, and Clarence was apologetic. Beyond that, I have no idea what they said about us.

After their argument, a young White girl who had been listening to the whole conversation, hiding behind Geoffrey, the male slave in the house, pranced out and hugged her daddy's legs.

I looked at Suraya and pointed my chin to the reddish mop on the girl's head, smirking. The girl hugged and smiled at her papa. I learned later that Susannah asked to have Suraya as her maid, and the wish was granted.

Suraya and Susannah looked each other over—one as white as a cloud, the other dark as a black serval. I felt like an outsider, looking at them as they assessed each other. Powerlessness was becoming a normal condition, though I continued to fight it. I didn't like Susannah on sight, maybe because she had a home, and a family—the very things denied me. I also didn't like her because she liked Suraya. Susannah's red, curly hair seemed wild and untamed, compared to Suraya's neat braids lying flat against her head.

Then the tall, ugly man turned to Clarence and continued to berate him. I learned later that Mr. Cross—that was the name of the tall, white man—was upset that Clarence brought home girls, when Mr. Cross wanted men. He gave Suraya to Susannah, who promptly named her Sarah. I thought it was a bit odd that she came up with a name so close to Suraya. Maybe she heard us talking to each other. I didn't like the name, though. There was nothing wrong with Suraya.

Suraya, however, was quite pleased with the name, so like her own, and abandoned her given name with aplomb. She seemed altogether too pleased with her situation for my liking. I vowed to never accept my lot, and only adopted the outward actions of a slave. If they told me to work, I would work, but in my heart, I was back home with my family, and in my mind, I was plotting a way of escape.

At this point we were unchained; my wrists were bruised and raw from the chafing of the irons. My left wrist was bleeding, and my right wrist was swollen. My chest still burned from the branding. But these slight, passing pains were nothing compared to my anguish upon realizing I would probably never see Ledu or my family again. I lived in a foreign country, owned by a man who looked like he would just as well kill me or sell me as feed me, and I had no way of getting home.

My thoughts were interrupted by Clarence, instructing us in loud, unintelligible language, to stay put. He told us not to wander anywhere, but as we had no understanding of the word, we were clueless about what we were supposed to do. He yelled and by his motions pointing away and vigorously shaking his head and shouting 'no,' he almost got his point across. It was more comical than frightening because he looked like such a buffoon. We weren't dumb or hard of hearing; we simply did not yet speak English.

Miss Martha was summoned from the kitchen and met us behind the back doors of the house. Miss Martha was brown-skinned, not dark like Suraya and me. She was short and a little plump, with wide hips and an even wider smile. Her hair was braided in cornrows and wrapped around her head like a crown. She looked us over as Clarence instructed her to wash and clothe us. Miss Martha clucked her tongue at our spindly frames and unkempt hair—tch, tch, tch. The dirt blended in with our skin, but nothing could disguise my bony knees and twig-like arms. She drew Suraya and me up to her generous breasts and gave us a quick hug. We were so shocked at the kind human touch, we recoiled. But she was so big, warm, and sweet smelling, we gave up our anxieties and allowed ourselves to be briefly smothered by her fleshy arms and motherly love. Miss Martha muttered to herself, looking us over, turning us around, patting our hair.

Miss Martha disappeared for a few minutes, coming back with a small bowl. She scooped up a handful of the brown, creamy substance and very gently applied it to our blistered skin—shock and pain gave way to a cooling sensation.

Miss Martha then led us to the well.

Martha laughed as she kept up a steady monologue. We understood few of the words, but we understood, somehow, she was on our side. Never having seen a well, Suraya and I were shocked to see a bucket rising out of the ground, filled with sweet, clean, clear water. My only thought was that I wish we had enjoyed one back home, to preclude daily trips to the river. We washed infrequently at home, so when Miss Martha removed our clothes and poured a cupful of water over our heads, it took all our self-restraint to remain still and not run, screaming for help. Where would we go, anyway?

Miss Martha decided to cut our hair before washing it. Once our hair was so short we were almost bald, she turned her attention to our bodies—filthy from weeks on a ship without bathing. Suraya had worse sores than I did on her wrists, because she was heavier than me, and I saw Miss Martha gently cleanse them. Using a rag and homemade soap, Miss Martha cleaned us from the top of our ears to the soles of our callused feet. After a while we relaxed and reveled in the pampering. When we were as clean as we were going to get, she wrapped each of us in an oversized blanket, led us to the kitchen, and sat us down on a bench in the corner. The aromas in that kitchen remain to this day the best I have ever smelled in my entire life. Then my stomach growled loudly. Suraya giggled, but I was so embarrassed I tried to cough to cover up the sound. Miss Martha clucked her tongue.

As she was fixing us a meal, we gaped up at the shining pots and pans hanging from the ceiling, and the open hearth. The fireplace took up half the wall, with a stone hearth extending out in front. The pantry was lined with food—eggs, flour, sugar, greens, potatoes, tomatoes, onions, rice—in burlap bags, baskets, and tins, filling the shelves and promising hearty meals for days to come. Cabinets with glass doors revealed stacks of plates, mugs, cups, and bowls.

Miss Martha retrieved one plate, one bowl, and one mug from the cupboard. Pointing to the plate she said, "plate" and had us repeat after her. With words we didn't understand, and explanatory hand motions, she said, "This is a bowl."

"Ball," we said obediently.

"No, say bowwwl." Miss Martha stretched out the word.

"Bowwel," we said together.

She said something else, ending with "soup."

"Sup?"

Miss Martha shook her head, talked some more to herself, then motioned for us to stay seated and left the room.

Suraya looked at me and smiled. We both liked Miss Martha and knew intuitively she would help us if she could. Miss Martha came back with two old frocks Susannah no longer wore. They were faded and a bit short, but we tried them on gingerly and looked at each other in amazement.

"Olu pretty!" exclaimed Suraya.

"Suri pretty!" I said.

Then we laughed together for the first time in over a month.

That night, after eating a meal of roasted potatoes, roasted corn, and rice—the best meal since our kidnapping—we were given oversized shirts to sleep in and taken to a small attic room. The mattresses on the floor were small and hard, stuffed with straw, the bedding was minimal, and the room was hot, but it felt luxurious to us in comparison to every place we had been since we were taken from home.

Reader, do not be lulled into the false impression that slavery was a preferable state. But for the moment, with each other, and Mama Martha, we were as content as it was possible to be.

We slept well—due not to comfort, but exhaustion. The rooster crowing and rays of sun woke us at dawn, and the abated fear returned.

Suraya murmured something, and I tried to comfort her.

Suraya repeated the phrase I didn't understand, tapping her hand to her chest as she spoke. I knew we were both thinking of home and our families. I still hoped I would find my brother. But I didn't know where I was, and where he might have been taken. I hadn't seen or heard of him since we were last together. The chances of finding Ledu seemed slim.

We didn't know what to do, nor what was now expected of us, but we had to relieve ourselves, so we snuck downstairs and headed to the outhouse, about fifty yards behind the main house. Miss Martha had shown us where it was the previous evening. Halfway across the yard we were stopped by the night watchman and his large dog.

He yelled at us, asked us a question, and laughed. It was a mean laugh and terrified us. The dog resembled a wolf, or a hyena, an animal we hated. Mute, I pointed to the outhouse.

The watchman nodded, motioned for us to go, and waited for us to return to the house. We went in together, emerging quickly and scampering back to the house. It would take weeks for us to learn all the prescribed behaviors of a slave.

When we entered the house through the kitchen door to return to our room, Miss Martha was humming, moving about the kitchen preparing breakfast. The smell of frying ham and tomato filled the kitchen, as Miss Martha cracked eggs over a bowl for griddle cake batter. Suraya and I inhaled the enticing odors and stared. Miss Martha gave us each a scrap of ham, which felt like abundance, and scolded us. I imagine she was telling us not to go outside, but how were we supposed to relieve ourselves. At the time we had no idea what a chamber pot was or what it was used for, but we understood we were not to leave the house. The concept of rules was also foreign to us.

Miss Martha talked to us, making hand motions to accompany her words so we would understand. She tried to make it clear we should not leave the house for any reason. A short time later, once we had dressed and washed up with the water from the bowl in our room, Miss Martha burst into the room followed by a dark-skinned woman.

She introduced us to the other woman, calling her "Mary." Then she pointed at me. She pointed to herself, "Miss Martha." She pointed to the woman, "Mary." And pointed at me again. She asked me something and I heard the word *name*.

I knew the word *name* and at last could reply to a question spoken in English.

"My name Oluchukwu, sir." I was so proud of myself. I had learned that on the second ship.

Miss Martha laughed. I couldn't figure out what I had done wrong. I pronounced all the words just as I had been taught.

"Sir!!! No, no, no." She said something else, laughed again, lifting her ample breasts to exaggerate the difference between a sir and a ma'am.

Mary took the opportunity to introduce herself to us. She pointed to me and said words that included "maid" and Mrs. Cross. I asked her if she was African, and she said "no." That is one word I understood. I tried to ask if my brother Ledu might be here, and Miss Martha just shook her head, frowning, dispelling any hope I had of reuniting with my brother.

Without understanding all the words, I understood the sentiment. Miss Martha didn't think Ledu was anywhere near us. I knew in my heart it was probably true, but it was so hard to give up that last thread to home.

Miss Martha continued, gentle but firm. She talked for a few minutes, and I understood only a few of the words. She called me by an unfamiliar name, Olivia.

"My name Oluchukwu," I replied, thinking Miss Martha was confused.

"O-li-vi-a. O-liv-ia."

"O-liv-a." I didn't like the way it sounded.

"No. O-liv-Ia." Miss Martha repeated the name, emphasizing the second "i."

"O-liv-Ia?"

"Yes. No Oluchuchu. Your name Olivia."

"No Olivia. Oluchukwu."

Miss Martha just shook her head.

# CHAPTER FOUR

## Joanna

### March 1807—Audley household

"Ouch!" I cried and pulled back as Deirdre, the Irish maid, assistant cook, and occasional hairdresser, attempted to tame my unruly, thick, curly dark brown hair.

"Ach, hit a tangle that didna want to let loose," Deirdre said.

It may seem odd for a maid and kitchen helper to dress hair, but Deirdre was quite skilled at it, better than the cook, Annie Farmer. Deirdre came from a large Irish family, with six sisters, and all of them had unmanageable, frizzy red hair. My hair usually yielded itself to Deirdre's brush and her soft Gaelic curses.

After the excitement of the Wilberforce celebration, I stayed with Uncle John for several leisurely days spent reading, embroidering, walking in a nearby park, and bird watching. Papa and Uncle John had been good friends, and Uncle John had helped him find subscribers to his book. I learned Papa had a lot of friends, and the English men who helped him, like Uncle John and Mr. Wilberforce, aided his success. I like to think Papa was so serious and ambitious he could have succeeded on his own, but I'm sure their advocacy augmented his drive. When Papa died, I lived with Grandmamma for a time. But as she aged, she found it more and more difficult to care for me. Papa had appointed his friend John Audley, a barrister in London, as my guardian. So it was that I alternated between living with Grandmamma in Ely, and Uncle John in London, or Ely in Cambridgeshire—he owned two homes. I liked each of them for different reasons, but I came to prefer staying with Uncle John as there was more to do and I enjoyed playing chess and birdwatching with him. I call him Uncle John because though we are not related, he feels like an uncle to me.

Uncle John often thought how agreeable it would be for me to live with him year-round. He wished to hire a governess for me, enabling me to live with him year-round, but my papa's will clearly prescribed the parameters of my education. Papa had the means and motivation to provide for my formal education. He had earned a huge sum from the sales of his memoir, making him probably the wealthiest African living in London when he died. Papa stipulated that I attend boarding school from the age of 11 to 18. Maybe Papa thought it would be good for me to be with other girls my age. Uncle John had no choice but to acquiesce to Papa's clear instructions and enroll me in boarding school. He was dreading my departure and had already filled up his schedule with evening engagements for the next fortnight to avoid coming home to an empty house.

My emotions were mixed. I looked forward to meeting girls my age, but I wasn't sure how I would fit in, not being a typical English lass. My brown skin and riotously curly hair were obvious clues to my mixed heritage. I tried to look upon boarding school as an adventure, hoping it would be a good one and not a disaster.

For a reserved man, never married, with a small family, only one sister and two nephews still living, I tried to soften the lonely edges of Uncle John's life, laughing at his jokes, expressing interest in his business, and joining him on birding walks. I was an ideal companion he often said—and though he assumed I would one day marry and set up my own house, he hoped the nuptials would be many years in the future.

In the evening we often settled down in the library and engaged in a competitive game of chess. Uncle John possessed a fine, handcrafted chess set—pieces made of ivory and ebony. He taught me the names of the pieces when I was seven, their moves when I turned eight, and I bested him for the first time when I was ten. That night, business dealings distracted him, or so he said, offering an excuse for his compromised concentration.

On this cold March evening, I asked, "Uncle John, where have you hidden the chess set?"

"Oh, my dear, Richard has taken it for a thorough cleaning and polishing. He claims that I lost the last game because the piece was dusty, and I didn't see it clearly!"

"Pish, posh! Your eyesight is better than mine—I won the game fairly. Skill—not sight—won the game!" I declared.

"Yes, yes. But alas, the set is unavailable tonight."

"What about the other chess set?" I looked around the library.

"The wooden one? Yes, you learned on that one, did you not?"

"I'm still partial to it."

"I believe it lies here in the credenza." He moved across the room, pulling out the board and a velvet bag containing the old wood chess pieces.

"Oh yes—let's play! I love that old set!"

"I wonder why? Could it be because you reached checkmate before me for the first time on this set?"

"Don't be gruff, Uncle. Here, let me help you set them up."

We played, as was our custom, in silent thought—our minds progressing four and five moves ahead, anticipating danger before it arose. I had learned to read Uncle John's unintended signals—a raised brow, dilated pupil, stroke of the beard, or crossing of the legs. These clues would prevent my king from an early death or alert me to the perspicacity of a move.

However, after losing three pawns, a knight and then my beloved queen, I was convinced my doom was nigh. But after a misguided move by Uncle John's bishop, I nimbly drew the rook alongside, and protected by a remaining knight, checkmate was secured.

"When the pupil excels the teacher, it's time for a new lesson!" Uncle John exclaimed. "Your papa would be immensely proud of you. He was a skilled chessman himself."

"Really? Who would win when you played together? Papa, or you?!"

"Our wins were evenly divided, but he may have had a slight advantage. He used to play strategy games with his sister Olu."

When Uncle John mentioned Papa's sister, it caught me off guard. But then our conversation moved on as he congratulated me on my win, and I thought no more about it.

"Uncle John, it's only because you're such an excellent teacher that I have become a true chess-woman!"

"Not quite a woman, Joanna. At eleven you are yet a girl." He smiled at me.

"I do dislike this age. Not a girl, nor yet a woman. Such an in-between-ness. Neither here nor there. I don't like it a bit!"

"Enjoy it, my dear. You have few responsibilities, good health, friends—be content with what you have, what you are. You'll soon be a beautiful young woman and your suitors will be standing in line at the door. I'll need to hire an additional butler to control the mob—in fact, this may be a job for Odysseus!" His eyes widened in mock horror.

"Don't be silly, uncle. I don't expect a line of suitors. And as for Odysseus—didn't he kill the suitors?"

"Indeed, he did. I wondered if you remembered the conclusion of *The Odyssey*."

"It was wonderful and dreadful all at once. Those men shouldn't have bothered Penelope—but truthfully, he didn't need to kill them."

"Yes . . . wonderful and dreadful. The prospect of your marrying and leaving me."

"Uncle, I don't expect to marry at a young age. I'll still be around for many years to take your king in checkmate!" I reached out and patted his hand, smiling in victory.

## 15 September 1807—Ely

"Joanna, have you laid out all your dresses?" Grandmamma was a quintessential English lady—proper, quiet, deferential . . . and White. She took care to wear a hat to avoid any hint of color in her cheeks or freckles to mar her pale skin. The English prized fair skin, but I personally thought the dark skin of Africans more beautiful.

"Yes, Grandmamma. I have six dresses that still fit me."

"You are growing so. You're my height now, and when I see you again, I may have to look up to see you!" Grandmamma put her hand up to shade her eyes.

Grandmamma had dealt with many losses, yet she kept a firm eye on the future and didn't dwell on the past. My mama, her daughter, died quite young, soon after I was born, and of course my sister died when she was a baby. Then Grandmamma's husband died not too many years later, and her other daughter, my Aunt Mary, was arrested for shoplifting and sent to Australia! So much bereavement and loss, but Grandmamma soldiered on, stoic and uncomplaining.

"Oh, Grandmamma, I'm not growing so very fast."

"But you are, dear, and you're growing nicely too. Your manner and deportment reflect well on our family."

"Thanks to you, Grandmamma."

"And Mr. Audley. Your guardian has been wonderful. He's lavished all the attention he would have given his own daughter, had he ever married and had a family. He's waiting for you downstairs. Let's get your things packed."

My six dresses were folded with care and packed in alternate layers with slips and underthings. My one pair of dress shoes was sandwiched against the side of the trunk, and sturdy shoes and half boots were on the bottom. My favourite blanket, knitted by Mama, lay gently covering all. I carried Miss Sissie, my beloved African doll, replete with a bright red and green head scarf and matching dress, a cherished remnant of Papa's love, handmade by a fellow abolitionist, a free African woman.

Grandmamma fingered one of my dresses, a floor-length peach dress with lace on the end of the sleeves and at the hem. "Your mother wore this dress when she was your age. She loved pastel colors . . . peach, pink, lime green, light blue. She was wearing a peach dress when she met your papa." I listened intently whenever Grandmamma spoke about my mama.

"Really? Where did they meet?" I leaned forward awaiting Grandmamma's response.

"Your papa was on a book tour here in Cambridgeshire. He sold his memoir by having book tours and getting subscribers to pay for reduced price copies of his book in advance. The subscribers' fees paid for publishing the book. He was a smart businessman as well as a good writer."

"He didn't use a publisher?"

"No, dear. His book was self-published. And it sold very well, especially when he travelled on book tours. He travelled all over England, Scotland, and Ireland. Your mama loved to read, and she was interested in various causes, so she went to one of his stops on the book tour here in town. Her name is listed as one of the subscribers."

"Really?! I didn't know that."

"Oh, yes. We have a copy here somewhere. It was. . . I believe. . . the third edition of his memoir." Grandmamma walked over to the bookcase and lightly fingered the spines of the books until she found it. She opened the book and showed me Mama's name in Papa's book. I touched her name as a tear wet the page.

"Take this copy with you, Joanna. You'll have both your parents near you with this book in your possession." I carefully tucked the book in with my dresses and closed my suitcase.

## CHAPTER FOUR: JOANNA

Uncle John came up to gather my bags and carry them downstairs. With the carriage safely packed, I hugged Grandmamma, accepted Uncle John's hand, and stepped into the carriage to embark on my school career.

Uncle John said the journey to the boarding school at Highbury would be less than two hours; I gazed out the window as Ely receded. The familiar sight of the occasional stream, flocks of geese, and mile upon mile of rolling hills with grazing sheep and cows, soothed my nervous heart.

Lulled to sleep by the rhythmic clopping of the horses' hooves and swaying motion of the carriage—I dreamed. I was riding a horse, galloping toward a village. All the people in the village were black and the men all looked like the portrait of Papa on his book—dark-skinned, frizzy black hair, eyebrows arched over oval eyes with brown irises, a broad, slightly flattened nose, and generous, unsmiling lips. The women resembled my doll, Miss Sissie—come to life, singing in unison with a chorus of drummers rising in echo.

I awoke disoriented when the carriage stopped. I peeked outside to see where we were and read the large wooden sign to the right of the front door—Mrs. Limebear's School for Young Ladies. Ahh . . . yes. Today was the first day of boarding school. No welcome from African villagers here.

Down the steps marched a tall, thin man, with a short black moustache, pointed shaven chin, ears that refused to lie against his head, and dark, questioning eyes. His eyebrows formed a permanent question, while his nose stood guard over all his features, lending a stern, disapproving look.

Still waking up, I watched from my seat as Uncle John dismounted the carriage and greeted the odd, thin man, dressed soberly in black. They shook hands and spoke to one another, though I couldn't hear their conversation. Moments later, the carriage door opened, and Uncle John helped me down and introduced Mr. Harding.

"How do you do, sir?" I curtsied as I had been instructed.

"What pretty manners. Welcome to Mrs. Limebear's School for Young Ladies. You are the third girl to arrive. Please follow me."

He led us to the front door, but not before I took in the aspect of my new abode. One large Scots pine tree stood erect in front of the windows on the left side of the school, reaching up above the roof, providing beauty, scent, and shade. The school was large, three stories high, with a wide front porch, constructed of brick, and several chimneys rising above the roof, boding well for heating.

I looked up at the school, wondering which room would be mine, when the headmistress, Mrs. Limebear, appeared at the entrance. Uncle John strode over and bowing slightly, introduced himself. He also presented a copy of Papa's memoir to Mrs. Limebear.

"Joanna, dear," Uncle John said, "Come and meet Mrs. Limebear."

My gaze reluctantly left the tree and landed on Mrs. Limebear. First impressions were immediately registered by both of us. I saw a large, imposing woman, standing straight, with graying hair braided up under a black cap, a shelf-like bosom and wide hips; black eyeglasses perched on the end of her nose. Her mouth formed a smile without pleasure—only appraisal.

Mrs. Limebear probably saw a well-dressed young woman, with good posture, pecan brown skin, a wide, rather flat nose, and large brown eyes. She attempted to mask her initial surprise with a nod.

Looking back, I know Uncle John told Mrs. Limebear I was mixed race, but I'm not sure what she envisioned—maybe someone 'less brown.' Africans and people of mixed race mingled among the upper and middle classes in London at that time, as now. It was not unheard of for English men to take African brides, or as in my parents' case, African men to take English brides. In the early 1800s in England, I heard there were over 20,000 Africans and people of mixed-African heritage. But when Mrs. Limebear saw me, her widened eyes and raised eyebrows marked her shock. I wonder what she expected.

"How do you do Mrs. Limebear, ma'am. It's a pleasure to meet you." I curtsied.

"I'm delighted to welcome you to the School for Young Ladies. You are all most welcome. Some of the girls have arrived and are already settling in. Mr. Harding will bring your things up to your room. I hope your trip was pleasant."

"Yes, ma'am. So pleasant that I fell asleep in the carriage!" I smiled.

"Well now. You are rested and ready to begin your school career. As I said, some of the girls are here already."

Uncle John joined the conversation. "I have heard only good reports of your school. I know many in the county are pleased to see you have re-opened."

"You're most kind. We usually have eight to ten girls; we have but seven young ladies this term. Due to some unfortunate circumstances the school closed for two years. With this incoming class I only accepted girls ten to twelve years old. But as the good Lord ordered it, they are all eleven and twelve. Three of the girls have returned—the twins and Miranda."

We stopped outside a large room to the right of the entrance hallway. In a large house this would be the drawing room, but Mrs. Limebear referred to it as a parlour. The room held an assortment of small tables, with high-backed cherry wood chairs, sans cushions. A chess set lay on one table, on another baskets with spools of thread and material, on the third table a basket contained charcoal pencils and an easel stood behind the table.

"The young ladies of our school will become mistresses of their own households. They must learn how to entertain, hold engaging conversations, and ladylike endeavors such as embroidery and drawing. This room and the activities engaged therein will prepare the young ladies to move in society with manners and skills befitting their station in life."

I later learned the "station in life" of the other girls. Most of their fathers were in some profession or other, barristers and solicitors, bankers and merchants. They would have been considered upper middle class, like Uncle John.

Mrs. Limebear gestured with her hand to the features of the room. I wondered if this were to be the extent of my "education." I did not need to come to school to learn chess, drawing, and embroidery. Uncle John taught me chess, my grandmamma taught me embroidery, and why do I need to learn drawing anyway?! As I contemplated the limits and uselessness of such an education, Mrs. Limebear drew us over to the opposite room.

"This is our classroom," she stated proudly. "As you can see, it's divided into two rooms. Unfortunately, the fireplace heats this side more efficiently, but the girls rotate sides often. Here to my left is our history room." The area to which she pointed had a long rectangular table with ten hard-backed chairs placed evenly around the table. At each place lay lined paper, quill, and an ink stand. In the center of the table stood a most unusual globe etched in wood and painted with bright colours. England was prominent, larger than life, and the only country painted purple. Two unlit lamps sat on either side of the globe. At the end of the table a large map of Europe was displayed on an easel. I wandered over to take a closer look.

"You have an interest in geography, Miss Joanna?" asked Mrs. Limebear.

"Yes. I find other countries fascinating. My father wrote about Africa, and I would love to learn more."

"How interesting. Mr. Harding teaches history and geography. We focus mainly on England, and Europe, but we do touch on other continents—Asia, Africa, Australia, North and South America. Little is known of Africa. Some explorers and missionaries are only now bringing back reports of the land and customs there."

Mrs. Limebear walked quickly to the other side of the room, separated by a four-foot-tall wooden screen, which folded like an accordion.

"Over here I teach grammar, writing, French, and arithmetic." An identical rectangular table surrounded by ten chairs stood in the center of the room. Noticeably cooler than the other side, large windows facing east caught the morning sun. At each place a book, charcoal pencil, and paper were neatly arranged.

I looked around, wondering if I would be happy in this new, ordered, soul-less environment. I thought longingly of the trees and garden outside, preferring their wild beauty and asymmetry to the enforced pattern in the classroom. I hoped the stables held horses we could ride.

Mrs. Limebear brought me back to the present by asking, "Do you enjoy reading, Joanna? We have an extensive library here."

"Yes, ma'am. I enjoy it very much. I read the bible every morning and Uncle John has a wonderful library. I read *Camilla* by Mrs. Burney, *The Mysteries of Udolfo* by Mrs. Radcliffe, and *Emmeline-The Orphan of the Castle* by Charlotte Smith. I want to read Shakespeare, but Uncle John doesn't believe I'm ready!"

"In a year or two some of Shakespeare's plays would be more appropriate. There's an excessive amount of dying and debauchery in most of his plays, not proper for young ladies. In fact, I'm not certain Mrs. Radcliffe's novels are quite appropriate either!" Mrs. Limebear frowned.

As we discussed novels and plays, a striking young girl appeared in the doorway. Her blond hair flowed loosely around her shoulders, and her face was perfectly symmetrical—almost too perfect. Two blue eyes looked into my brown eyes, wearing a stunned expression. Light blue ribbons attached under the bodice of her white dress hung down almost to the floor. I imagined the girl swirling around a festive maypole and could not suppress a grin at the image.

She curtsied slightly to Uncle John, addressing her remarks to Mrs. Limebear. "Please excuse me, ma'am. I finished unpacking and came to see if you needed any assistance."

# CHAPTER FOUR: JOANNA

"Miranda, come in and meet our new pupil. Miranda, this is Miss Joanna Vassa. And this is her guardian, Mr. Audley."

"Pleased to meet you," Miranda said.

"Nice to meet you," I replied.

"Your room is next to mine. May I show her, Mrs. Limebear?" Miranda asked.

"Yes, please do, Miranda. My legs are tired, and I happily relinquish the task of walking up two flights to you. Mr. Harding has already deposited Miss Joanna's trunk in her room. Miss Vassa can see the library and the music room another time." Turning to Mr. Audley, she asked him, "Would you care to stay for a cup of tea, or a glass of something a bit stronger?"

"Thank you, ma'am, but duties call me homeward. I'll say my goodbyes and head back down to London—hopefully, I'll reach home by nightfall." Mr. Audley turned to pull me aside to say goodbye.

Out of hearing of Miranda and Mrs. Limebear, Uncle John leaned in and said softly, "I know you're worried about fitting in, but I'm sure you'll be fine. This young lady seems friendly, and Mrs. Limebear has an excellent reputation. Write as often as you like. Your first break is Christmas, and your grandmother and I will be fighting for the pleasure of seeing you first."

Tears formed and clung to my eyelashes; I gripped Uncle John's arm. "Oh, Uncle John. I miss you already and you haven't even left! I hope I can make a friend. I hope I don't make any awful mistakes. Sometimes I feel so out of place."

"Just be yourself. They can't help but like you," Uncle John said, as if it were obvious.

"Pray for me, Uncle John?" I pleaded.

"Certainly, my dear. As I do every day. When you retire and say your prayers, I'll be thinking of you and praying for you. My dear girl, be strong! You've faced new experiences before and acquitted yourself admirably. I know you'll do well here. No tears," he added as the tears threatened to spill out onto my cheeks. He put his thumb up as one tear rolled out and blew it away—our secret sign that God would blow my troubles away.

"I'll . . . be fine. Thank you, Uncle John. Do write. Won't you? I promise to write every week—no—every day!" I proclaimed.

"Every week is fine, my child. I'll tell you all the news of London and home. This young lady is ready to show you your room, perhaps you have a friend already," he said in parting.

I braced myself for uncle's departure, gave him a fierce, quick hug, wished him Godspeed, and turned to Miranda, ready to be led to my new life. Uncle John bowed to Mrs. Limebear and departed for his London home. He had told me I was the first non-White girl to attend the school, and he had informed Mrs. Limebear of my mixed background, but she still looked surprised when she saw me. I guess hearing you will have a half-English, half-African girl doesn't adequately prepare you to meet her in the flesh.

Miranda sashayed over to me, putting the blue ribbons in motion, and asked me to follow her upstairs. "You will adore your room. It is simply divine! There is a heavenly canopy over the bed, and the loveliest mauve curtains. Here, I'll show you my room first."

Miranda stopped at a door and opened it with a flourish to show off her room. Two beds sat side by side, separated by a small night table. A lamp and a bible graced the table. Both appeared well used. One large dresser stood at an angle in the corner, with room for a few dresses, and four drawers for undergarments. Across from the dresser, a table holding a bowl and pitcher stood against the wall—with a small oval mirror hanging on the wall above it. Each bed was covered with a quilt, made of green, blue, and orange squares. The curtains were burnt orange, held back by ties, revealing a view of the front drive and hemlock trees across the street.

"This is a lovely room! I hope my room is like this. Is there another girl staying with you?" I asked.

"You'll like your room even better. This is plain compared to yours. Anne is sharing the room with me. She's new like you."

"You've been here before, at the school?"

"I was here before the fire, two years ago."

"There was a fire . . . here? I wondered why the school had closed. I don't think my uncle knew about the fire."

"It was terrible. The fire started in the parlour and Mr. Limebear tried to put it out. It grew big fast. He had no chance to get out. We girls were rushed outside—in our nightdresses! He battled the fire, with Mrs. Limebear yelling for help, urging him to come out."

Miranda paused, seemingly caught in her memories. "Mr. Harding and Miss Maisie came with buckets of water, but by that time Mr.

Limebear had been overcome by the smoke and was unconscious on the floor. The two of them managed to pull him out, as Mrs. Limebear started directing everyone. I couldn't believe she could be so calm with her husband dying right there. She just took charge, ordered Mr. Harding to send for a doctor, and Maisie to get all of us girls in a line with buckets, almost emptying the pond to put the last of the flames out. Mr. Limebear never recovered. Mrs. Limebear didn't go to him and cry over him, or faint, or any of those things ladies supposedly do in a crisis."

I wondered what kind of woman could be so cold, so callous, that she would not collapse in grief over a dying husband. But what I said was, "How tragic. I never would guess there was a fire here but two years ago. There are no signs."

"No," said Miranda. "There wouldn't be. She threw out everything the fire touched and repaired and restored the floor and walls. Mrs. Limebear is very businesslike—no fuss, no muss, no tears."

If Mrs. Limebear was so unfeeling when her husband died, I thought, I can't expect to find any sympathy or solace from her while I adjust. I'll have to be strong and keep my feelings and tears to myself.

# CHAPTER FIVE

## Olu

### 3 November 1754—7 months later

Every day I learned new things—how to sew and mend; sweep and dust; empty chamber pots and fireplaces; chop and dice; wring out wet sheets and fold dry ones. There was a specific way to do each task, and sometimes it made no sense to me. Every night I looked forward to the solitude of my hard, straw mat. Once upon it, I cried.

Now that I understood the rules, and most English spoken to me, I managed to avoid punishment—dinner withheld, extra chores, threats to put me out in the fields with the 'hands.' The list of things we could not do was so lengthy, at times we thought we'd never learn it all—but we did.

DON'T GO OUTSIDE WITHOUT PERMISSION
DON'T TALK FIRST—TO ANYONE
DON'T TALK BACK TO MASTER OR MISTRESS
DON'T LOOK MASTER OR MISTRESS IN THE EYE
DON'T LEAVE YOUR ROOM UNTIL YOU'RE DRESSED
DON'T GO ANYWHERE WITHOUT PERMISSION
DON'T TALK ABOUT HOME OR FAMILY IN AFRICA
DON'T SPEAK AN AFRICAN LANGUAGE
DON'T STOP WORKING UNTIL YOUR JOB IS DONE
DON'T TOUCH ANYTHING IN THE HOUSE WITHOUT PERMISSION

I heard slaves speak of harsher punishments from other masters, but Mr. Cross allowed whipping only on rare occasions, not due to the goodness of his heart as much as to the belief that it led to less productive slaves. Pragmatism and expediency ruled Mr. Samuel Cross. He wanted the most amount of work done in the shortest amount of time with the least amount of trouble producing the greatest income. I wouldn't call him a fair man, as I was privy to his darker side, but others might.

I heard he visited other plantations and homesteads and observed how other overseers treated slaves. Comparing methods and results, he concluded that the best run, most productive plantations had somewhat well-treated slaves who were given enough to eat, a day off a week, and permission to marry. At the plantations where slaves were whipped, cursed at, deprived of food, and forbidden to marry, the slaves died often and early, requiring more money spent on new slaves. Witnessing this discrepancy in treatment and output, Mr. Cross decided upon the former approach. Thus, I did not fear beatings or starvation. I did fear the lustful eye and roving hand of Mr. Cross, and separation from Suraya.

We soon settled into a routine. After a few weeks, the enormity of the house—especially compared to our two-room mud house at home—ceased to overwhelm us. Miss Martha took us all over the house, from the attic where I shared a room with Suraya, I never did call her Sarah, to the cellar, where vegetables and grains were stored. I grew accustomed to the labyrinthine hallways and knew the quickest way to get in and out of any room. This came in handy when Mr. Cross took it into his mind to pursue me.

Those first few weeks we made many mistakes, and both Suraya and I felt we couldn't get anything done right. The water was too hot, or too cold; we didn't look down enough, or we looked down too much; we didn't curtsy or bow properly; we rushed too much or were too slow. No matter what Suraya and I did we could never satisfy Mrs. Beth or Master Cross. Although I was by no means comfortable at the Cross household, my greatest fear was being sold. I heard slaves talk about life on other plantations, with other masters. I counted my blessings.

The third day after we arrived, we were expected to begin our regular duties. Still learning English, our mistakes were often the result of misunderstanding directions. Mrs. Beth and I developed an elaborate, exaggerated sign language in those first few weeks. I donned my new (to me) dress—frill-less, dark brown, mid-calf length, collarless, mid-length sleeves—defined more by features it lacked than by any laudable qualities. It was not shapely, pretty, fashionable, or flattering. It was serviceable.

Nervous and unsure of myself, I tapped lightly on Mrs. Beth's door, as I had been directed to do by Miss Martha, and waited with one ear close to the door for a reply. Upon hearing the muted "yes," I opened the door and stood in the entrance to the room of the mistress of the house, eyes cast down.

Mrs. Beth spoke and motioned for me to come to her. Understanding the tone, but not the words, I tentatively entered the room, eyeing the large canopy bed, so high up I thought I would need a stool to even get on the bed—not that I would ever be permitted. The drapes on two long windows were thick and velvety, a deep shade of green, held back by carved wooden stays. Two large chests of drawers flanked the bed, one topped with combs and razors, coins, and handkerchiefs, and the other with ribbons, brushes, a small vase of dried flowers, and a framed drawing of Susannah on horseback. In the corner a large bowl with a matching ceramic pitcher rested on a small blue table. My eyes lit on the pitcher, twice as big as the one in my room, as Mrs. Beth picked it up and thrust it at me.

I understood from her motions and tone that I was meant to fill it with water. I took the pitcher, with a firm grasp in both hands, nodded, and fled down the stairs.

I could hear her speaking to me as I ran down the stairs, but before Mrs. Beth finished the sentence I tripped over the carpet at the bottom of the stairs, dropped the pitcher, and fell hard, ripping my dress in the process.

On my hands and knees at the bottom of the staircase, pitcher pieces digging into my hand, I was trying to figure out where the blood was coming from on my bruised body when I heard Mrs. Beth yell and complain, ending with one word I knew, "Martha!!"

Miss Martha was already on her way out of the kitchen, having heard the crash, and she reached me before Mrs. Beth did, although Mrs. Beth was in no hurry to help. Miss Martha assessed the situation at once, taking in my position, bloodied hand, torn dress, and the smashed pitcher. The offending carpet, the true culprit in my first disaster, was pushed out from its place at the bottom of the stairs and lay in ignominy against the wall.

Miss Martha murmured to herself, lamenting the broken vase more than my wounded hand, I think, pushing my hand away when I tried to help her clean up. She called up to Mrs. Beth with apologies and calming words, attempting to placate her. At the end of Mrs. Beth's diatribe, she yelled, "You hear, gel? NO MORE ACCIDENTS." Hearing wasn't the problem.

## CHAPTER FIVE: OLU

Miss Martha lifted me up gingerly, avoiding my bloody hand, and led me into the kitchen, talking all the while. She talked as she washed off my hand, and I made out a few words—vase, Mrs. Beth, fix, a'ight.

I took slow, deep breaths, trying to calm myself down; listening to Miss Martha helped. I wanted to explain to her what happened but couldn't find the words. I demonstrated slipping on the rug, falling forward, dropping the pitcher, and landing in its shards. Unfortunately, my performance was a little too life-like, for when I landed, I hurt my hand again.

Miss Martha grabbed a small square of a handkerchief and pressed it on my hand. I winced but tried to hold back a cry of pain. The bleeding stanched, Miss Martha rubbed a peeled potato on the cut, an old remedy to aid healing and prevent infection. This was the first of many remedies I learned from Miss Martha, who had learned them from African slaves—African remedies for a new world.

Miss Martha eyed my dress and motioned for me to get my only other dress. I would be up late that night washing and mending this dress. Miss Martha filled the new pitcher from the well while I cleaned up the fragments of the broken vase. Once the vase remnants were gathered, the rug returned to its position at the bottom of the staircase, and my new (old) dress in place, I asked Miss Martha, "What now do?"

"What do I do now?" Miss Martha responded. Funny how she could speak properly when she was teaching me how to speak English, but most of the time she chose to speak her own form of English.

"What do I do now?" I drew out each word as I spoke.

She continued to speak, and pointed upstairs, nudging me.

I walked with careful, deliberate steps up the stairs, holding the newly filled pitcher tightly in my sore hands. Mrs. Beth was already dressed, but the back of her dress was unbuttoned. She sat at a dressing table, brushing her long blond hair. Spotting me in the mirror, she handed me her brush.

As I sat the pitcher down on the stand, she pointed to the back of her dress, which needed buttoning up, and pointed to her hair, saying "braid." I understood she wanted me to button her up and fix her hair. I apologized again for breaking her vase. "Sorry, vase, ma'am," I said as I buttoned up her dress, trying to ignore my throbbing hands.

As I began to brush her hair, I had to ask what "braid" was, as it was a yet unfamiliar English word. "Braid? Ma'am?"

Mrs. Beth reached back, grabbed three handfuls of hair, and began to weave them into a loose braid to demonstrate. I was so relieved and happy at that moment. I knew how to braid hair and I did it well. I didn't have any sisters, only brothers, but my mama taught me to braid hair and I practiced often on my friends' or half-sisters' hair. For certain ceremonies, elaborate braids were called for, and I could braid hair in several styles. I hesitated, not sure which style Mrs. Beth would prefer, and wondered how her fine hair would hold a braid.

I decided narrow, tight cornrows would not work on her hair, so I began to weave her hair into large, loose cornrows, ending in a braid that would hang down onto her shoulders. Judging the thickness and length of her hair, I figured nine braids would be about right, three in each of three sections. As I braided, Mrs. Beth haranguing, and I made out the words "simple" and "braid." I wasn't sure what "simple" meant. I eased up, thinking to myself how silly it was to go to the trouble of braiding hair, and not doing it so it would last more than a day.

After I had finished with one third of her head, the right side, and moved to the center, Mrs. Beth began to wiggle and squirm. I continued braiding, my stinging fingers moving slowly over her fine hair. As I braided, I thought back to the last time I had braided hair—as different as night and day.

Imani and I, my half-sister by our father's third wife, sat outside gazing at the goats. Our brother Ezinzwe was standing near the goats, leaning on a large stick, drawing a design in the dirt with his bare toe. Imani and I giggled together about how skinny he looked—tall, thin, and gangly like a baby giraffe—unsure how to navigate in its growing body. Then I began to braid Imani's hair, which when pulled out straight reached out to about the width of my hand. Pulling tightly, ignoring Imani's whimper of pain, I braided an intricate design resembling intertwining coiled snakes onto Imani's stretched scalp. We continued to make fun of Ezinzwe and other boys in the village as I spent the afternoon braiding. Hours passed. When I finished, Imani bolted up and ran to the pond to admire her reflection—reaching up to touch the braids as she ran. Gazing back out of the water was a beautiful, dark-skinned girl with an elaborate, intricately braided head. The original design delighted Imani, who hugged me fiercely when I arrived at her side by the pond. Mrs. Beth's blond braids replaced the vision of Imani's head reflected in the water, as I focused on the task before me, reining in tears. I finished and admired the braids lying against Mrs. Beth's head and hanging down onto her shoulders.

Mrs. Beth did not reach up to pat her head or run to the mirror, but she rose in slow motion and walked to the mirror. She looked at her reflection, and I thought she must be pleased with the pretty design and evenness of the braids. I was mistaken. She looked at her reflection—and screamed.

Mrs. Beth snatched the brush from my hand and began beating me with it on my arms and head. A man appeared in the doorway. Ashamed and frightened, and clueless about what I had done wrong, I bowed my head, dropped into a clumsy curtsy, and withdrew to the window.

I was fascinated to hear him use the same placating tone Miss Martha used with Mrs. Beth. The man seemed to assess the scene quickly, taking in Mrs. Beth's newly braided hair, me cowering by the window, and Mrs. Beth's scowling face. He diffused the tension and anger in the room with his calming presence.

Mrs. Beth pointed at me and at her hair as she began a diatribe, no doubt telling him about the broken vase and how much she detested the braids. The man just smiled, and seemed to compliment Mrs. Beth, maybe telling her the braids looked pretty. I couldn't believe my eyes. I still stood by the window but glanced up to see Mrs. Beth's reaction to this strange, smiling man. Her eyes softened and her anger seemed to dissipate. She smiled—something I had not seen before. If I didn't know better, I would think she had feelings for him.

Mrs. Beth looked in the mirror again, reassessing her braids. As she gazed at her reflection, I glanced up at this tall smiling man, just as he looked over at me—and slowly closed only his right eye! I had no idea what that meant, but accompanied by his slight smile, I took it as a good omen.

Pulling all the braids back behind her head, Mrs. Beth called me over and motioned for me to tie them all back in a ponytail. I wondered at the odd phrase. Why would Americans call hair a pony's tail? I gathered up the braids into one braid at the nape of her neck, and braided the smaller braids into one, tying the end with a blue ribbon lying on the table.

"What's her name?" the man looked over at me, and I met his gaze, although I knew I should continue looking down. He had a slightly sunburned face with small brown specks dotting his nose and cheeks peeking out from between the bushy moustache and beard dominating his face. I was unused to facial hair and thought it looked odd. His eyebrows were thick and dark brown, and his hair was a wavy mass of light brown curls reaching his collar. His nicest feature by far was his smile. I had seen so few smiles since Ledu and I parted. Slightly crooked teeth added to his charm. He looked much younger than Mr. Cross. I was grateful to him for his intervention, knowing that he saved me from a worse beating, or whipping, or selling.

Mrs. Beth told him my name was Olivia and called him Teddy. Teddy and Mrs. Beth continued to converse in English as I observed. I later learned he had just finished a job and often stopped by to see his brother, Mr. Cross, between jobs. I had a hard time believing this friendly man was brother to Mr. Cross; still do.

This exchange between my mistress and her husband's brother made me uneasy. I didn't understand the harmless flirting Teddy engaged in with Mrs. Beth—I would later learn he disarmed all women with his charm and wit.

Once Teddy left, Mrs. Beth resumed the examination of her new braids. She mumbled to herself, smiling, and dismissed me.

I moved with careful deliberation down the stairs, stepping gingerly on the offending rug at the bottom. Once in the kitchen, I exhaled.

Miss Martha looked up, eyebrows raised, "Yes, chile?"

"Mr. Teddy," I pointed upstairs.

"Mr. Teddy be here?" Miss Martha grinned.

"Nice . . . Mr. Teddy."

"Yes chile. He's nice."

Miss Martha added griddle cakes to the breakfast menu of fried tomatoes and porridge, and bread. She knew he could eat two large stacks, so she asked me for the large bowl and set me to breaking eggs. "Break?" I asked.

"Yeah," Miss Martha chuckled. I believe she was amazed at how little I knew—she didn't realize all the helpful things I knew about African life that were unnecessary here in America. I could scare off a lion, of little use here. I could braid hair into elaborate styles; my efforts here earned me a beating. I could weave a basket; here they used ceramic bowls. I could make elaborate necklaces and bracelets for engaged women—but somehow, I doubt the American women would be interested in our jewelry. I needed to learn skills useful in this new country, and Miss Martha could teach me.

I cracked four eggs into the bowl, fishing out a few errant eggshells. Miss Martha added milk and flour, some white powder, and sugar. She showed me how to beat the powder with a tool made of many rounded stalks of straw—a whisk, I later learned. I beat the mixture with all my might, ignoring the pain in my hands, emptying my frustrations and anger into the bowl, leaving no clumps intact. Miss Martha marveled at my skill with a whisk. I felt proud to have finally done something right and felt I would be more useful in the kitchen than serving Mrs. Beth.

Miss Martha added blueberries to the batter and ladled scoopfuls onto the grill, while I set the table, careful to follow the one place setting Miss Martha had set down as an example. The table was set for four— Mr. and Mrs. Cross, Mr. Teddy, and Susannah. As I came back into the kitchen I asked Miss Martha, "We eat?"

She nodded and pointed me to the rough wooden table there in the basement, and pointed upstairs saying, "Mrs. Beth, Master Cross, Miss Susannah." I understood I was to eat downstairs. It would take me some time to learn my "place." Back home I was always treated as a loved member of the family, the village, and the tribe. Here I was a producer of work, not worthy to eat with the master and his missus. I continually thought of home and my "place" there.

Miss Martha brought all the platters out, setting them on the sideboard. She directed me to observe and help serve, observing me with a slight frown marring her face. After ringing the bell, she retreated to the kitchen to grill more cakes.

Mrs. Beth was the first to appear, followed by Susannah and Mr. Teddy. Suraya joined Miss Martha in the kitchen. Susannah was admiring her mother's hair as they sat down at the dining room table.

I went downstairs and met Suraya in the kitchen. Her morning had been uneventful, and when I tried to explain my mishap with the broken pitcher and Mrs. Beth beating me with her brush, her eyes widened. As we whispered to each other in the kitchen, Mr. Cross entered—stomping his boots to loosen the mud and grass. He pointed at Suraya and me and asked Miss Martha a question.

Miss Martha flipped a griddle cake, catching Mr. Cross's attention and arousing his hunger. Miss Martha defended us and distracted him with breakfast. When Mr. Cross saw the blueberries, his expression changed from anger to anticipation.

Teddy pushed open the door, strode into the kitchen, and walked over to greet his brother. Juxtaposed, their differences, and similarities, were striking. They were both over six feet tall, and where Teddy had a face full of hair, Mr. Samuel was clean shaven. Teddy's long and curly hair contrasted with Mr. Samuel's straight, short hair. Teddy had slightly crooked teeth, but Mr. Samuel's rare smile revealed perfectly aligned white teeth. But their eyes were the most strikingly different. Teddy's eyes glimmered, especially when he smiled. Mr. Samuel's eyes pierced and commanded, softening only when he was with Susannah. Teddy had full smiling lips, underneath all the facial hair, while Mr. Samuel had thin, firm lips. One could tell simply by looking at the two men who was optimist and who pessimist, flexible and rigid, loving and stern.

Teddy patted his brother on the back and grinned at him. He waved his hand over the breakfast table as he talked and closed one eye as he looked at Miss Martha. I asked Miss Martha what that meant later, and she smiled and said it was a wink, like a private joke between friends. I had never met Teddy before, so I wondered what joke we shared when he winked at me over Mrs. Beth's braids.

Teddy came closer to Mr. Samuel and whispered a warning. I heard the word 'compliment,' and knew somehow, he was again trying to protect me. Mr. Samuel asked Teddy what he meant, more loudly than necessary. Teddy urged his big brother to compliment his wife.

Mr. Samuel led the way into the dining room, followed by Miss Martha, carrying a creamer brimming with fresh cream and a dish of sugar, and me bringing in more griddle cakes. Teddy entered the dining room in time to hear his brother exclaim over his wife's new hairdo.

What Teddy missed, but I glimpsed as I was putting down another platter of griddle cakes on the sideboard, was the expression of shock and puzzlement on Mr. Samuel's face as he saw the braids. He recovered quite well and delivered the line with sincerity. Mrs. Beth believed her taciturn husband, and reaching up to pat her braids, blushed and smiled.

Mr. Samuel took his place at the head of the table, Teddy seated himself at the other end, and mother and daughter sat across from each other. Miss Martha enlisted me to help serve and she put Suraya to work in the kitchen chopping vegetables for dinner.

From the soil of this inauspicious beginning—shattered vase, uncommon and unwelcome braids—I learned to become a helpful and indeed, if I say so myself, indispensable maid. The daily routine became a source of some comfort and predictability, but also a cause of restlessness. The physical labor was tiring—lifting, washing, cleaning, sweeping, chopping, mending—but my mind was often back home. I had given up the dream of returning home, but still harbored hope of finding Ledu. I couldn't reconcile myself to slavery, and never considered myself a slave. Suraya didn't share my yearning for the North and freedom, and hushed me when I spoke of it, so slowly a wedge formed between us, and I learned to keep my ambitions to myself.

# CHAPTER SIX

## Joanna

15 September 1807

I HAD ONE AMBITION—TO make a friend. Miranda led me to my room, and I realized I was the only one in a room alone. With an uneven number of girls, Mrs. Limebear left only me, the half-African girl, without a roommate. Even at the time, when I was twelve years old, I didn't think it was a coincidence that only I was alone. The room was lovely, but I would have preferred a simple room with a roommate.

The canopy over the single bed in the room lent a fashionable flair to the room, with curtains in the same shade of mauve as the canopy. The large dresser had silver handles, and the royal blue pitcher and bowl perched on an ornate cherry stand. I could view the side yard and garden from the window. Although my room was not "divine," nor did I "adore" it, it did become a peaceful refuge.

After we all settled in, the bell rang for supper. Mrs. Limebear sat at one end of the table and gestured for me to sit to her left. Mr. Harding sat at the opposite end, flanked by the twins, Rose and Violet. No one sat next to me; Anne sat on the seat next to Rose, one empty seat away from me. Miranda sat across from me, then Candace, and Samantha sat next to Violet. This seating arrangement would be permanent. Only if another student arrived would I have a meal mate other than Mrs. Limebear. Miss Maisie, cook and maid of all work, placed a soup bowl before each of us. Maisie was dark-skinned, with large hips; a generous bosom; wide, often smiling lips; a broad, flat nose; and earlobes with elongated holes.

"Now that you are all here, I have the honour of welcoming you, and welcoming you back," Mrs. Limebear said, nodding to Miranda, Rose, and Violet, "to Mrs. Limebear's School for Young Ladies. As you know, we had to close two years ago after a very . . . unfortunate fire. Sometime after the grievous loss we were able to restore the school to its former glory. So now I welcome you most heartily to our *new* school."

Mrs. Limebear paused to give us a chance to finish our soup, observing our etiquette. "Girls, I would have you observe Miranda as she eats her soup. She is most properly filling the spoon away from her, not completely, and leaning forward ever so slightly, delicately bringing the soup spoon to her mouth. Most proper. The manner in which you eat soup says much about a young lady, and I would have you accomplish every task in the most refined way, as befitting a girl at my school. There are no small, unimportant tasks to be ignored or brushed aside. From dress, to deportment, to eating, to conversing—all reflect on the young women you are becoming."

"Thank you, Mrs. Limebear. My mum is most insistent that I do not slurp my soup," Miranda nodded demurely. Violet stifled a laugh and ended up blowing her soup right off the spoon. As the other girls giggled softly, Mrs. Limebear scowled at Violet. "My dear girl, that is exactly the sort of behavior we do not entertain at this table!"

Violet began to sip her soup in a very ladylike manner. She looked up at Mrs. Limebear and asked, "Mrs. Limebear, will we be allowed to take riding lessons this year? I think Miranda would love to ride Seamus." Miranda coughed into her soup spoon, blowing the contents across the table, and right into my soup bowl. Violet told us later about an incident before the fire when Miranda took Seamus, one of the stable horses, out at night for a ride without permission.

"Oh!" I exclaimed.

"My gracious! Miranda, after I just complimented you on your fine manners. Your soup landed right in Joanna's bowl." Lifting her voice, Mrs. Limebear called out, "Maisie, another bowl of soup for Miss Joanna."

"Oh, thank you, ma'am, but I was almost finished. It really isn't necessary," I demurred.

"Well, you should be able to have your full bowl of soup. You needn't finish this bowl," she added, as Maisie laid a fresh bowl down in front of me, picking up the tainted bowl. "How careless of you Miranda. We're not getting a very good start to our first dinner, are we girls? I think I will omit the soup from our next dinner menu and give you time to remember your table manners."

Miranda leaned back to scowl at Violet at the end of the table, in vain as Violet focused on her soup, spoon by slow and careful spoon. I sensed the undercurrents between Miranda and Violet, and surmised they were friends, but not knowing the private joke they shared at the time, I felt excluded. Returning to Violet's query, I said, "I love to ride. My Uncle John has given me some lessons. He has a gentle mare, easy to learn on."

"Seamus is the opposite of gentle," Violet exclaimed.

Mrs. Limebear cut in, "I had not planned on offering riding lessons, but you girls may be approaching the age at which riding lessons would be appropriate. I do, however, have a most exciting trip planned which involves horses."

The girls erupted at once, having forgotten all their carefully learned table manners.

"To Mr. Astley's, is it?" cried Samantha.

"Oh, to the Amphitheatre to see Mr. Astley?" echoed Candace.

"Mr. Astley's amazing horses—how fun!" exclaimed Rose.

"Yes, to all of you. You have guessed aright. We will be taking a fun, educational trip to Mr. Astley's Amphitheatre. This is something I hope you will all look forward to, and it goes without saying that only girls who show proper behavior in the next few months will attend." The girls whispered quietly among themselves, but I had a hidden reason to see Astley's—one I didn't want to share with these new girls yet.

Mrs. Limebear shifted the subject back to her introduction. "For some of you, this is your first time away from home. I'd like to welcome our new girls, Joanna, Anne, Candace, and Samantha. You may miss your family for the first few days, or even weeks, but mark my word—you will become accustomed to school life and make new friends.

"Most, if not all of you, will become mistresses of your own households. When you leave this establishment, you will be introduced to eligible gentlemen, some of whom will no doubt be enamored by your fine manners, although today is no indication, your deportment, your knowledge of the world, and ask your father for your hand in marriage."

Of course, Mrs. Limebear did not consider her sole fatherless student. I had no kind father to accept proposals or give me away in marriage.

"You will marry gentlemen and have children and will require skills to run an efficient household. Accounting skills, cooking skills, sewing skills are all necessary. You will not have to personally perform all these tasks, but you should be acquainted with them all, so you can supervise those who do. If you have a competent knowledge of bookkeeping, no one can swindle you. If you know the difference between a well-cooked and an under-cooked goose, you do not have to rely on a cook's defense of poor cooking. If you know how to sew and mend, you can expect the best stitches from those who make or repair your clothing. You need not become chefs, but you do need to become familiar with menus and basic cooking skills. You will not become housemaids," Samantha interjected "God forbid" as Mrs. Limebear silenced her with a look. "You will not become housemaids," Mrs. Limebear repeated, "however, you will learn to apply standards of cleanliness and what is required to maintain a clean home, free of dust, smoke, smells, and mildew. You will not become laundresses," she paused waiting for another interjection, which did not come, "but must be familiar with the steps involved in cleaning clothes, bed sheets, curtains, towels, and such.

"Most importantly, you will learn history, government, and geography. Thus, when your husband's business associates, family members, or neighbors are invited to dine, you will be able to join in the conversation, not humiliating your husband with a lack of knowledge, but impressing all with your well-rounded knowledge of England and her position in the world.

"I have talked enough. Go ahead and finish your supper now," Mrs. Limebear said.

The girls were finishing their meat and bread and began to chatter amongst themselves. Miranda turned to Candace, seated next to her. "Aren't you excited?! You will adore this school. I attended before the fire and my father wouldn't dream of sending me to another school. I've had a tutor for these past two years."

"Really? I had a tutor also—I was quite happy staying at home, but Father thought I should go away to school. I'm an only child. He thought I would enjoy being around girls my same age," Candace replied, although as I listened, I received the distinct impression that Candace would be happier not being around girls her age.

"An only child. I envy you. My little sister can be such a pest. She follows me everywhere and wants me to braid her hair and play with her dolls," Miranda complained.

"That's funny. I would love to have a little sister, I think. I guess we always want what we don't have," Candace replied.

## CHAPTER SIX: JOANNA

Rose was telling Anne about the school, while Violet regaled Samantha with stories about the girls who attended before the fire.

Mrs. Limebear monopolized me, asking about my family.

I told her I was orphaned when I was two, as my mama, papa, and sister had all died within the span of one year. She offered condolences and asked about my Uncle John. I explained I had lived with my grandmamma—on my mother's side—in Ely until I was eight. Then I moved in with my Uncle John, but often visit my grandmamma. Uncle John was appointed by Papa as my guardian in his will, and he's not my real uncle.

Mrs. Limebear knew the basics about my parentage, that I was half English and half African. I told her my mother's name, Susannah Cullen and that my father was from Igboland in Nigeria. After he worked as a slave on British naval ships during the war against the French in the 1750s, he was sold to a West Indies planter. Eventually, he earned enough money to buy his freedom.

All the girls were listening intently by this time and my words carried to the end of the table. I assumed they might be trying to place my accent. It's mostly British, but with a twinge of something foreign. An indescribable lilt. Not a Yorkshire accent, an Irish brogue, nor a London twang.

The girls seemed fascinated with my story and curious about my background. My mixed parentage explained the pecan skin tone, and wide nose. I looked like a brown-skinned African but behaved as a proper English girl, or at least I believe I did. All the other girls had standard English mums and papas, and had probably never even known an African, or seen one up close, other than the occasional servant. Mr. Harding stared at me from the end of the table. His expression, vaguely menacing and unpleasant, caused me to stumble on my words.

"How old was your father when he became a slave?" Miranda asked.

"Oh, um... he, my papa... he was kidnapped when he was almost eleven years old," I replied.

Anne and Candace exchanged glances. "I'm eleven," Anne said softly.

I realized during William Wilberforce's speech that I was older than Papa had been when he was kidnapped. I couldn't imagine being kidnapped, but I did know what it felt like to be separated from parents. The girls were all silent for a few moments.

"So how did he get free?" Samantha asked.

"He would buy goods in the West Indies—fruit, sugar, rum—and sell them in America for a profit. He saved up enough to buy his own freedom." I repeated what I had learned from others and read in Papa's memoir.

"That's amazing. How much did his freedom cost?" Anne asked.

"Forty pounds."

"How do you know all this about your father, if he died when you were only two years old," Candace wondered.

"My papa wrote a book about his life. I read it twice." I looked around at the girls' openly shocked faces and wanted to change the subject. I wanted to fit in at the school, not be on display like a statue in a museum.

Mrs. Limebear looked at me thoughtfully. "Your Uncle John gave me the book and I will enjoy reading it. Maybe we can incorporate some of the information into our lesson plans."

"I'm surprised he knew how to write," Mr. Harding whispered, but I heard him loud and clear.

"Joanna," Candace chimed in again, "were his parents slaves, too?"

"No, only my papa and his sister were kidnapped."

"You have an aunt!" Anne smiled at me.

An aunt! I suddenly remembered Uncle John talking about Papa's sister. When I read Papa's memoir, the part about the kidnapping included brief mention of his sister. I thought of her almost like a character in a book—remote, imaginary, never aging. This new thought, this chance my aunt might still be alive, overwhelmed me. I wanted to stop this conversation, go to my room, and ponder all the ramifications of this new possibility.

Mrs. Limebear, noticing the tone had become somewhat melancholy, attracted the girls' attention. "There now, girls. Enough questions for Miss Joanna. Her family story is fascinating I dare say, and we can learn more about it in her father's book."

"So, your father became a writer," Anne said.

"Umm, you could say that. Mostly he was an abolitionist," I replied.

"An ablution who??" Violet ventured.

"An abolitionist. Someone who fights against slavery. Like Mr. Wilberforce in Parliament." I mentioned the most prominent person I knew.

Half the girls looked puzzled, and the others smiled or nodded their heads, possibly too ashamed to admit they had no idea who Mr. Wilberforce was, but they all turned back to their plates to see if there were any morsels left untouched. Mrs. Limebear rang the bell, and Miss Maisie came in to clear the dishes and set down the pudding. I eyed Maisie, without looking directly at her, wondering what her life had been like, how she came to England.

After eating all the pudding, and asking for more, the girls filed into the parlor for chess and reading. I sat with Mr. Harding before a cribbage board. He didn't speak at all and glared at me with a firm expression and furrowed eyebrows. I couldn't figure out if it was just me he disapproved of, or all the young ladies, but he made me quite uncomfortable. Rose, Violet, Anne, and Candace were playing casino, and Miranda and Samantha were playing a game of chess. Mrs. Limebear went into the kitchen to review the menu for the following day with Maisie.

An hour or so later, alone in my room, I tried without success to undo the buttons on the back of my frock. At home, whether at Grandmamma's or Uncle John's house, a maid was always on hand to assist with my dress and hair. Frustrated, tired and lonely, I didn't want to seek help. I resigned myself to sleeping in my frock when I heard a soft tap on the door.

"Come in." I was greeted by the smiling face of Miss Maisie, bearing a pitcher of warm water for washing up.

I looked up and gave her a shy smile. "Miss Maisie. I was wondering how I would get out of this frock. Could you help me with the buttons on the back?"

"Oh, you poor chile. You all alone—all them others have somebody to help. Turn around there. I'll have these done quick'r than a man can woo a maid." Miss Maisie unbuttoned the frock expertly and quickly—then turned me around and placed her calloused hands on my shoulders. Maisie vowed to help me dress and undress and asked me to call on her whenever I needed help. She was busy, but not too busy to help me out, especially as I was the only girl in a room alone. She patted my shoulders, wished me a good night and bustled out of the room, taking her cheering presence with her, leaving me more bereft than I felt minutes earlier. Mrs. Limebear walked down the hallway, calling out to the closed doors, "Lamps out, girls. Good night. Breakfast is at 8 am. The bell will wake you at 7:15."

I removed my frock, folded it and gently placed it in the wardrobe. I pulled on the muslin nightgown and examined my face in the small mirror above the wash bowl. Small portraits of my parents provided the only clues to my features. My skin, the colour of a roasted chestnut, blended the very dark brown complexion of Papa with the milky white tenor of

Mama. My nose resembled Papa's, though a little less broad and a little higher, and my eyes and forehead were Mama's—although my eye colour was the same dark brown as Papa. My lips were neither as full as Papa's, nor as thin as Mama's. I freed my full, thick, long, dark brown hair which Grandmamma's maid had wrestled into a bun this morning—was that only this morning? Undoing the combs and pins, I fingered my hair out, reveling in its freeing fullness.

I thought of all the girls I had met and wondered who, if any, would become friends. As I often did, I felt my in-between-ness acutely. Neither fully African, nor completely English—not a girl, nor yet a woman—no living parents, but a devoted uncle and grandmamma—alone, yet not unloved. My mind wandered back to the evening at the Wilberforce home, and I remembered the pinky pledge with Barbara and Lizzy. I smiled remembering the unusual assortment of animals and people Wilberforce seemed to attract. I didn't feel out of place at all with the Wilberforces. Quite the contrary—I felt at home. My mind wandered from subject to subject as I blew out the lone remaining candle and climbed into bed. Aunt. Hmmm. Although I knew Papa had a sister with whom he'd been kidnapped, for some reason I never gave it much thought. For the first time I began to wonder who she was, where she was, if she were alive . . . How could I ever find her? My papa's sister. It suddenly meant everything in the world to me to find her. We were both related to and loved by Papa—we had that most important thing in common.

# CHAPTER SEVEN

# Olu

### 17 May 1757

Suraya and I had everything in common but were nothing alike. Three years after our arrival at the Cross plantation—now fifteen years old—events conspired to deepen the wedge between us. Our days were routine, blending into one another with little variation and no excitement, except when Teddy or someone else came for a visit, which also meant extra work. All of us looked forward to Teddy's visits. Me, because he would brighten my day. He had taught me to read in clandestine meetings before dawn and after bedtime. Each time we met in the cellar he had a candle, and I snuck down from my attic room using the back staircase to meet him. Or he would meet me as I hung sheets on the line outside. I remember well how it started. I was dusting the bookshelves in the library and took one book out to look at it. Of course, I couldn't read any words, but as I stood there, gazing at the book, trying to decipher it, Teddy walked in.

"What book do you have there, Miss Olivia?" he asked.

"I don't know, Mr. Teddy. I can't read."

"Would you like to?" He reached over and turned the book right side up.

"Yes! I would."

Teddy contrived to get some early readers, and whenever he came, three to four times a year, he would pick up with our reading lessons wherever we left off. He began with letter recognition, sound, and writing the letters, then progressed to short phonetic words: *The fat cat ate the rat; the mouse in the house has a louse.* In between I would try to read on my own. He not only taught me to read, but he also taught me to speak more like the Whites than the slaves. Mrs. Beth and Mr. Cross didn't seem to notice as my speech improved.

Mrs. Beth also cheered up whenever Teddy visited, which made my days easier. I still believe she wished she had married Teddy instead of his brother. But she couldn't live without her large house, slaves, and respectable position. Teddy refused to keep slaves and he traveled a lot—almost wandered. He followed his work. Wherever a house needed building, he would go. Mrs. Beth couldn't live like that. But I think she liked to believe she could. Mr. Cross liked his brother's visits because they would sit and talk for hours. Miss Martha loved to cook for Teddy, and he was always appreciative of her efforts.

My days would begin with assisting Mrs. Beth with her morning rituals. I never ceased to wonder why White women insisted on wearing dresses they couldn't put on without help. They seemed so helpless; I don't think anything would have gotten done without slaves around. Mrs. Beth needed assistance choosing her clothes, dressing, fixing her hair, bathing, and adorning herself with jewelry. All she seemed to manage on her own was telling others what to do. She needed no help to shout orders. After Mrs. Beth was ready to face the day, I would hurry downstairs to help Miss Martha in the kitchen.

Midday we would help Miss Martha prepare dinner. I had learned through many conversations with her that Miss Martha's mama was from Africa. Miss Martha was born on another plantation and came to the Cross plantation when she was a teen. She didn't know who her papa was, but he wasn't African—anyone could tell by looking at Martha that she was mixed, or as they said, colored. Looking at her daughter Elsie, several shades lighter than her mama, one could tell she was also mixed. It was common to see slaves with children of varying shades—from very dark to very light. The secret was on display for all to see—masters raped their female slaves. Miss Martha and I didn't speak of it but once when I was helping a slave birth her baby she whispered the baby was "got on her by the massa."

After Suraya and I helped Miss Martha prepare dinner, in the late afternoon we were often together in the vegetable garden—watering, weeding, and gossiping—my favorite part of the day. I loved the outdoors, and if I looked up at the sky, blocking out the house and the slaves in the field, I could almost, almost imagine I was back home in Igboland. Especially on a hot, hot day, when the humidity was low. Miss Martha had begun the garden years ago but had so little time to work on it that when Suraya and I offered to help, we ended up taking it over. We were quite proud of the size of the collard greens, yams, eggplants, potatoes, peppers, and tomatoes. Not to mention the beans, peas, and turnips.

Now that Susannah was twelve, she had a tutor most days. Noah, an eighteen-year-old from Philadelphia, had received his education largely from his father, a math professor at the newly founded College of Philadelphia. He had some notions that didn't quite fit in down here in South Carolina, and in turn, I believe he found Southern ways difficult to understand, and even more difficult to accept. Susannah harbored a secret crush on Noah, unaware that he, Suraya, and I knew all about it. Twelve-year-olds, well at least twelve-year-olds who live at home and are spoiled, do not tend to hide their emotions well. When I was twelve, I swiftly learned to hide my feelings very well. Susannah was gleeful when Noah arrived three days a week, and despondent each afternoon when he left. She was especially angry when he ended lessons early one day. I was right outside the room, dusting picture frames that seemed to never remain clean, when I heard them conversing.

"Susannah, this geography will wait until the morrow. I don't believe any continents will be moving about during the night, so I'm going to conclude our lesson early today."

"Oh, but Mr. Noah. They might move. What if there is an earthquake?"

"Ha! Leave it to you, precocious Susannah, to think of that!"

I could sense Susannah smiling, even though I'm sure she didn't know what precocious meant. "It's possible, you admit it, don't you? And why, Mr. Noah, do you have only one dimple when you smile?"

"Counting dimples now, hmm? Math is not on the schedule till the morrow. But today is lovely. Let's take a walk outside in the garden before I depart."

His timing was perfect. As Noah and Susannah walked to the garden, Suraya was already there, and I joined her. Suraya was watering thirsty tomato plants and plucking ripe tomatoes, and some still green for frying. Dressed alike in our simple white muslin dresses reaching far below our knees, our hair was braided in rows against our heads, elaborate mazes with no escape. Our heads were together, and we laughed over something Mrs. Beth had done, when Noah and Susannah approached us.

Susannah never did anything quietly, so she ran up to us, tugged on Suraya's sleeve and mock whispered so everyone could hear, "Noah ended lessons early today. He wanted to take me for a walk in the garden!"

"That's sweet, Susannah," Suraya said, but I knew what she was thinking. *You are going to get hurt, you little twit. You're but 12, and Noah is 18.* As Noah reached us, Susannah tucked her hand into the crook of his arm and said sweetly, "Let's walk over here, Mr. Noah."

"Yes, Susannah. But what are the girls doing?" Noah craned his head to look at us.

"Oh, nothing important. Just giggling. They're not even working." Susannah tried to pull Noah away.

"It looks important if you want to have fried tomatoes with your dinner." Noah raised his eyebrows.

Suraya and I suppressed a laugh and smiled sweetly instead.

"We pickin' tomatoes for tonight's dinner, and breakfast tomorrow," Suraya replied, looking directly at Noah. As slaves we had been taught to never look directly at a White person, especially a White man. Looking down emphasized our humble state. Suraya usually followed this dictum, and most of the time one did not even know she was in a room—she blended into her surroundings, making little noise, and never calling attention to herself. Her direct gaze at Noah startled me but didn't seem to shock him. He looked right back at her. Full in her eyes. I was stunned; my mind reeled. The content of her short speech was unremarkable, but her unspoken language revealed volumes.

Already in shock, what Suraya did next almost elicited a gasp.

"Do you likes the red ones?" Suraya handed Noah a ripe tomato, her fingers touching his palm as she placed it in his waiting hand. She talked to him as if no one else were around and touched him purposefully.

"This is my favorite kind. I could eat it right now." Noah grinned, bringing the tomato to his mouth.

"Oh, I don' think . . I mean . . . well, the Missus. . . ." Suraya stumbled over her words.

"On second thought, I don't want to deprive the family of tomatoes at dinner this evening," Noah recanted. Noah handed the tomato back to Suraya by taking her wrist in his hand and placing the tomato gently in her open palm, oblivious to the rules prohibiting such behavior.

Susannah, impatient with her bystander role, yanked on Noah's arm, pulling him down the path to the carrots and turnips abutting the stable yard.

## CHAPTER SEVEN: OLU

"Caesar, why didn't you brush Mr. Noah's horse?" she complained, as they reached the fence where Rosie was tethered.

"Yes, miss. I did brush her, miss. Head to tail," Caesar said.

"She don't look brushed. Did you exercise her?" Susannah demanded to know.

"Yes, miss. Rosie had a good 'n long run in the yard."

"Don't wear her out!" Susannah cried.

Noah, tired of Miss Susannah's complaints and sulking attitude, turned to Caesar himself, smiled, and said, "Thanks, Caesar. She looks well. I'll be off now." Turning to Susannah, Noah said, "Susannah, study the countries and capital cities we reviewed today."

"Yes, Mr. Noah." Susannah frowned.

Noah mounted his horse in a quick, fluid motion, and with a grin and wave, he kneed her gently and Rosie began walking.

Susannah left the stable yard, grumbling under her breath about the incompetence of slaves. She often did so, and I wondered how Suraya could be so sweet to her, and not see past the "we're like sisters" nonsense Susannah would spout, and into her mean heart. Once Susannah was gone, Noah steered Rosie back toward the garden. He drew his horse up alongside the fence, carefully avoiding the garden itself. Suraya told me Noah was only attracted to African girls. He couldn't abide White girls with their fussy ways, and concern only for dress, manners, and well-behaved slaves. Noah found the "pretty White girls" cloying and annoying. But Charles Town was not Philadelphia. And Suraya, normally meek and compliant, would not stay away from him. Noah seemed restless to me, and I didn't believe he would be content with tutoring for long.

Rosie snorted, and Suraya looked up to see Noah sitting atop his magnificent horse.

"Have you picked the best of the crop, ladies?" Noah asked.

"Yes, sir," I replied. I picked up my basket and set it on top of my head, balancing it between my braids.

"That's a neat trick. How do you keep it up there?" Noah asked.

"Balance. Straight back—straight head."

"Mmmm. I see you have strawberries, Miss Sarah. That little one won't be missed—could you not spare it?"

"You don' give up easy, Mr. Noah. I suppose one small berry won' be missed." Suraya walked the few steps to the fence, hesitating before the magnificent horse, looming above her.

"Don't fear Rosie. She's big, but gentle," Noah reassured her.

Suraya stepped over the rock border and extracted a small berry from the basket, handing it up over the fence to Noah. She held it by the stem, but Noah reached down and slowly ran his fingers over hers before retrieving the offered fruit. I felt as if I were intruding on something intimate. Flustered, Suraya nearly toppled her whole basket, full to the brim with strawberries. As Noah popped the berry into his mouth, and Suraya regained her composure, Rosie turned around swiftly and planted her muzzle in Suraya's basket—rising with a mouthful of strawberries.

"You naughty horse!" Suraya's anger replaced her fear. Laughing, Noah dismounted, swung Rosie's head around, and secured her halter to the fence. Swinging one leg over the fence, followed by the other, Noah reached down and picked up the basket Suraya had dropped, gathering the errant strawberries rolling on the ground before Rosie could sweep them up as well.

"I forgot to warn you. Rosie likes strawberries even more than I do!" Noah laughed.

"Oh dear, Martha won' have near enough for the strawberry pie now! What'll I do?" Suraya asked.

"Let me," Noah said. He began picking more strawberries without another word.

"Oh no, you needn't," Suraya cried. "I'll just pick a few more. Rosie didn't get much, though her mouth's huge!"

"You noticed, did you?! You hear that, Rosie? You have a big mouth. I'm afraid she did get a nice big mouthful. I'll help you pick some more so Martha will have enough for two strawberry pies. It's my duty."

"Suri, I need to help Martha with dinner. I'll tell her you'll be in shortly." I sent a warning glance her way.

"I be there soon's we fill this basket."

I nodded to Noah and left, trying with all my will not to turn around and look at them as I approached the house. Curiosity won. I turned and observed them bent down, heads together, picking strawberries, talking, and laughing. Later, Suraya told me what transpired after I left.

Noah and Suraya reached for the same strawberry and his hand grasped hers, enveloping both her hand and the berry. Noah calmed her fears about his horse Rosie and boasted that he could reach Philadelphia in three days on her back. Noah told Suraya about his mom's cooking, his favorite lemon custard pie, and praised Miss Martha's biscuits but

# CHAPTER SEVEN: OLU

said his ma's bread—thick, with a slab of butter—was better even than Martha's biscuits.

They had all but abandoned the pretense of strawberry picking, more intent on learning about each other. Noah spoke to her like he would speak to any White woman or man, using words she didn't understand and explaining them, instead of using simpler words. Suraya explained how she was kidnapped, how she was unsure if her brother was taken as well, and how much she missed her family—her mama, papa, papa's other wife, her two sisters and four brothers.

Noah explained that he was an abolitionist, people from the North helping slaves escape. Talk of escape scared Suraya, so she changed the subject right quick. Right then, as they talked about escape, Rosie pulled her halter loose, neighing loudly, trying to escape. Noah ran to Rosie, rolled over the fence, speaking to her soothingly all the while. At this point I looked out the window, alerted by the loud neighing of Noah's horse. Noah grabbed her halter and pulled it tight.

He turned back to Suraya, who looked about to fall over. Suraya thought it was a bad omen—she didn't want any more talk of escape. She asked Noah why he was so nice when all the other White men were mean to her, and Noah's demeanor abruptly changed. His kind eyes now glinted with suppressed anger, confusing Suraya. She decided not to tell Noah about Clarence patting or grabbing her behind, or Samuel brushing his hand nonchalantly across her breast.

# CHAPTER EIGHT

## Joanna

16 September 1807

THE NEXT DAY I woke with the sun before the bell rang, got out of bed and walked quietly to the window, not wanting to wake anyone. Drawing back the curtains, I took in the view of the pond, flowering shrubs and trees and could barely make out a large, barren garden behind the stable.

I sat down on the hard-backed chair next to the compact writing table and opened the bible to the Psalms, comforted by the familiar words. A soft knock, followed by the arrival of Maisie, brought me out of my meditation. Maisie emptied out the old water in the bowl, replenished it with fresh water, and then offered to help me dress. As Maisie buttoned up the frock, we could hear Miranda and Anne talking on the other side of the wall.

". . . and her father a slave," one said.

"She has an English grandma," the other one replied.

"And an African father. She can't possibly fit in. She's not like us. She's an orphan! I'm surprised she's not in an orphanage. Mrs. Limebear put her in a room alone so's not to contaminate anyone. Don't know why she accepted her at all. Must be the money. I guess the colour of money is more important to Mrs. Limebear than the colour of her father."

"I wouldn't want to be . . . "

Their conversation became unintelligible as the girls moved to the other side of the room.

Maisie and I both heard the girls' gossip. Maisie said, "Don' you worry none about them, Miss Joanna. That Miss Miranda always has something mean to say, leastways when she thinks no adults are listening. She friendly as can be when she with you, but when you not around, then she true feelings come out."

I stayed quiet, suppressing tears.

"You be jes' fine here. Be strong, girl. Don' let them girls see you weak. That won't do. Be strong and be sweet. That be the only way to shut 'em up," Maisie said.

Maisie continued talking, soothing me as she buttoned up my fresh frock. "I be here to help you. Say . . .you need help dressing up this lovely hair? So much of it—and so long!"

"You're so sweet, Miss Maisie," I cried, hugging her around the waist and resting my head on one breast.

"There, girl." Maisie set me back.

"I got work to do—but jes' let me pull this hair into one braid here—in the back, like this. Okay?"

"Thank you. I have a hard time with it myself."

Right then the bell rang, and Mrs. Limebear tapped on the doors alerting the girls that breakfast would soon be ready. Maisie opened the door and stepped into the doorway and I could hear Mrs. Limebear, who was already fully dressed in a gown and cap, say, "Maisie, there's work to be done. Don't linger long in the girls' rooms."

"Yes ma'am. I be helping Miss Joanna here with her frock and hair, seeing as she the only one in a room alone," Maisie replied, in explanation and reproof.

"Finish quickly and have breakfast served at 8:00 am."

"Yes, ma'am."

"Where your comb?" Maisie asked. I handed back the comb and looked in the mirror, wincing, while Maisie separated my hair into a braid taking less time than it took me to comb it.

"It's lovely." I hugged Maisie again.

"Leave off, girl. That weren't nothing. But I'm glad you like it." Miss Maisie lifted my chin with her index finger. "Remember child. Be strong and be sweet. Don' let them girls know they hurt you."

"Thank you, Miss Maisie."

Maisie left to finish preparing breakfast. I could hear the girls next door again, chattering as they dressed, and fought the urge to cry. Strong, sweet. Strong, sweet. Placing a cap on top of my head, slipping on house slippers, I sat down in my chair to resume reading—awaiting the breakfast bell.

Fall passed uneventfully. We fell into a daily routine—rising, eating, going to class, lunch, reading, supper, studying, gathering in the parlor. Saturdays were spent resting, reading, studying, writing letters, and practicing—piano, drawing, and embroidery. Sundays we were required to attend church. We had a choice. We could attend the nearby Congregational church or the local parish church. Anne, Miranda, Violet, and I attended the Congregational Church (non-conformist, as it didn't 'conform' to the rules and regulations of the Church of England) accompanied by Mr. Harding. It was less than a mile from the school, so in most kinds of weather, we walked. Samantha, Candace, and Rose attended the parish church—the official Church of England, accompanied by Mrs. Limebear.

One Sunday in November the weather had turned sharply colder. Mr. Harding instructed Anne, Miranda, Violet, and I to dress warmly, and wear boots. I put on two petticoats, a high-waisted cream muslin dress with a high neck and long sleeves, a navy-blue redingote, kid gloves Grandmamma had given me two Christmases ago, and a fur hat! Bundled up in layers, I met Anne, Violet, and Mr. Harding downstairs. Miranda was late, as usual.

The five of us headed to church. Miranda and Violet walked ahead, with Anne and Mr. Harding behind. The wind froze my cheeks, but the layers protected my head, feet, and body. We kept up a brisk pace and I could hear Miranda and Violet chatting, but Anne and Mr. Harding were silent. The gray, cloudy sky reflected my subdued mood.

"I can't believe they let Joanna sit in the main church right in the front," Miranda said loudly enough for me to hear.

"She should be in the balcony. Africans are always in the balcony," Violet added.

I heard Mr. Harding mumble his assent.

"She acts like one of us. Inserting herself into everything—our school, our church. But she's not. She never could be like us. I don't know why Mrs. Limebear accepted her."

"She could have gone to a public school or had a governess. If her father had so much money, he could have afforded a governess. Then we wouldn't have to have a half-caste at our school."

I kept looking down to avoid the ubiquitous potholes and pebbles on the road, and as I listened to Miranda and Violet, I watched a teardrop plop onto my shoe. My steps slowed as I put distance between us so I couldn't hear their insults. Their words chipped away at my self-esteem like stone masons. I wasn't a beautiful African-English girl; I was a half-caste. I was no longer a lovely pecan brown, but a mongrel. I pictured my mama and papa, in the one lone portrait I had of them together, but for the first time it brought no solace.

Anne joined me and asked if something was wrong. Her question was so softly spoken I could barely hear her. I didn't say anything for a minute or two. Finally, I mentioned I heard Miranda and Violet saying hurtful things about me. She put her arm in mine and said not to mind them—they had no sense and no taste. Whatever they said, the opposite was probably true. We continued to walk arm-in-arm to the church.

I suddenly felt tired, older than my twelve years and in desperate need of a mother, or at least an older sister, maybe even an aunt. I didn't want to think about Miranda and Violet. I shivered and sped up—we were almost at the church.

"Are you cold, Joanna?" Anne asked.

"A little. Sit by me in church?" I asked.

"Of course." Anne tightened her grip on my arm.

We arrived at the church after Miranda and Violet—they sat in the fifth row, with Mr. Harding beside them. I started to sit at the end of a pew in the back, but then I lifted my chin, motioning to Anne to join me at the front. We sat in the second pew. I looked up at the cross and asked Jesus to give me strength. I closed my eyes briefly, allowing the organ's melodious tones to soothe my disturbed spirit. I joined in the hymns, listened attentively to the sermon, and put Miranda and Violet's words out of my mind.

That night I was alone in the library with a book open on my lap. I was thinking, not reading. Could I avoid Miranda and Violet? Did the other girls feel the same way about me? How long would it be before I could go home to Uncle John's in London? Was there any hope of finding my aunt? Miss Maisie entered, interrupting my reverie.

Maisie apologized for interrupting me and began to sweep the floors. Maisie looked over at me, asking if everything was alright. She encouraged me to tell her what was bothering me, promising to keep it a secret.

"What goes in these ears don't come out this mouth."

I repeated Miranda and Violet's words and watched Miss Maisie's perpetually placid face harden and her eyes widen. She waited for me to continue.

"That all, chile?" Miss Maisie asked.

"That's all I heard."

"Miranda's a sneaky one. Sucks up to Mrs. Limebear, ignores me, and cozies up to the girls who come from the richest families. Don' mind nothing she says. Violet's jes' following her lead. You so pretty, they jes' jealous."

"You think so?"

Maisie resumed sweeping. "I know so. They never met no one like you—half English and half African. You got the best of both. Be proud of that."

I never thought of myself that way. "Thanks, Miss Maisie," I said.

"Course, chile." Maisie came over and patted my shoulder. I closed the book I wasn't reading, said "good night" and went up to bed. In this case, sharing troubles did halve my sorrow.

I spent many evenings with Maisie, following her around, and helping a little—as Maisie would allow me. One evening, Mrs. Limebear observed me dusting in the library while Maisie mopped the floor.

"Miss Vassa!" Only when she was angry did Mrs. Limebear refer to us by our last names. "What is this? Is that a duster I see in your hand?"

"Yes, ma'am."

"This will not do. May it never be said that my girls were forced to do housework." Mrs. Limebear stood with her hands on her hips.

"Oh no, ma'am. I was only keeping Miss Maisie company."

"It's not seemly. Please put the duster down. Go upstairs and keep company with the other girls. Study your lessons. Maisie does not need help or distractions."

Sending Maisie a helpless look, I nodded, curtsied, and walked upstairs to my empty, quiet, cold bedroom. During the day the lessons provided enough stimulation to maintain my interest and attention. But in the evening the girls retreated to their rooms, leaving me alone, lonely, and bored.

Maisie would not allow me to do any dirty tasks, like emptying the fireplace or chamber pots, but I think Maisie enjoyed my company as much as I enjoyed hers, so she didn't discourage me from helping with small tasks. Deprived of this small solace, I felt more alone than ever.

After that evening, Maisie and I fell into a routine which allowed maximum interaction and minimum interference. Miss Maisie came earlier in the morning to refresh my washbasin and help me dress, allowing time for a morning chat. In the evening I sat with my lesson books in the room Maisie worked in, allowing further time for talking. One evening as Maisie was sweeping the library floor, I read poetry to her aloud. John

## CHAPTER EIGHT: JOANNA

Donne's words leapt off the page as I read Holy Sonnet XVII: "Since She Whom I Loved":

> Since she whom I lov'd hath paid her last debt
> To nature, and to hers, and my good is dead,
> And her soul early into heaven ravished,
> Wholly in heavenly things my mind is set.
> Here the admiring her my mind did whet
> To seek thee, God; so streams do show the head;
> But though I have found thee, and thou my thirst hast fed,
> A holy thirsty dropsy melts me yet.
> But why should I beg more love, when as thou
> Dost woo my soul, for hers off'ring all thine,
> And dost not only fear lest I allow
> My love to saints and angels, things divine,
> But in thy tender jealousy dost doubt
> Lest the world, flesh, yea devil put thee out.

Maisie ached to read, but she grew up a slave and reading was forbidden. This is the first I heard she was a slave—I wanted to know more. Maisie was kidnapped when she was 10 or 11, she didn't know her exact birthday. She was the slave of Mr. Limebear's brother—a mean bastard, so she said. He bought her, worked her, mistreated her—never paid her. He died like he lived, mean, angry and alone. When he was buried, his four slaves were brought to Mr. Limebear, the husband who died in the fire.

Maisie described Mr. Limebear as the kindest, gentlest, most charming man. She said half of London came out to bury him, which I assume was an exaggeration. He gave all four slaves their freedom. The other three took their five pounds and left, but Maisie offered to stay and help Mrs. Limebear with her school. The other three died young—one from alcohol, one from hunger, and one, a woman named Mollie, whose story she claimed I was too young to hear.

I realized I should be thankful for my blessings instead of moaning over the mean words of the other girls. I thought about how much I loved to read and had an idea.

"I can teach you to read, Miss Maisie."

"Oh no, chile. You have your own learnin' and book work and what not. You too busy—I be too busy, too. Now Mr. Limebear, he would've taught me to read. But not the missus."

"Well, she doesn't need to know. We could be, you know, secretive." I looked at the closed door to the library.

"Ach, Miss Joanna. I ain't aimin' to get you in trouble."

"No trouble, Miss Maisie." My eyes widened with glee and my voice softened to a whisper as I contrived a way to meet with Maisie for reading lessons. Maisie's schedule made finding a time challenging: up at dawn to pray; empty out the ashes from the previous day's fires; add more coal to all the fireplaces and build the fires; empty the chamber pots; refill the pitchers with fresh water. By this time, Mrs. Limebear would ring the 7:15 wake up bell. Then Maisie makes breakfast, serves the food, and cleans up. By 9:00 she's already tired. Just telling me about her schedule wore Maisie out! She leaned on her broom.

"You work so hard. I wonder Mrs. Limebear doesn't find someone to help you out."

"Someone else would cost money, and Mrs. Limebear likes to hold on to the money she brings in, not spend it lessen' she must. She do get a laundress to come in to wash once a week."

Maisie had a little break after dinner, so we planned to meet in the unoccupied room next to mine, for which Maisie had a key. Although reluctant to agree to my plan, Maisie got excited about the prospect of reading on her own.

"I'll go to my room, get out my books and study for a few minutes. Then I'll slip next door, meet you and teach you to read."

"It be tempting."

"Just think, Miss Maisie. You could read Donne, and Johnson, the bible, even Shakespeare."

"I ain't aiming to do all that. I'd like to read the Psalms, and John, Matthew, and Genesis. Read about all the saints 'n sinners in the good book. Yes, I would." Maisie began to sweep again, her smile growing.

"Let's do it! We can start three days a week. And if that works, move to four or five."

"Three days be more n' enough."

Thus, at the age of twelve, I persuaded Maisie to meet for reading lessons. I hadn't thought of the actual methods of teaching, only the opportunity. I supposed it couldn't be too difficult, as I was an excellent reader myself. But when my excitement subsided, I realized I had taken on a task needing further preparation. I appealed to Uncle John for help. He was always there when I needed him. He will know exactly what to do, I thought. Throughout that evening, and the next day, I puzzled over my dilemma—how to get help without revealing what I needed help for, but without lying too badly. I finally settled on a solution and composed a letter to Uncle John.

> Dear Uncle John,
> 	I hope you are well. I pray for you every day, and though I do miss you, I have made friends and settled in. Who do you have for a chess partner now that I am away? I have been playing with Anne. Though she is not as good as you, she is teaching me a few moves, and I am becoming a better player. Watch out! I do miss our walks and I miss bird watching with you. Just yesterday I saw a bright blue bird, with streaks of orange on its wings, but Mrs. Limebear could not identify it and she does not have a bird book. Keep adding to our bird list and I hope you can show me some new species when I visit again.
> 	I am doing well in all my subjects. Mrs. Limebear is strict, but fair, and very knowledgeable about writing and arithmetic. Is it not odd for a woman to know so much about numbers? Soon we will all be ready to go to work as accountants or bankers! Mr. Harding is teaching us about England, France, Germany, and Italy. I hope he teaches us about Africa.
> 	In addition to our basic subjects, we have special projects to complete. The project I have chosen is teaching an illiterate person to read. Mrs. Limebear has no young children, and no beginning readers. Could you please find me an early reader—a reader for a beginner-—and send it by post?
> 	There is one other thing I want to ask of you. I do so wish I could sit down and talk to you, but this letter will do for now. As I was talking with some of the other girls here, one of them asked me about my aunt, my father's sister. Honestly, I have never thought much about her, but when the question came up, I could not stop wondering who she is, what happened to her, and if she is still alive. Is there any way, Uncle John, you could inquire about slave ships leaving Africa about the same time my father's did, and if there is any way to find out who my aunt is, and if she is still alive? I know it may be impossible, but if you could try, I would be forever grateful.
> 	My health is good, and I am eating well. I read my bible every morning and pray morning and night. I miss you,
> 	Joanna

I folded up the letter and put it in the envelope addressed to Uncle John. I hoped and prayed he would grant my request, and he would find my aunt. It felt good to have some goals—teaching Maisie, finding my aunt—and it took my mind off Miranda and Violet's cruel words.

# CHAPTER NINE

## Olu

### May 1759

MARTHA NOT ONLY TAUGHT me to cook, but also how to grow and apply various balms and healing remedies. One day, after I had cleared the breakfast dishes and hauled them downstairs for washing, I noticed a young man sitting by the fireplace in the kitchen area, sitting on a stool with his feet propped up on another stool.

Martha called me over to observe. Leeches clung to his ankles and bites swelled the skin from his knees to his feet. I itched simply looking at him. I hadn't met him before and inclined my head in greeting. I did not know then that I would come to know him quite well in later days. Martha introduced us:

"Samson, this be Olivia. I'm teaching her the potions and poultices I use to heal y'all."

"How do, miss," Samson said in greeting, nodding to me.

"Fine, I thank'ee. What happened here?"

"These here suckers liked the looks of my ankles, and then I accidentally stepped a bit close to an ant hill. These here ants tried to bite my foot off leaving nothin' for the leeches to suck!"

I winced before I could check myself. Then, composing myself, I addressed Martha, "What can I get you to aid Samson? Oils, aloe, cream?"

"Yes, oil and aloe be needed. Firstly, I need to get these leeches off him. Light that yonder small stick in the fire and hand it to me—gentle like," Martha commanded.

## CHAPTER NINE: OLU

I lit the twig, handed it to her, and was surprised to see Martha put the fiery twig right next to the leech. The leech dropped off Samson's leg immediately and he reached down to scratch.

"No, you don't." Martha slapped his hand away. I could see drops of blood forming in the spot the leech vacated. Whilst swatting his hand with her own, Martha took a white cloth in her other hand, dipped it in water, and gently applied it to the now leech-less spot on Samson's leg. She got the other leeches to detach themselves in a similar manner.

"Olivia, throw them leeches into the fire."

As I reached down to pick it up, she cautioned, "No, no girl. Don' pick it up with your fingers. Flick them into the fire with that twig."

I was relieved and picked up the now extinguished twig. I flipped the leeches into the fire, as my stomach flipped along.

"Do you know," Martha said as she applied oils to Samson's leg, "those crazy White doctors use leeches on sick folks. They don' know they do more harm n' good. You must," Martha addressed me now, "take them off gentle like. Don' never pull a leech off. The craziest ways them so-called doctors has. Bleeding a sick one and putting suckin' leeches on them. That don' do nothing but make a sick one sicker. Plenty of rest, plenty of tea, and some of my good herbs—that'll set them right."

When Martha had an audience she tended to become didactic and there was no stopping her theories and philosophies. I listened as I went into the storage room for aloe and oil.

"Problem is, they send slaves right back to work before they healed. Weak slaves can't work hard as healthy slaves, so they be punished. Don' make no sense—working 'em to death."

Martha talked as she worked. I handed her the aloe stalk and watched as she split it open and dropped some aloe juice directly onto Samson's leg. He almost fell off the stool, but he didn't cry out. I had seen Martha minister to field workers who had been whipped. Mr. Cross didn't sanction whipping for minor offenses, but he wasn't against severe punishment for what he considered severe offenses. Men, mostly, who came in with shreds of skin sagging from their bare backs and blood dripping onto their pants, knew Martha was the only one who could ease the pain.

Martha instructed me to rub the oil over Samson's legs. This was the first time she had asked me to assist with a man, and I was embarrassed, hesitating to touch him in what seemed like an intimate manner.

"Go ahead girl. Rub the oil over those bites, gentle and smooth," Martha urged me.

I began to rub the oil into Samson's calves, palpating the multitude of bites, hoping I wasn't increasing his pain. On my knees, I leaned over his legs as I worked and glanced up to see if I was causing him pain, I noticed Samson slightly grinning as he gazed down my frock!

Restraining the urge to slap him, I asked in as sweet a voice as I could muster, "Does this help?"

To his credit, Samson averted his eyes and replied, "Yes, miss. Thank ye."

Martha left to gather the ingredients for lunch—freshly caught rabbit, stewed with potatoes, greens, and celery. A few minutes after she disappeared into the pantry—a whole room devoted to fruits, vegetables, grains, and the like—Martha returned to inspect my work. I was finishing massaging the oil into Samson's leg and she came over making noises I could not interpret as she examined his leg: "Um hmmm. Ah, hmmm. That'll do, Olivia."

Martha told Samson she would have a word with Jones and tell him Samson needed some time off the fields. She asked him what his skills were. Samson said he could carve bowls out of wood, maybe make a few bowls for the missus. Martha thought that was a great idea and sent me to find Jones and ask him to come and see her, with the added incentive to sample the freshly baked biscuits.

Samson sat on the floor now, with his feet on a log, Martha began to cook lunch, and I went to find Jones. I loved going outside. The house felt constricting, stifling. The grounds surrounding the house were stunning. Looking out the back of the house, one could see the wide lawn sloping down like very wide stairs all the way to the river. The expanse of graduated lawn was bigger than our village back home. Martha heard it took one hundred slaves over ten years to dig out that pattern in the ground, plant and tend the grass, landscape the borders. The effect was magnificent. In the winter children from the surrounding plantations would come and sled down the terraced slope, stopping right before they reached the icy river.

Back home the land was broken by trees, an occasional pond or stream, often dry, with very few flowers or flowering trees. Shades of brown and grey with a dusting of blue painted my landscape back home. Here at the plantation, green was everywhere—in myriad shades. The green of the grass, a shade lighter than the green leaves of the magnolia, hanging with Spanish moss, which were shinier than the maple tree leaves. The pines and evergreens grew all year round. There must be dozens of shades of green, I thought, as I gazed out on all the grass, trees, shrubs, flowers, and moss. Some of the trees were so large they eclipsed even the massive house, with trunks so enormous I could count to five as I ran around them—yes, I did. And in the spring . . . the flowers erupted in a blinding kaleidoscope of color.

Mrs. Cross was a woman I neither liked nor admired, but even I could admit she had a good eye for a garden. Years ago, Mr. Cross took Mrs. Beth on a trip to England. Apparently, she complained endlessly about the ship. However, when they arrived in London, the happy couple visited many gardens, formal and wild, and Mrs. Beth obviously learned enough to know what she wanted for the grounds at Cross Hall.

I was often sent to meet Captain Thomas at the dock. He's a slave whom Mr. Cross trusted to pilot the schooner down the Ashley River, back and forth between the plantation and Charles Town. I never quite understood why he trusted Thomas, or Jones for that matter.

When I'm sent by Martha to the dock to retrieve the fruits, vegetables, and grains Thomas brings back from Charles Town, I walk down the allée, over the ha-ha, to the dock, and I notice everything. I notice when the azaleas begin to bloom, first pink, then red and white. I notice when the maple trees begin sprouting leaves. I notice when the magnolias bud, and I notice when the birds begin to hatch their young—nesting osprey, eagles, and hawks; great blue herons and little blue herons; tufted titmice and cardinals. I developed a love for the grounds and all the inhabitants.

Now I walk through the garden beside the reflecting pool and out to the nearest rice field. This was planting time, so all the enslaved women were out with a bag of seed slung around their necks, barefooted and bare-headed, planting seeds. There were two large rice fields, and this was the bigger one. I couldn't say exactly how big it was, but it would take me ten minutes to walk its width, and twenty its length. And I walk fast. There were at least twenty women out planting today.

With their big toes, each woman would slightly depress the soil, drop a seed in the hole, then press it in with her heel. Toe . . . drop seed . . . heel. Toe down . . . drop seed . . . heel down. All day in the relentless heat of the sun, soaking with sweat, bodies aching for rest and food. Whenever I came out to the fields, I was thankful anew for my role in the house. The only benefits to being in the field were days off for harsh weather, distance from the Master and Mistress, and the community of fellow slaves.

Shielding my eyes from the sun with my hand, I glanced out across the field to see if I could spot Jones. All I saw were women. Then I spotted him coming up from the dock. Thomas must be in with the boat. Jones came up to the field and looked out at the women—I could tell he was counting them. When he looked in my direction he strode over.

"Afternoon, Miss Olivia," he greeted me in his baritone voice. Picture this, reader. Jones stood a whole foot taller than me, and he was two shades darker—I guess from being out in the sun, while I stayed mostly in the house. From the Kingdom of Dahomey, a neighbor of Igboland, Jones knew all about cultivating rice—one of the reasons he was promoted to driver. His people knew everything about rice, much more than any of the White masters. They knew the different types, how often it could be planted, how to flood the field, how to harvest it. When the Crosses first came to Charles Town, they planned to plant sugar cane, as at their plantation in Barbados. But it wouldn't grow well here in South Carolina. They tried indigo and that didn't work either. The fields were too wet, or it was too humid—the conditions were not conducive to sugar cane or indigo. As I heard it, the Crosses were so frustrated they almost gave up their plans to become rich in this new colony and prepared to move back to Barbados. Then Jones—bless him, curse him—mentioned rice. Rice!

"Why don' you grow rice, Massa Cross?" Why did he ask that simple, life-altering question? Of course, I wasn't there; I wasn't even born yet. But one naïve question led to a new enterprise, a successful plantation, riches for the Crosses, and misery for Africans. I never could forgive Jones for that.

On the next ship from Africa, Mr. Cross bought seed to grow rice. And twenty years later I stood here in front of Jones to ask for mercy for another slave whose legs were so bitten up he could scarcely stand.

Jones' people in Dahomey spoke a dialect like mine, so we tended to communicate in a hybrid language—part English, part Yoruba, part Fon, part Igbo. I'll relay the conversation here in English.

"Good afternoon, Jones. Thomas is in with a fresh load from town I see."

"Yes, miss. I was needing more seeds and got more'n enough now."

"The women are working hard."

"As they should." Jones looked out over the rice field as if to confirm it.

"Yes, well. I came to see you about Samson."

"What's wrong with Samson?"

"He stepped too close to an ant hill and got bit up. Some leeches also attached to his ankles. His legs are swollen up and very painful." I grimaced to convey Samson's pain.

Jones grunted something unintelligible.

"Miss Martha asked if you could step down to the kitchen to see and maybe allow him to do other work—not in the fields—for a few days. Miss Martha also asked if you could taste her biscuits to make sure they're light enough to serve at lunch."

"She did, huh? She thinks I'll jes' come runnin' to taste her biscuits, and forgive all, and give slaves days off to do nothing? As if I don' have more important things to do?"

"Well . . . I . . ." I stammered.

"She knows me well." Jones smiled, resembling an alligator's invitation to lunch. "I'll check on 'im. And those biscuits. Good day."

Before I could respond, Jones was striding away toward the house. I called after him, "Please tell Martha I'm down to the dock to check our food supplies."

"Yes, miss."

As I walked back through the rice field, I overheard two female slaves talking. I slowed down and listened in as they discussed a cousin at another plantation who had just escaped. She took a boat down the river at night. She hadn't returned to the plantation, but they didn't know if she had reached freedom. When they glanced over at me, I kept walking.

As I walked the allée, with the stream alongside, I noticed a new baby alligator, only the end of its long nose protruding out of the water. I could see the boat at the dock, and Thomas lifting out barrels and sacks, so I pulled my eyes from the beauty and danger around me and focused on the task ahead.

"Afternoon, Miss Olivia. It be a fine day, don' it?"

"Yes, Captain Thomas. It's a beautiful day."

"You always talk so proper like—where'd ye ever learn to talk like that?" Thomas asked. Lowering his voice he said, "Even the massa and missus don' talk so fine."

"Thomas, that's not true, and even if it were—you know you shouldn't say it aloud. The trees have ears. Maybe the river itself can hear you."

"True. But beggin' the question, where'd ye learn how to talk so good?"

"Mr. Teddy teaches me when he's here." I lowered my voice to match his. "He also taught me to read and write."

"No kiddin'! Ain't that something. What you be needing that for?"

Thomas began to move about the boat as we talked, pulling out sacks and crates meant for the kitchen, or the stables, or the workshop. I leaned in and whispered, "I don't plan to stay on this plantation my whole life. One day, I don't know how soon, one day I'm leaving. And not looking back."

"You mean escaping?"

"Hush, Thomas. I thought I could trust you."

"Yes, miss, you can." Thomas hesitated, looked around, then leaned closer to me and said, "When you ready—you let ol' Thomas know. I know this here river better'n anybody. Better even than the massa. This be the best way off. Truth be told," he whispered, "I already helped a few out of here. You tell me when you ready, miss—I help you."

"I knew I could trust you. The river—hmm. Talk no more of it now. When the time is right, I'll know. I'll come to you."

Thomas turned his back to me, ending the conversation and finished unloading the boat.

"You be needin' some help with these sacks—this one of flour, and this one of oats be heavy."

"You tell me that every time Thomas. Who would help me? Everyone is busy. I can manage—I'll just take them one at a time."

"Well, here then. I'll jes' take this heavy crate of sugar."

Thomas hefted the crate filled with paper cones of sugar upon his shoulder, after he helped me lift the bag of oats and place it on top of my head. We walked, slowly and carefully, back up the allée toward the house.

As we approached the swiftly moving stream adjacent to the ha-ha we startled the baby alligator. It turned and slowly strode down the bank. Thomas had a well-founded dislike of alligators, and almost dropped the crate of sugar. But he righted himself, muttering under his breath, and continued to the house.

When we entered the ground floor Samson was asleep on his mat by the fire and Martha was busily finishing the rabbit stew. The wooden spatula she had pulled out of the fire was not quite full of biscuits—two were missing. Martha turned her head as we ducked in through the low door.

"Ahh. What you got there, Capn. Thomas?"

"Afternoon, Miss Martha." Thomas gazed at the hot biscuits, lowering the crate of sugar to the floor.

## CHAPTER NINE: OLU

"I see what you lookin' at. Jones already had two. If anybody else comes in here there won't be enough left for lunch. Oh, go on. Only one, mind you."

"Thank ye, Miss Martha. Ain't nothing so fine as your biscuits." Thomas grinned.

"Go on with you."

"Mmmmmm."

As Thomas and Martha talked about what supplies and foodstuffs he had on the boat, I dropped off the bag of oats in the storage room and came out to see how Samson fared. The swelling had not decreased, but he slept soundly.

Martha told me Jones had looked him over, but didn't even wake him, too busy enjoying biscuits to fuss over Samson. He did say a few chairs need repairing, so Samson could work on those the next few days. Samson would rest here for the remainder of the day.

I turned to Thomas. "Can I get the rest of the goods after lunch?"

"Don't worry miss. I'll have a few field hands bring them in for ye."

"Thank you, Thomas." I smiled at him, thinking about the river.

Thomas left and I helped Martha by putting the biscuits in a bowl and bringing them up to the sideboard in the drawing room. Suraya was already setting the table.

"Suraya, how are you?"

"Great! Noah will be here this afternoon." Suraya smiled widely.

"Suraya, be careful with him." I glanced at Suraya.

"Why don' you trust Noah?"

"I'm not sure. He's very friendly, but he's a bit too free and open. And he's young. He doesn't understand how things are here. He's from Philadelphia. There are many free Africans there. That's what he's used to."

"So what! He knows I's a slave. He still likes me. And you know what else, I like him too!"

"Just be careful Suraya."

"You saying that 'cause you care about me, or you just jealous?"

"Jealous! I'm not jealous, Suraya. He's young and, and . . . well he seems like he doesn't know what he wants. Believe me when I tell you a relationship with him can only lead to trouble. I do care about you. That's why I'm warning you."

"You wrong about him. And the warnings too late. I's already in love with him."

I went back downstairs to get the stew, wondering if Suraya was right. Was I jealous? Well, not because of Noah—I had no attraction to him. There was something about him I didn't trust. Why was he attracted to African girls? No, I didn't trust him at all. But I hoped I was wrong.

I was not wrong.

After Suraya and I cleaned up after lunch, she went off to help Susannah prepare for her lessons, while I sorted out the sacks and bags of goods Thomas had brought from Charles Town. In addition to the traditional fare of flour, sugar, oats, onions, potatoes, and cabbage, there was a small crate filled with dark blue, shiny, juicy blueberries. I glanced out the doorway, then popped a few blueberries into my mouth—chewing them slowly, savoring the tangy sweetness of the juice as it ran down my chin.

"Are them there blueberries sweet as they look?" Martha asked me, grinning.

"Yes, ma'am. They're very sweet. Perfect for your delicious blueberry pie—with fresh whipped cream."

"Um hmm. Flattering me, is it?" Miss Martha tilted her head and gave me a half smile.

"Only saying what's true." I wiped the blueberry juice off my face.

"Mmm. What else did Cap'n Thomas bring us?"

"All the regular staples, plus these berries, two new fishing poles, a crate of oranges, and one of lemons."

"Good, good. The missus likes fresh orange juice and Mr. Cross likes his lemonade. If Jacob brings me some fish, we'll fry it up for dinner. Eitherwise, it's turkey again."

"I hope he gets the fish."

"Yes, that'd be tasty. Only if they bitin' today. Come back to help me about 5:00."

"Yes, Miss Martha."

As I turned to go, Martha's daughter Elsie came bounding into the storage room. Her eyes widened as she saw the blueberries.

"May I have some berries, mama?"

Martha laughed, tousled her hair, and handed her two blueberries. Her daughter's complexion was several shades lighter than hers, and I could almost swear her ears looked just like Mr. Cross's, sticking out a bit with a little indentation on the top.

I said goodbye to Martha and Elsie and went up to my room. As I approached the door, I heard muffled sounds, and paused with my hand on the doorknob. I knocked twice, and waited for a minute or so, hearing swishing, rustling noises.

I opened the door and saw Noah pulling up his breeches and slinging his red suspenders over his shoulders, glancing up to see me in the doorway. He didn't look apologetic, embarrassed, or guilty—he looked satisfied. I felt like slapping him—and almost did. Suraya was sitting up on her mat, wide-eyed, holding up a thin sheet to cover her naked body, her flyaway hair out of its pins, dress thrown across my mat, her shoes strewn across the floor.

"Olivia," Noah said. "We didn't expect you."

What an understatement.

"Oh, my Lord. Olivia. It's not . . . we didn' . . . it's not what it seems," Suraya stuttered.

"Noah, you will be missed downstairs. Susannah cannot concentrate for more than five minutes on any assignment." I gave him the sternest look an enslaved woman could give a White man, with a hand on my hip for emphasis.

"You're so right." Noah laughed. The urge to slap returned.

Noah put on his ubiquitous hat, kissed Suraya—and hurried downstairs.

Suraya had hurriedly put her dress on but buttoned it up incorrectly, so it was uneven.

"Suraya, what are you thinking of?"

"You don' understand. Noah loves me."

"Does he? Does he really? What will he do? Marry you?"

"He . . . he would. He will. Not yet, of course, he's young, and I's too young. He don' care I's a slave. He'll buy me, free me, and marry me. I know it." Suraya's hesitant expression belied her confident words.

"You know it! Did he promise you these things? Did he?" I was losing my temper and my patience. Noah was not to be trusted. I would bet Suraya was not the first girl he had seduced. Undoubtedly, she would not be the last.

"No . . . not exactly. He tells me I's his special girl. I's beautiful. He wants to be with me."

"Well, he has been 'with you.' Suraya, have you taken any precaution? Is it a safe time of month?" I hoped she had at least been careful.

"I don' bother with that. I don' keep track. My monthlies come and go, and then I forgets about it till it comes again. Anyhow, this is only the third time we been together."

"The third time. Lord help us. If you insist on being with Noah, you need to keep track. Tell me, I'll write it down. And keep him away when I tell you it's a bad time."

"I can't do that, Olu. You don' know mens like I do. When they want us, they want us. We can't tell them, not now—it ain't a good time. They don't understand."

"Suraya, listen to me." I was only a few months older than Suraya, but I felt like her mother right then. "If you're with child, Noah will deny his relationship with you and Mr. Cross will sell you."

"No, no, you wrong, Olu. You don' know Noah." Suraya's eyes pled with me, and the absent Noah.

"Be careful, Suraya. I only tell you this because I love you."

"I know. But so does Noah."

Suraya turned to allow me to button up her frock correctly, ending the conversation.

# CHAPTER TEN

## Joanna

December 1807

I RECEIVED A REPLY from Uncle John in October.

> My Dear Joanna,
> 
> Thank you for your recent letter. I am happy to hear that you are adjusting and doing well with your studies, as I knew you would.
> 
> My daily walks are not as pleasant without your company. Even the birds' singing seems to have lost its luster. I'm not the only one missing you.
> 
> I must encourage you to not raise your hopes too highly regarding the search to find your aunt. Your father only referred to his sister, your aunt Olu, a few times. I know they were separated after they were kidnapped together, and as far as I know, he never saw her again. Although slave records are generally kept meticulously, even if we locate your aunt, you must remember she is in all likelihood a slave. To secure her freedom, and passage to England, may encompass a sum beyond my means of accomplishment. But I digress. Firstly, finding her in and of itself may prove to be an insurmountable task. I write this not to discourage you, but to ensure you do not hold falsely high expectations of finding your dear aunt. Having written this, I will promise to do my utmost to locate her. At least I have her name, or possibly a nickname—Olu.
> 
> In regards to your other inquiry, I have enclosed a reader as you requested. I am surprised Mrs. Limebear does not have

this resource, but I suppose all her books are at a much higher reading level. I wish you well on your project.
    With affection,
    Uncle John

As I read his letter, I could hear Uncle John's voice. I missed him so! I craved his protection—from Miranda and Violet and their hateful remarks; from Mrs. Limebear and her stern manner; from Mr. Harding and his cold looks. Miss Maisie had become my refuge. If I didn't have her, I don't think I could have survived, and I had only been here three months.

Maisie and I had met secretly for a fortnight before we were discovered. One night Mrs. Limebear decided to check on all of us to ensure we were studying during study hour, 8:00–9:00 p.m. A few of the girls had performed poorly on a recent exam, and she thought either they weren't studying, or needed extra help.

Maisie and I sat in two chairs, with our heads bent together over a book. Maisie read each word in a slow, deliberate, loud cadence. The door opened, our heads shot up bumping each other, and we looked up at Mrs. Limebear, guilt and pain reflected on our faces.

"Mrs. Limebear, ma'am," I began, "I finished my studies and I'm . . . I'm helping Miss Maisie read."

"I don't know who I'm more disappointed in. Maisie, you know better than to take Joanna from her studies. I'm surprised at you. And is your work done?"

"Yes, ma'am. It's my fault, ma'am—don' blame Miss Joanna. I got too excited 'bout learnin' to read."

Mrs. Limebear appeared momentarily at a loss, a rare event. She hated surprises, preferring control in all situations.

"Let me hear you read, Maisie," Mrs. Limebear commanded.

"I's just learnin', ma'am. I can't really read good yet."

"You can't read well yet. Yes, fine. Let me hear what you *can* read."

I pointed to a line in the book in Maisie's hand, smiling at her.

"The boy ran. The boy feel. The boy cried," Maisie read.

"I think the boy fell," Mrs. Limebear corrected her.

"Yes, ma'am. Fell." Maisie nodded.

After an awkward silence, Mrs. Limebear addressed me. "You have obviously worked very hard with Maisie. It's very difficult to teach an adult to read."

"Yes, ma'am."

"While you haven't broken any written rules, other than using study time to do something other than study, you have been secretive and dishonest. You should have asked my permission to teach Maisie to read. I would have granted it. As it stands, your behavior cannot go unpunished."

"I understand, ma'am." I looked down, waiting.

"And by the way. Where did you procure that reader? I have no beginning readers in the library." Mrs. Limebear looked at me with her head tilted.

"Ma'am, my Uncle John sent it to me."

"He knows you were teaching Maisie to read?" Mrs. Limebear asked.

"Not exactly."

"Not exactly? Exactly what did you tell him?" Mrs. Limebear raised her eyebrows and tilted her head, determined to ferret out the truth.

"I said I needed it for a school project," I admitted.

"I see. So, in addition to not being forthcoming with me, you also deceived your uncle."

"I didn't mean to, ma'am." I lowered my head.

"Well, you did. For the next two weeks you will have study time in the library along with Miranda, and Mr. Harding will supervise the two of you. I'll write to Mr. Audley, informing him of your behavior, and he may take whatever actions he deems appropriate. I will decide if and when reading lessons may resume. And Maisie, your Christmas holiday is reduced to three days."

"Mrs. Limebear, please don't punish her; I talked her into it," I pleaded.

"She's a grown woman, Miss Vassa. She is responsible for her own actions, as are you."

"Yes, ma'am." I felt my pulse throbbing in my head.

"Maisie, come with me. Miss Vassa, prepare for bed." Without another word, Mrs. Limebear pivoted and left the room.

I lay down that night with a mixture of guilt, remorse, and pride. Maisie was learning to read, but now that we had been found out, the lessons were terminated, and might never resume.

When Maisie appeared at my door the following morning, she said, "I hope you ain't worrying bout me, Miss Joanna. I's fine. She shortened my days off, and gave me a few extra chores, but that ain't nothing. I's fine," Maisie promised me.

"Oh, thank you, Miss Maisie. I do feel bad. You're doing so well with your reading, too."

"I can keep going a bit on my own. Up with you now, here's water for washing. Let me get your frock off."

After breakfast, Mrs. Limebear called all of us into the parlour and declared we would put on a program for the vicar's birthday in February. During the months of November and December, the afternoon hour normally devoted to drawing and practicing piano would be spent rehearsing for the program. Mrs. Limebear decided each girl would showcase a musical talent. On that rainy Tuesday afternoon, Mrs. Limebear made the assignments.

Rose and Violet, who had sung and played together since they were four or five, would perform together. Rose played piano adequately, while Violet had a lovely soprano voice. Candace played the violin and Samantha was learning piano, so they would play a simple duet. That left Miranda, Anne, and me. Miranda and I both played piano, while Anne sang well. Mrs. Limebear decided I would accompany Anne, and Miranda would play a solo.

"Mrs. Limebear, I may need some help," Samantha said.

"I've already spoken to a young lady who is an excellent pianist and gives piano lessons. Miss Catherine will come two afternoons a week to help all of you who are playing the piano for the program."

"Rose, what shall we do?" Violet asked.

"Maybe a hymn. Vicars like hymns."

"Oh, piffle. I don't want to play some boring hymn. Let's do an aria. I enjoyed singing that Mozart piece, and you played so nicely. I want a challenge. Not some simple hymn," Violet responded.

"Fine. Let's look at the music and see what Mrs. Limebear has. Then we can decide." The twins departed to the music room.

Miranda said aloud to no one in particular, "I don't know why she had to assign us. I think I should accompany Anne; she's my roommate."

Candace looked up and said, "Maybe that's exactly why. Joanna is always alone. You're not. So maybe she put Joanna and Anne together purposely."

"Well, that's stupid," Miranda announced. "She should put us together by how well we play. What does Joanna know about classical music, anyway? She's not even English!" Miranda glanced at me in a challenge, arms folded, chin raised.

Candace asked Miranda, "What do you mean, she's not English?"

"She's not. She's African. You can tell just by looking at her. She's not like us." Miranda lowered her voice as though she were telling a secret, or a curse. "She's practically black." Miranda hastened out of the parlour like a dark cloud, taking her negative energy with her. An awkward silence ensued.

I looked down at my *practically black* hands folded in my lap. I wondered, can I not be *practically black* and English? Oh, how I wish my mama or papa were here. Uncle John was wonderful, but we didn't speak about these things. He had no idea what it was like to be a young woman of colour in England.

In this initial foray out into the world—I had led a sheltered life thus far—I encountered attitudes and opposition I didn't expect and didn't know how to deal with. Where did I fit in? How did others view me? Was I English or African, and are those mutually exclusive?

Samantha broke the awkward silence. "Candace, let's go to the music room and decide what we want to do." Candace looked relieved and left the parlour with Samantha.

Anne looked over at me and winced. "Miranda is self-centered and mean when she doesn't get her own way."

"I noticed that. Do you want to play with her, instead of me?" I hoped she would say "no."

"No, I'm happy to sing with you. I'm always with her."

'Thanks, Anne."

Anne looked at me and said, "Can I ask you a question?"

"Of course."

"Has Miranda said other mean things to you?" Anne asked, speaking softly.

"Not really. But I am upset about something," I admitted.

"What is it?" Anne leaned forward.

"Don't tell anyone!" I asked her.

"Of course not."

"Well, I got caught teaching Miss Maisie to read—we met during study time in the room next to mine, the empty one."

Anne raised her eyebrows and asked, "Miss Maisie can't read?"

"No, but she's learning fast. The thing is, we got caught, and I have to stop teaching her. Mrs. Limebear also shortened Miss Maisie's holiday. I feel so bad. On top of that, I must study in the library for the next two weeks, with Miranda. Mr. Harding will supervise us." I looked at Anne to see how she would react.

"That's awful!"

"I know."

Anne didn't respond immediately. Then her eyes widened, and she grinned. "I know! I'll tell Mrs. Limebear I need extra help. I'll join you. She won't be so bold with Mr. Harding and me there."

"I don't know. You don't have to do that, Anne."

"I want to. We'll stick together, look out for each other. Right?" Anne asked, eyes sparkling.

"Yes!" I smiled and wiped a stray tear. It occurred to me this is what friends do, stand by each other. Maybe Anne would be my friend.

Anne asked if I had any sisters. I told her my only sister, Anna Maria, died before her fourth birthday, before I was two, and I didn't remember her. Anne reached out and put her hand over mine. We kept talking.

"I always had my own room, far as I remember. But I thought when I came to boarding school, I'd have a roommate. I thought that would be so lovely, to have a girl to talk to at night, to stay up late talking." I remembered my dreams of making friends and talking late into the night.

"You must have been so disappointed—when you got your own room."

"I was. Especially since I'm the only one in a room alone. It rather makes me stand out, which is the last thing I want to do." I looked down.

"I see what you mean."

"Do you have any sisters, Anne?" I was ready to change the subject.

"No, I'm an only child."

"Like me." I was happy we had something in common.

"Yes, and my mother died when I was nine years old."

"Anne, how hard that must have been. I don't remember my mama at all. I was barely walking when she died."

"You're better off. Let me tell you something. Promise not to tell anyone." Anne leaned closer to me.

"I promise."

"I was . . . relieved when my mama died." Anne tilted her head down and glanced up at me to gauge my reaction. I hoped my shock didn't show.

"She was very ill?" I asked.

"Yes, she was sick for . . . well I don't really remember her being well at all. My papa tells me she used to read me stories, and take me for walks, and have tea parties with me, but I don't remember any of that. All I remember of my mama is her lying in her sickbed, sleeping, moaning in pain, looking out the window, asking me to read to her."

"Anne . . ." I held her hand.

"Every day, for two or three hours, I was made to sit by her bed, talk to her, read her poetry, and novels. To tell the truth—I dreaded it!"

"That's a lot to ask of a nine-year-old." I wondered why her father put her through that.

"Well, Papa always said be brave, smile. He said Mama needed me; she looked forward to my visits. He promised me my visits would help her get better. But she didn't get better. She slept more and more, got thinner and thinner—until she died."

"You were a good daughter, Anne."

'Not really. I was there, but I didn't want to be. Isn't that terrible?"

Mrs. Limebear burst into the room.

"Well, girls. Samantha and Candace will play *Ode to Joy*, that's a Beethoven piece. Violet and Rose have decided upon the Bach, *My Heart Ever Faithful*—such a transcendent song, and Miranda has wisely chosen a Handel sonata. Have you girls chosen yet?"

"Not yet, ma'am," I replied.

"Well, then, let's see what we can find that would be suitable."

Mrs. Limebear pulled out a rather large selection of piano and voice duets, and after discarding some that were too common, and some that were too difficult, Anne and I chose Handel's *Susanna: Chastity, Thy Cherub Bright* and *Go, and on my truth relying*.

"Excellent choice girls. Practice both and we'll decide if you'll do one or both for the vicar's birthday. Miss Catherine will help you as you practice. I'm sure the vicar will be delighted with these."

On Monday evening Miranda and I had to retire to the library to study with Mr. Harding "supervising." He frowned at me occasionally but didn't speak. She kept to herself. I guess without an audience, she couldn't be bothered to harass me. I wondered what motivated her—hate, fear, jealousy, discomfort. I guess I'll never know. I didn't hate Miranda, but I didn't like her either. At that time in my life, as a girl on the brink of becoming a woman, I had limited experience and had never heard anyone call me practically black or half-caste or disparage my skin colour. Uncle John didn't prepare me, either.

On Tuesday, Anne joined us. Anne and I sat together, and Miranda continued to keep to herself. With Anne beside me, the evenings were pleasant, not torturous. Thursday evening Miranda left early, complaining of a headache. Anne whispered to me she found out Miranda had tattled on me, telling Mrs. Limebear I was teaching Maisie to read.

Apparently, she also said some unkind, derogatory remarks about Africans and slaves, the reason for her punishment.

I could have easily done a second week, but on Sunday afternoon, Mrs. Limebear knocked on the door of my room as I wrote a letter to Barbara Wilberforce.

"Come in," I called out.

"Miss Joanna. The first week of your supervised study time is over. I'm prepared to offer you an alternative to an additional week of study time with Mr. Harding," Mrs. Limebear said.

I didn't want her to realize it wasn't really a punishment, so I proceeded with caution. "Yes?"

"Maeve, our laundress, found out you're teaching Maisie to read, and she would also like to learn to read. In lieu of an additional week of study time in the library, would you be willing to take on another pupil, and teach Maeve to read?"

"I'd love to! Thank you, Mrs. Limebear." I was so excited and relieved, for the first time I felt like hugging Mrs. Limebear. But she was all business.

"That's settled then. You may resume your study time on your own, and you may meet with Maeve once a week on Saturday, after she finishes her work."

"Thank you for trusting me with this responsibility," I said.

"You are a mature, intelligent young woman, and it's never too early to be of service to others who are less fortunate. If you need any resources or materials, you may ask me. No need to inquire of your uncle again. Good night, Miss Joanna." Mrs. Limebear left the room and closed my door.

I found out when I went to Uncle John's for Christmas vacation that he had responded to her letter upbraiding me for teaching Maisie by praising my initiative and selfless service. Apparently, Uncle John implied Mrs. Limebear should be proud of me instead of punishing me—hence her change of course.

# CHAPTER ELEVEN

## Olu

### July 1759

Two months later Suraya had not gotten her monthly courses; we both realized she was with child. Seventeen, a slave, expecting—a damning combination.

Three months later, now five months along, Suraya was obviously showing. Noah had ceased his attentions, and Suraya still claimed he loved her and was simply protecting her.

"When I has the baby, he'll come. He'll take us with him—up to Philadelphia," Suraya repeated this mantra—believing it, convincing herself.

One morning as I helped Martha with breakfast, our heads turned together when we heard a familiar voice.

"I would ride all night for a taste of your griddle cakes, Miss Martha." Teddy strolled into the kitchen.

"Mr. Teddy!" Martha laughed. "You never knock, or let a body know you comin'?"

"Never, Miss Martha. Though I'm a bit more predictable now. Seems my wife likes to plan ahead, not move on a whim," Teddy said with a chuckle.

"You looks healthy, Mr. Teddy. That wife of yours must be feedin' you right."

"She's the best cook in South Carolina—after ye." Teddy bowed.

They continued talking as I bustled around the fire, pulling out the griddle cakes, and putting new ones in, mixing up some fresh batter. Teddy was exactly the person I needed to talk to about Suraya. I could always talk to Teddy. I trusted him. But now that he was married, I wasn't sure how to relate to him or approach him. Not that our relationship had ever been sexual. It wasn't. Not that I wasn't attracted to him. I was. But he acted like an older brother, if that were even possible.

I listened while Teddy and Martha chatted, waiting for my chance to talk to him alone. It came when Martha went to check on one of the pregnant cows; Martha checked on her several times a day, wanting to be present at the birth to ensure there were no complications. She felt responsible for the mama cow even though it wasn't her job.

"How've you been, Olivia?" Teddy asked.

"Teddy, so good to see you." I had grown a few inches since Teddy was last here over a year ago, so I didn't have to tip my head back quite as far to look up at him. Teddy looked content. I was happy to see it. He had always seemed, had always been, so restless.

"I'm fine. Martha's teaching me more of her remedies and giving me lots of chances to help. I've watched her birth a few babies, too." I smiled at Teddy.

"That's wonderful. You're good with people, and have a way of putting others at ease, which can only help the healing process."

Embarrassed, I changed the subject.

"I've been journaling and reading every day."

"That's great. Your paper supply must be low," Teddy observed.

"It is actually, ink too."

"I've been neglecting my star pupil!" Teddy put his hand on his forehead in mock despair.

"Not neglect. You have a family now. How's Lydia?" I asked.

"She's well, thank you. Although she's given me cause for concern a few times. She's so vibrant, but when she takes ill it hits her hard and recovery is slow."

"Sorry to hear it. Do you have an herbalist or a doctor nearby?" I asked.

"The doctor's not much use that I can see." Teddy frowned.

I continued to bake the griddle cakes as we talked and finished up all the batter. As I moved the cakes onto a platter, Teddy offered to help bring them upstairs.

"No, no. You know your brother would have a fit if he saw you doing my job. I can manage, thanks, but I do need help with something else."

"Whatever it is. Let me help you." Teddy put his hand over his heart.

"Can I speak with you after breakfast?"

## CHAPTER ELEVEN: OLU

"Yes. Where shall I meet thee—you! Oops, I still use the Quaker tongue at times when I'm not with Quakers." Teddy laughed at himself.

We agreed to meet after breakfast at the laundry line. With a grin, Teddy took the stairs two at a time, and surprised his brother Samuel, who had recently wandered downstairs seeking coffee.

Martha came back convinced that the cow would be calving this day or the morrow.

"Teddy looks fine, don' he? Marriage be what he needed, I declare. He's always movin' about here to there. I's glad he's settled down."

"Yes, ma'am. He does seem content. It's good to see him so."

"Let's get these cakes upstairs afore the Missus yells down for us. Where's Sarah? That girl is gettin' slower and clumsier. I surprised as can be the Missus ain't figured out she's 'spectin. True she ain't pokin' out too much yet, but still and all, the Missus don' miss much." Miss Martha shook her head.

Martha could do three things at once, four if one included talking. Now she was heating up some fresh maple syrup, handing me a bowl to fill with blueberries, lifting the platter filled with griddle cakes, and stoking the dying fire. I filled the ceramic bowl two-thirds full of berries and brought up a small creamer filled with syrup. As I placed the berries and syrup on the sideboard, covered with a newly embroidered runner in shades of maroon and gold, I noticed Teddy and Mr. Samuel conversing in strident, muted tones.

Martha came up next with the griddle cakes, and sausages, and right before it was time to ring the bell, Suraya arrived. She looked droopy—with dark, puffy skin under her eyes.

Mrs. Beth and Susannah came down as soon as they heard me ring the bell. They were usually hungry in the morning and rarely late. As they came in, Teddy turned away from his brother to greet them.

"How are you, sister and niece? You're looking positively glowing this morning!" Teddy greeted his brother's wife and daughter with a compliment.

"Uncle Teddy!" Susannah ran over for a hug.

"Oho, look who's been growing. You reach up to my shoulder almost. Soon I'll have to teach you to dance!"

"Uncle Teddy. You say the silliest things. I'm only fourteen, not dancing age yet!"

The Cross family sat down to eat, Suraya and I served, and Martha retired downstairs to put her feet up for a minute before beginning lunch preparations.

"I'm learning about the kings and queens of England, Papa," Susannah announced.

"Good, good. I wonder how long we'll be beholden to the king of England."

"What Papa! Why?" Susannah asked.

"Oh nothing. Just some laws and taxes I don't reckon with. Did you know that Charles Stuart, called the Young Pretender, tried to take over England? But he couldn't do it." Susannah nodded her head as her father spoke.

"He went back to Scotland with his tail between his legs," Teddy murmured.

Mrs. Beth then asked after Lydia, and Teddy shared his joy in marriage, and concern for Lydia's health.

"After she has her first child, she'll be strong. Women need birthing and babies. It's how God made us," Mrs. Beth pronounced.

"Well, we may be anticipating a larger family fairly soon." Teddy smiled.

"Teddy, how wonderful," Mrs. Beth said.

"Congrats, brother. Nothing like a child to make a family complete," said Mr. Cross.

I was silently happy for Teddy, standing by the sideboard, ready to replenish any empty plates. I couldn't help but think of Suraya. She was doing what God made her for, but what would become of her and her child?

After I'd washed all the dishes, bowls, mugs, cups, silverware, and platters, I took the laundry out to hang. The line was shielded from the house by a row of magnolia trees, and this is where Teddy would often meet me, where he taught me to read and write. I looked forward to Tuesdays and Thursdays every week unless it rained. I could be outside, away from the constantly watchful eyes of Mrs. Beth, and often Teddy would show up and continue our lesson, wherever he had left off.

Today was different. We had something serious to discuss. And he was a married man now. I was glad that didn't seem to affect our relationship. I began to hang the sheets, and Teddy peered out at me from behind a blooming magnolia tree.

"Ready for your lesson my star pupil?" Teddy asked.

"No lesson today, Teddy. I have a pressing matter to discuss."

"So serious. Olivia, what is it? I hope I can help." He turned his full attention to me.

"I'm not sure you can, but I don't know where else to turn." I clamped a sheet to the line with a clothes pin.

"So, I'm either your first choice, or your last."

"First, definitely first, and *only* for that matter. I don't know if you noticed anything different about Suraya."

"Suraya. You don't call her Sarah?"

"I don't care for slave names."

"I never asked. What's your given name?"

"Oluchukwu, it means walk of God. My brothers all call me Olu."

"Oluchukwu, an unusual name." Teddy pronounced it right the first time and I loved the way it sounded in his baritone voice.

"It's common back home."

"Olu it is. I like it. Yes, to the point. I did notice something different about Sarah—Suraya—or should I say someone. She's obviously expecting. I only hope it's not—that is . . ." Teddy didn't offer up a name.

"The father is Noah," I said.

"Noah! I didn't expect that! Was it an ongoing, hmm, friendship?"

"Mm hm. She claims he loves her. I don't trust him. I don't know what Mr. Samuel will do when he finds out." I glanced over at Teddy around the sheet I was hanging.

"Oh, he knows."

"He knows? No one has said a word." I whispered, though apparently the news was out.

"He's waiting and deciding."

"That's what I dread—what he will decide." I looked at Teddy.

He sat on his favorite log, watching me as I hung the linens, sheets, and shirts. I paused, with a clothes pin in my hand, and looked over to Teddy. He straddled the log, his legs filling out his breeches, his face a reddish brown from traveling by horse for a few days. He had a long piece of rice stalk in his mouth—he liked to chew on things. His hat was on the ground beside him, one arm crossed his belly, the other hand was cupping his chin—deep in thought. He was a handsome man—I always thought so. He wasn't like his brother, or other slave owners who bedded slave women randomly and at will. I never heard any slave say a negative word about Teddy. Now he was married. He was always out of reach, now even more so.

"You're right, of course. I want to think well of my brother, but he continually disappoints me. He knows how strongly I disapprove of slavery, and yet . . ."

"And yet?" I waited for Teddy to continue.

"He offered Sar. . . Suraya to me! As a slave for Lydia. I would take her, not as a slave, but to save her from a worse fate. But Lydia won't abide having a slave, or even a maid. She insists on doing the cooking and cleaning herself. Maybe when the baby comes she'll agree to have help, but that doesn't help Suraya now." Teddy looked down in defeat.

"I'm happy for you, Teddy. You'll be a fine father."

I didn't know what else to say. I went back to hanging linens, thinking about what Teddy had said. Suraya going with Teddy and Lydia would be an ideal solution, but having two babies in one house might not work well. And I admired Lydia's stance against slavery. I couldn't fault her for that.

"I struggle with this decision Oliv. . . Olu. To honor my wife's conviction, and my own, may put Suraya in harm's way, but I will not trample on Lydia's beliefs. I knew when we wed she would not accept a slave, or even a live-in maid. It's the Quaker way. But that doesn't mean I can't help Suraya. I can focus on convincing Samuel to find her a suitable home."

Teddy told me how he met Lydia. Teddy built houses for a living, and when he built a house for Lydia's neighbor, he employed Lydia's brother. Lydia would bring over lunch from time to time. About the fourth time providing lunch, Lydia had filled up her saddlebag, not with oats or carrots for her horse Grace, but with cheese, bread, and fruit for the men— and smoked turkey. She rode up to the site, dismounted, and leaned up to retrieve the heavy bag, but Teddy reached it first, and smoothly lifted it off the horse's back.

Lydia remonstrated with him, letting him know she was grateful but not incapable. Then he asked if she would accept more assistance and offered to assist Lydia by emptying the contents onto the blanket, and into his stomach.

"That sounds like you, all right," I interjected.

Teddy laughed. Lydia has four brothers and a father, so she was aware of the capacity of males to eat a great deal in one sitting. After they ate, Teddy assisted her brother Jacob with leveling the window frame. Teddy asked Jacob if his sister was engaged to be married, and Jacob replied, "No, who'd want her?"

I laughed. "That sounds like something a brother would say," thinking of Ledu, as I often did.

Teddy related his conversation with Jacob, finding out Lydia's age, twenty-two; previous marriage offers, two; and religious persuasion, Quaker. Lydia hummed an old Quaker hymn Teddy wasn't familiar with as she laid out the food. Teddy and Lydia talked as they ate and got to know about each other's families and religious beliefs. By the end of the day Teddy found himself sprinkling 'thee' and 'thou' into his conversations.

After discussing language, they discussed their views on slavery—both ardent abolitionists. Lydia finally asked Teddy what he believes of the bible and what was his favorite verse. They both had the same favorite verse, Habakkuk 3:19. Teddy told Lydia it was fate. Teddy had not planned to marry, but once he met Lydia, he realized something was missing in his life.

Teddy stopped his recital of meeting Lydia. "I'm boring you," he said.

"No, not at all. Please go on." I urged him to continue.

"I told her what was missing was a house I built, a home, with a roaring fire and in it a beautiful young woman, rocking back and forth, knitting a baby blanket . . . the woman in the rocking chair looked like Lydia."

Teddy continued. "I was persuasive enough to gain her father's permission to marry me, after I began attending the Quaker church."

"It's a lovely story, Teddy. And Lydia sounds like the perfect wife for you." I paused, focusing on placing the clothespin on the sheet, hesitant to change back to a more serious subject.

"You're sure Mr. Samuel means to sell Suraya? No matter what?" I asked Teddy.

"Yes, he does. And once Sam makes up his mind, it's nigh impossible to sway him. I'll see what influence I may have with him."

"Thanks, Teddy. How long will you be staying this time?"

"Not long. I'm concerned for Lydia's health, and though she's not due for some weeks yet, I hate to be away for long." Teddy looked off into the distance.

"She needs you now."

"How is it a teenage girl is so wise?"

"I'm seventeen in years, but much older in life experience, in longing."

"What do you long for, Olu?" Teddy tilted his head and gazed at me.

I stopped hanging up sheets and turned to look at him.

"Freedom. To wake up in a place of my choosing, to decide what I want to wear, what to eat, what to do. Or even to turn over and stay in bed if I so choose. Every minute of my day is determined by others. I remember my childhood, with my family, and I didn't even realize I was free. I didn't appreciate it. Now I do." I didn't tell him I also longed for him, or someone like him, to picture me in a rocking chair knitting for our child.

"Hmmm. I never thought of it like that. I've always abhorred slavery—it makes no sense for one person to own another when we are all children of God. But what it means to live as a slave day by day, I never really considered."

"I sometimes wonder if those born as slaves aren't slightly better off. It's all they know. Their whole life has been un-free," I said, thinking aloud.

I took up the now empty basket and placed it on my hip. Teddy glanced around, rose from the log, and said, "I should be going as well. I'll talk to Samuel, see if I can sway him at all. But I'm afraid he's bound and determined to sell Suraya before she delivers."

"And I'm helpless to prevent it." I looked at Teddy.

"My brother makes most people feel that way," Teddy said.

Teddy left to talk to his brother, and I went back to the house to help Miss Martha with lunch preparations. Two days later, as Suraya and I were going to bed, she turned to me with tears in her eyes. "Mr. Samuel sellin' me. Say he don' want no slave babies around."

"Suraya, oh my sweet Suraya." I reached out to touch her arm.

"I ain't scared of being sold. I figure one massa's as good or bad as the other. It's only . . . I believed Noah would take care of me and his baby. I did. And he won't. I don' know if I's more angry or just feeling poorly."

"Did you speak to Noah?" I asked.

"I did. And he right surprised me. You were so right Olu, and I didn' see it. I said Mr. Samuel was sellin' me, and what should we do. You might never believe what he said. He says, 'Sarah, I'm sorry to hear it, but there is no we.'" A tear slid down Suraya's cheek.

"No 'we' I says. No 'we'? Who was that makin' love, makin' a baby if it weren't 'we'? And he says, 'How do you know I'm the father?' Well Olu, I didn't like Noah much right then. He knew I was a virgin. I felt like slappin' him. Hard. I look back at him, stared right at him. He knew. I knew he knew he was the only man I been with. He said he couldn't do nothin' for me, and if I was smart, I wouldn't tell Mr. Samuel he be the father. He even tried to give me five pounds."

"This is too much. He tried to pay you?" I sighed in exasperation.

"Maybe I should've kept it. But I ain't no whore." Suraya shook her head.

"No, you're not."

"I threw his money on the ground and ran back in the house."

"I hope your new master won't be harsh. I hope you can stay in the house."

"I can't think. I just had to say 'goodbye.' I don't imagine we see each other again. Leastways not this side o' heaven."

"You never know, Suri. I'm planning to escape."

"Olu, don' talk 'bout escape!" She backed away from me.

"I know how you feel now, but you may change your mind. I can try to get word to you once my plans are set."

"God knows where I'll be—me and my chile. Pray my chile and me can stay together. That be the only thing I fear. Not being with my baby."

"I will pray, Suri. I'll always pray for you."

"I gotta go. I don' know how Miss Susannah will get along without me!"

A lot better than you will, is what I thought, but what I said was, "She'll be fine."

"I s'pose she will. Olu, I'll miss you so. You be like my sister—my family."

We embraced, and cried, and promised to always pray for each other and never forget each other. She didn't want to let go, and neither did I. Suri was such a sweet girl, but for all we'd been through she was still ingenuous and too trusting.

It was the last time I saw Suraya.

# CHAPTER TWELVE

## Joanna

December 1807

Michaelmas term was almost over; I looked forward to going home to Uncle John in London and visiting Barbara and the Wilberforce clan. I was more than ready to leave the school and Miranda's damaging words behind. My thoughts were on the future as we gathered for dinner at the school a fortnight before the final day of term.

No soup tonight—a beet salad followed by boiled fish, potatoes, and peas. The twins Rose and Violet were talking about their grandmamma and what to make her for Christmas; Miranda complained about the dinner—no taste and not hot enough; Candace and Samantha talked about their favourite Christmas tradition, stockings on Christmas Eve; and Anne asked me where I was spending Christmas.

Mrs. Limebear cleared her throat and said, "Girls, may I have your attention."

We all turned to her; I expected some new assignment or chastisement for unsatisfactory work.

"Our term is over soon, and you girls have performed very well. I am most pleased and proud of your progress." Mrs. Limebear gave her version of a smile, mouth closed, right side of her mouth slightly raised.

I braced myself for the "but."

"I mentioned on the first day that all of you who displayed proper behavior and a good work ethic would be treated to a special outin. . . ."

"To Astley's! Yay!" Rose cried out.

"Rose, I hope I won't have to change my mind. Your enthusiasm is noted."

I looked around the table—all of us had irrepressible grins on our faces. Dinner was forgotten and all eyes were on Mrs. Limebear. I couldn't wait to see the majestic horses, but I knew the girls were mostly interested in the performers.

"I will be taking all seven of you to Astley's Royal Amphitheatre on 11 December, after final exams." Mrs. Limebear nodded as if congratulating herself.

Miranda asked, "How will we get there?"

"I will retain two carriages for the trip. I have arranged for all of us to stay over in London, either with your own families or at my sister's home," Mrs. Limebear replied.

"How fun! A carriage ride and Astley's all in one day," Samantha said.

"Will we have a box?" Candace asked.

"Yes, indeed. I will purchase tickets for a box, and of course I have approval from your parents, and guardian." Mrs. Limebear glanced at me.

Anne looked at me and said, "This will be so fun!"

"I can't wait to see the horses," I said.

Then we all started talking at once—only Mr. Harding was silent.

I awoke long before the bell rang on the day of our trip to Astley's. I couldn't decide what to wear! Pulling the curtains aside, I watched as the soft silver enveloping fog crept up the fields, an uninvited guest casting a spell over the day. Undeterred, I let the curtains fall and turned my attention to my clothes. Choosing from outer to inner, I decided on the red merino wool cloak, then I pulled out my ivory spencer jacket, a muslin white gown with a peach inset (which was a bit short and would not get soiled brushing against the ground), my chemise, and petticoat. I chose my half-boots, the only wise choice for an outing with lots of horses and other animals! The final touch was my amber cross on a plain gold chain, given to me by my mother.

We all met in the parlor after breakfast, giggling and chattering. Anne and I stood together, hoping to be in the same carriage. Mrs. Limebear divided us into two groups for the two carriages—Anne, me, Candace, and Mrs. Limebear in the first carriage, and Miranda, Violent and Rose, Samantha, and Mr. Harding in the second carriage.

After a three-hour journey, our carriage pulled up behind a long line of carriages, coaches, and curricles. Crowds of people surged forward, rocking our carriage. Once we had moved only a few carriage lengths forward, after several minutes of waiting and rocking, Mrs. Limebear rapped her knuckles on the front of the carriage to get the driver's attention. He jumped down, squeezed around the crowd to open the door, and stared at Mrs. Limebear, eyebrows raised.

"We'll get out here. Is it always this crowded?" Mrs. Limebear yelled to be heard over the shouting, squealing, laughing, raucous crowd of adults and children.

"Yes'm. Always crowded for Astley's. Very popular it is. I be waiting for ye over yonder by that tree when ye come out." The driver handed Mrs. Limebear and us girls out of the carriage, and then went to tell the driver of the other carriage what was happening. The fog had not lifted, but the cheery crowd imbued it with an exuberant lightness. Mr. Harding came forward, followed by Violet and Rose, Miranda, and Samantha.

Mrs. Limebear led the way with Mr. Harding beside her, forcing her bulky body through the masses to the ticket booth. Atypically, she shouted for us to hold hands with our roommates and stay close, forgetting one of us had no roommate. I sandwiched myself between Anne and Violet and tried to avoid being squished and shoved by strangers.

Once we were all through the gate, Mrs. Limebear turned again, yelling, "Box Eleven, follow me." After getting an elbow in my stomach, a reticule swung at my head, and a child's hand pushing my derrière, I wedged my way through an opening to a tunnel which smelled of horse poop, sweat, and sawdust. I glanced back to see in what direction the girls were going, and walked a little way down the tunnel, deserted except for an errant rider, acrobat, and clown. This is what I had looked forward to since Mrs. Limebear mentioned Astley's in September—a chance to see these magnificent horses up close. An enormous light gold Palomino with a dazzling white mane and tail was tethered to a railing. I made my way to her, looking back to see if anyone might stop me.

I reached the majestic horse and stood still in front of her—talking softly, murmuring horse sounds, and humming—*harrumph, wheeeehunhhunhhunhhunh, hushhushhush, erruruerruru*. Uncle John claimed I spoke 'horse'—a language horses use to communicate with each other, and their favourite humans. All I know is I have a connection with horses.

After standing still and whispering to the mare, I reached the back of my hand to her muzzle. She breathed out on my hand, flapping her lips, and inhaled my scent, then she lifted her head and whinnied. She nudged my hand, recognizing a kindred spirit. One of the riders walked by and looked at me askance, asking, "What ye be doing back here, missy? The seats be out thataway." He pointed up the tunnel and kept walking.

I stayed beside the lovely lady, stroking her braided mane, when I smelled the most unwelcome scent of all—Mr. Harding.

"Miss Vassa, you should not be here." He stood right behind me, pushed up against me. I ducked under the mare's neck and stood on the other side, the Palomino now between us. She pawed the air with her front legs, high-stepping up and down, landing at least once on Mr. Harding's foot. I heard his grunt of pain and whispered to the mare—she threw her head to the side knocking Mr. Harding to the dirty floor, where he landed on a pile of horse poop in pain and disgrace. I promptly kissed my new best friend and walked swiftly up the tunnel to find Box Eleven.

I didn't encounter crowds as I looked for Box Eleven. Most people were already seated and the show was about to begin. I glanced behind me, but didn't see Mr. Harding, so I continued around part of the inner circle beside the open seating, and finally found Box Eleven. We were adjacent to the ring, separated from the performers by only a short wall. Anne waved at me and showed me a space beside her, so I stepped through an opening in the wall and squeezed up to my seat. Mrs. Limebear frowned at me, but no one else paid any attention; they were too busy gazing at the people, the ceiling, columns, and chandeliers, decorated in white, gold, lemon yellow, and green. Crimson red curtains bracketed the more expensive boxes.

I smelled Mr. Harding before I saw him. He held his offensive jacket in his hand and stepped over the wall, sitting in the front row next to Mrs. Limebear, who turned to him grimacing, moving as far away as she possibly could. The laughter, talking, and shouting ceased immediately when Mr. Philip Astley himself entered the ring seated on an enormous black horse with gold ribbons braided through his mane. Mr. Astley looked both tall and wide, a striking figure in a military uniform consisting of a black and gold waistcoat with tails, gold epaulets, black breeches, and black boots.

"Ladies, gentlemen, and children of all ages!!" he began, to the cheers and shouts of the crowd. "Welcome one and all to Astley's Royal Amphitheatre!" He paused for the clapping and shouting to subside. "Let the show begin!" On the word "begin" drummers began tapping out a rapid beat while Mr. Astley stood up on his horse which was cantering around the ring in a wide circle. He waved at the audience while standing on the horse, and after three circles around the ring, he dropped onto the horse's back, quite gracefully for a tall, rotund man. Then he called out, "Welcome to the ring my beautiful wife, Patty!" I saw my horse, that's how I thought of her, a woman with a flounced, knee-length dress sitting astride. She, too, rose and stood on her horse, now cantering behind Mr. Astley's horse. Anne pointed to Patty Astley and asked me, "what's that on her arms?" I leaned forward and looked at what appeared to be a kind of muff, but it was moving. We heard someone exclaim in the box next to us, "she's got bees on her arms!"

The buzzing in the audience drowned out the buzzing of the bees circling both her arms. Patty Astley took her seat on her horse, then slid to the floor. The Palomino came astride the black horse Mr. Astley was riding, and he pulled up the reins of both horses, standing with one foot on each. Oh my! I never saw such a sight in my life, and it seems the audience hadn't either, as we all gasped in unison. To see that large man, decked out in a military dress uniform, with one booted foot on the black horse and the other on the golden horse, what a sight! Mr. Astley proceeded to pull a reed pipe out of his pocket and play a tune whilst standing on both horses as they cantered around the ring.

One act followed another, acrobats flying above us only to barely grasp a ring or a hand, dogs dancing and doing tricks, clowns entertaining the crowd. At one point a clown came right up to Mr. Harding, bowed low, then came up holding his big red nose, his whole face scrunched up in disgust! Anne and I couldn't stop laughing!

I was especially impressed by a dark-skinned circus performer. He was darker than me, with a bushy full moustache and was introduced as Pablo Fanque. He rode into the arena on an impressive black steed, he stood up and flipped to a seated position, then continued to turn around and ride facing backwards. Anne patted my arm, "Can you believe this?"

"I know. He's amazing."

Anne and I remained riveted by all the acts. We saw Pablo Fanque again later in the performance, but this time we had to lean back and look up. He walked on a wire stretched between two platforms above the central arena, holding a long pole for balance. The audience hushed, afraid to startle him and cause him to fall to the ground. I held my breath until he safely reached the other platform at which point the whole audience exhaled and erupted in applause.

The acts came one after another in rapid succession, like a mama cat giving birth. A tall clown with large floppy shoes, a red wig and rubber nose, and white and red-striped pantaloons made his way around the ring, pulling pranks on audience members. I watched him pull a bouquet of flowers out of a lady's hat, extract a handkerchief from behind a man's ear, and sneeze confetti on a little boy. Laughter followed him as he pranced around the ring. The clown reached our section and mimed falling in love with Mrs. Limebear. He looked at her, batted his fake long eyelashes, leaned back and held his heart, took his cap off, and bowed to her. I watched as Mrs. Limebear's perpetual scowl softened to a smile, and when he handed her a flower that squirted water in her face, Mrs. Limebear laughed—big guffaws as she put her hand on her chest. I wouldn't have believed it if I hadn't seen it.

A short while later a large wild cat came out in a cage, a leopard I believe. The tamer opened the cage and motioned for the leopard to leap over a small wall, turn in circles, and stand on a huge ball. The audience gasped as the man put his fist in the big cat's mouth, but he removed it unscathed.

At the end of the performance, Anne and I walked arm-in-arm back to the waiting carriage, following Mrs. Limebear. We were all staying in London for the weekend. Candace went in the other carriage, and Anne came with me to Uncle John's. The excitement of having a roommate, even if only for a few days, almost equaled the excitement of Astley's . . . almost.

We giggled and laughed and talked about our favourite acts on the one-hour carriage ride to Grosvenor Square. The carriage crossed the bridge over the Thames River and wound through St. James. By the time we reached Uncle John's home, Anne and I had both succumbed to slumber.

"Girls, we're here," Mrs. Limebear said, waking us.

I opened my eyes, stretched my arms up, and saw Mr. Blake coming down the front steps, followed by Uncle John. Mr. Blake helped Mrs. Limebear out of the carriage, then Anne, and me last of all. Uncle John bowed slightly to Mrs. Limebear, "So nice to see you again, Mrs. Limebear. Thank you for taking the girls on an adventure they won't soon forget."

"We'll never forget it, Uncle John!" I said, before Mrs. Limebear could respond.

Mrs. Limebear gave me a mildly disapproving look and said, "It was my pleasure. Everyone had a most enjoyable evening." Then Mrs. Limebear did something extraordinary—she smiled! Not a half-smile or a smirk, but a full-on, eyes lit up, genuine smile.

Uncle John asked, "Would you like to come in for a cup of tea, or a glass of sherry?"

"Thank you, Mr. Audley. I believe I would," Mrs. Limebear replied.

Uncle John and Mrs. Limebear retired to the drawing room, and I took Anne up to my room. Deirdre showed Anne the room she had prepared for her, but I begged her to make up the daybed in my room so we could be together.

"Ye be comf'table on the day bed, miss?" Deirdre asked, looking doubtful.

"Oh my, yes. I'd much rather be in here than in a room alone, all by myself," Anne said, using her acting skills to look very forlorn.

"Let me get Mr. Audley's approval," Deirdre said.

Anne and I sat on my bed and talked about the beautiful horses, the scary rope walk, the hilarious clown, and Mr. Harding getting knocked over by the Palomino. We were laughing when Deirdre came back in to make up the day bed.

Uncle John called us downstairs to say goodnight to Mrs. Limebear. We thanked her profusely and she shocked us again by pulling us in for a quick hug. Maybe it was the sherry! Once Mrs. Limebear left to go to her sister's house, Uncle John asked us if we wanted hot cocoa.

"That's perfect, Uncle John. But can we have it in my room?" I knew this went against one of his few house rules.

"I'll make an exception for tonight." Uncle John put his arm around me and kissed the top of my head.

Anne and I undressed, put on our nightgowns, and sat on the day bed, warmed by hot cocoa and the fire.

"I wish *you* were my roommate instead of Miranda," Anne said.

"Me too. I'm used to being alone, but I don't like it. I wish you could stay longer than only a few days."

"I know. But we'll have fun while I'm here!" Anne smiled.

We finished our cocoa, talked about school and our favourite books until the fire died out and we couldn't keep our eyes open any longer.

Anne and I woke up late and wandered down to breakfast at almost 11 o'clock. Uncle John was in his study, so we ate alone, chatting about what we wanted to do. After breakfast we both buried our noses in a book; Anne read a novel by Maria Edgeworth, and I was reading *Robinson Crusoe*.

Uncle John accompanied us on a walk to Hyde Park where we engaged in some serious people watching—commenting on the horses, carriages, gowns, and handsome men! When we returned, Uncle John's sister greeted us.

"Sister! I didn't realize you would come so early. Forgive me for not being here when you arrived." Uncle John kissed Aunt Jane on her cheek. His sister Jane was a few years younger, married to a banker, and she had two sons—one was a few years older than me, and the eldest was at Oxford. I hadn't seen Aunt Jane (not my real aunt) often growing up, but when I did she was always sweet and encouraging, interested in whatever I was doing. I found out later Uncle John and Aunt Jane had discussed my living with her. I'm glad I ended up with Uncle John, both for his sake and mine. It was a perfect match.

"That's fine, John. I made myself at home." Aunt Jane turned to look at me. "Oh, my! Joanna, you're becoming a beautiful young lady." Aunt Jane held my arms in her hands and gazed at me.

"Thank you, Aunt Jane," I said, blushing.

"And who is this lovely young lady?"

"Aunt Jane, this is Anne Knight, my friend from boarding school."

"It's a pleasure meeting you, ma'am," Anne said, with a slight curtsy.

"Such nice manners. It's lovely to meet you, Miss Anne." Aunt Jane led us into the drawing room. "I want to hear all about Mr. Astley's Royal Amphitheatre," Aunt Jane said as the three of us sat down. Uncle John excused himself to retire to his study to prepare for a big case.

Anne and I took turns telling Aunt Jane about our favourite acts, though I omitted the escapade with the Palomino and Mr. Harding's smelly disaster.

Mr. Blake knocked and informed Aunt Jane there were two women requesting to speak with the 'lady of the house.'

"How curious! I guess that would be me, at least for today. Please show them in," Aunt Jane said.

Anne and I stood as Aunt Jane welcomed the two women. One was white, younger than Aunt Jane, tall and thin, wearing a modest white muslin dress with a matching bonnet. She introduced herself as Frances Whitehall, a member of the Ladies Anti-Slavery Society of London and handed Aunt Jane a pamphlet. When I looked at the other woman, I backed up and leaned against the sofa, momentarily stunned. I recognized her from the gathering at Mr. Wilberforce's house.

"I'm Sadie, Sadie Cross. Frances and I are visiting all the ladies in the neighborhood to enlist their support and signatures for our petition."

I tried not to stare at Sadie, who looked like she could be my older sister. She seemed to be about the same age as Frances, late twenties or early thirties, a little shorter, with hair the same colour and texture as mine, and skin a bit darker than my medium brown tone.

"Welcome, ladies. It's a pleasure to meet you. I'm Jane Audley and this is my brother, John Audley's home. These two young ladies are Miss Joanna Vassa, my brother is her guardian, and her friend, Miss Anne. . . I'm sorry, I don't know your last name, dear," Aunt Jane said.

"Knight. Anne Knight."

"Do come in and sit with us." Aunt Jane gestured to two chairs and the women came in and sat down.

Annie Farmer, Uncle John's cook, appeared in the doorway and asked with a curtsy, "Would ye like me to bring in tea for you and your guests, Miss Jane?"

"Yes, thank you, Annie."

I kept sneaking glances at Sadie, and a few times I caught her looking at me with a thoughtful gaze.

Sadie began, "Thank you so much for welcoming us, Miss Jane. It's also heartening to see the young ladies here. You're never too young to raise your voices and make a difference in the world."

Miss Frances added, "Though they do appear too young to sign the petition."

"Yes. A pity. How old are you, Miss Joanna, Miss Anne?" Sadie asked.

"I'm eleven ma'am," Anne replied, looking in awe at the women.

"And I'm twelve," I said.

"Certainly not too young to know what's going on in the world, and especially here in England and England's colonies," Sadie said.

"I agree," Aunt Jane added. "I think they should stay and hear what you have to say."

Anne and I squeezed each other's hands.

"As you may know, the Houses of Parliament abolished the slave trade almost a year ago," Sadie began. As Sadie spoke, I heard an echo of Mr. Wilberforce's speech ringing in my ear; ". . . the cargo on these ships is not sugar or rum, but women, men, and children."

"That was step one. An important step, to be sure, but only the beginning." Sadie paused and looked at Miss Frances.

"Men have formed societies, fought in parliament, and distributed petitions. Men like William Wilberforce, Granville Sharp, and Thomas

Clarkson," Frances said. I wanted to boast and tell them I'd met these men, but I kept silent.

"We women, and girls," Frances added, nodding to us, "are now joining the fight." Frances glanced at Sadie.

"To that end, we recently formed the Ladies Anti-Slavery Society of London. Our goal is to end slavery in the British Colonies—for good. We aim for immediate, not gradual, abolition," Sadie said.

Aunt Jane's intent gaze moved from Frances to Sadie as they took turns speaking.

Annie came in with a pot of tea, teacups, strainers, a plate of scones, clotted cream and preserves, and sugar and cream for the tea.

Aunt Jane poured tea for the guests and herself. "Milk and sugar?" Aunt Jane asked.

"No, thank you," Frances replied rather brusquely.

I served tea for Anne and myself, adding a generous splash of cream and two teaspoons of sugar to mine.

Sadie continued, "Isn't it lovely to sit together with other ladies and enjoy a cup of tea?"

"Oh, yes! There's nothing finer!" Aunt Jane agreed. "Especially when accompanied by a flaky scone."

"Frances and I have visited dozens of homes over the past few months and enjoyed tea with many wonderful women. But unfortunately, one ingredient in this English tradition is problematic."

I thought I might know where Sadie was leading the conversation, but I wasn't sure. I leaned in to hear better.

"What's that?" Aunt Jane asked, her head tilted to the left.

"Sugar," Frances said.

"Would you prefer honey?" Aunt Jane asked, confused.

"Miss Joanna," Sadie said, turning to me. "Do you know where the sugar comes from that we put in our tea and coffee?"

"Yes, I . . ." I put my teacup down so hard some of the tea sloshed onto the saucer. Aunt Jane's eyes widened and her head arched back in surprise.

"It comes from sugar plantations in the West Indies. The slaves produce the sugar, working twelve-hour days in the hot sun."

"Well done, Miss Joanna. Most girls and even women are unaware of the origins of the sugar in their tea," Sadie said.

"What are you proposing, Miss Sadie? If your goal is to end slavery, what difference will it make to stop adding sugar to our tea?" Aunt Jane asked.

"Excellent question, Miss Jane. One we in the Society have debated for months. It may not make a difference, you're right. But picture this. Ladies stop using sugar in tea and other dishes. They stop buying sugar. The local markets end up with sugar sitting on the shelf, going bad. They order less sugar. The plantations no longer have a market for their product. Without a need for slave-produced sugar, we decrease the need for slave labour." Sadie presented a concise argument.

Anne asked, "So if I stop using sugar I can contribute to abolition?"

"Yes, Miss Anne. Exactly!" Sadie smiled.

Frances joined the conversation. "The goal, our goal as we go door-to-door talking to ladies young and old, is trifold. First, we want to educate, to raise awareness. Second, we want ladies to reduce the amount of sugar they buy and use. And third, we are gathering signatures for a petition, to show Parliament how many women support an end to slave-produced sugar."

"How old do you have to be to join the Society?" Anne asked.

Sadie and Frances looked at each other. Sadie nodded to Frances.

"I believe our youngest member is twenty years old, but you can certainly contribute to the cause in many ways, with parental approval, of course," Frances said.

Annie came in to replenish the tea, and Anne and I asked her to empty our teacups. When Annie brought back our new cups, we tried tea without sugar. The bitter taste wasn't pleasant, but a sip of tea in between bites of scone made it more palatable.

Uncle John showed up in the drawing room doorway and bowed slightly.

"Good afternoon, ladies. No, no. Don't rise. I don't want to interrupt."

"Brother, may I introduce Miss Frances Whitehall and Miss Sadie Cross, from the Ladies Anti-Slavery Society of London," Aunt Jane said.

"It's a pleasure to meet you. Although, Miss Sadie, I believe we met at the Wilberforce home after the vote on the slave trade, if I'm not mistaken."

"Yes, we did! How wonderful to see you again. And we have so enjoyed chatting with your sister and these two young ladies," Sadie said.

"I'm glad," Uncle John said.

## CHAPTER TWELVE: JOANNA

"Mr. Wilberforce might not be so welcoming if I visited Barbara to get her to sign a petition instead of caring for her in her confinement," Sadie said.

"Is that so?" Uncle John asked.

"He doesn't believe women should be political!" Sadie said.

I was listening intently, trying to decide how I felt. I had the utmost respect for Mr. Wilberforce, but as a girl, a young woman of colour, I wanted to believe I could contribute to important causes like abolition, not simply by taking care of the men. Why shouldn't women speak up, sign petitions, go to rallies?

Sadie continued. "His views are informed by his interpretation of scripture. This is one of the few areas where we disagree, so I don't share my abolition activities with him."

"I can't say I agree with him. Why shouldn't Jane, Joanna, and Anne lend their voices to the fight? Joanna would be following in her father's footsteps," Uncle John said.

"Oh, who was her father?" Sadie asked, leaning forward.

"Gustavus Vassa, a freed slave who aided in the abolition movement, and a dear friend of mine."

Frances added, "These young ladies are the future of the movement, and we welcome their involvement."

"Hear, hear!" Uncle John said. "It was an honour to meet you ladies. Thank you for your dedication to the struggle." Uncle John bowed and left the room.

"We don't often get such a nice welcome," Sadie said.

"Oh really? I imagine you have stories to tell." Aunt Jane leaned forward.

"Yes, indeed," Frances said. "Doors have been shut in our faces, we have been invited in by a curious butler only to wait interminably in a parlor or drawing room..."

"And then invited to leave," Sadie finished. "We have discovered that Frances is more likely to gain entry. I think some assume I am her maid." Sadie frowned.

Frances laughed. "As if Sadie would be a maid to anyone!"

"But that's simply awful," Anne said, aghast.

"Maybe, but it's also the way things are, at least right now here in England." Sadie looked directly at me, signaling sisterhood and a warning.

No one spoke as we munched on scones and drank unsweetened tea. Aunt Jane broke the silence.

"You've given us a lot to think about. Thank you for the work you're doing."

"It's a calling," Frances said.

"We can't *not* do the work," Sadie added. She pulled a tied up scroll out of her large reticule and spread it out on a nearby table. "This is the petition we're circulating. We already have 321 signatures. Would you like to sign, Miss Jane, and commit to not buying sugar produced by slaves?"

"I would," Aunt Jane said, standing. I had never seen her with such a serious and determined expression. She took a quill, dipped it in an inkstand, and signed her name slowly, with a flourish.

Anne stood up, walked over to the scroll, and examined all the signatures. Frances handed Anne a card and said, "You and Miss Joanna are the future. Your time will come to sign petitions and march in protests."

"I wish I could join right now!" Anne said.

"Hold on to that enthusiasm, young lady." Sadie laughed.

I came to stand beside Anne, wishing we could form our own abolition society.

"It has been a joy meeting all three of you. Thank you, Miss Jane, for your help with our cause. I think you'll find it easy to give up sugar and drinking tea will be a constant reminder of the struggle," Frances said.

"Yes, thank you so much for your gracious hospitality. It was lovely to meet you all," Sadie said, shaking hands with Aunt Jane and Anne, and giving me a light hug.

Frances rolled up the scroll, we all said our goodbyes, and Aunt Jane escorted them out.

Anne turned to me and said, "I want to be like them when I grow up."

"Me, too, Anne. Oh, me, too!"

# CHAPTER THIRTEEN

## Olu

August 1765

Days blended into one another, becoming weeks, months, stretching to years. Suraya had been away six years now. Mr. Samuel didn't buy a slave to replace her. Instead, Elsie, Martha's eleven-year-old daughter, was pressed into service to help Susannah dress in the morning. I continued to help Mrs. Beth, assist Martha in the kitchen, tend the garden, and help clean the house. I felt much older than my twenty-three years. I still thought about escaping... every day. When I visited the 'quarters,' I heard stories about slaves who had escaped, even whole families. Not everyone was successful. If they were caught, punishment was always severe—flogging, imprisonment, or being sold down South. I was waiting for the right time and opportunity. I would know when it came.

Every night I prayed for my family, for Suraya and her child, and especially for Ledu. I would not give up my search to find him. Teddy had made several inquiries without success.

Teddy was a father now and visited the Cross plantation less frequently. Before he wed, he would come in between each job—every two to three months. Now he comes but twice a year, usually alone, occasionally with his family.

Mrs. Beth suffered a miscarriage a few years back and somehow it brought us closer. I never liked her, and she could barely tolerate me, but through the ordeal we came to understand each other a bit more. She suffered and I helped, one woman helping another through a crisis.

Now it was a smothering hot day in August—not that South Carolina offers any other kind of day in August—where you want to find a breeze, drink something cool, dip in the river—anything to avoid the sweltering, steaming, suffocating heat. I worked in the kitchen preparing lunch, washing greens, chopping onions. Martha had gone down the river with Captain Thomas to get some fruits from a nearby plantation for fruit pies. I heard a thud, an incongruous sound, a harbinger signaling trouble or pain. I left my chopping and hurried up the back flight of stairs to the main floor. When I reached the stairway to the second floor, I heard a moaning "no" emanating from Mrs. Beth's room. She and Mr. Samuel had never shared a bedroom.

I knew Mrs. Beth was almost three months along as there had been no monthlies to prepare for or clean up after. She hadn't mentioned it, and it was not a subject Martha and I had ever discussed.

I reached Mrs. Beth's room and stopped at the doorway. Mrs. Beth lay on the floor on her side moaning incoherently, blood staining the back of her dress. Realizing I alone could help her, thinking back to her last, lost pregnancy, I steeled myself to the task at hand, sent a silent prayer to God for grace and guidance, and knelt beside her.

"Mrs. Beth, let me help you." Mrs. Beth looked at me through eyes glazed with dread, shining with unshed tears.

"I'm losing my baby. God is punishing me." Mrs. Beth pronounced her own judgement.

"Here, let me help you." I lifted her to a sitting position, and then slowly, cautiously, to her feet. I unbuttoned her night dress, as I had on many other less traumatic occasions. Mrs. Beth put her head down, staring at the floor.

"Martha back?" she asked.

"No, ma'am. She isn't. I can help. Miss Martha has taught me the herbs to stanch the bleeding and ease the pain."

Once I removed the night dress, I grabbed a nearby towel and pressed it to the spot between her legs where blood continued to trickle out. Quickly covering the embroidered seat cushion with two more fresh towels, I sat Mrs. Beth down, and urged her to breathe slow, deep breaths, counting her into submission. I grabbed a nearby shift and pulled it down to cover her as modestly as possible.

I knew the hip bath was in Mr. Samuel's room. Pushing aside the heavy drapes, I yanked up the window and shouted down to Jeremiah, emerging from the tool shed. "Jeremiah, get some help and heat up water; bring it up for the bath. Quickly, please."

Jeremiah squinted up at me, holding his hands over his eyes to block the early morning sun and identify which female was yelling at him so early in the morning.

"Yes, miss. I be there quicker 'n green grass through a goose," Jeremiah yelled.

I encouraged Mrs. Beth to continue her slow breathing while I ran down to the kitchen for some shepherd's purse. Miss Martha had shown me how to both brew it in a tea and apply it as a poultice.

Mrs. Beth pleaded with me to "hurry, please," and as I couldn't remember her *ever* saying "please," I tried even harder to get what I needed quickly. I ran downstairs, holding my dress so I wouldn't trip, and dropped the blood-stained night dress into the laundry room, almost colliding with Jeremiah, who rushed by with a pot of water to put on the fire. I said Mrs. Beth was feeling poorly and he regretted that both Mr. Samuel and Miss Martha were gone.

"It's on me to help. When the water is more than warm, please bring it up." I continued to the pantry for the shepherd's purse. I found the shepherd's purse in a labeled jar on the pantry shelf, among all Miss Martha's healing remedies, took a clean square cloth and dropped a handful of the herb in the middle of the cloth. I had to wait for the water to boil—I busied myself by straightening the supplies in the pantry. Finally, I dipped the cloth-encased herb in the almost boiling water and pulled it out quickly. I then filled a mug and added three teaspoonfuls of the herb to the mug, praying it was the right amount. Going back upstairs I was prepared with tea, poultice, and some extra cloths.

Jeremiah followed close behind me and we parted ways on the second floor—he to fill the hip bath in Mr. Samuel's room, and I to enter Mrs. Beth's room. Mrs. Beth's arms were crossed, her hands cupping her elbows, and she was shivering, despite the heat. Her knees pressed together trying to prevent another loss. While Jeremiah ran downstairs for more hot water, I vigorously rubbed Mrs. Beth's arms, to both warm and calm her. It was the most intimate physical contact we had in the eleven years I had lived at the Cross plantation. Yes, I had dressed and undressed her, fixed her hair, poured water for her bath, but I had never touched her so deliberately, nor so tenderly.

"Is there . . . could there be a chance . . . have I lost the baby?" Mrs. Beth inquired quietly, unbidden hope lighting her eyes.

"I don't know yet. Jeremiah is preparing the bath. I've made this tea for you, which should help. I can't promise it will taste good, but it may help stop the bleeding."

Mrs. Beth took the mug in both hands, tentatively sipping the bitter tea. Neither of us spoke. Jeremiah knocked, calling through the closed door, "Bath's ready, miss."

"Thank you, Jeremiah," I replied. "Okay. Mrs. Beth, sit for another few minutes, finish the tea while I ready the bath."

"You've used this before? You know it works?" Mrs. Beth leaned towards me, gripping my arm.

"Miss Martha uses shepherd's purse for the slave girls who have problems with their monthlies. It seems to help stop bleeding. I'm going to put some in the bath, too."

Mrs. Beth relied on me only because she had no other alternatives. As I emptied the herbs into the steaming bath water, I thought of the slave girls I knew who asked Miss Martha for herbs to end a pregnancy, not wanting to bring a slave child into the world. I thought of all the African mothers who lost babies—to death, disease, hunger, slavery. And I wanted to walk out. I looked out the window to the river below and I wanted to go to the dock, get in a canoe, and leave. Without a plan, without Thomas helping me—I was ready then and there to leave. But I feared leaving more than I hated helping Mrs. Beth. I had a complicated relationship with Mrs. Beth, and I did not want to help this wife of a slave owner keep her baby. But I did.

We walked through the connecting door to Mr. Samuel's room, and I helped Mrs. Beth remove her underclothes, step over the rim and ease down into the tub. I noticed a small gush of blood, and Mrs. Beth cried out "oooohhh."

"The bath will help. You'll need to stay for almost an hour. I'll change the water to keep it warm. If you keep bleeding, I'll send one of the slaves for the doctor. We'll know soon if that's needed." I spoke with authority inculcated by Miss Martha.

"Maybe you should send for him now. Samuel will be displeased if I lose this baby." Displeased was putting it mildly, most likely he would blame me.

"I can send for Doctor Sheffield, but he can't prevent you from losing the baby."

"How can you be so sure?" Mrs. Beth asked, her eyebrows dipping together over her nose.

"I know I'm young, Mrs. Beth, but I've seen Miss Martha work cures that no doctor could. And I've seen doctors make their patients worse by bleeding them. It may be, it's possible . . . but I won't know yet. We must wait."

"Know what gel? Tell me!"

She had the strength to yell at me, so I knew she was improving.

"I've seen girls bleed and go on to deliver a healthy baby. Miss Martha says it's sometimes a silent twin."

"A silent twin? You mean it's possible I'm carrying two and miscarrying one?"

"Possibly. We'll only know in a few weeks. If you grow, have symptoms, no more bleeding, and sense the baby moving, then yes."

I drew out the reddish water and went down the two flights of stairs to the kitchen to retrieve freshly boiled water. Mixing it with cold water till the temperature was nicely warm, I hauled up fresh buckets of water and refilled the bath. Two trips later my arms were aching, but I smiled when the water no longer turned red.

"The bleeding stopped," I said.

"That's good. But what does it mean?" Mrs. Beth leaned back in the tub.

"We'll know in a week or two. Or maybe Miss Martha will be able to tell."

I helped Mrs. Beth get out of the bath, dried her with two large towels, applied the poultice to her womanhood, and helped her dress.

"I'm feeling a bit weakly."

"I'm sure you are. Rest today. Don't go down the stairs. I'll bring up your food."

"Fine."

Mrs. Beth looked at me and nodded, and I knew our relationship had subtly, permanently changed. She was still the mistress, and I the slave, but my ministrations and her frailty yoked us to one another in a bond neither of us expected nor desired. Her vulnerability and my ability upset the 'natural' order of our relations.

Mrs. Beth stayed in her bedroom, and I continued to apply the poultice. When Martha returned that evening, I relayed to her what happened and what I had done. Miss Martha checked on Mrs. Beth and told her I had done all anyone could do, what she herself would've done had she been here, and now all that we could do was wait. I believed I had done the right thing, but it was a relief to hear Miss Martha confirm it.

Martha came back down to the kitchen and said, "Ain't nary a thing I would've done different. You becomin' a fine herbalist, Olivia. Good thing you didn' use the black cohosh. She'd've lost any hope of a baby. That'd clean her right out—'xcusing my expression."

"I remember you told me the difference between shepherd's purse and black cohosh, and I wondered if I should have added anything else in. But I could hear your words in my head 'when in doubt, leave it out.' So, I did."

"Good, good. You be a quick learner, Olivia. And you be growin' me some fine herbs, too. I can teach you to use 'em but seem like you can teach me a thing or three about growin' 'em."

"Sunlight and water. No secret there. Just plant them in a sunny place and water 'em often. Also, keep somebody out there hunting the rabbits to keep them out of the garden, and in the stew!" I replied.

"The herb garden never did look so fine." Martha smiled.

"Miss Martha, do you think Mrs. Beth is still carrying?"

"Yes, chile. I do. I ain't touched her or examined her as I would one 'o the slave girls, but it seem she still carryin'. She ain't bled since. Time will tell."

Time agreed with Martha. Mrs. Beth may have lost a baby, or not, but one month later her belly, appetite, and bosom were all growing. One morning in late September, as I was getting her dressed, I had trouble buttoning up her gown.

"The dress no longer fits. Praise be!" Mrs. Beth laughed. I laughed with her. Mrs. Beth's rare contentment made her company tolerable.

Susannah had married earlier that year, and I knew Mrs. Beth missed her, so I was happy she'd have another child in the house. I loved babies but knew I would be too busy with my other duties to spend much time with the new child. And I didn't plan to be around much longer. I knew the best way to escape was the river, and Thomas was ready to help me on a moment's notice. I was waiting for a sign or confirmation—I would know when it was time to leave. The time had not yet come.

## May 1766

The following May several events converged; I wouldn't learn the significance until years later. The previous year, March of 1765, the Stamp Act passed. I didn't know what it was but heard Mr. Samuel complaining about it over dinner with neighbors or friends, or Teddy. I once asked Teddy what it was, and as best I understood, the British required all documents to be stamped—marriage licenses, deeds, slave documents. No problem there. However, the stamps cost money, and the money went to the British. In essence it was a tax added to other taxes. The White South Carolinians were outraged.

Groups of angry colonists marched in downtown Charles Town, holding up large signs proclaiming "Liberty." Captain Thomas, the slave who piloted the riverboat, mentioned an incident he witnessed from the docks. He was loading up the boat with goods—molasses, coffee, tobacco, potatoes, flour, oil—when he heard loud shouting and marching on Broad Street. A large group of White men marched down the road waving flags and banners proclaiming themselves "Sons of Liberty." Thomas saw old men and young boys chanting and shouting 'Liberty.' They were a motley group, some dressed well, but most in worn, faded, ill-fitting breeches and loose shirts, some with tri-corner hats.

Thomas spied a small contingent of slaves, one of whom picked up a dropped 'liberty' flag. They began their own melodious chant for freedom. Within minutes, before Thomas had finished loading up the boat anyway, a group of White militiamen on horseback swooped down, threatening the Blacks, confiscating the sign. Apparently, liberty was only for Whites. Thomas wished he would have marched with the Blacks.

Teddy had recently arrived on one of his rare twice-yearly visits. I had not yet had a chance to speak with him—to see how his wife and son kept, or if he had any news of Ledu. Dinner had been served, eaten, and cleared away, leaving only Teddy and Mr. Samuel drinking coffee and eating peach pie. I heard knocking at the back door, unusual at any time, but especially at night. Martha was in the back room, tending to Sula, who worked in the rice fields, and I strained to hear the conversation upstairs. Mind you, the kitchen is right below the first floor, and sound travels well, so if I placed myself near the stairwell, I could hear muted tones.

BOOM! Startled by the loud explosion, I went to find Martha, who was bending over Sula's feet. Her feet were swollen, darkened, and reddened by bites, and she moaned in pain. I almost forgot why I had come to Martha, but then another blast, louder and closer than the first, shook me and the ground we stood on. The vegetable and grain bags jumped up on the shelves, and one of Martha's favorite platters slid off the shelf and cracked into pieces on the floor.

"Miss Martha, excuse me, what's that noise? Is it gunfire? Cannons? Why does it seem to be getting closer?"

"The White folks be celebratin' the end of the Stamp Act. That be fireworks. If'n you can see out this window, you'll see flowers of light up in the sky. It do be pretty."

I walked over to the small window, carefully avoiding Sula's feet and the broken platter, and heard another loud blast, followed by a shower of small white lights up above the trees.

"Ohhhhh. I've never seen anything like it!"

"They don' be settin' em off too frequent—but they sure is pretty. Awful loud, though."

From my vantage point, leaning half out the window, which was only a few inches above ground level, I could hear the raised voice of Mr. Samuel, and a quieter, but insistent voice of a young African man. Mr. Samuel was angry, as evidenced by his vociferous, harsh tone.

"I paid you what them limes and bananas is worth," Mr. Samuel insisted.

"Sir, you paid me for three crates, but I gave you six crates," the African replied.

"Are you callin' me a liar, boy?" shouted Mr. Samuel.

"No sir. I thought maybe . . ." The African's words were cut off by another explosion. I thought for a moment he sounded like Ledu. Of course, I hadn't seen or heard Ledu in thirteen years, and it was an older, deeper voice. Maybe hope colored my hearing. And the African spoke in English, very good English actually, which I had never heard Ledu speak. But I sensed a very familiar tone in that voice. I leaned even further out the window, to hear better. Then Martha called out, "Chile, what you doin' over there? You about to crawl out that window? They'll think you escapin'. Best get back to finishing dinner clean up."

"Yes, Miss Martha."

I longed to tell her I thought possibly my brother was upstairs, but I didn't. How could it be possible for Ledu to show up here in Charles Town, at this plantation? But . . . I wanted to hear that voice again to reassure myself the man was not Ledu. I stayed by the window. Voices were still raised, and then I heard Teddy's voice reasoning with his brother.

"Samuel, it's not an unreasonable amount. Why don't you split the difference?"

"Split the difference—split the difference? I'll split his lip or maybe split open his head—split the difference?" Mr. Samuel yelled.

## CHAPTER THIRTEEN: OLU

"I'm sorry, but I think you'd better leave," Teddy said to the African.

"Thank you. Is there no . . .?" Another blast cut off his words. I longed to run up the stairs and look him in the face to see if it were my dear Ledu. I crept upstairs and as soon as I reached the first floor, Mr. Samuel ordered me to go back to the lower level and bring up a bottle of bourbon. I looked longingly at the front door and went back downstairs.

Mr. Samuel was stomping around the house, and I could hear doors slam. I had to go upstairs to bring him the bourbon and retrieve the last serving dish. I walked upstairs gingerly, so as not to be heard or noticed by anyone, deposited the bourbon bottle on the table and grabbed the serving plate, but before going back down to the kitchen, I stood at the front door entrance and could barely make out an African man getting in a canoe and taking off down the river toward Charles Town. Was it Ledu?

Teddy must have walked him to the dock. He now walked slowly back up the allée, looking down in thought. He looked up to see me standing in the doorway and quickened his pace.

"Olivia . . . Olu, how are you?"

"Same as always. Who was that man, Teddy? He was African? Did he say his name?" I looked at Teddy and glanced down at the river.

"Olu, slow down. So many questions. You overheard the conversation?" Teddy asked.

"Well, yes, bits of it, between the blasts."

"Yes, yes, the happy celebrations of the end of the Stamp Act. Freedom and liberty—for the colonists," Teddy said, his voice laced with sarcasm.

"Who cares about that? Who was that man? Did you get his name? His language? Is he a slave?" I couldn't wait for the answers.

"Again with the questions. I wonder why you are so curious. But let's go downstairs before my brother detains me." Teddy led the way downstairs.

Martha was in the pantry, selecting food for tomorrow's breakfast. Sula sat by the fire with her feet in a bucket, filled with steamy water and oats to relieve itching. I turned around to Teddy, with my hands on my hips (I couldn't help myself) and said, "Well?"

"First, I have a question for you. Why are you so interested in finding out about this African?" Teddy peered at me from beneath his hat.

"Teddy, I think it's possible, I think he may be . . . it's possible he's my brother Ledu."

"Oh! I wasn't expecting that! What makes you think so?" Teddy leaned back in surprise.

I told Teddy the voice I heard reminded me of Ledu. Teddy asked me what Ledu looks like, and I said Ledu has no facial scarring, a small gap between his two front teeth, skin as dark as mine, thin and shorter than me. As I tried to remember Ledu's features tears formed, obscuring my vision.

"This man did have a small gap, and no scarring, but that could be true of thousands of Africans. I did notice his ears. They were small and seemed to have an extra bit of cartilage in the middle—a ridge."

"Cartilage?" I asked, unfamiliar with the word and impatient to get answers.

"Not as hard as bone," Teddy replied.

"Oh, Teddy. Ledu had that. We used to tease him. What if that man is Ledu? And just feet away from me. Oh, Teddy."

I collapsed, sobbing, into Teddy's outstretched arms. My normal composure fled, along with any rational arguments against the man being Ledu. I was convinced. But what could I do? Why didn't I go up the stairs when he was here—to know for certain. Why?

I couldn't stop crying—great heaving sobs I tried to restrain but holding it in only made it worse. My chest hurt, my head ached, my eyes swelled. Our lives as happy siblings filled my mental vision, until the last time we were separated replaced my happy memories and I convulsed in sobs all over again.

"Ledu, oh my Ledu—Ledu, is that you?" I cried out to him, knowing he couldn't hear me, regretting not crying out to him when he was here, cursing my timidity, realizing taking risks is all about timing.

Minutes passed, maybe an hour, I don't know. Teddy held me, I cried and pictured my brother as I last saw him. I knew what I had to do.

"I'm going after him," I declared.

Teddy sat me down, grabbed a rag, wet it, and wiped my tear-swollen face.

"Olu, you can't do that. I'll go." Teddy held my arms and looked me in my eyes.

Right then Martha emerged from the pantry.

"What's this? Mr. Teddy come for a visit and going off already?"

Teddy explained to Martha what had happened.

## CHAPTER THIRTEEN: OLU

"My poor darlin'. May it be he's Ledu? God knows. How strange if'n it were him. Teddy'll find out." I cried anew held against Miss Martha's ample bosom.

Teddy didn't take the schooner and arouse suspicion. He jumped in a canoe, and paddled fast toward Charles Town, hoping to catch up with the African. It was a clear, moonlit evening, so he could see the way easily and reached Charles Town by midnight, he told me later. The festivities and celebrations had ended, and the streets of the city were almost empty, save for a few drunken colonists stumbling home. Teddy didn't find our African, but he did learn his name from someone who worked at the docks.

Teddy reached the house just before the sun rose. I had cried myself to sleep and Martha and I ended up sleeping on the ground floor, bundled up on burlap sacks by the fire. Martha also kept an ear open for Sula through the night.

I immediately awoke when I heard Teddy's footfalls on the stairs. I sat up and eased myself away from Martha. I couldn't discern Teddy's mood from his expression. I didn't speak, afraid to have my fears and hopes confirmed or denied—delaying the inevitable knowledge of identity.

I stood. Teddy approached me, and taking my hand, pulled me into a side room, where logs and coal are stored. He held one of my hands in both of his hands and looked at me intently. I focused on the vivid green irises in his eyes, his bushy mustache and beard, his sandy curly hair.

"Olu, the man who was here reached Charles Town before me and disappeared. I couldn't find him." He gazed at me, seeming to prepare himself for my reaction.

"I see." I breathed in deeply.

"The ship he boarded left shortly before I reached the dock."

"Teddy. You rowed through the night. Thank you. You've done so much for me. I probably only imagined it was Ledu. I want so badly to find him, to see him, that I heard in the man's voice an African lilt." I didn't believe my words—I knew it was Ledu.

"I did find out something."

My stomach tightened, and my heartbeat quickened. I stood as still as possible, not wanting to disturb even the air around me as I waited in anticipation. Fickle hope flared. "Yes?"

"The name of the slave, the African who was here is a slave, is Gustavus Vassa."

"Hmmm. Gustavus Vassa. I knew it would be hard to trace Ledu with his given name, Olaudah Equiano, but is it possible to find out the original African name if we have a slave name?" I wondered aloud.

"It's easier to trace the name backwards, starting with the slave name. You know I've tried for years to trace your brother, but it's near to impossible to find a slave using only a given African name, even though we had the month he left Africa narrowed down. With a slave name one can backtrack—find the location of a slave and trace him or her back to the slave ship, and records showing original names alongside slave names. Most slave owners keep meticulous records."

"So . . . you may, you might be able to find out if this Gustavus Vassa is Ledu?"

"I will try, Olu. I will try."

It was all I could ask for and try as I might to squash the seed of hope, it germinated in my traitorous heart. I knew the African arguing with Mr. Samuel was Ledu. But would I ever see him again?

"Teddy, what can I ever do for you? You've done everything for me! Taught me to read, write, speak; searched for my brother; intervened and appealed to your brother for Suraya. You've done so much for me, and I so want to do something for you, but what can I do?"

"Just keep sneaking me extra pieces of Miss Martha's cherry pie—and I will be a happy man." Teddy winked.

"You jest. Be serious, Teddy."

"Yes, well. There is something you can do for me." Teddy's expression turned serious.

"Oh good! What is it?"

"Make me a promise."

"What's the promise?" I wondered what I could possibly do for him.

"Promise me you won't leave without saying goodbye." Teddy gripped my arms.

I didn't want to make a promise I might not keep.

"But what if the time comes—a perfect chance, and you're not here?" I asked, hedging.

"Get word to me. Let me know when you leave—somehow—what your plans are. Can you at least promise me that?"

"Yes, Teddy. I promise." I hoped I could keep that promise.

# CHAPTER THIRTEEN: OLU

## November 1766

Several months after Gustavus Vassa was at the Cross plantation, Teddy reappeared. We met in our usual spot, out of sight of the house, by the laundry line.

"Teddy, I didn't expect to see you for months yet. Did you finish the house so quickly?" I hoped he had news of Ledu but wanted him to initiate that discussion.

"No, no. I've weeks yet to finish the house, with less help than I was promised. I came to bring you news."

"News, of . . . of Ledu?" My hands stilled on the tablecloth, while my heart pounded out a drumbeat, the call to come home.

"Yes, but it's not the news you hope for. I'm so sorry." Teddy spoke gently as he broke the news. He came over to me and stood across the line of tablecloths and linen napkins. He put his rough hand over mine, willing me to remain upright, his eyes intent on mine.

"I found out Gustavus Vassa was slave to a man named Robert King, of Montserrat, in the West Indies."

The staccato drumbeat of my heart slowed, becoming erratic.

"Well, that's good. We know where he is?!"

"We know where he was," Teddy said, emphasizing 'was.'

"Was?" I felt hot, and shaky, and leaned back against the wooden fence for support—removing my hand from underneath Teddy's.

He leaned under the line, ending up with a wet napkin on his head. I laughed.

"Olu, you are so sweet; I wish I had better news. Shortly after this man, Gustavus Vassa, possibly your brother, soon after he left Charles Town he was freed." Teddy's mouth lifted on the right in his signature half-smile.

After exhausting all his avenues of information, he was able only to discern that Vassa was a slave of Robert King of Montserrat. Later that year, in 1766, Vassa received manumission papers—he was a free man. I hoped this Gustavus Vassa was my dear Ledu, and now a free man, even though it meant it would now be nearly impossible to trace him. From the time a slave boarded a slave ship in Africa, he or she could be traced to owners—until he or she died or gained legitimate freedom. There the records ceased.

"He's free. If he was Ledu, if he is Ledu, then he's a freed man. Praise the Lord! That is *good* news, Teddy," I said, attempting to convince myself.

"It is indeed good news, for Mr. Vassa, whether he is Ledu or not." He paused, and I wondered if my heart would survive the motion sickness—heights of happiness to depths of despair. "However," Teddy continued, "it does make it nearly impossible to trace him now."

"I know. Just another freed African, no one buying or selling him. Well, I must say I'm happy for him—Mr. Vassa—or Ledu. He's free. If it means I can't continue the search for my brother, or if it means I'll never find him, that's in God's hands. His freedom is more important than our togetherness. I would rather one of us be free, and we apart, than for us to be slaves together."

"I agree, Olu. But it's hard to give up. I know. I'll not abandon my search, though I harbor little hope of success." Teddy even offered to go to Montserrat to determine if he could find where Gustavus Vassa traveled to, and if he was indeed Ledu.

If it really was Ledu, he's free. It's time. It's time for me to be free as well. I resolved to put a plan together, talk to Thomas, and escape—soon. I wouldn't ask Teddy to look any longer, but maybe when I was free . . .

"Teddy, it's been thirteen years. You need no longer look. I must go on without my family, as I have these many years and counting." As I said the words, I tried to make myself believe them. My heart hardened a bit—buffering my soul against future loss, decathecting.

# CHAPTER FOURTEEN

## Joanna

### Winter 1808

When we returned to school after the Christmas break, all of us girls participated in the vicar's birthday party presentation. Miss Catherine Bromley had helped us practice. Her elegant and effortless piano playing inspired us, and her suggestions and techniques helped all of us who play piano. Her brother Henry accompanied her the last few practice sessions to constitute an "impartial audience." He looked about my age, though a little taller than me, with brown hair and eyes. Henry managed to give us feedback that was helpful while avoiding criticism—like medicine on a silver spoon. He coated his remarks with praise and his sweet, shy smile enlivened his face. Miss Catherine and Henry's presence at the performance caused us to play at our peak. I thought Anne and I were phenomenal, and we did get a lot of applause.

Epiphany term was short and when we all went home for Easter break, I stayed with Grandmamma. I helped her with her gargantuan garden—Grandmamma loved to grow flowers, including roses, lilies, hollyhock, foxglove, and delphinium. I especially liked the peonies, large and vibrant. Grandmamma also loved sewing, but I found no pleasure in it, so I sat nearby handing her thread or scissors, engrossed in a book. I always enjoyed hearing stories about Mama, and this time she confessed that while Mama loved gardening, she abhorred sewing—just like me! I gathered up these tidbits about my mama and stored them in my memory to take out and cherish later. This is also about the time I started journaling, so I wouldn't forget anything Grandmamma, Uncle John, or William Wilberforce, said about my parents.

Easter term, from April through June, included studying for final exams and polishing our musical skills. At the end of the school year, Miss Maisie whispered what Mr. Harding had done right before we left school for the summer break. I always felt threatened in his presence, though I couldn't pinpoint what I thought he might do. A vague discomfort and heightened vigilance arose whenever I endured his snide comments or surly stare.

"I'll surely miss you, Miss Joanna. Let me help you pack up your things." Miss Maisie helped me layer dresses and underthings in my trunk.

"I'll miss you, too, Miss Maisie." I paused and looked up at her. "I'm curious. I haven't seen Mr. Harding the past few weeks. Where is he?"

"The devil got his due!"

"What do you mean?"

"He was always up to no good. Turns out. . ." Miss Maisie shut the door completely, "Turns out he got Maeve in the family way, but he warn't no family!"

"My goodness! Maeve is expecting??" I leaned back in shock.

"Yes, miss. Soon as Missus Limebear heard, she fired that devil quicker 'en a bad cook can burn a meal. It be like they say, he who injure somebody injure hisself. Mr Harding is gone, and good riddance!"

With Mr. Harding gone and a friend in Anne, school became more than bearable. It became enjoyable. I excelled in my studies, gravitated towards history, and became a decent piano player. Anne and I grew closer as we both harbored a desire to join an anti-slavery society. We followed the news about the abolition movement and talked about what we might do with our own anti-slavery society. I corresponded with Aunt Jane; she had joined a local anti-slavery society. She kept us abreast of all that they were doing. Anne and I were excited every time a letter from Aunt Jane arrived at school.

As my grandmamma got older, she felt less and less able to look after me, and I spent more and more time with Uncle John, both in his London and Cambridgeshire homes. I loved Grandmamma, but as I got older I felt like a burden to her, and Uncle John so clearly enjoyed my company, it was more pleasant to stay with him.

After Uncle John met Mr. Wilberforce, he would often be invited to gatherings there, and I tagged along. Uncle John told me once how much Mr. Wilberforce had affected his life.

"Joanna," Uncle John said, "I enjoy my work—researching, strategizing, arguing a case. Some of them are serious cases, life and death. But much of what I do is mundane—trusts, wills, estates. When I met your father, he inspired me. I wanted to aid the abolition movement, but other than subscribing to your father's book, and signing a petition, I had no idea how to be useful, until I met William Wilberforce. He has a way of pulling people toward him, like a powerful, irresistible, yet genial magnet."

Uncle John's growing partnership with Mr. Wilberforce provided many opportunities for me to visit the Wilberforces and become close friends with Barbara. I visited two or three times a year and saw Fredrik on several occasions. I continued to harbor a crush—I'm still not sure if I was enamoured by Fredrik himself, or by Fredrik the African. Spending time with Fredrik fed a longing in me to know more about Africa and my family.

## June 1814

Seven years after I came to the school, graduation day finally arrived. I was more than ready to leave the confines of school and figure out what I might do for the next stage of life. I was not in a hurry to marry, Fredrik didn't show any signs of proposing, and I had not met any other eligible men. Uncle John's predicted hordes of suitors never materialized.

The plan was for the guests, family mostly, to gather at the school and walk to the nearby church for the graduation ceremony, then return to school for a late breakfast. We assembled in the parlour.

Miranda's dad came, along with both of Candace's parents. Violet and Rose were talking with their parents, while Samantha's parents questioned Mrs. Limebear about her plans for the school. Anne came over to where I stood alone, near the unlit fireplace, a serene expression glued firmly on my face—or at least I hoped so.

"Joanna, I'm so sorry Uncle John couldn't come. I'm sure he's devastated," Anne said.

"He is. I said I didn't mind, but now that graduation is here, all of you have your parents, I . . . I miss him."

Mrs. Limebear said, "It's time we were off, graduates, ladies and gentlemen. It's a lovely day for a walk, but some of you may prefer to ride in your carriages. We have a carriage available as well. The ceremony will begin promptly at 10 o'clock, and it's now 9:30, so let's make our way to the church." Mrs. Limebear directed all of us and the parents out of the school and into carriages. Anne and her father and stepmother, Candace and her parents, and I chose to walk.

We settled in the front pew, with the proud parents in the pew behind us. I noticed Catherine and Henry Bromley sitting a few rows back. I was surprised and happy to see them both. Mrs. Limebear, and the minister, Rev. Wombwell, walked down the center aisle to the strains of Bach on the organ.

Rev. Wombwell rose to speak. "We welcome to St. John's the graduating class of Mrs. Limebear's School for Girls. We welcome all the proud parents and family members and friends in attendance. This is indeed a joyous occasion, and we are here to give thanks to God for the accomplishments of these seven young ladies."

As he continued a short speech the church door opened, and three people came down the aisle, taking seats several pews behind the parents. Anne craned her neck around to see who it was and nudged me. I turned around to see Rev. William Wilberforce, his wife Barbara, and Sadie Cross. I turned back around to face the reverend, so as not to be rude, but I couldn't suppress my smile.

All of us marched up, received diplomas and hearty congratulations from Rev. Wombwell and Mrs. Limebear. The ceremony concluded with prayer and the graduates, family members and friends assembled in the narthex, the lobby of the church.

"Joanna, we're so sorry to be late. We wanted to surprise you, but not at the graduation ceremony itself! Wilby couldn't tear himself away early enough for us to get here on time," Mrs. Wilberforce explained.

I hugged Mrs. Wilberforce. "I'm so happy you came. Uncle John and Grandmamma were not able to come—so you are my honorary family."

"You must mean your honready family," William Wilberforce said with a grin.

"Yes, indeed," I said, smiling.

"And we brought a dear friend of the family with us. Joanna, this is Miss Theodosia Cross," Mrs. Wilberforce said.

Sadie and I shook hands politely, and she said, "It's so nice to meet you, Joanna." She emphasized "meet you" and I remembered her telling

Anne, Aunt Jane, and I that Mr. Wilberforce was unaware of her activities in the Ladies Anti-Slavery Society. She must not have mentioned she visited us at Uncle John's home. We had a secret, and I wasn't going to reveal it!

"Please, Miss Cross is much too formal, and no one calls me Theodosia. Call me Sadie."

"Sadie is a dear friend of our family, Joanna, and the best midwife in England, or possibly all of Europe." Mrs. Wilberforce smiled at Sadie.

"Don't stop there, dear. Nowhere else in the world can there possibly be such an excellent midwife as our Sadie," Mr. Wilberforce said.

"They exaggerate highly," Sadie said.

"Not at all, Joanna. Sadie not only delivers babies, but she mothers the mothers after the birth," Mrs. Wilberforce said.

"I've never heard of that before," I said. The more I learned about Sadie, the more I wanted to know. I felt an unexplainable kinship—I wished she were my older sister, but at least I hoped we could be friends.

Mrs. Limebear called out to us graduates and our families, "We will now return to the school for a full breakfast to commence in one half hour."

I walked over to Miss Catherine and Henry and said how happy I was to see them. Catherine hugged me and Henry smiled awkwardly. Mr. Wilberforce joined us and gave Henry a hearty handshake. Apparently, Henry and his oldest son William were in school together. What a coincidence!

As we started walking back to the school, Sadie drew up next to me, followed by William and Barbara Wilberforce.

"How delightful to see you again, Joanna," Sadie said quietly. "Mr. Wilberforce and Mrs. Barbara don't know we met—I didn't tell them about our petition."

"I figured. I won't tell!" I promised.

"None of your family members could come to the graduation?"

"Aunt Jane is unwell. And Uncle John has a case he couldn't postpone."

"I'm so glad we're here for you!" Sadie said, smiling.

"Me, too. I'm curious. May I ask you a question?"

"Certainly," Sadie said.

"Are you English?"

"No, I'm American."

"Really?! Where in America are you from?" I adjusted my views of Sadie's background.

"I was born off the coast of Virginia—on a ship! My mama and papa had recently been married by the ship's captain, and then I made my appearance."

"I've never heard such a story before." I'm sure my mouth and eyes were wide open. By this time, we had reached the school and were ushered into the dining room. Both the dining room and drawing room were used to accommodate all the guests.

William Wilberforce touched me on the shoulder.

"We wanted to see you graduate dear, but I'm afraid we must be off now. I have a pressing appointment in London, and I must accompany these two lovely ladies home first. Well done, my dear. Many blessings on your graduation." The Wilberforces left, taking Sadie with them, and I felt the loss. Another ending and a new beginning, of what, I didn't yet know.

## 4 January 1815—seven months later

William Wilberforce invited Uncle John and I to join the family for Twelfth Night. They had moved to Gore House, in Kensington Gore, during the fall of 1808 to be closer to the Houses of Parliament, reducing traveling time for Mr. Wilberforce. The house was bigger, to accommodate the family of eight, plus the numerous servants. Mr. Wilberforce never fired his servants or let them go. Even his 87-year-old butler, who could no longer perform his duties, had a home at Gore House.

Twelfth Night was always a special occasion for the Wilberforces. The celebration on the eve of Epiphany—the arrival of the three kings with gifts for the baby Jesus—included singing, eating, and games. Wilberforce enjoyed playing with his children and deemed games appropriate even for adults!

I was staying with Uncle John in his Cambridgeshire home, and during the half-day carriage ride to Gore House, Uncle John informed me of a missive he had recently received. His attempts to find my Aunt Olu were tedious and slow, but he did ascertain that O. Equiano left West Africa in 1754, and the ship she was on landed in Barbados. I was bursting with hope as Uncle John continued. He drew out his recital, in a lawyerly way. After 18 months of searching, he finally tracked Aunt Olu to a ship that landed in Charles Town, America in April 1754.

The wonderful news was overshadowed by the reminder that Aunt Olu would now be a much older woman. If she was still alive. Papa lived to almost the end of the century. I held out hope to meet, to see another member of my family, of my papa's family.

Uncle John said, "that's not all." I was sitting so far on the edge of the carriage seat I would have tumbled off had the carriage wheel hit a rut. Uncle John gently took my hands in his, moving me back on the seat.

"Your aunt's full name is Oluchukwu, Olu was a nickname I guess, but when she was sold, she was renamed Olivia."

"Oluchukwu." I sounded out the name slowly, savoring each syllable.

"She was bought by a Mr. Samuel Cross, Cross Plantation, Ashley River, South Carolina."

"So we know where she is!! Do you have an address? Can I write to her? Can we do something to free her?"

"Slow down, child. I have traced her thus far, which as you know has taken several years. But the next phase of our search should be easier if the owner's still alive, and if he's willing to tell us your aunt's whereabouts." Uncle John's grim, straight-mouthed look warned me not to get my hopes up.

"I recently sent off a short inquiry to Mr. Cross. But of course, who knows if he's still there. South Carolina suffered much during the American Revolution. Many slaves escaped, many plantation owners died and some fled. But we can hope and pray that Mr. Cross is still alive, or a descendant who knows where your aunt is."

"I can't tell you how much it means to me to have you search for her so diligently. Do you think there's any hope . . . we . . . will find her?" I asked.

"My sweet Joanna, I have cautioned you from the beginning not to raise your hopes too highly. But this recent development is promising. Now we need to find out—is she still there? Or do Mr. Cross or his heirs know where she is?"

We were silent for the next hour of the journey, each immersed in thought. I prayed my Aunt Olu was still alive. I also looked forward to a week with the Wilberforce family, time to renew my friendship with Barbara.

I turned my attention to the passing scene as the carriage progressed through London to the gates of Gore House. We had skirted the city of London, passing St. Paul's Cathedral, past the Houses of Parliament and Westminster Abbey, alongside the Thames, with a view of St. James

Park and Buckingham Palace. I had visited Gore House a few times a year since the Wilberforces moved there in 1808, so it felt almost like a second home. I had become accustomed to living in various places and had learned how to adjust quickly. Shuffling between Grandmamma's, Uncle John's, and Mrs. Limebear's school for the past eight years, and visiting the Wilberforces, I became a chameleon, blending into each environment, being helpful without being intrusive; adapting to household schedules, meals, customs, unwritten rules—making myself as agreeable as possible. I grew to enjoy the change of setting and scenery and could scarcely imagine living in one place for years on end. I was in no rush to marry. However, as I approached my 20th birthday, others were beginning to prod me to think about marriage and be open to welcoming prospects. Grandmamma's awkward attempts to introduce me to local, eligible men, recent Cambridge graduates, failed miserably.

I assumed Fredrik would be at the Wilberforces, and still often thought about him. But he was several years older, and we had no understanding. Fredrik seemed to enjoy our time together, but he hadn't even hinted at marriage. His charming, courteous demeanor and attractive dark complexion had attracted me to him, but a fondness for Fredrik replaced my earlier girlhood crush. I knew, however, that any interest on Fredrik's part would quickly reignite the spark of romance I let die out. I had recently seen Henry Bromley on my visits to Gore House, he often came home with William (the son) on school breaks. I enjoyed our conversations—he always made me think and smile—an appealing combination. Two very different young men, both appealing in very different ways.

I stood to inherit a substantial sum on my 21st birthday, bequeathed to me by Papa. This would attract some suitors but might discourage Fredrik as he had so little to bring to any union. He came to England from Africa as a boy, and while he now earned a living as a barber, he didn't have any property or investments. I still hoped Fredrik would be visiting this week, so I could determine the depth of his regard.

The carriage stopped and I looked out at the large, cheery house. It was half again the size of Broomfield, with larger grounds in the back, only a short walk from Hyde Park. Uncle John stepped out first and helped me down. The coach driver tied up the horses and retrieved the suit cases. The door opened before we could even knock, and I smiled to see Barbara rushing to greet me.

## CHAPTER FOURTEEN: JOANNA

"Here you are at last! I've been looking out for you, waiting impatiently. I'm so happy you could come! Hello, Mr. Audley. Welcome, welcome!"

"Thank you, Miss Barbara." Mr. Audley bowed over her hand. "It's always a pleasure to see you. You look more like your charming mother every day."

Barbara smiled and curtsied and took my hand. "Mama, Joanna is here and we're going out back," she called to her mother, who stood in the doorway.

"Joanna, nice to see you again. Did you have a nice Christmas?" Mrs. Wilberforce inquired.

"Yes, ma'am, it was lovely."

"You girls enjoy the grounds while the weather is nice." Mrs. Barbara waved us on.

Uncle John and Mrs. Wilberforce entered the house, while Barbara and I held hands and walked around to the back of the house, taking a stroll around the perimeter of the yard. I had grown in the past few years and stood a full head taller than Barbara and Mrs. Wilberforce. My figure had filled out, top and bottom, often attracting unwanted male attention.

After years of struggling to tame my unruly hair, I finally found a cream to subdue the frizz, resulting in shoulder-length, full, tightly curled, brunette hair. Barbara, walking beside me, mirrored her mother's petite, small-boned frame. Her hair was dark blonde, curling around her face, the longest part tucked up in her bonnet. We walked together, tall and short, dark and fair, an orphan and a girl surrounded by a large loving family.

Barbara and I talked as though we'd never been apart. She was sorry her illness prevented her from attending my graduation. I related how excited I was to see her parents and Sadie. Barbara looked out across the lawn and bemoaned never going away to school.

"Oh, I wish you could live with us. We'd have such fun together!" Barbara reached out and put her hand over mine. We talked about our very different living situations—she, surrounded by siblings, me with no siblings; she had two parents—I had a guardian, and a grandmother who was no longer able to care for me.

"Well, we always seem to want what we don't have. I actually want a big, noisy family and you want a quiet house. I'll ask Uncle John if you can come and visit us for a week. Then you'll see how much you enjoy not having brothers and a sister all around. I bet you'll miss them," I said, smiling.

"Oh, of course I will. I do complain, but I love them all, even little Henry, who just broke the arm off my favourite doll."

We had walked quite a distance, and decided to sit on a bench, near a juniper tree.

"Those birds are noisy!" I exclaimed, hearing the song thrush and bullfinches vying for eminence.

"They love the ... ooof ... oh fiddle!" A ripe juniper-berry plopped down on Barbara's clean white frock, a midday snack dropped from the beak of a thrush.

"Dear me, that stain won't come out easily," I said, glancing at the purple stain.

"Let's go back. Maybe I can get Miss Betty to wash it before my mama sees it."

As Barbara rose, the juice of the berry dripped down the skirt of her dress, leaving a long, purplish line.

"This is even worse. I'll never be able to hide this!" Barbara looked down, frowning at the spreading stain.

"Let's go quickly, before the stain sets in," I suggested.

We walked back to the house briskly. I told Barbara that Uncle John found out where my aunt lived, she grabbed my hands in excitement. When I explained Uncle John had traced Aunt Olu to a plantation in South Carolina, she encouraged me to write to her.

"I know how much this means to you. To find your family. Your father's family. I hope, I pray you find her."

"Me, too. But I'm trying not to get my hopes too high. There's little hope that we'll find her. And even if we do, she's across the ocean in America. It would be too expensive to bring her here, or to go there."

"You're coming into your inheritance soon—don't forget," Barbara reminded me.

"True, but I mustn't spend it all immediately! I may be on my own, so I need to be very careful with my inheritance. And it might not be that much." I kept my expectations low.

"Well, you'll marry a wealthy man, so that will simply be extra. Right?" Barbara grinned.

"Oh really? Please introduce me to this anonymous wealthy man."

"You can marry William. He'll be wealthy, I'm sure," Barbara winked at me.

"William? Your brother?" I asked, astonished.

"Yes, of course. Don't you like him?"

"I like him fine. As a brother. Not as a husband. And besides, it's not too common for a White Englishman to marry a woman of colour. I know my parents married across racial lines, but it's rare here, right?"

"I guess so. I don't know of anyone who married someone from another race. Do you like someone else . . . as a husband?" Barbara leaned closer and peered at me.

We neared the house and slowed down, engrossed in our conversation.

"Well, you know I'm fond of . . ." I began.

"Good afternoon, ladies," Fredrik said, slightly bowing as he approached us. I looked pointedly at Barbara and approached Fredrik with mixed feelings—hope tinged with reticence.

"Hi, Fredrik," Barbara replied. "I'm on my way to repair my frock."

"I hope you have not met with an accident. That is not . . .?" Fredrik started.

"No, nothing that serious. Merely a juniper berry!" Barbara laughed.

"Good, then. Well, not good, but I'm glad you're not injured." Fredrik nodded.

"Thank you. Joanna, come up to my room later, so we can finish our conversation." Barbara waved goodbye and entered the house.

Fredrik said, "Please forgive me for intruding."

"Oh, don't worry."

"How have you been, Miss Joanna? I haven't seen you in, oh, has it been a full year?" Fredrik asked.

"Yes, I believe it has," I said, knowing it was a full year.

Fredrik gestured to a bench on the back porch, where I sat down, while he took a seat in a nearby chair. He was only a little taller than me and seemed thinner than he was last time I saw him. He now sported a mustache and had on a nice pair of breeches and a waistcoat.

"You graduated, I believe?"

"Yes, last summer we all graduated. Mrs. Limebear has a fresh batch of girls to mold," I said, with a half-smile.

"I'm sure she'll enjoy that. From all you've said about her, she seems to greatly enjoy molding girls into women. And I think she's pretty good at it, too, judging from the example I see before me." Fredrik nodded to me.

I never knew how to interpret his remarks. Was he sincere, or only flattering me? And why? When it came to Fredrik, I tended to evaluate every phrase and every look carefully, pondering them for days. Was this infatuation? Love? Or friendship?

"Thank you. I can now play the piano, speak passable French, tell you all about the history of England, parse Latin verbs, and compute elaborate sums."

"Like you, my French is passable. But I did not learn how to play the piano!"

"No, but you can cut hair," I said.

"Yes, I can. I can cut it, curl it, shape it, colour it, even shave it off. Mr. Macaulay and Mr. Wilberforce will not let anyone but me cut their hair."

"You're in demand, I see. And do you have many customers now?"

"More than I can attend to in a week. I may be leaving the Macaulays and finding a small place of my own."

"How nice. Though I'm sure the Macaulays would miss you. Here in London?"

"Yes, of course. In Clapham Commons alone I have about 20 customers—men and women. And as I cut their hair, they ask me about my home. Every one of them is an abolitionist. Sometimes I think they believe they're helping the cause by using an African barber."

"Aren't they? In a way? They're demonstrating that Africans are productive members of society, not only slaves or servants."

"I never thought of it like that. I see Mr. Wilberforce has had a positive influence on your thinking."

"He has. As have others, like women in the Anti-Slavery Society."

"Have you joined a society, Joanna?" Fredrik looked at me closely. Fredrik had joined the Sons of Africa abolition society a few years back.

"Not yet. But I hope to soon. I heard Mr. Wilberforce is not in favor of women politicking! So please don't tell!"

"I think you should join. Your father would have approved."

"Yes, I think he would," I said, thinking about what legacy means.

Fredrik said he was staying several days, but then he had to return home and attend to his clients. He hoped he wouldn't be the blind man in Blind Man's Buff, and when I said I enjoyed the game, he said he preferred chess.

"Fredrik! At least say you like cricket," I prodded.

"To appease you. I'll claim to enjoy cricket."

"You know you like the game," I teased.

"Yes, well, I do like it, in small doses. I really don't like endless games of cricket." Fredrik motioned his hand out in a circle.

"You're right, there."

Fredrik looked up. "Well, the sun is close to setting. Barbara will be waiting for you. I'll see you at dinner?" Fredrik asked, rising, and putting out his hand. I took it, and as I rose to my feet, he moved closer, so we were mere inches apart. I looked into his eyes.

"You have grown into a beautiful young woman, Joanna, if you don't mind my saying so." Fredrik looked serious and thoughtful.

"I . . . I don't mind."

"You will make someone a lovely bride."

I looked down, unsure how to respond. But will I make you a lovely bride, is what I wanted to ask. Fredrik stepped back, and went to the door, opening it for me to enter the house and rejoin Barbara. When I knocked on Barbara's door, it opened immediately.

"What took you so long?" Barbara asked, wearing a fresh, clean white frock.

"Was I long? I was talking to Fredrik."

"Talking, hmmm? Not kissing?" Barbara wanted to know.

"Barbara! No, we weren't kissing." Though I wish we were, I thought. His full lips looked to be perfect for a first kiss, and many more to follow! I tried to stop my thoughts progressing in this direction.

"But you want him to kiss you, don't you?" Barbara looked closely at my face.

"What has gotten into you? Why all this interest in kissing suddenly?" I asked.

"I'm a young woman. And even though Mama and Papa shelter me, I see things, I hear things, and I read things. Isn't that what men and women do when they're attracted to each other? They kiss!"

"I suppose so. But they should only kiss if they have an agreement."

"An agreement. You mean an engagement?" Barbara asked.

"Yes. Otherwise, well, it's simply not right. You and I are not the type of girls to kiss any man we take a liking to."

"So, he didn't kiss you?" Barbara looked disappointed.

"You're incorrigible!"

"And you still haven't answered my question, have you?" Barbara stared at me.

"No. . . . he didn't kiss me. But . . ." I began.

"Go on, but. . . what?"

"He looked like he wanted to," I admitted, smiling. "And I kind of wished he had."

"You will tell me when he does, won't you? I must live through you until I get my own beau."

"If he does. Yes, I'll tell you. Now, what happened to your frock?"

"Fine. Change the subject. Although I'd rather talk about kissing than frocks! I came in through the kitchen and Miss Betty helped me out. She's not sure she can get the stain out, but if anyone can, she can."

"That's good, then."

"You want to marry an African?" Barbara asked, returning to her favourite subject.

"Not . . . necessarily. I like Fredrik, but I'm not sure how he feels. It would not be considered a good match for me, and that might deter him. I don't know. I don't need a lot of money. I want to marry a man I love and admire, not just a man who's wealthy, and not necessarily an African," I replied, thinking aloud.

"I know I wouldn't want to be poor. I like having a nice house, servants, and a carriage. I don't imagine a barber could afford all that?" Barbara questioned.

"You don't like Fredrik?" I asked.

"I like him fine. He's practically a brother. Come to think of it, he came to England the year I was born, and living with the Macaulays, we were always in each other's homes. It's not Fredrik I object to. I think it would be hard to live with little money. I wouldn't like it, I'm sure." Barbara shook her head.

"Well, I'll have money of my own next year, when I inherit."

"Yes, but you don't know how much it will be, nor how long it will last. Better to marry a man of means." Barbara was adamant.

"Isn't love important?" I asked.

"Do you love Fredrik then?"

"I don't know, to be honest. I've never loved a man before. I like him. I think he's handsome. I admire him." I wasn't prepared to say I loved Fredrick yet.

"So not quite love," Barbara replied.

"Maybe not."

"But even if you did love him, would that be enough?" Barbara wondered.

# CHAPTER FIFTEEN

## Olu

### 1766–1775

SLAVES FELL IN LOVE, but love didn't form a family and couldn't keep one together. Slave women got pregnant and either gave birth, aborted their babies, or miscarried. Women carrying to term birthed a new generation of slaves. Martha got older, continuing to teach me all she knew about the restorative powers of herbs, plants, bark, roots. Her daughter Elsie, now twelve, began to work around the house helping Mary—the slave and maid of all work—with cleaning. Mr. Samuel continued to keep his distance from me.

With every passing year I thought of escape, prayed for an opportunity, and waited. Each new year I thanked God for my life, and prayed for my family, not knowing who still lived. In my prime child-bearing years I rebuffed the Africans who tried to woo me or seduce me. I refused to bring a child into slavery, and honestly, none of the men attracted my interest. I remained a rare anomaly among slave women—a virgin. I vowed to remain untouched till I was free. I began to wonder if I would die a slave.

### November 1775

In November we all heard rumors of war. Talk of war, hushed planning for freedom, and debate over which side would win permeated the slave community. News traveled over land and river, from plantation to town house. Good news traveled fast, bad news even faster. Back in August, colonists tried, convicted, hung, and burned a free Black man. Thomas Jeremiah was accused of inciting rebellion—*with* the British *against* the Colonists. I heard Mr. Samuel talking about it one night at dinner with a neighboring plantation owner.

"Cut and dried—that nigger is guilty as sin," Mr. Samuel grumbled.

"Aye, no doubt of it. We can't trust none of 'em. I wonder you let that slave o' yours pilot your schooner on 'is own," the other man said.

"Cap'n Thomas. He's all right. He's reliable. You need to trust a few—but keep the majority down. The way I see it, give a little power, a little freedom, to one or two; they stays happy and helps me keep the others in line. Yes sir, with goin' on 100 slaves it's the only way. I can't hire more Whites—too costly." Mr. Samuel shook his head.

"It may be costly, but I don't trust a single one 'o mine. Not one." The guest put up his index finger for emphasis.

"Jones keeps 'em working in the rice fields and Thomas moves my goods. I keep a close eye and they know it."

"How did that fellow, Jeremiah fellow, how'd he get the guns?"

"I heard he stole 'em, one by one, from various houses. Believe me, he had some help. They should be hanged, too." Mr. Samuel crossed his arms over his chest.

"Damn right. You think war's coming here to Charles Town?"

"No doubt. Too many of us are agin' the Brits, and they ain't leaving peaceably. No sir. They want to hold on to this land. But I predict the fighting will be short, and we'll win." Mr. Samuel was half right.

The slaves had one perspective and the Whites another. The *slave owners* wanted freedom—from the British. The *slaves* wanted freedom—from the owners. Slaves ended up fighting on both sides, some for the colonists and more for the British. Whites and Blacks fought against Whites and Blacks. I knew which side I was on—the British. I didn't trust any slave-owning patriot one whit. They promised freedom, better conditions, even pay—I believed not one word.

The rumors continued. One gained prominence. Slave gossip had it that Lord Dunmore, the British Governor of Virginia, was offering freedom to any slave who joined him in battle. Then on 7 November 1775 Lord Dunmore issued a proclamation:

> . . . And I do hereby further declare all indented Servants, Negroes, or others, (appertaining to Rebels,) free that are able and willing to bear Arms, they joining His MAJESTY'S Troops as

## CHAPTER FIFTEEN: OLU

soon as may be, for the more speedily reducing this Colony to a proper Sense of their Duty, to His MAJESTY'S Crown and Dignity...

GIVEN under my Hand on board the Ship WILLIAM by Norfolk, the 7th Day of November in the SIXTEENTH Year of His MAJESTY'S Reign.

DUNMORE

By November 8th every slave from Virginia to Florida had heard the proclamation, usually uttered verbatim from one slave to another. Hundreds, maybe thousands of slaves fled, escaping certain servitude for an uncertain future, freedom glimmering in the distance. When I heard the proclamation, from Cap'n Thomas who heard it in Charles Town from another slave boat pilot, I thought, now, now is my time to leave. Maybe I couldn't bear arms, or maybe I could, but I could cook, catch babies, and heal folks. I convinced myself my services would be welcomed by the British.

As I planned my escape, talked to women in the rice fields and to Cap'n Thomas, a black envelope arrived by post for Mr. Samuel, delivering the sad news Teddy's wife and son had died of smallpox—five months ago. The letter preceded Teddy by one week.

Martha and I were preparing lunch when Teddy walked in. How can I describe how different he appeared—I almost didn't recognize him. His beard was longer than usual, scruffier, flecked with gray. His eyes no longer sparkled with humor but glazed with sorrow. His shoulders slumped, and subdued silence replaced his familiar joviality. His normally tight breeches hung loosely on his hips, and his shirt was hanging out, wrinkled and dirty—unlike his normally clean, fresh, tucked-in look. He looked beaten up, defeated, worn. Crushed by harsh waves in an angry ocean, grief had shaken him, battered his body, and thrown him lifeless on the shore.

"Oh, my dear boy. So sorry. So sad to hear of your loss. Come here, Mr. Teddy," Martha spoke to Teddy as if he were five, not forty-five. And he came. Even lifting his feet and walking seemed to take more energy than he possessed. Martha met him halfway and enveloped him in her arms. Martha's head did not even reach up to his chin, so Teddy laid his head on top of hers, heaved a sigh, and let out a tormented moan of anguish which throbbed through our own bodies, a drumbeat pounding a note of unbearable grief.

Unable to watch any longer, uncertain of what to do, I turned back to the hearth, using the long wide wooden paddle to pull out the biscuits right before they burned, set them in a basket, and check on the fish stew. Several minutes later Martha led Teddy to a cane-back chair beside the hearth.

"I knows food can't heal the soul, but it do help the body recover. Grieving's physical—you know it, I do too. I reckon this fish stew needs a tasting to see if I put enough onions in't, and mercy me, I made too many biscuits. Lordy, what was I thinking?"

Martha went on talking, and I'm sure Teddy wasn't minding the words, but her low, melodious voice must have comforted him, as did the food. He ate slowly at first, then ravenously. "What you been eatin' these past months, Mr. Teddy?" Martha asked.

"Not much, Miss Martha. Not much. Seems I lost the knack of cooking and the desire to eat when I lost Lydia and Thaddeus."

I hadn't spoken yet, but now I said, "We were all heartbroken to hear of your loss, Teddy. The card only arrived last week. I only wish we had known or could have helped you."

"Ah . . . I've been no fit company. Raised a house these past three months, working sun-up to sun-down to take my mind off . . . well, it didn't work, but the house got built."

I ladled another large spoonful into his bowl, along with two more biscuits. He showed no signs of slowing down.

"They were my life, Lydia, and Thaddeus. I never thought . . . I never even imagined I'd outlive her. Sometimes I . . . sometimes I can't even remember what she looks like," he barely got out the last few words through his throat choking up.

"Think on the times you had with her, Mr. Teddy. She were a lovely lady and I's glad to have met her. Remember the laughter, the joy. Thank God above for knowing her, lovin' her. Don't none of us know how long we got. Each day, count it a blessing—slave or free. That be all we got— today. Okay, no more preaching. I'll leave that to the minister. You knows I get carried away. I just hates to see you so sorrowful-lookin'."

"You're the best cure, Miss Martha. Your cooking and kindness can put a man to rights."

"Ah, Mr. Teddy. Go on with you."

Teddy said he would probably stay at the plantation for several weeks. With fighting popping up here and there, he had no desire to build a house only to see it get burned to the ground. Teddy continued to spoon stew into his mouth, some of it landing on his beard.

I was happy to hear that. I always enjoyed Teddy's visits, and I knew he needed to be away from his home, with reminders of Lydia and Thaddeus. He needed to heal. There were no herbs or roots or barks in the pantry to cure what ailed him. Time, love, food, prayer, the outdoors—healing would come.

I postponed thoughts of escape and focused on being helpful to Martha and Teddy. Mr. Samuel was away from the plantation, meeting with other planters in Charles Town, debating how to respond to British threats. That left more time for Teddy and me to talk—without always listening or watching out to see if we were being observed. He ambled down in the morning when he smelled breakfast and managed to lift off a griddle cake or sausage before it made the serving dish. Martha didn't even scold him.

Late morning, he would find me in the vegetable garden, or hanging laundry on the line, or chopping vegetables in the kitchen. One afternoon, the house was uncharacteristically empty. Martha was visiting one of the new mothers in the slave quarters, Mrs. Beth and her son Sammy had gone down to Savannah to visit her sister, and Mr. Samuel was staying in town. Only Mary and Geoffrey, the lone male slave in the house, remained behind, and they were down at the "village" enjoying rare free time with other slaves.

Teddy and I sat in the morning room. With windows all along one wall and on the adjoining wall, the long rectangular room was awash in late afternoon light. The aroma of freshly baked bread drifted into the room. Teddy's healing had begun. He had shaved his beard and put on a few pounds. We sat together on the divan.

I broke the silence. "Teddy, where will you go when you leave?"

"I'm not sure. I guess that's why I haven't left yet. I can't face returning to the house, our house. I built it for her: window seats and stained glass, a fireplace in every room, vaulted ceilings, stone exterior. Her ideas—my skill. I can't go back. Too many memories."

Teddy began to weep—tears wet his boots, his shoulders heaved up and down, and he groaned. I moved closer to him, unsure of myself, wanting to comfort. I put one hand on his knee, the other gently rubbing his back. I didn't speak.

After about five minutes, he stopped crying, wiped his eyes roughly with the back of his hand, wiped a handkerchief over his nose and turned to me. He looked at me in a way he had never looked at me before. His grief shifted to passion, quickly and subtly, from a bereft pride lion to a frisky lion cub. The depth of emotion remained constant as the focus shifted from the past, what he had lost, to the present, me. He looked at me as if he'd never seen me before, shaking his head.

"All the time you were here—I never knew."

"Knew what, Teddy?" I was alarmed—he looked at me so fiercely, held my face in his strong, callused hands. He gripped me tighter.

"I thought I was helping you, like a project, a good deed. I would teach you to read and write, track down your brother, tell Samuel to leave you alone."

"You did all that, Teddy. You did help me. I'm not ungrateful."

"I didn't see it—I didn't realize it. All this time spent with you . . ."

I looked away. His eyes were too intense. I felt he could read my thoughts, my yearning.

"Olivia . . . Oluchukwu . . . I think, I believe . . . I love you."

"Love? Me?" Incredulous, thrilled, I couldn't construct a rational response.

"Yes, my sweet Olu. You."

I was speechless. My eyes must have registered my disbelief, tinged with hope. I had loved Teddy since he rescued me from Mrs. Beth when I was twelve years old, I was now thirty-three. My love had only deepened over the years. But he was White, the brother of my master, and then a married man. He was always out of reach.

Teddy looked at the top of my scar, where my chest began to rise, SCP, and gently lowered my frock, exposing the mark that sealed me as a slave, the property of a man. I expected him to turn in disgust or cover me back up . . . instead he traced the sign of my slavery with his finger—as if he were a blind person and he wanted to learn the contours of my soul. He kissed it. And the scar that scorched my soul, depriving me of dignity, became an emblem of love and hope. He kissed the wound, and I was running, in my mind, back home in Igboland, flying over the countryside, chasing the antelopes with Ledu—I was running back home to hug Mama and Papa—I was loved.

The same spot that sealed my fate as a slave, now opened to me a door back to myself. It may not make sense, reader, and even as I write this, the words do not come easily. How can I explain how one kiss gave me permission to be myself? Teddy didn't see a slave girl; he saw a woman whom he had come to love. And through his eyes and through his touch,

I saw myself as I truly was—carefree, loveable, and loving. Independent, strong-willed, determined, I was not Olivia—I was Olu once again.

He opened a torrent of emotion in me, which escaped in an overflow of tears. Now I was the one crying. One gentle touch and I was undone. I wept . . . and wept. He held my head in his hands—he didn't ask why. I couldn't have explained it at the time. Now it was he who waited.

"You are something special, Olu. Oh God, you're so beautiful. I want to—may I kiss you?"

I think I said "yes" but I'd be surprised if he heard me. The mouth that had kissed my scar, tasted my lips, and I couldn't get enough. I'd been kissed a few times, awkwardly, always wondered what the point was. I see it now. His kiss lingered on and on, he was murmuring something about sweet lips. Then his hands began to roam over my body, and he showed me what it was to love—body and soul. He took me, and I reveled in it—I was his.

Still in the morning room, in an empty house, we slept naked, my back against his chest. He woke me by rising. The room was dark now, so it must have been hours later. I looked at him as he stood and thought, I wished we could stay together, be together. I pushed the thought aside. The impossibility of our ever being together seemed impenetrable. His brother owned me. And if I did manage to escape, what kind of life would I have? On the run, an escaped slave? I would enjoy the present, and love Teddy with all of me—my body, my mind, my spirit.

"How do you feel?" he asked me now.

"Wonderful. You?"

"Well, I thought you might be, you know. . . sore. It was your first time?"

"Um hmmm. I'm glad it was you."

"Me, too." Now he grinned and pulled me up to stand in front of him. I was a bit embarrassed to be standing there naked, but he seemed to love looking at me, so I looked right back at him.

"Come to my room, Olu. No one will be back tonight. Let me love you. Love me."

So, we did.

In the morning before Teddy awoke, I went up to my attic room, changed into one of my three day-frocks, and went downstairs to the kitchen to see if Martha had returned.

"Don' you look cheery today?" Martha said.

Could she see it, smell it, I wondered? Did she know I was no longer a virgin?

"I'm feeling well. I slept soundly and it's so nice to have an empty house."

Martha directed me harvest the herbs and go to the quarters to get more country pots. She asked me to make Teddy's breakfast, too.

"I wonder if he'll be able to tell my griddle cakes from yours." I teased Martha.

"Oh, he can tell. He's no fool, that man. And he surely knows his food." Martha grinned, confident her griddle cakes surpassed mine.

Teddy came down a half hour late, looking like a lion that just ate a hearty gazelle—eyes glazed with contentment and satisfaction.

"Good morning, Mr. Teddy." I greeted him as if I had not gotten out of his bed an hour ago.

"Mornin', Olu. Did you sleep well?" Teddy winked. How audacious! Thankfully, no one was in the room, or even on the first floor.

"It's about the best 'sleep' I ever had."

"Is that so. How delightful!"

"I hope I *sleep* as well tonight." I couldn't believe my brazen reply, but I wanted to keep our repartee alive and keep the grin on Teddy's face.

"I firmly believe you will. Yes, I predict you'll sleep very comfortably tonight." Teddy fondled me with his eyes.

I leaned over his shoulder to pour his coffee, purposely brushing my breast against his back.

In a fierce whisper, Teddy said, "You left my bed too soon. I had another lesson for you."

"I hope you will *instruct* me later today."

"How 'bout right now?" He put his hand over mine on the coffeepot handle and placed the pot on the table.

Martha walked in to see us in this position, me leaning over Teddy, him gazing up at me, with his hand over mine on the coffeepot.

Martha asked, "How'r them cakes, Mr. Teddy?"

"Oh, ah, I haven't tasted them yet. I'm sure, ahem, I'm sure they're delicious as always."

Teddy looked sunburned for a few moments.

"Here, let me serve you a nice tall stack—see if theys good as always." Martha challenged me with her eyes behind his back.

Teddy put a large bite of cakes, molasses, and blueberries in his mouth.

## CHAPTER FIFTEEN: OLU

"Mmmm. They taste good, though a bit different. Something's missing—but there's a new ingredient as well. They're not quite as fluffy as usual." Martha smirked.

"Well, be they as good as usual?" Martha asked.

"Mmm. As good? Yes, but different, in a nice way," Teddy said around bitefuls.

"Oh, you're impossible—couldn't you just say they're better or worse?"

"Nope. Why all the fuss?"

"I didn't make 'em—that's what!" Martha admitted.

"I see. You let Olu make 'em. And you wanted to know if they're as good as yours. I refuse to get between two ladies in the kitchen, especially two ladies whom I admire, who feed me. I will always come running for a taste of your griddle cakes, Miss Martha. But you have taught your pupil well."

Martha raised her eyebrows, and carried herself back downstairs, calling over her shoulder, "Don't forget they's still work to be done, Miss Olivia." She mumbled under her breath, "Pupil. Hmph. She be your pupil, too—or more'n that from the looks of it!"

"Yes'm. I'll clean up here when Mr. Teddy's done and get right to work."

I sat down beside Teddy, our knees touching.

"You're happy, aren't you?" Teddy asked, his green eyes firmly fixed on mine.

"Yes, Teddy. I am."

"You can't stay here, Olu. Come away with me? We can go north." Teddy took hold of my hands and held them fast in one of his.

"Teddy, do you forget? Your brother owns me. How can I run away with you? I'd put a rift between you that would never mend."

"You're more important to me than Sam, for God's sake. The loss of him is nothing compared to the loss of you—now that I've found you."

I let Teddy know I'd been planning to escape but waited for the right time. I didn't share the specifics of my plan yet. I asked if he'd heard of Lord Dunmore's proclamation.

"Yes, of course. Why?" Teddy peered at me.

"It's a way out for me. He's offering freedom, legitimate freedom to slaves."

"Yes, for those who want to fight. For male slaves. Not for females." Teddy shook his head.

"They must need cooking and nursing on those ships," I reasoned.

"It's too dangerous, Olu. How would you get all the way to Virginia?"

"I haven't worked it all out yet." What I had worked out, I didn't want to share with Teddy. Cap'n Thomas was ready to help me, and we had talked about tides and timing. A few other slaves were also ready to escape, and it could be any day now. I'd pack up one bag of provisions and meet Thomas at the river. Freedom was so close, yet so far.

"You could come with me—pretend to be my slave, till we reach the North."

"Pretend to . . ." I reared back, pulled my hands away, and put my hand on my chest, considering what Teddy said.

"I didn't mean it like that, Olu." Teddy pursed his lips and tilted his head.

I wanted to see his smile again, but his plan unnerved me. I wanted to stop being a slave, not escape by pretending to be someone else's slave, even if it was Teddy. I was hurt by his words but wanted the closeness we had recently enjoyed. I said, "Let's not speak of it anymore for now. Let's enjoy our time together."

We did.

For the next four days we lived in two worlds. With Mr. Samuel and Mrs. Beth both away, the house seemed less oppressive, more like a home than a prison, but I knew it was only temporary. I imagined it was our home. I resolved to enjoy these days together—the memories of our time together would have to last the rest of my life. I cherished every touch, memorized each loving word, captured every expression on Teddy's face.

Too soon Mr. Samuel returned, and our time together became stolen moments, rather than languishing hours. We were ever conscious of being caught or interrupted in our trysts. Teddy tiptoed up to my attic room in the early morning and left before dawn.

Three weeks after Teddy and I first made love, I missed my monthly. I never missed my monthly—not once. I knew what it meant, and I knew what Teddy would do if he knew, so I resolved to show my love for him in the only way I could. I planned my escape.

## 6 December 1775

Two days later I met Thomas at the dock as he unloaded goods from Charles Town. We spoke quietly about Lord Dunmore's proclamation, and Thomas said he had spoken to boat pilots at other plantations. Several were planning escapes via the river, some leaving soon. They were heading to Norfolk, Virginia to put themselves at the mercy of Lord Dunmore. I said I was ready to go, too. After questioning me about my ideas to offer services of midwifery and cooking, he agreed it might work. Nothing was holding me here. Well, nothing except my love for an exceptional man and the fact that I was carrying his child.

Thomas decided to stay. His freedom on the river, his wife and children were among his reasons. He'd take me to Charles Town to meet up with another boat pilot who would take me all the way to Virginia. Two days. I needed to be ready in two days.

I finally had an escape plan. I only hoped I could go through with it. My love for Teddy compelled me—there could be no life for us together. I was only doing what was best for him, so he could move on with his life. And I refused to give birth to a slave. My child would be born free. I harbored a small hope that we might find each other again, once I was free. But I had to be free first. I didn't want to continue our relationship while a slave. And I refused to birth our child to be a slave. It was time to leave. I had to place our future—Teddy, our child, and me—in God's hands.

Teddy inadvertently made my escape easier. He had agreed to go down river with his brother to check on some property Mr. Samuel was considering. The rice crops flourished, and he had extra ready cash, so he wanted another house farther inland. It could also be a place of refuge if the British invaded Charles Town.

I could not deny the perfect convergence of events—Teddy and Mr. Samuel gone, a warm spell, a schooner captain ready to go, and my pregnancy not yet evident. I knew if I didn't leave now, I probably never would; I thought it must be God's will for me to leave.

The night before Teddy left with his brother, he came up to my room in the early morning hours, as he was wont to do. The moon was almost full, bathing my room in soft light. I heard the floor creak, and the doorknob turn, and my heart paused, then quickened—the thought of spending our last night together infused my spirit, heightening my sensations and deepening my love. Without a word Teddy showed me how much he adored me, and I gave him all I had to give—one last time. He sensed the frenzied, painful joy, the severe sweetness of our lovemaking, and asked me, "Is everything all right, Olu? You know I love you?" Teddy asked.

"Yes, my love. I know, and I love you. Tonight, this morning, here in your arms . . . this is all I need."

"And tomorrow?" Teddy wondered aloud.

"Let's not talk of the morrow. Love me, Teddy." Exhausted by a love we couldn't quench, we slept. When I awoke, Teddy was gone.

The hardest part was not telling Teddy or Martha. But I couldn't endanger Martha and Teddy would either talk me out of leaving or accompany me. I bundled up my sparse belongings and food for the first leg of the journey and secreted away some potions. I rolled up my two frocks and some linens and inside I tucked a few country pots with healing herbs and roots, some rolls, cheese, nuts, and dried beef. The provisions were enough to last six people about three days. I didn't risk bringing any more. I did grab a pocketful of seeds, not knowing if I'd be in one place long enough to see them grow.

I trusted Thomas enough to put my life in his hands—and he risked his position for me. As it turned out, I was not to be the only passenger in the schooner that night. Samson, whose leg I had helped heal, his wife Maybell, and two slaves I didn't know would also be in the boat, along with Letty, one of the field slaves.

Minutes after midnight on December 8th I left the Cross Plantation for the last time. I wanted to leave Martha a note, but she couldn't read, so I left her a picture in the pantry on the shelf with all the herbs and roots. She was the only person who ever looked there, so it would be a safe place. I poorly drew a mother goose with six goslings trotting behind. One of the goslings was spreading her wings and taking flight. I only wish I could convey how much I loved Martha—my second mother.

# CHAPTER SIXTEEN

## Joanna

### 4 January 1815

Dinners at the Wilberforce home tended to be long, loud, loving affairs. This night was no different. Barbara and William, at seventeen and nineteen years of age, now ate with the adults, so I sat next to my best friend. Henry Bromley was there as William's guest, and there were a few guests I didn't know, but I was happy to see Sadie again. After the turtle soup and roasted pheasant, the main course, mutton stew, was served. Mr. Wilberforce and Uncle John were deeply engaged in a private conversation when Mrs. Wilberforce said, "Wilby, tomorrow is Twelfth Night."

"Ah, tomorrow, is it? So soon. What do we have planned for festivities, my dear?"

"If the weather holds out the boys will no doubt want to engage in races."

"Of course. Only the boys? What about the men?"

"Wilby dear, you may race as well." Mrs. Wilberforce smiled at her husband.

Fredrik added, "I'd like to join that race."

"Ha! I'm glad I'm not a betting man anymore. I'd have to decide whether to put my wager on Fredrik or William. William has the advantage of youth, no offense to you Fredrik," Mr. Wilberforce said.

"None taken, sir." Fredrik nodded.

"However, Fredrik has the advantage of longer legs, and a wider stride. This will be a true competition. Henry, I hope you will join in," Mr. Wilberforce lifted his head in Henry's direction.

Henry replied, "I'm better on long distance, but I'll do my best."

Mrs. Wilberforce directed her husband and Mr. Macaulay to plan the games. Mr. Wilberforce reminded her they must play Blind Man's Buff and looked over at Sadie and me. Barbara explained the game: One person has a blindfold and is turned about this way and that. Then the blindfolded person must find and touch another player. The one who is touched becomes the blind man. Mr. Wilberforce claimed Fredrik secretly loved Blind Man's Buff and declared Fredrik would be the first one to be the blind man.

As we ate dinner, I quietly asked Barbara if she knew Sadie was born in Virginia and if she thought she was pretty. Barbara thought Sadie was born in England. She glanced at Sadie, who was speaking with Mrs. Wilberforce. "Her eyes are a bit rounder, and closer together. And her nose is more pointed, not stretched out like yours."

I kicked Barbara under the table.

"Ouch!" A few heads turned in our direction.

"Her eyebrows are thinner, and her forehead is smaller," Barbara continued.

"I'm sorry I ever said anything," I mumbled.

"And her hair." Barbara looked closely at me, then back at Sadie, who was now looking at us with a hesitant smile.

"Stop looking at her." I nudged Barbara with my elbow.

"How do you expect me to determine how pretty she is without looking at her?"

"Please forget I mentioned it," I pleaded.

"I'm almost finished. Her hair is a bit lighter than yours, more of a medium brown. And it looks softer."

"She's prettier."

"She's different, in some small ways, and you're both beautiful. It's amazing really. She could be your mother."

"Except for the fact that my mother was a White woman," I reminded Barbara.

"Yes, except for that!" Barbara laughed.

Dessert arrived, a tasty bread pudding. Barbara and I stopped talking while we savored dessert. After dinner, the men retired to the drawing room, and the women went to the morning room.

Mrs. Wilberforce claimed she wouldn't have such a big healthy family without Sadie. Sadie delivered all six of her children—calming her, walking with her, allowing her to act very undignified. She recommended

# CHAPTER SIXTEEN: JOANNA

Sadie to all her expecting friends. She said the best decision Sadie ever made was to leave Nova Scotia and come to England. Mrs. Wilberforce reached out and patted Sadie's back.

"I've had enough patients to keep three midwives occupied," Sadie added.

"But everyone wants you, dear. Well, let's join the men in the drawing room."

I walked with Sadie into the drawing room.

"It's so nice to see you again. I thought you were from Virginia. You lived in Nova Scotia?" I inquired.

"Yes. My mama, papa, and I moved to Canada at the end of the war. I don't remember Virginia at all. I don't remember New York City either. Nova Scotia is much colder than England. And not nearly as green, nor as pretty." Sadie shivered a little.

"If you don't mind my asking, I thought Nova Scotia had only Canadians."

"Mostly. But there are a few villages of free Africans who settled there in the late 1700s."

"That's fascinating. It seems like most of what we learned was all about England and our history."

Right then Fredrik came over, bending slightly and greeting me and Sadie. He claimed we looked like sisters. Sadie patted his arm and said she was probably old enough to be my mother. When Fredrik asked Sadie if she was staying for the games tomorrow, I glanced over to see her response. Sadie laughed and said she wouldn't miss it, unless of course she was called away for a patient who was already confined. She let Fredrik know Blind Man's Buff was loads of fun and we should all expect a lot of laughter, and running, and some falling—but hopefully the falling would be done by the children. Sadie advised me to wear sturdy shoes and a plain dark frock—to hide the grass stains!

When I awoke the following morning, I smiled as I drew back the curtain. The sun shone brightly in the cloudless sky and no dew wet the grass—a perfect day for outdoor games. I felt a bit giddy, like a girl instead of a young woman, nearing the mature age of one and twenty. When I heard a knock on the door, I quickly donned my robe and said, "Come in."

Barbara rushed into the room taking both of my hands in her own. She exclaimed over the glorious day, marched me over to the window to look outside, and rushed me to dress for breakfast. She had already consumed her cup of chocolate and reminded me to go to the parlour in fifteen minutes for morning devotions.

I quickly washed up and dressed, in a light-coloured morning dress and slippers, and went downstairs to join the morning devotional. Mrs. Limebear did not emphasize spiritual discipline. We girls had to attend church on Sunday and offer thanks at meals, but no further devotion was expected or encouraged. From the age of fourteen, I had formed the habit of reading the bible nightly and praying. I knew both my parents were devout Christians, though Uncle John and Grandmamma's religious life consisted solely of attending church. As I read Papa's memoir, and books by other Christian writers, my understanding of and love for God grew. All the losses I experienced in my life drove me to the grace of God. And the godly influence of William Wilberforce was more potent than I realized at the time.

Mr. Wilberforce greeted us all and praised the fine morning. He had already taken a walk in the garden and proclaimed the day auspicious for outdoor activities. Mrs. Wilberforce agreed, reminding him of the previous year when there were several inches of snow on the ground.

Mr. Wilberforce led out in prayer from the Book of Common Prayer. When he concluded, everyone chimed in "Amen."

Then he read a passage from Romans chapter five. Mr. Wilberforce explained that Paul's letter to the Romans clearly laid out the doctrine of salvation through faith and faith alone. In chapter three Paul explains how all have sinned, and no one is found righteous. And in chapter four, he reminds the Jews that the law, circumcision, and works will not help one obtain salvation. Paul begins chapter five with, 'Therefore being justified by faith, we have peace with God through our Lord Jesus Christ.' He asked his son Sammy, "what is peace?"

"Not fighting, Papa?" Sammy asked.

"Yes, yes. That's true. But peace is more than the absence of conflict."

"May I?" Henry Bromley asked.

"Certainly. What say you, Henry?" Mr. Wilberforce asked.

"Peace is positive. It is . . . the presence of calmness, joy, serenity, contentment."

"Indeed. All the aforementioned. Well done, Henry. I hear you have an interest in becoming a minister. Maybe you would like to lead the devotion tomorrow morning."

Henry said he would be honoured, and I looked at him, thinking he seemed grounded, mature beyond his years.

## CHAPTER SIXTEEN: JOANNA

"Children. A few minutes of silent meditation please," Mr. Wilberforce called out.

The boys looked down at their feet, counting off the seconds. After about two long minutes, Mr. Wilberforce said "amen"—the cue to go to breakfast. Little Henry and Sammy raced upstairs, while Robert and Lizzy followed slowly. The four younger children still ate their meals in the nursery with Miss Lindsay.

Barbara, Sadie, and I filled our plates with fried eggs, fried tomatoes, biscuits, sausages, and potatoes. As we ate, Mr. Wilberforce said the games would commence mid-afternoon, after it warmed up a bit outside. Sadie mentioned visiting a friend in the neighborhood on the other side of Hyde Park. She asked if Barbara and I could accompany her. Mr. and Mrs. Wilberforce consented, so the three of us prepared for a walk.

I tried hard not to let my feelings show, though inwardly I was smiling widely. Sadie said we were going to see Miss Frances—I hadn't seen her since she came to Uncle John's with the petition. I longed to know more about the Anti-Slavery Society. Maybe I was old enough to join now. The three of us were soon ready to go; we met downstairs by the front door.

Sadie said Miss Frances remembered me and Anne well. Out of the hundreds of women they visited, we made an impression on her. Being a woman of colour might be a factor, I thought. I mentioned that Anne had already contacted some of the women of the Chelmsford Ladies' Anti-Slavery Society. Abolition had become her passion ever since she met Sadie and Miss Frances.

Barbara wondered aloud if her papa would approve of their visit. Sadie doubted it, which is why she referred to Frances as a friend instead of the leader of an Anti-Slavery Society. Within a half hour we had reached Miss Frances' home and were ushered into the drawing room, where at least a dozen women were seated, excitement and animation infused their conversation.

Miss Frances came over and greeted the three of us, hugging Sadie and me. Sadie introduced Barbara.

"Charmed! To have the daughter of William Wilberforce, who has fought as hard as anyone for abolition, is truly an honour. May I ask, does he know you're here?" Frances tilted her head.

"He knows I'm visiting a friend of Miss Sadie's. He doesn't know I'm visiting the leader of the Ladies Anti-Slavery Society of London!" Barbara admitted.

"I'm incredibly happy to have you in my home." Miss Frances turned to me. "Miss Joanna, you are a young lady now. You graduated from school?"

"Yes, last year. I'm nineteen now. Am I old enough to join the Society?"

"You are! Come with me. I'll introduce you to some other young ladies around your age." Miss Frances took me by the hand.

I met four young ladies who ranged in age from twenty to twenty-three. I noticed that everyone in the drawing room was White, except for Sadie and me. I also noticed that we didn't get any surprised glances or stares. I saw a few petitions spread out over tables and women engaged in reading the names and counting the signatures.

"Ladies, many of you already know Miss Sadie Cross, my partner in the parliamentary battles, and this is Miss Barbara Wilberforce and Miss Joanna Vassa. Let's sit down and begin our discussion, shall we?" Miss Frances had all the ladies' attention.

Barbara sat next to me and gazed out over the room full of women dedicated to the same cause her father had fought for over many years. I saw a tear slide down her cheek, and I squeezed her hand. Barbara said she often saw men come and talk to her papa, but she had no idea so many women were involved. I told her I planned to join the society and encouraged her to join.

"I want to, of course. But I don't think I could hide this from Papa. I would have to get his permission," Barbara said.

"You might be surprised. He might encourage you," I said.

Miss Frances summarized the latest petition campaign and called on various women to read out the numbers of signatures they had gathered. After about ten minutes, we were interrupted by the butler standing in the drawing room doorway.

"So sorry to disturb you, Miss Frances. There is a Mr. William Wilberforce here for a Miss Sadie Cross."

Sadie asked, "Is he an older gentleman or a young man?"

"He's young, ma'am," the butler answered.

"It must be your brother, Barbara. I imagine my patient Mrs. McCorkle needs my services," Sadie said. "I'm so sorry ladies, but my midwifery duties call. I'll see you at the next meeting." Sadie gave Miss Frances a quick goodbye hug, and Sadie, Barbara, and I left quickly to see William, who was pacing in the front hallway.

William said a page had come to the house with an urgent note that she was needed at Mrs. McCorkle's home immediately. William was out of breath and spoke quickly. Sadie asked him how he got here; William had ridden the mare. Sadie looked thoughtful, and asked William if she could take the mare, while William walked me and Barbara back to the house. William looked doubtful.

"I've ridden bigger and wilder horses than Grace. Trust me, William. I need to get there quickly, and this is the best way." Sadie assured William she would be fine and had everything she needed. She promised to send the horse back with a servant. William helped Sadie mount the horse while holding her bag, and she rode off to catch a baby.

We watched Sadie ride down the road and I was thinking what an amazing woman she was—an abolitionist, a midwife, and a horsewoman! William walked with Barbara and I back to Gore House, Barbara quietly asking me questions about the Society, disappointed at having to leave so quickly.

When we got back to Gore House, William went into the house, while Barbara and I quickly changed into dark frocks and sturdy shoes. I told Uncle John I was joining the outdoor games; he was working on a case in Mr. Wilberforce's study. When we walked to the backyard, we could hear the laughter and yelling of Barbara's younger brothers, and we saw Mr. Wilberforce, Fredrik, and Henry Bromley.

"Let the games begin!" Barbara yelled. Sammy and Robert were rolling hoops on the ground—Sammy was ahead. When Sammy turned to brag to his brother he lost his hoop, which rolled a few feet and fell over. Robert swished on past and won the race.

"Focus on the goal, Sammy, not your opponent," his papa encouraged him.

Sammy frowned and challenged his brother. "Let's do it again."

Barbara came over and grabbed a hoop and stick. "I'm in," she declared.

"No girls!" yelled Sammy.

"I'm not a girl, I'm your sister!" Barbara insisted.

"You look like a girl to me," Robert grumbled.

"You can't be afraid a girl will beat you?" Barbara teased.

"Come on, then," Sammy said, predictably.

Hoops at the ready, their papa counted down and the race began. As they neared the finish, all three close together, Sammy looking straight ahead, their dog Wolf ran out from the side of the house and into Barbara's hoop, knocking it over. Sammy won.

"Yipee! I won!" Sammy cried.

"That's not fair. Wolf knocked mine over. That's interference," Barbara complained.

"I think Barbara wants a rematch." Mr. Wilberforce grabbed his own hoop and stick.

By now, Mrs. Wilberforce, William, Henry, and Fredrik were all looking on, along with Joanna. The fearless foursome, Mr. Wilberforce, Barbara, Sammy, and Robert, began the race—after William did the countdown: " 3 — 2 — 1 — GO!"

Mrs. Wilberforce cheered, "Wilby, go Wilby, do be careful, dear—go Wilby."

"Come on, Sammy; you can do it," cheered Fredrik.

"Go Barbara! Go Barbara!" I yelled.

"Ro-bert, Ro-bert!" William chanted. No dogs or mishaps marred the race, so the boys had no one to blame when Barbara won.

Barbara grinned, holding up her hoop. Mr. Wilberforce patted her on the back. Sammy grumbled, "Beaten by a girl."

Robert replied, "She's not a girl; she's our sister!"

After hoops, the pillowcases came out for the three-legged race. Barbara was paired with Lizzy, Robert with William, Sammy and his papa, little Henry with Fredrik, which left me with Henry Bromley. I smiled at Henry and said, "welcome to the madness!" We each put one leg in the sack and held it up with our hands.

"Line up here, a straight line, if you please. Now you will run, or walk, or limp, swiftly to the walnut tree. Touch the tree (you must both touch the tree) and return to the starting line. If you fall, simply get up and keep going. No bumping or pushing! All set?" Mrs. Wilberforce asked.

"Yes mama," "Yes ma'am," "Let's go," they all chimed. Mrs. Wilberforce counted down, "3. . .2. . .1. . .GO!" Barbara and Lizzy started out ahead, but then they started giggling uncontrollably, slowing them down. William and Robert were neck in neck with Sammy and Mr. Wilberforce, so when the girls slowed down, William and Robert pulled ahead. Little Henry and Fredrik were making a run for first place, and Henry and I were in the rear, as it was the first time either of us had played the game.

"We need to move our inside legs together" Henry suggested, as we struggled to move forward without falling.

"Oh . . ." I said, almost falling, and leaning against Henry for support.

"Here." Henry helped me stand, "Let's count so we move together. On one we move the outside leg, on two, the inside leg."

"One, two; one, two." We got a steady beat and pulled ahead of Sammy and Mr. Wilberforce, and alongside the laughing sisters.

"Joanna?! How did you catch up? Let's go, Lizzy!" Barbara urged.

Lizzy and Barbara stopped giggling and sped up, causing Henry and I to go back to counting. I was distracted by the cheering, and lost count, stumbling into Henry, who fell into Barbara, who toppled Lizzy. The four of us stacked on top of each other, with Lizzy on the bottom and me on top. We were laughing so hard it took some time for us to get up. Meanwhile, Robert and William had reached the tree and were racing back to the finish line, unscathed. Henry and I got up first, helping each other up, holding hands, briefly, and repositioning the pillowcase. We quickly continued racing. Barbara and Lizzy hopped up and raced after us, not to be outdone.

"No fair, Mama. They fell on us." Barbara complained loudly, still running and grinning.

"All's fair in a three-legged race. Keep racing."

Henry and I reached the tree and pulled up right behind Sammy and Mr. Wilberforce. First to reach the finish line ran William and Robert, followed by Sammy and his papa, with Henry and I, laughing and panting close behind. Barbara and Lizzy and Fredrik and Little Henry tied for last place. Henry looked quite handsome with his hair windblown, slightly out of breath, laughing. I noticed gold flecks in his brown irises. Yes, quite attractive.

"Blind Man's Buff is next. Fredrik, if I recall correctly, has graciously agreed to be the blind man first. Now, let's set the rules. We cannot use ALL the grounds, but only from the back of the house to that line of trees on the east, to the garden on the west, and the pond on the north. Mrs. Wilberforce will alert the blind man if he or she nears a tree or other obstacle," Mr. Wilberforce explained.

Mrs. Wilberforce came forward, pulling out her long, dark scarf with a flourish. The younger kids gathered around full of excitement and energy. Fredrik, William, and Barbara held back a bit, but Barbara nudged Fredrik forward. "You're up, sir. The day of reckoning has arrived."

Fredrik went forward, Mrs. Wilberforce turned him around and reached up to secure the scarf around his eyes. Fredrik had to bend his knees a bit so she could reach. Mrs. Wilberforce turned him once, twice, three times around. Fredrik counted down from ten slowly, while the kids, old and young, including Mr. Wilberforce, scattered, and Fredrik began his quest.

Barbara, Lizzy, Henry and I walked swiftly but quietly back towards the pond. William ran to the trees on the right, Sammy and Little Henry ran around the fountain right in the middle of the game area; Robert wandered over to the garden, while Mr. Wilberforce planted himself a little north of the fountain to keep an eye on everyone else.

"Ready or not, here I come," Fredrik hollered, and struck out to the right, by the trees. "I'm the blind man, and I'm coming to get you," Fredrik called out. As he approached the pond Mrs. Wilberforce said, "Have a care, Fredrik. The fountain is ahead of you." Fredrik started walking awkwardly, arms extended, toward the back, where Barbara, Henry and I were. "Well done, Fredrik, you're doing fine," Mr. Wilberforce called out. Fredrik turned in the direction of his voice, only to be distracted by the sound of running feet. Sammy and Little Henry were running right toward Barbara and me. Fredrik followed the sound of their footsteps, and could hear Barbara's hushed voice, "Go away. You boys are cheating. Scram!"

Fredrik picked up the pace, following the sounds, extending his arms, hearing breaking twigs and grunts and . . . "Aahhhh." His right hand connected with a . . . head! Fredrik snatched off his scarf to see a red-faced Sammy, looking upset.

"That was a bad idea, Henry!" Sammy said.

"Wonderful. Now we have a new blind man. Here you go, Sammy." Mr. Wilberforce fastened the scarf around his head. In less than five minutes Sammy collided with Robert when Sammy turned abruptly and reached out his arms. Robert caught his papa, who relished being the blind man, though his wife fussed over him.

"Careful there, dear. You're approaching a tree. Go off to the right, Wilby; Barbara's right there. No, left dear," she intoned, on and on, until Mr. Wilberforce finally caught Lizzy. We played for over two hours, until everyone had been the blind man, Mr. Wilberforce twice, and we were all tired and happy. I thought, not for the first time, that I would love to have a large family. I glanced over at Fredrik, and then at Henry.

Mrs. Wilberforce, who had watched and warned and guided from the sidelines, led everyone back into the house, where the cook had prepared tea, and chocolate for the children. Miss Lindsay brought Robert, Sammy, Little Henry, and Lizzy upstairs to change and have a snack. We young adults went up to our rooms to change.

It took me an hour to get dressed. I wore a sage green, long-sleeved gown, with matching slippers and my hair up in a French braid. I came downstairs with Barbara, who wore a pale blue gown, with short puffy sleeves, and dark blue slippers.

"Aren't you girls as pretty as a picture?" Mrs. Wilberforce declared, greeting us from the drawing room.

At dinner, I sat next to Fredrik and across from Zachary and Selina Macaulay.

"How is the settlement in Sierra Leone faring, Mr. Macaulay? I haven't heard you speak of it in quite a while," Fredrik asked. I knew Papa had been involved in early efforts to repatriate slaves to Sierra Leone. The plan was to send freed Loyalist slaves who fought on the side of the British in the American Revolution to Sierra Leone. The freed slaves would form a colony in Sierra Leone, with support from the British government and private donors. Salaries for a minister, doctors, and educators were all arranged. I knew from conversations with Uncle John and Mr. Wilberforce that Papa had reservations about the plan, as slave dealers were still active on the West Coast of Africa. The 'back to Africa' movement was flawed from the start, as most of the freed slaves had never even been to Africa. I also knew that when Papa questioned what some of the English men were planning, how funds were being used, and how the ex-slaves were being treated, he was dismissed from his position. The first attempts were a dismal failure, and more than half of the freed slaves who went to Sierra Leone died of disease.

Mr. Macaulay said the colony in Sierra Leone was doing well, the ex-slaves were adjusting, and the fishing and farming were sustaining the people. Fredrik inquired if ships were still going over with people wanting to emigrate.

"It would be quite something to see Africa again. I often think of my childhood there, and wonder what has become of my family," Fredrik said.

"Well, Fredrik, if you're serious, there is a ship going over in a few months. May, I believe. There are free Africans, and even some British going out. Some will stay, and some will return with the ship. As you know, that was the original plan when you came over for schooling. That you would return home and lead your people."

"It's tempting, I'll admit. Though I have established myself here, speaking the King's English. I hardly even remember my native tongue, Susu." Fredrik looked pensive.

"That would come back quickly enough."

England was home and the thought of moving to Africa held no appeal for me. If Fredrik went back to Africa, I would miss him, but we had no formal understanding. And besides, even marriage to Fredrik would not be enough to entice me to move to Africa.

"Now, then," Mr. Wilberforce said, "our outdoor revels have ended, but the night is young. Who is ready for a chess tournament? We have two boards, so let's say . . . round one I'll play . . . Macaulay, who else is in?" Mr. Wilberforce asked.

"I'll play Joanna, Papa," ventured Barbara, "though she's sure to beat me."

"Splendid. Who else? Audley? Fredrik? Henry?" Mr. Wilberforce asked.

"Certainly, William," Uncle John replied.

"I'm ready, sir," Fredrik answered.

After dinner ended, the chess games began. In the first round I beat Barbara, and Macaulay won the game with Mr. Wilberforce, after he was distracted by the cat and lost his queen. Then Fredrik played me, and Uncle John played Henry.

"I didn't know you've thought about returning to Africa," I said to Fredrik between moves.

"Yes, I do from time to time. More, lately, I think. As I get older, I think about my family more, and the desire to see them grows."

"I can understand that. Family is important. I think you should go," I said, despite my wishes to the contrary.

"You do?" Fredrik looked at me and leaned forward.

"Yes, I do. It's important to you. You would regret it if you didn't go."

"It's all just a dream. But it's nice to dream," Fredrik said.

As I prepared for bed that night, I thought about Henry and Fredrick. Henry's open countenance reflected his emotions: wide smile and laugh conveyed joy; furrowed brow meant confusion or contemplation; tilted head conveyed pondering. Without being overt, his actions and gestures showed his interest in me. On the occasions we had been together—practices, performance, graduation, Gore House—whenever I glanced at him, he was already looking at me, assessing and admiring. Fredrik was polite and deferential to everyone, not preferential to me. Though older than Henry, he seemed restless, less settled, admiring but not pursuing me. And Fredrik may soon return to Africa. I fell asleep wondering—if it were my choice, whom would I choose??

# CHAPTER SEVENTEEN

## Olu

### 8 December 1775

CAPTAIN THOMAS HAD A plan for us to meet him at various checkpoints along the Ashley River. My meeting point was a ten-minute walk away, past the rice fields, a third of the way to the neighboring plantation.

Leaving my attic room, I walked barefoot down the hall to the back stairs, tiptoed down to the first floor and out the back. I made my way to the front of the house, turned right, and glanced back at the house one last time, only to see Mrs. Beth gazing at me from her bedroom window. Then the curtains closed, and I wondered if I had seen her at all. It was a dark night, clouds obscured the moon and it had turned colder. I turned to the path and trudged ahead, praying beyond hope Mrs. Beth would not give me up.

Much later I learned Mrs. Beth had indeed not given me up. While she approved of slavery, she still protected me. She kept my secret while Teddy and Mr. Samuel were gone, alerting no one. When they returned a week later, she still didn't inform her husband for another day.

Reaching the meeting place before Captain Thomas, I sat on a rock—up away from the river, on the edge of a grove of trees. I heard the hooting of an owl, no, two owls, and the deep burp of frogs. I sat immobile, tucking my bare feet under my dress—hovering between slavery and freedom.

I imagined Martha's reaction when I didn't appear to help with breakfast in the morning, her discovery of my crude picture. Unlike my parents' doubtless grief at losing Ledu and me, I pictured Martha shaking her head, clucking her tongue, and smiling. Or something like that.

My reverie was interrupted by the soft, swishing sound of the schooner approaching. It glided on top of the water, leaving barely a ripple, like the long-legged bugs that walk on water. Carefully climbing down from the rock, I noticed Captain Thomas in the front and another man, whom I soon learned was Will, holding a steering instrument of wood in the back. I scrambled down to the river as the schooner slid up near the bank, gathered my skirts, held up my boots and belongings, and waded out to the boat.

No words of greeting were given, but nods of welcome and gestures that I should lie down under a canvas tarp. My feet and legs were cold from the water, so the covering felt good. The schooner was larger than I remembered. Of course, I had only seen it at the dock, and I'd never been on it. The bottom was hard, and I felt powerless, not able to see where we were going.

A short time later we stopped, and I heard two pairs of feet board the boat. Not much later two more pairs of feet came aboard, and then the covering above me lifted and I was joined by Letty and Maybell, two of the female slaves who worked in the rice fields on the plantation. The seven of us left the Cross Plantation on the Ashley River.

I must have fallen asleep. Letty nudged me and whispered, "Miss Olivia, we getting off here—going to that boat yonder. Cap'n Thomas say be quiet, get your things. He be goin' back. Nathaniel's the new pilot taking us upriver."

I emerged from the tarp cocoon and saw Letty and Maybell on a bench in the middle of the boat, arms wrapped around their meager belongings. Samson and Ambrose, the first pair to come aboard, had hopped out and waded knee deep in the water, carrying ropes, while Captain Thomas and Will were moving about, tying down sails.

I checked to make sure I had all my things, craned my neck back to look up at the moon, trying to determine the time. "How long've we been gone?" I asked no one in particular. Ambrose said we'd been on the river two hours and needed to get as far from Charles Town as quickly as possible to avoid recapture. Letty was glad Mr. Cross was away but didn't trust Mrs. Cross. I kept quiet.

Captain Thomas said to all of us, "I'm heading back. It won't do to give y'all away and get in trouble myself besides. Here's Nathaniel. He's a good man—I's known him these fifteen years. He be ready to go, too—and he knows these waters. He'll take you up the coast, by night, then upriver, into the Great Swamp, and on up to Norfolk where Lord Dunmore be stationed. Godspeed."

I hugged Captain Thomas hard, surprising him. "Thank you, Thomas, for risking your life for us. I'll never forget you." I leaned close and whispered, "About a week after Teddy returns, tell him I've gone north." Thomas looked at me, his brows furrowed over his nose, then a slow grin lit his face. "Yes, Miss. I tell 'im."

I had kept my promise. I didn't know if I'd ever see Teddy again—if he would ever meet his son or daughter. But I knew I had to escape. I wouldn't look back.

Thomas turned back to the others, helping Maybell and Letty off the schooner and onto the next boat. Back in the water, skirts lifted high, we walked to Nathaniel's sloop. It was a little more than half the size of the Cross schooner with only one set of sails. I had a sudden premonition it wouldn't carry us all to freedom.

Captain Thomas waved us on, gathered up the ropes, and turned about to head back upriver to the plantation before he was discovered missing. Nathaniel was younger than Thomas, darker than the night sky, and serious about his role in our escape. We were putting our lives in his hands, and I wasn't sure my trust in Thomas extended to him—but I had no choice. Thomas was already sailing away. We were committed.

Nathaniel tersely ordered Ambrose, Will, and Samson to untie ropes and secure ropes as we women sat hunched over on the only bench. Without the covering, the ubiquitous mosquitoes began biting me. Nathaniel said we had to skirt Charles Town, get around Sullivan's Island, and up the coast before pulling in and hiding out during the day. Charles Town was quiet and dark, sporadic streetlamps on the major roads lit houses resting side by side. An occasional horse with a single rider trotted by. The narrow houses were all two stories, painted in a rainbow of pastel colors. Only a few houses emitted light. As we cruised the docks, a drunken soldier staggered down the road beside us. Hatless, shirt hanging out of his breeches, bottle in one swaying hand's grasp, he sang poorly and looked up as we passed.

"Ha, a slave ship—comin' or goin'—good rid . . . riddance!"

The men ignored him, but we women were frightened by the possibility of discovery. We passed the drunken man, saw him trip, stumble and fall over into a tree. The last time I saw him he was hugging the tree and singing loud and off-key.

At least he took my mind off the mosquitoes temporarily, now insidious, finding any exposed skin and feasting away. I swatted one on my cheek, then my arm. Nathaniel laughed at me. "Don' mind these mosquitoes—don' you know some of them be bigger than a bird. Only one thing keeps 'squitoes away."

"What's that?" I couldn't wait to hear, slapping myself on the forehead to kill another one.

"Garlic. Wear it round your neck and eat it. 'Squitoes don' like no garlic. I brought some, but it'll get worse than this, so we'll wait on't." I didn't believe him, but he was right. It did get worse.

Nathaniel expertly piloted the sloop by himself, occasionally asking for a hand from one of the men. Before dawn, he maneuvered the boat into an inlet, almost a cave. The whole time, since we left Charles Town at midnight, the boat hugged the shore. We could see fields and plantations past the sandy shore, but they were few and far between. The land we passed now appeared uncultivated; the trees were thick, giving way to marshy grass. It didn't look inviting, but it was devoid of human activity, so Nathaniel deemed it safe, and we pulled up alongside the shore, hiding the sloop in the swampy grass. Nathaniel jumped out and secured the boat to a tree. I almost wished we were back at the plantation.

Letty saw something move in the water and stifled a scream. I saw it too and hoped it wasn't a bad omen. A large alligator, at least six feet or more, slithered through the water defending his territory. I didn't want to get out of the boat. We waited minutes, which felt like hours, until the alligator moved on. Then you never saw three tired runaway slaves move so fast. We nimbly and numbly stood up, lifted our legs to jump out of the boat and into the cold water, skirts held high, all our earthly goods wrapped up tight and balanced on our heads. Ambrose took the liberty to put his two large, rough hands on my waist—a bit too high. It really wasn't necessary for his fingers to rub up against my breasts. He lifted me out of the boat, swinging me over the side and plopping me in the water. I mumbled "thank ye kindly" while fuming inside. Samson carried Maybell to land, a benefit of married life, then Ambrose lifted Letty out of the boat as well. She was a bit more grateful than me and gave him a quick hard kiss on the mouth—delighting Ambrose and angering Will.

Once we were all on a patch of dry land, Nathaniel led us into a grove of trees to set up camp for the day. This became our routine for the next several weeks—travel at night, hide out and sleep during the day. The mosquito bites were itching something awful, but Letty and I seemed

## CHAPTER SEVENTEEN: OLU

to have it worst. On our short walk I looked for any plant that might ease the itching. I didn't find any aloe, but I did spot a tubular plant that looked promising, so I stopped to pull off some stalks. I was desperate and ignored Martha's advice to never use an unknown plant. I figured I'd test it on myself before I used it on Letty or anyone else.

Nathaniel led us, followed by Samson, then Maybell, Letty, Will, me and finally Ambrose. When I stopped to pluck the leaves, they continued, leaving Ambrose and I separated from the rest.

"Whatcha got there miss? Fitting to make a potion? I hope it's a love potion!" Ambrose grinned.

I placed the stalky leaves in my pack and continued walking, to catch up with the rest. "More like mosquito poison. I'm focused on only one thing right now. Getting as far away as possible from the Cross plantation and as close as possible to Lord Dunmore."

"Lucky Lord Dunmore," he mumbled. "That don' mean we can't enjoy the trip!?"

I didn't know how to respond, so I simply picked up my bundle and headed off down the path where I had last seen Will, who appeared on the path in front of me from the left, walking toward us.

"We need to stay together, Nathaniel says. Keep up you two," he winked at Ambrose as he spoke.

"Hmph," was all Ambrose had to say.

The sun began to peek over the horizon, adding a faint patina of pink to the air. The marsh smelled of wet linen; an unmistakable womanly, musty scent; a warm poultice all rolled up in a humid mist. As dawn broke, birds greeted the sun, chattering and singing in the new day—reveling in their freedom, as we all did. I found out later that on this day, December 9, as we greeted the welcoming dawn, looking forward to freedom through Lord Dunmore, that selfsame Lord Dunmore was beaten badly in a fight with Patriots south of Norfolk.

Nathaniel dragged a tarp from the boat and tied it to three trees in a small clearing—forming a triangle of shelter. "We's best get some sleep. Any o' you men's got weapons?" Nathaniel inquired.

Ambrose had Mr. Cross' hunting rifle, and a small handgun; Will had a knife; and Samson sneaked off a shotgun and Jones' best whip. They also had bullets and munitions. Nathaniel told the men they would take turns guarding the women and their provisions. He took the first shift.

"I have a question," I volunteered, already annoyed at being relegated to "the womens" and not even asked if I had a gun. Nathaniel shot me an annoyed look. "Yeah?"

"What's the plan for our route?"

"Well miss, I plans to travel by night, up the coast of Carolina, till we reach Winyah Bay. We be on the ocean till then. Then go inland on Waccamaw River to the lake. Then we needs to find smaller rivers up to the Great Dismal Swamp, and from there we leaves our boat and travels by land till we gets close to Norfolk. Then we probably needs to take small rowboats, through the swamps, to the shore, and out into the harbor to Lord Dunmore's ship. That's the plan, but we needs to be flexible."

Letty wanted to know how long it would take—two to three weeks or more. Maybell wanted to know what we would eat—whatever we could kill, fish, trap, or steal. As we 'womens' were questioning Nathaniel, the men finished tying up the tarp and laying down palmetto leaves to cover the dirt and rocks. We were surrounded by water, but I didn't know if it was safe to drink. I asked Nathaniel if he planned to light a fire, so I could boil the water. He looked at me askance and replied tersely, "No fire. I don' wanna draw attention on our first day out. The water's fine . . . I 'magine."

Maybell had brought two tin cups, which we took turns using, walking back to the swamp and dipping it in—I prayed we wouldn't get dysentery and drank a full cup myself. I pulled out the leaf and rubbed it on the most bothersome bites.

Sleeping accommodations were tricky. I preferred to sleep next to Letty or Maybell, as I didn't trust any of the men, except Samson, and maybe not even him. We ended up sleeping side by side—for warmth and safety. The men slept on the outside, Nathaniel and Ambrose were bookends. Next to Nathaniel was Will, then Letty, me, Maybell, Samson and Ambrose. Hard ground, cool air, sunlight shining through the trees, and fear of capture all kept me awake briefly. But soon exhaustion set in and I slept.

During the day I snuggled up to Maybell, who generated warmth, and Letty and Will looked inseparable. When I opened my eyes, Ambrose was sitting up with the rifle across his lap, and Nathaniel was gone. Everyone else slept. I hurried off into the bushes, and when I returned Maybell and Samson were getting up. Ambrose nodded at me—I smiled in return. I didn't want animosity between us for the long journey, but I didn't want to encourage him either. I looked through my bundle and pulled out some hard rolls and a small wedge of cheese. I handed one roll to Maybell, broke mine in half and handed half to Ambrose, along with a small piece of cheese—an olive branch.

"Thankee, miss," Ambrose offered.

"I didn't bring much, but it should last a day or two," I said.

"We needs to hunt and fish," Ambrose replied.

"You catch it—I'll cook it," I promised.

"Ye have yourself a deal, missy." Ambrose winked at me.

When everyone was up, Nathaniel and Will took down the tarp, folded it up, and Ambrose messed up our sleeping quarters. I looked at my arm where I had rubbed the leaf, and it seemed a little better than the bites I hadn't applied it to; there was no negative reaction. I gave a leaf to Letty, and one to Maybell.

We settled into a routine over the next several days—sailing at night and sleeping by day. I remembered my trip into slavery, walking by night and sleeping by day. Now I was on a reverse path by water, baptized into freedom.

We all got along well, except Will and Ambrose, who still vied for Letty's affections. Thankfully, I was left alone. The foreboding of recapture became less acute and at times our vigilance flagged. One night Samson fell asleep on his watch. We were all sleeping, tucked up against each other to ward off the chill, when I was awakened by a scream.

"Ahhhhhh," Maybell practically summoned Mr. Samuel with her piercing scream. I sat up quickly, bumping heads with Letty and we muttered "ouch" simultaneously.

Nathaniel had a knife in his hand, and I barely saw it before he thrust it into the ground, right above where my head had recently lain. "What the . . ." Samson swore, eyes bulging. Samson grabbed Maybell and pulled her away. Will pulled Letty up into his arms and carried her a short distance off. Ambrose had pulled out a knife, and helped Nathaniel finish killing the long, thick, ugly, black snake—the source of all the commotion.

I crawled away, sat at the edge of our sleeping area, wrapped my arms around my knees, rested my head on top of my knees, and whispered a silent prayer of thanks. Nathaniel called out to me, "You reckon you can make a meal out o' this carcass?"

"I . . . I don't know. I've never cooked snake before," I admitted.

"No? Roast it over the fire; it'll be mighty tasty."

I thought "if you say so," but I said, "I'll try."

The snake had been cleanly chopped in half, but part of its tail still wiggled. Sick to my stomach, not for the first time, I struggled to stand and stumbled off to the bushes to vomit. Maybell came over and put her arm around my shaking shoulders. I began to weep and weep . . . and weep.

I prided myself on staying in control, focusing on the task at hand. But the snake opened the gate to a childhood nightmare. I had seen two men in my village bitten by a black mamba and die within hours. Once I started crying, I couldn't stop. I cried for my mama, papa, my brothers, and especially Ledu. I cried for Miss Martha. And I cried for my sweet Teddy. I was separated from everyone I ever loved. I had never felt so alone.

Maybell had never seen me in such a state. She began crooning in a soothing sotto voice, "It's a'ight honey, the snake's dead. You don't have to eat it. It's a'ight. We be moving on soon. Hush, there." Maybell led me back, and lay down next to me, holding my hand. I slept.

When I awoke, Letty and Maybell were roasting the snake over a fire, Will was getting water to boil, Ambrose and Nathaniel were gone, and Samson was adding logs to the fire. Now fully awake, I hurried off to the bushes, and down to the water to refresh my face and wash my hands. I felt remarkably well.

We fed on roasted snake and some berries I had found the last few days. I never would have believed snake could taste edible, but it wasn't bad.

A few days later, as we were walking from the boat to our new campsite, we all saw a "Runaway Slave" poster nailed to a tree. It advertised for a

> Runaway—one stout wench, short hair, slight limp, dark skin, answers to Bess, and a tall, healthy negro male, scarring on his forehead, goes by Jim.
> REWARD £25.

We all stopped and stared at it—I didn't know who could read, so after a few minutes of silence I read it aloud. No one moved.

## 17 December 1775

We moved on every night and slept during the day. The days were getting colder, and a freezing rain fell on the tarp tent during our daytime sleep. The soft beating of the rain hitting the tarp lulled me to sleep. I woke up freezing. Opening my eyes, I saw only Nathaniel's sleeping form—an empty space where Letty and Will should have been. It was early for them to be up. Glancing at the way the sun slanted in on us, I guessed it was still early afternoon. The rain had stopped. Letty and Will must have gone off together. I wasn't surprised. I wouldn't be surprised if they quietly and surreptitiously made love amidst the rest of us while we were sleeping. Imagining them finding warmth together, away from the rest of us, I turned toward Maybell and went back to sleep.

When I woke again it was dusk, Nathaniel was stoking a fire, and Letty and Will had not returned. The men brought in dry wood to add to the fire, and Maybell gathered up her blankets. I sat up and stretched, tired and queasy, wondering how much longer we would be on the run. I walked over to the fire, warming myself on its low flames—we used fires as needed to cook or for warmth, but still tried to keep them to a minimum and with low flames.

"Nathaniel, how long have we been out? I've lost track," I said.

"I been keeping track. Nine days. Should be about another week to ten days to Norfolk. We might have to go by foot for a bit, up by the Dismal Swamp. It might take a bit longer with you womens, depending on how fast y'all can walk."

I was tempted to offer a curt reply, but I didn't. I couldn't resist a hint of sarcasm though. "We'll try not to slow you men down too much."

"Hmm, well, then maybe five more days over land, till we spot the British flag of Lord Dunmore's fleet."

"Fleet?"

"Yes, miss. I hear he got many ships—not only one. We ain't the only slaves escaping, ye know."

"I never really thought about it. I guess I always pictured one big ship," I said.

"No, no. I imagine there be ten or twenty by now." Nathaniel shifted a log on the fire. "Where's Will and Letty? We be eating and leaving soon. We can't wait around for them."

Everyone glanced around as if turning their heads would bring back the missing couple. Everyone but me. Nathaniel missed nothing.

"Olivia, do you know where they are?" he asked me.

"No . . . I noticed them missing a few hours ago when I woke up, but I figured they'd be back by now."

"You figgered. . . you figgered!" Nathaniel raised his voice in anger—waving his hands in the air for emphasis. I didn't reply.

Ambrose cut in. "What're ye yelling at her for?"

"She should've waked us up—we could've searched then," Nathaniel glared at me.

"Searched to find their love nest? To disturb their mating?" Ambrose matched Nathaniel in volume and anger.

"We can't wait. It ain't safe. We're leaving when the sun sets, if they be back or not."

Now I had to speak up. "We can't desert them."

"They deserted us," Nathaniel retorted.

Ambrose said, "I'll look for 'em while y'all eat and pack up. Save me some food, will ya?"

He strode off into the nearby trees, while Maybell and I finished roasting the food. An hour later we had finished eating, put the fire out, and packed—no Letty, no Will, no Ambrose.

Nathaniel was already at the sloop, untying the sail, setting the tarp under the bench, while the rest of us hesitated, waiting for the return of Ambrose at least, if not all three of them. Then a shot rang out, and another. No one moved.

Quiet panic set in. Paralysis gave way to frenzy. Samson picked Maybell up in his arms and ran, high stepping in the tall grass out to the boat.

I stood alone—torn between my desire to escape and guilt over not alerting anyone to the missing couple's absence. "God, what should I do" I cried aloud in Igbo. Then I thought of my baby, and I made my way to the boat. As I began walking, I heard feet pounding on the ground behind me—running toward me. My heart stopped beating, then raced faster than the footfalls. I began to run, not knowing if it was Letty or Will, or Ambrose, or whoever shot the gun. But I couldn't run fast, and soon the footfalls were right behind me, and I heard loud grunting as well.

"O. . . liv . . . ia. Slow down."

I turned to see Ambrose approaching, alone. He ran to me, grabbed my hand, and we ran out to the boat together.

Nathaniel was already preparing to sail. He wasn't waiting for any of us. Ambrose swept me up in his arms and walked through the water out to the boat. I clung to him, wishing I could love this man who always seemed to be there when I needed him, but instead I saw Teddy's face when I closed my eyes.

Ambrose dropped me on the bench none too gently and glared at Nathaniel. "You couldn't wait even for Olivia?" he demanded.

## CHAPTER SEVENTEEN: OLU

"We can't wait for no one. Our names be on a poster somewhere too, you know. They's a reward for you, and Olivia. Guns go off, we need to move. Who's here—we leave."

"What happened, Ambrose?" Samson asked.

"I was looking for 'em and followed footprints. After the rain the prints stood out like. I gets through the trees and comes to an open field. I didn't see a house, but it were a plantation, I's sure. Someone must've seen me. And I see a tall White man with a big beaver hat holding up a shotgun aimed at me. I didn't stay to look. I turned and ran. He missed me—thank ye Lord—I just kept running till I got back to camp to see Miss Olivia all alone."

"Ah, poor Letty," Maybell said softly. Nathaniel had already turned his attention to sailing and we were moving out of our inlet, back onto the river. The guilt and grief combined to overwhelm me; I began to cry. I cried easily these days.

It was a cloudy night, starlight dimmed by mist and clouds and a half-moon barely visible. The feeble light reaching the water guided Nathaniel as he piloted the boat. No one spoke. I'm sure the others were thinking of Letty and Will, as I was.

The wind blew harder, first in gusts here and there, then a steadier bluster. Our whole journey we had managed to stay in rivers deep enough so we hadn't grounded the boat. This river was larger than most; subsequently the waves were larger. Although my esteem for Nathaniel sank further day by day, I knew he was an excellent boat pilot.

I thought of Teddy, wondered where he was, what he was doing, if he missed me. Lost in my thoughts, I didn't notice that we had moved into an even larger river, the largest I had seen.

Disturbed from my reverie by shouts from Ambrose and Samson, I looked up and our quiet, orderly boat erupted in chaos. We were no longer sailing north, but due east, out into the open sea—where the waves swelled as high as the top of the plantation house, higher than our sail.

Nathaniel intently directed the boat farther and farther from shore and I could just make out the hazy outline of a large ship in the distance, lit up by lanterns on the deck.

"What the hell are ye doing?" Ambrose yelled.

"Are ye daft man?" Samson added.

Nathaniel ignored them, holding the tiller tightly, the boat dipping and rising over larger and larger waves. Water splashed into the boat, startling Maybell. Ambrose moved to the front of the boat, positioning himself beside Nathaniel. Samson tried to wrest the tiller from Nathaniel's hands. Nathaniel held fast and said to us all in a deathly calm voice,

"That there's a British ship. Can't you see the British flag? We've no need to travel another fortnight to Dunmore. Here's our refuge. Right here. Any British ship'll do. That White man who shot at Ambrose knows we here. He'll send out slave catchers. We need to get to safety . . . now."

Before my mind could process what my eyes beheld, Nathaniel was in the water, Ambrose was turning the boat around, the sail came about, and Samson threw a rope out to Nathaniel.

What happened, you ask? After Nathaniel's calm pronouncement Ambrose and Samson began yelling and cursing at him, Ambrose shoved him and grabbed the tiller, and Nathaniel fell overboard.

Nathaniel flailed about in the freezing cold water, while Samson tried to throw the rope to pull him back on the boat. Nathaniel reached up an arm to grab the rope, and a large wave crashed on top of him, yanking him under. Nathaniel didn't surface. We waited.

"Can't none of you swim?" I pleaded. Silence. No one was willing to risk his life for Nathaniel. The waves continued to batter the boat and Ambrose steered straight for the shore.

"He's gone," Samson declared. "God have mercy on his soul."

"Amen," I added.

Letty and Will were gone—none of us knew if they were alive, free, recaptured, or dead. Nathaniel was gone. Now we were four.

# CHAPTER EIGHTEEN

## Joanna

11 April 1816—London

IN THE YEAR SINCE the Twelfth Night gathering with the Wilberforces at Gore House I hadn't seen or heard from either Fredrik or Henry. I harboured little hope of renewing our acquaintance as my twenty-first birthday approached. I focused on my imminent inheritance. Uncle John didn't know the precise amount of money Papa left me, but he knew it to be significant. He tried to prepare me not to underestimate or overestimate the total. My birthday dawned on a foggy day. By 10:00 o'clock on that Thursday morning I had dressed, breakfasted, had my devotion, and sat in the drawing room, ready to go. We weren't scheduled to depart until 11:00 o'clock. I dressed in a modest mauve morning dress gathered above my waist and falling gently to my ankles, with puffed sleeves reaching down to my elbows. I carried a gold reticule and wore matching gold slippers, which seemed appropriate as the sun had now burned away the fog, and the few wispy clouds overhead did not look capable of producing rain. I sat upright in an armchair in the drawing room with an open, unread book in my lap.

Uncle John entered the drawing room a few minutes before 11:00 o'clock.

"I see you're ready to go, my dear. You'll soon find out the extent of your inheritance. Shall we be off?" Uncle John carried a leather letter case, put on his hat, and took my arm.

"Yes!" I replied.

Mr. Blake brought the carriage around and I lifted my dress and sat on the seat facing front. On the short carriage ride I related the news I had recently heard—Fredrik was returning to Africa. Uncle John took my hand and asked how I felt about Fredrik leaving. Though I had encouraged Fredrik, I was still surprised he left so quickly. And without saying goodbye. Uncle John reminded me we had no understanding, we were not engaged, so it wouldn't have been proper for him to write or visit. I knew he was right, but I was still miffed.

The carriage ride ended at the law office of Edward Ind and Frank Forsythe. Uncle John handed me down from the carriage, told Mr. Blake we wouldn't be too long, and we both looked up at the old brick building and its imposing sign. A liveried doorman swung the front door wide and ushered us into a small, elegantly furnished waiting room, replete with a landscape painting of a stormy sea, and two vases of peonies. I again sat on the edge of my seat, while Uncle John set his letter case beside him on the settee and looked over some legal papers. After about twenty minutes, an inner door opened, and a tall man, with swinging jowls, a broad red nose, and suspenders stretched over a wide girth holding up too-short pants revealing grey shoes, strode forward extending his hand to Uncle John.

"And you must be, must be, you must be Mr. John Audley. Am I correct sir, correct?"

"Yes, I am John Audley, and this is Miss Joanna Vassa."

"Such a pleasure," Mr. Forsythe said, nodding furiously. "What a pleasure, such an honour. Miss Vassa, yes, an honour. Please do come in, come in, follow me, come right in."

I glanced over to Uncle John with raised eyebrows as we followed Mr. Forsythe; Uncle John simply shrugged. Mr. Forsythe sat himself down in a throne-like chair, before an enormous cherry wood desk, piled up with stacks and stacks of papers, files, and books.

"Yes, now, Miss Vassa, Miss Vassa is it, yes, I have the will, that is Mr. Vassa's will, I have it right here, yes right here." As he talked Mr. Forsythe moved some papers around, and shifted files over, to uncover the will. "Ah yes, right here, here it is, right here where I left it, as it should be, yes?"

"Yes, sir," I replied. My nervousness gave way to stupefaction. Could this man really be a skilled lawyer?

"Now, now then, Mr. Audley sir, Mr. Audley, sir, yes, your name appears, Mr. Audley, here, right here, on the will of Mr. Vassa, Mr. Gustavus Vassa, next to Edward Ind, my associate, my associate Edward Ind."

"How is my friend Edward? He's not in today, I gather?" Uncle John asked.

"Mr. Ind, Edward, yes, your friend, my associate. No, he's out of town, yes, out of town. Out of country, actually, yes, he's gone to Barbados, don't you know? Off to Barbados."

"I see. Yes, he did tell me he was joining some others on a fact-finding trip to the West Indies." Uncle John nodded.

"Yes, that's it. Fact finding trip. Not a holiday. A trip to find facts. Yes. Fact finding. Indeed, to scout out the facts."

"Yes, so Mr. Forsythe, shall we commence with the reading of the will?" Uncle John prodded.

"Yes, yes, of course. Of course. I will read the will. Now, I'll read it. Right here. Um hm. Yes. Here I go." Mr. Forsythe adjusted his glasses and held the will in both hands.

Uncle John and I listened attentively while Mr. Forsythe read the will, thankful he read only the printed words, without repetition. I especially treasured the part of the will where papa provided for "the Board Maintenance and Education of his Daughters" and when we (I) reached the age of twenty-one I would inherit my papa's "Estate and property I have dearly earned by the sweat of my Brow in some of the most remote and adverse Corners of the whole world." What a papa!

Mr. Forsythe finished and looked at us expectantly.

"So, a princely sum, I would say—a very healthy sum, or queenly, shall I say. Yes, hmmm, queenly."

"Mr. Forsythe, so this is the remainder after Joanna's schooling and other expenses?" Uncle John asked.

"Yes, yes. Exactly so. Yes. The sum of £950. Very respectable. This will cover your expenses for several years, yes, indeed. With wise investment, very wise, mind you, these funds can last many, many years. Such a lofty sum! And the land, you see, according to the will of Mr. Vassa, the will states Miss Vassa will receive, will inherit the two acres, only if Mr. Vassa outlived Mrs. Anne Cullen, which did not happen, no, that did not occur. No, most unfortunate, but Mr. Vassa died before Mrs. Anne Cullen. Your grandmother, am I right?" I was trying hard to follow his winding speech.

"Yes, sir. My grandmother is still alive," I offered.

"Yes, just as I thought. So, the land, that is, Mrs. Anne Cullen's land, well that shall be, will be determined by her will. Therefore, at the present time, today—oh, and happy birthday to you Miss Vassa, and many returns of the day. I must say, there are many returns today, aren't there? Ho ho! Yes, at the moment, today, you now have the inheritance of £950 and some of your mother's dresses. Lovely, isn't it? Your mother's dresses. And finally, yes, at the end of the will it here states, finally at the end, a silver watch, silver teaspoons, and books. What young lady would not want teaspoons? Aha! Spoons for tea. And books to read whilst she drinks her tea! Is that not delightful, Miss Vassa? Hmmm? Delightful, is it not? Oh, yes, one last thing. This is the final item, the last item, indeed. One quilt! This is to put over her knees whilst she reads her books and stirs her tea! What a pretty picture, indeed. A quilt to top it all off! Aha!"

I was speechless, which no one really noticed, as neither Uncle John nor I could squeeze a word in during Mr. Forsythe's rambling soliloquy.

## 1816–1821

After I turned twenty-one and inherited a small fortune, nothing much changed in my life. The sum which would make me "quite comfortable" was not enough to buy property or to live on for the rest of my life. I had a few choices, including getting married and looking for employment. I rather hoped marriage was in my future . . . my near future.

I still alternated between Uncle John's homes in Ely and London, and Grandmamma's home in Ely until she died in 1820. There was a small family service for her in the local parish. The last time I saw her before she died, several months earlier, she was sleeping a lot, not getting out of bed much. Although we weren't that close, her death saddened me—another family member gone. I was too young to grieve when my parents died, so as I mourned Grandmamma, I also grieved for my other family members who died so many years ago—Mama, Papa, sister Anna. And I longed for Papa's sister, my aunt, hoping she was alive and could be found.

Uncle John's efforts to find Aunt Oluchukwu reached an impasse when he discovered she had escaped during the American Revolution. Good for her, I thought, but it meant we would probably never find out what became of her—we would never meet. Her freedom was my loss. The careful records kept by slaveholders would not help us find a free woman. I thought my heart had become immune to loss—I was wrong. Aunt Oluchukwu's escape, her freedom, gutted me. I would never know any of my papa's family unless I traveled to Africa, which I did not plan to do. I felt adrift until I received a letter from Anne.

Anne was still single, like me, with no prospects or even desire to marry. The spark Miss Frances and Miss Sadie had ignited ten years ago became a steady flame. Anne became an official member of the Chelmsford Ladies' Anti-Slavery Society, and her letter invited me to visit her for a week or more.

For the next five years, I visited Anne for one or two weeks every year. We went out together to visit women in their homes, encourage them to discontinue using sugar, and sign our petition. Miss Frances and Miss Sadie mentored us well and we became part of their living legacy. I had begun plans to form a Ladies' Anti-Slavery Society in Cambridgeshire.

## February 1821

"You'll enjoy this reverend, Joanna. He studied at Cambridge and clearly knows the Word of God," Uncle John said as we rode in the carriage to church.

"With your ringing endorsement, I'm sure I'll enjoy the preaching," I responded.

"We met him several years ago, at the Wilberforce's Twelfth Night celebration. Henry Bromley."

Henry! I thought of him from time to time, wondering where he was, what he was doing. My anticipation at seeing him again teetered between happy expectation and pensive reflection. I turned to look out at the passing countryside, enjoying watching the fields, cows and sheep, and grazing horses—a perfect panorama of English country life. Unmarred by clouds, the sky and air had a crisp, clean chill to it. The carriage turned sharply, throwing me against my seat.

"Ho there, Blake! Take your time!" Uncle John called out the window.

"Sorry, sir!" Blake yelled back.

"We're almost there, Joanna," Uncle John assured me.

As the carriage came to a stop, Uncle John hopped out, still full of energy at seventy years of age. I stepped out and looked up at the church. The church building, made of brick and stone, seemed welcoming, with a small steeple, evergreens lining the walkway to the entrance, and outer doors swung open wide. Two men and two women stood near the entrance, greeting members and visitors, smiling, shaking hands.

I tucked my arm in Uncle John's, and we proceeded into the church to the ringing tones of an organ. I looked around as we sat in a wooden pew about halfway down the aisle, noticing many children, most well-behaved. I was not surprised to be the only person of colour in the congregation. I had inured myself to maintain a placid, friendly exterior, but still felt a little awkward, out of place, in the all-White settings which characterized most of English society.

The service began. The congregation sang the hymns loudly and lustily, and exchanged the peace quickly, but amiably. During the offering a young woman, accompanied by the organist, sang an aria in a strikingly beautiful soprano voice, then I sat back, opened the bible, and prepared to hear Henry's message.

Henry, rather Rev. Bromley, had grown taller and he wore simple vestments, with no ornate velvet trimmings—almost too simple for my taste, used to the more lavish clergy dress of the Church of England. I remembered Henry's voice, a soothing, musical, deep voice. I looked at his striking brown eyes and recalled rather than saw the gold flecks in them. His frequent smile revealed one deep dimple in his left cheek. He had no facial hair, but the unruly, curly brown mop of hair on his head declared he certainly would if he didn't shave. As Henry began, he acknowledged the singer and organist by name.

"Thank you, Sister Jean Simpson, for that lovely rendition, and thanks to the organist, Sister Miriam Doolittle. It's a pleasure to be with you again here in Horningsea. Thank you for inviting me back. If you have a bible, please open it to the Gospel of John, the 14th chapter, verses 1–6.

"Jesus begins by admonishing his disciples, 'Let not your heart be troubled.' In other words, He was saying don't fret. Don't worry. Don't be anxious. Why not?"

Henry paused, and a boy about five or six years old raised his hand. To everyone's chagrin, Henry acknowledged the boy.

"Yes, son. Do you know the answer?"

"Cause we's posed to trust God," the boy said.

"Yes, that's it exactly. Your parents have taught you well."

The parents visibly relaxed, beaming under the praise of this guest speaker. I was impressed. I had never seen such an interaction in church, and wondered if it was common in dissenting congregations, but somehow, recalling my years at the Congregational Church in Highbury, I thought not. After the closing hymn, congregants filed out slowly, talking quietly, donning cloaks, holding children's hands so they wouldn't run off. Henry stood outside the entrance, greeting people, offering blessings, promising to pray for the sick, answering questions. Uncle John and I approached him.

"Excellent sermon, Rev. Bromley. It's a pleasure to see you again. Do you remember Miss Joanna Vassa?" Uncle John shook Henry's hand.

"Thank you, sir. It's nice to see you again," Henry said to Uncle John. "Miss Joanna, what a pleasure to see you again. How fortuitous as well. I recently read your father's memoir."

"How wonderful. It's an amazing account, isn't it?" I looked up at his face.

"Not only is it a fascinating firsthand account of slavery, but his conversion narrative is riveting."

"Thank you so much, Hen . . . er . . . Rev. Bromley. It's one of my favourite parts of his memoir." I beamed every time someone mentioned his book. Papa was so entrepreneurial, buying and selling goods while he was a slave, enabling him to buy his freedom. He traveled to such faraway places as the Caribbean and Central America, Turkey, and almost made it to the Arctic Circle, going on many expeditions. He was an amazing man, and I was so proud to be his daughter.

People were still streaming out of the church, so we had to move on.

"Again, it's a pleasure, an honour, to see you again, Miss Joanna." Henry gazed directly into my eyes with his own piercing brown eyes, and I could now see the flecks of gold. We moved on, though I would have preferred to stay, and talk, and examine those brown eyes more closely. My feelings were firmly in the happy expectation camp.

## April 1821

A few months later I attended a christening at the parish church in Chesterton, not far from Ely, where Grandmamma used to live. The mother lived in the neighborhood, and with Grandmamma gone, I went to represent the family.

I arrived at the church right when the service began, taking a seat at the back. St. Andrew's boasted beautiful dark wooden pews, polished to a shine, pillars set between every 3rd or 4th pew rising to an arch. The imposing figure of a hexagonal oak pulpit rose in the front, but my eyes were drawn to the arch separating the nave (where the congregants sat) from the chancel (where the minister stood). The stained-glass windows in the chancel, at the very front of the church, depicted Jesus, crowned as King of the church, surrounded by the four evangelists. Engaged in visually perusing the magnificent structure, I didn't notice the vicar performing the christening. I looked over, smiled at the baby, and looked up to see none other than Rev. Henry Bromley standing alongside the parents. I had no idea he would be there and was inordinately pleased. The mother must have requested his presence, as it was unusual for a dissenting minister to attend a parish church, and even more unusual for him to have a role in the service.

The christening concluded quickly, and the traditional service ended in less than an hour, with a forgettable sermon, but inspiring music. After the service I went over to greet the mother. The church emptied quickly, and I walked around the church reading the various plaques and memorials. As I exited, I noticed a plaque on the side of the church, high up, so that I had to crane my neck up to read it. I read the name on the top and gasped, covering my mouth with my hand, and began to weep. The plaque was for Anna Maria Vassa . . . my sister . . . and read:

Near this place lies interred Anna Maria Vassa, daughter of Gustavus Vassa, the African. She died July 21st, 1797, aged 4 years.

> Should simple village rhymes attract thine eye,
> Stranger, as thoughtfully thou passest by,
> Know that there lies beside this humble stone
> A child of colour haply not thine own,
> Her father born of Afric's sun-burnt race,
> Torn from his native fields, ah foul disgrace;
> Through various toils, at length to Britain came
> Espoused, so Heaven ordain'd, an English dame,
> And follow'd Christ; their hope two infants dear.
> But one, a hapless orphan, slumbers here.
> To bury her the village children came,
> And dropp'd choice flowers, and lisp'd her early fame;
> And some that lov'd her most, as if unblest,
> Bedew'd with tears the white wreath on their breast;
> But she is gone and dwells in that abode,
> Where some of every clime shall joy in God.

I have no idea how long I stood before the remembrance of Anna Maria, mourning her anew. I felt a presence behind me, a rustling in the grass, and took a deep breath to steady myself before turning around. Henry stood there; his hand extended a handkerchief.

"Please. Use this," he urged.

"Oh, thank you, Henry, Rev. Bromley. Forgive me. I'm simply . . . overcome."

"No apology needed. The plaque is for . . . your sister?" he asked.

"Yes . . ." I sniffed and held the handkerchief to my nose.

"I don't mean to intrude on your grief." Henry turned to leave.

"Don't go," I called out. "It's fine. I'm . . . fine."

"Are you sure?" Henry moved closer.

"Yes, I'm just shocked. I knew Mrs. Peckard had written a poem, but I had no idea it was made into a plaque and displayed here. I'm so . . . happy . . . to see it." Tears trickling down my cheek belied my words.

"I can see you are," Henry teased, smiling gently, putting his hand on my arm to comfort me. His hand did comfort, but I really felt like burrowing into his chest, putting my arms around him, and crying until my tears were spent.

I proposed a walk instead. Headstones sprouted up in the cemetery, surrounding the church like gladiolas in the spring, though not nearly as attractive. Shrubbery and trees dotted the area, lending a calm, pastoral air. Henry offered his arm, which I gladly took, tucking my arm under his.

We walked together, both acknowledging our surprise at seeing each other. We reminisced about the Twelfth Night games, our concert for the vicar, our recent meeting. When Henry inquired if I came alone, I told him the driver was waiting for me . . . at the pub. I wasn't in a rush.

Henry mentioned the christening and commented on his idea of a perfect family—one girl and one boy, like his own family. He asked me what I thought constituted a perfect family size. We had reached a bench, and Henry motioned for me to sit with him. I settled my cloak about me, Henry sat down next to me.

"The perfect size? I think six children is perfect."

"And do you know any families with six children?"

"I do. The Wilberforces have six children."

"I see."

"It's chaotic at times, but they all have someone else to talk to, to play with, to bother, to tease."

"I can see the benefits! Did you have other siblings, other than Anna Maria?"

"No. And my mama and papa died before I turned two."

Henry looked at me and held one of my hands in both of his. "How sad. I knew, of course, your father had died. But I had no idea you were... left alone? You have other family members though, your grandmother? And Mr. Audley. Is he a relative?"

"My grandmother died a year ago. Mama's sister, my aunt Mary, may still be alive, but she's down in Australia. There may be family members on Papa's side, in Igboland, but I don't know. Uncle John, Mr. Audley, is not an uncle, but he was a good friend of Papa's. He's my guardian; he's been looking for another possible family member—Papa's sister."

"And has he had any success?"

"Some. He traced her to a plantation in South Carolina, but it seems she escaped during the American Revolution. It will be almost impossible to find her now."

"I imagine you were very disappointed when the trail ended with her escape."

"Very much so. And we came so, so close. I'm happy for her. God willing, she's no longer a slave."

"You have a very mature attitude."

"Rev. Bromley, I have little choice."

"We all have choices, Miss Vassa."

"Please, call me Joanna." I hoped I wasn't being too forward.

"Joanna, we all have choices. And many choose to be angry with God, and rail against His will. Acceptance is the better road, but the more difficult one."

"Definitely more difficult." I nodded.

"You would know that far better than I."

I was silent.

"Joanna, where are you living now?" Henry inquired.

"With Uncle John."

"In Ely?"

"Yes."

"And may I... may I call on you there?" Henry tilted his head.

"Certainly, Rev. Bromley. T'would be lovely to see you again. And I must return your handkerchief, clean."

"Please keep it. I look forward to seeing you Joanna, in a week?"

# CHAPTER NINETEEN

## Olu

18 December 1775

Samson took over piloting the boat, explaining he had watched Nathaniel closely, and helped him out on occasion, so he felt he could keep the boat afloat. He acknowledged he didn't know the route Nathaniel was taking. Ambrose suggested skirting the shore all the way to Norfolk and recruiting an Indian guide. Ambrose and Samson debated the benefits and drawbacks of using a guide and decided without input from us 'womens' that a guide was needed.

Samson had maneuvered the boat out of the high swelling waves and closer to shore. He steered the boat north, the sail came about, and we settled in for a long night of sailing, up the River Neuse, north to Lord Dunmore. I hadn't slept well during the day, and the trauma of losing Letty and Will, and watching Nathaniel go under the waves, exhausted me. I slept.

When I awoke the rose-colored rays of dawn rained fingers of soft light over the land, the wind exhaled with a hush, and Samson steered the boat into an inlet. It was unlike the smaller ones we usually found, almost as wide as the Ashley River in parts. Samson and Ambrose guided the boat far in from the shore—almost grounding it on some rocks.

"Sorry y'all. I'm still learning how to sail this sloop." Samson apologized.

"You're doin' fine Samson," Ambrose replied. "Just fine."

Samson managed to get the boat off the rocks and closer to shore. We were almost right up against the shore bank so when Ambrose put out the plank, Maybell and I didn't even have to get our feet wet for once.

"You're a good pilot Samson. Or should I say Cap'n Samson!" I smiled at Samson.

He grinned and nodded his head, letting down the sail. Ambrose found a site larger than our normal spots, with a log fire pit that still emanated heat. Left by another runaway slave? Pine needles lay thick on the ground as if they had been carried in and laid down to form a natural mattress. I was more tired than hungry, and after helping set up the tarp, I burrowed under the blanket and fell asleep immediately.

Silence woke me. Or at least I woke to a stillness so pervasive it felt unnatural. Everyone else slept on, but as I sat up I saw our campsite had visitors—four Indian men looked down at us. One was quite tall, so much so that I had to crane my neck back to see his head. The other three were shorter. They all had on cloth fashioned like a skirt, and blankets around their bodies for warmth—no shoes. Their hair was black, and long, and they stood as still as statues. One carried a bundle, and another had a bow, with arrows slung across his back. They looked neither friendly nor threatening. I neither moved nor spoke. I wasn't as anxious as you might expect. I judged them to be harmless—I hoped I was right. The men stood still and continued looking down at us. A few minutes passed, then Ambrose woke up, sat up, and cursed loudly. His surprised outburst woke up Samson and Maybell and soon we were all awake.

One of the Indians stepped forward. In broken but understandable English he asked if we were escaping. Samson explained we were sailing to Norfolk, by river if possible. The tall Indian suggested taking the river we were on, the Neuse, almost all the way, avoiding land. They were going to Norfolk to trade and we could follow them.

With a mixture of words and gestures the men came to an agreement. To solidify the pact, Ambrose offered some ears of corn and a skinned possum, which the men looked delighted to accept. They offered Ambrose some banana-shaped food, which I could not identify, but turned out to be squash, delicious when roasted. I had reservations about following the Indians. However, we were more than halfway to Norfolk; we could not turn back, and none of us knew the way ahead. So, we forged ahead, following our guides.

The decision to follow the Indians was a wise one. We learned their names: Askuwheteau (he keeps watch), Chogun (blackbird), Etchemin (canoe man), and Huritt (handsome). After three days traveling together, and by the way, they showed us a much more efficient way to put up the tarp to keep out rain, cold, mosquitoes, two of them left to visit family. Chogun and Etchemin remained, and we were six.

## 22 December 1775

With only us four, and Chogun and Etchemin, our sloop became an impediment. With Chogun's help we were able to trade it for warm clothes—beaver coats and breeches for the men, long hide skirts for Maybell and me, food, and another gun. We all got into Etchemin's roomy canoe for the final leg of our trip—the Great Dismal Swamp. I hoped the name was not a harbinger of the days ahead. We were close to freedom. So close.

The sky is darkest right before dawn. My months into slavery and weeks out of slavery testified to this truth. With our topsy-turvy sleeping and rowing, I now knew the night sky intimately and when the moon sets before the sun rises the darkness blankets the land. Etchemin left us to go to a trading post farther inland, so only Ambrose, Maybell, Samson, Chogun, and I remained. I felt awkward as an unaccompanied woman with two single men in the group.

Chogun warned us when we broke camp that evening. The walk would be long with snakes, bugs, and ticks for companions. Dunmore was up to twenty ships, and when we got close, White men would be watching the shore—rough crossing. If we kept apace, we would reach the shore by morning.

Leaving the canoe and tarp, we took with us some cooked duck, squash, berries, and the remnants of our clothes. For the first few hours, our destination seemed so close, yet beyond reach. Chogun led, followed by Samson, Maybell, then me. Ambrose held up the rear.

I thought about the long walk away from home when Ledu and I were kidnapped. But that was a forced march to slavery, this a chosen walk to freedom. I forged ahead.

A light mist began to fall, and my feet were getting colder and colder. The makeshift moccasin shoes were slightly too big, causing my feet to rub against the back, blistering and bleeding. My energy flagged and each step felt like the last I could summon the strength for—then one more.

When I felt the first mosquito bite, I thought nothing of it. But after another half hour my arms had incurred the onslaught of a small army of mosquitoes. All I wanted to do was lie down, cover myself in a blanket, and sleep. With my sore feet, stinging arms, uncooperative legs, growing belly, and a mutinous attitude, I pressed on. No one spoke. Then we heard howling in the distance. Wolves or dogs? I feared the wolves, but dreaded dogs.Ced Dogs meant we were being tracked. Ambrose ran past me, and I saw him with Chogun and Samson, two dark fuzzy heads and one long haired. Three heads swam together in my mind. Their heads became pots, spinning around and around.

I opened my eyes to see the three heads, now as heads—two familiar black faces and Chogun, our guide, whose bronzed features I now cannot quite recall. Ambrose gave me a sip of something strong, Indian liquor, and I sat up, got up, and put one foot dutifully in front of the other, continuing our final march to Lord Dunmore. The howling had stopped, but Ambrose said we may have to separate if we heard it again.

By this time, it was about two hours before dawn. The sun had not yet risen, the clouds had blown off, and we could see clearly by moonlight—we could also be clearly seen. Chogun saw it first. The bay. How can I describe to you what that sight meant to my tired eyes, my aching feet, and my broken heart? In the distance, I could see faint outlines of ships. We were so close.

We all stood and stared through the opening in the trees at the ships anchored in the bay. We had lined up parallel to the shore, and the sight of our destination renewed our strength. Chogun told us the shores were lined with two kinds of men—slave catchers and ferry pilots. We could be caught or ferried to freedom. Chogun couldn't tell us how to differentiate—some White men were good, some evil. We needed a semaphore but had to rely on chance.

"You telling me we've gotten this far, and we have to just hope we pick the right canoe? I don't like this. I don't like it a'tall," Ambrose complained.

"Is there a way you could find out, and somehow let us know?" I ventured.

That's what happened. Or at least that was the plan. What really happened? Chogun left us to scan the shore, trying to find a friendly face, to determine if the boat owner would take us to freedom or capture us. The signal was to be one short whistle.

We heard the whistle, but so did the dogs. So as the four of us ran out of the swamp to the shore where the whistling sound originated, three large hounds began bounding out of the swamp after us. I hitched up my skirt, held onto my meager belongings with a tight grip, and ran out to Chogun. My fatigue forgotten, my malaise a memory.

Ambrose ran beside me, and I could hear him breathing hard. Maybell and Samson were behind us. Then a single shot blasted through the air. Ambrose and I reached Chogun and the waiting canoe, but the guide had fled. The three of us hopped in, and Chogun began to paddle out to the ship.

"Wait, what about Samson and Maybell?" I cried.

"No wait. Guns and dogs—no wait." Chogun was adamant.

As we pulled into the bay, I saw Maybell and Samson reach the shore. Samson held out his arms and yelled, "Come back. Take us!"

Chogun and Ambrose paddled on, while I prayed for God to forgive me for not caring more about abandoning Samson and Maybell. I continued to follow them with my eyes and saw them climb in a canoe further down the shore.

Relieved that they would reach the ships, I turned my eyes to what lay ahead. Ambrose and Chogun were right. There was not one ship, rather more than a dozen. They were all large, though none as large as the slave ship on which I came to America. Just the thought of that ship made me shudder. I felt my stomach rise in protest at the thought of getting on another ship, and I vomited over the side of the canoe.

"You alright?" Ambrose asked tentatively. After splashing some of the cool bay water on my face and wiping my mouth, I turned and said, "I'll be fine. I just don't like big ships."

Of the dozen or so ships in the water, the closest was also the largest. The ship was as long from bow to stern as the stable house on the Cross Plantation. The sails were down, and the rigging tangled. Leaning out over the bow, a beautiful, naked mermaid with long flowing hair, and tail fin wrapping around port side, promised to guide the men to victory and a safe return home. As we neared the ship, I heard a melodious sound. The British flag waved at us from the sky above, welcoming us to freedom, or so I thought at the time, and the men on deck were swaying, holding up tankards. They sang off key loudly.

We reached the ship, and a rope ladder was thrown over the side for us. A tall, white, forbidding officer called out to us, "Ahoy there—state your business."

Ambrose replied firmly, "We heard of Lord Dunmore's proclamation. We come to fight for the king."

"That slip of a girl is a soldier?" The men on deck laughed, and Ambrose frowned.

"No, she ain't. I am. But she can cook, and nurse the sick, and—and she can read!" Ambrose declared the last with such pride, I had to smile.

"Come on up then. We certainly could use some gel to read to us." More laughter from on deck. "What, an Injun too? A man, a gel, and an Injun. I never!?"

As Ambrose and I climbed up the rope ladder, Chogun and the Captain talked.

"I go back, Cap'n," Chogun said. "You trade?"

"Yes, yes. We trade. What you got?"

"Beavers, possum, pelts, fish . . ."

"Come back on the morrow. Bring goods. We trade."

Chogun nodded at the captain, said goodbye to us, and paddled back to shore. Now that we were on the ship, it seemed smaller than it had from the water below. The men resumed their singing, which I realized was a Christmas carol about ships! I looked at Ambrose. "Merry Christmas, Olivia," he said, giving me a kiss on the cheek. I had lost track of the days! Freedom on Christmas Day.

I hugged myself, prayed to God for the safety of those I loved, and looked about me on the deck. There were more Black soldiers than White, which surprised me. Their blue uniforms were a bit shabbier, and ill fitting, but across their chests on the uniform jacket was emblazoned *Liberty to Slaves*. Amen! I was caught up in the raucous, joyous, celebratory singing, and added my voice to theirs once I learned the tune and the words!

> I saw three ships come sailing in;
> On Christmas Day, on Christmas Day;
> I saw three ships come sailing in
> On Christmas Day in the morning.
> And what was in those ships all three,
> On Christmas Day, on Christmas Day?
> And what was in those ships all three,
> On Christmas Day in the morning?
> The Virgin Mary and Christ were there,
> On Christmas Day, on Christmas Day;
> The Virgin Mary and Christ were there,
> On Christmas Day in the morning.

At first I didn't see any women, then I spotted a few in the middle of the deck, sitting together, leaning against the center mast. As all the men were paying me no mind, and Ambrose sang and drank with a mug in his hand, I wandered over to the women.

"Morning," I said. The two women were younger than me. They appeared to be in their early twenties.

"Mornin'," said one. "M'names Sue."

"I'm Olivia."

"Where'd ye come from?" Sue asked.

"South Carolina. Charles Town."

"So far! We from down the road in Virginie. You escaped?"

"Yes."

"He your husband?" the other woman asked.

"Oh no. He's only—we're from the same plantation. How long have you been here?"

"Only a week" Sue said. "I regret leaving already. Ain't hardly any food and tastes awful. It so boring on this ship. And there ain't no good men!"

I could see what her priorities were!

"That some outfit!" the other woman said.

I had forgotten I was wearing what looked like an Indian woman's attire, complete with a deer hide skirt.

As the two women admired or ridiculed my outfit (I wasn't sure which), the deck grew quiet. Behind me I heard footsteps approaching from below decks. A White man in uniform emerged. He was small in stature, not much taller than me, with a slight build. His brownish hair was uncombed, but his uniform fit well. His presence preceded him—though small, he commanded attention. The men stopped their singing as he walked to the middle of the deck. Could this be the illustrious Lord Dunmore? I had never been in the presence of a person of rank, but had gleaned enough from Mrs. Beth and Susannah, Noah, and Teddy, to know how to act. Act as if they know everything and I know nothing.

He looked over at me and addressed the captain who had invited Ambrose and me aboard.

"Who's this, Captain? I instructed you not to bring any more women aboard. I have a devil of a time with the ones we have."

"Yes, milord. But this one claims she can cook—and nurse the sick. And read!"

"Hmmm. Let's see about it. Miss," he called out to me, "what's your name?"

"Olivia, my lord," I said.

"Well don't she speak right proper? Could be on the Queen's court. No miss, your given name, not your slave name."

Now I liked him. "Oluchukwu, my Lord. But people call me Olu."

"Olu it is then. I hear you can cook."

"Yes, my lord. Given the proper ingredients and tools, I can prepare a tasty meal."

"We often lack the ingredients on board, have but a few tools, but let's see what you can do. Cap'n, have one of your men take Olu here down to the galley. Set her to fixing breakfast."

I followed an officer down to the galley, breathing deeply to slow my rising heart rate. I focused on the wood, the narrow, winding staircase, the swaying of the boat—reminding myself we were on Lord Dunmore's ship, not a slave ship.

Lord Dunmore was right about one thing. The ingredients were scarce. No blueberry pancakes for this crew. The galley was cramped—a long wooden table straddled the room, with barrels, bags, and boxes lining the walls. Two large pots hung over unlit fires, with a small stack of wood precariously stacked up against a wall. With no windows it felt stuffy and hot, even though the fire was not lit. A few goods were in abundance, potatoes, onions, rice, while there was a dearth of meat. I needed a miracle to make enough food, delectable enough to please Lord Dunmore.

After scrounging around in the various barrels and bags I managed to find ingredients for cornpone. I also found a box full of neatly stacked eggs, a few herbs, parsley and basil, and some pork sausages. I cooked it up together, adding a splash of milk, salt, onion and a hint of pepper. It didn't look like it would feed even the men I had seen, and I assumed there were more onboard. I also made a pot of porridge, with some rice and honey, and nuts added in. Along with the cornpone, it should feed the whole ship, I thought. In my element, I found comfort in cooking.

Captain Williams, who welcomed us aboard, came in to smell, taste, and inspect the meal.

"Hmmmm." He hummed, tasting the porridge. "You done something to this here porridge to make it edible. This is mighty tasty. I declare, don' know how ye done it. Ain't much of a thing in this paltry pantry—ha! Like that rhyme? Ain't much a'tall. But ye finds enough to spruce up this here porridge. Um hmmm. What ye got in that there pot?"

"Eggs and sausage, Captain. Please try some." I smiled at him.

"Yes, ma'am. Ask me once, that's enough." Captain Williams took a large spoonful, ate it slowly, looked over at me and said, "You married?"

"No, Captain. I'm not."

"Marry me then!"

"Sir . . . I . . . well . . . I . . ." I was speechless.

"Relax, miss, I'm just teasing ye, sort of. But this here, this egg concoction is 'bout the best I ever had. Yes, miss, you wasn't lying. You surely can cook."

The captain called out to two of the men, one White and one Black. They got bowls and spoons to serve the 200+ men on board. The men were served in a dining room, of sorts, a long narrow room opposite the kitchen. They ate in shifts. Less than an hour later the men were fed.

After this first successful meal, I became the ship's cook. However, there were limited supplies, and I couldn't plan ahead because I never knew what would be available. Captain Williams explained where they got their food supplies. "Well, miss, we fishes some, and we hunts some, but most of the food the mens get when they raid nearby plantations, and farms, and such." I was so astonished I didn't know how to reply. What I thought was "they steal it?" but what I said was "is that safe?"

"Ha, no. I reckon it ain't too safe. We been shot at, but we shoot right back at 'em. Tis war, miss. If we don't 'procure' the meat and vegetables, grains and fruit, flour and sugar, we'll die of starvation. Thems the plain facts. And that ain't 'safe' neither."

"I see your point." As I cleaned up the pots and looked around to see what might be cooked up for dinner, having been informed only two meals a day were served, I could hear the men across the narrow passageway.

"Hoorah for the new cook!" "Hire the new dame!" "Where you been all my life?"

I smiled as I cleaned up. As I finished cleaning, Lord Dunmore showed up, smiling slightly, and said, "You surely can cook, Olu. And I'm guessing if you can make something edible with these slim morsels, given the right ingredients, you could prepare a feast."

"I do my best, milord."

"I'm sure you do," Lord Dunmore assented, barely holding in a burp.

Thus began my first day aboard the ship, and my first day of real freedom. Remember reader, I was used to sleeping during the day and traveling at night, so by the time breakfast was finished, I was ready for a nap. But I wanted to be as helpful as possible, so I put my things in the cramped, windowless cabin with Sue and June and set about to meet the medical person on board. As it turned out, there was no doctor or nurse on the ship. There were, however, three men in the sick bay, with very suspicious-looking red spots on their faces.

Lord Dunmore came down and found me in the sick bay.

I stepped into the narrow hallway and informed Lord Dunmore the men probably had smallpox. He agreed. Mr. Cross had inoculated all of us who worked in the house, to protect his wife and daughter, so I didn't fear contracting smallpox. I vividly remembered the doctor taking his scalpel, drawing it across my upper arm in a straight line, and tipping a spoonful of powder into the open wound—then closing it up with gauze and tape. It hurt like the dickens, but I'm sure not as much as smallpox. I offered to nurse the men and help the doctor when he arrived in a week.

"Thank you. I don't want it to spread. But it may already be too late. Many of the Whites have been inoculated, but not the Africans." Lord Dunmore shook his head.

## Spring 1776

After over two months, I had adjusted to the cramped quarters, Sue and June quarrelling, boisterous men, and rocking of the ship. I tried to get as much fresh air and sun each day as I possibly could, and my belly stretched to accommodate my growing baby.

March dawned and Lord Dunmore sailed his ship, followed by twenty others, into a nearby harbor. After a scouting party returned with the news that the island appeared to be uninhabited, the men began to ferry Africans to shore in small canoes. By the end of the day, one of the nicest days yet, with a bright strong sun, cloudless sky, and mild temperature, over 100 Africans were on the island. As I watched the canoes leave the ships, something struck me as odd. I could not pinpoint the source of my discomfort. As I continued to gaze upon the canoes unloading their human cargo on shore, I realized most of the men had something in common—the active stage of smallpox. We remained anchored right offshore that night, and I slept fitfully. By dawn I had come to a decision.

## CHAPTER NINETEEN: OLU

I didn't know how to approach Lord Dunmore, but my opportunity came unexpectedly one evening as I was cleaning up. He complimented me on dinner, and I asked how the men on the island would be fed. What were the plans for their care, their provisions? Lord Dunmore explained they must be separated from the healthy men. They came willing to fight but now they lay sick, unable to fight. Since none of the men answered the call to stay on shore and provide care, Lord Dunmore ordered some men to stay on shore. I offered to go to the island to cook and care for them, with no threat of contracting smallpox, I reminded him. He didn't like the idea of a woman alone on the island with all those men. And he didn't want to give up my cooking! I exaggerated when I mentioned Sue and June had helped me cook and could easily take over the cooking. Lord Dunmore stared at me. He agreed to confer with Captain Williams on my request and asked to have Sue and June cook supper the next evening. He wanted to see how well they did without me.

"Yes, milord. Thank you." I nodded.

"Thank you for your offer. Not many a woman, nor a man, would do as much." He gazed at me as if he couldn't put the pieces of my life together to fit—an escaped slave, a woman, a good cook, self-sacrificing, speaks well. I'm sure I didn't match his expectation of a freed slave.

The next night, I must confess—I cheated. Sue and June were capable but not creative in the galley, which was required considering the lack of foodstuffs; inventiveness was a key ingredient to success. For that inaugural supper on their own, they weren't really alone.

When Sue asked June what they should do with the rabbits, I might have mentioned where the onions and turnips were. I may have directed them to pepper and cloves. If I only mentioned the spices I thought would go well in the stew, Sue and June surely didn't notice. We went on in this fashion until the stew became quite tasty, though they didn't figure the proportions exactly right. They honestly thought they had done it all themselves, which was important to me. I felt their confidence would help them truly become better cooks. Dinner that night was hearty and tasty.

Lord Dunmore found me in the sick bay the following morning. The dinner was pronounced edible, so Captain Williams and Lord Dunmore allowed me to stay at Tucker's Point, under the protection of British soldiers. I would cook for all the soldiers and tend to the sick, who would be separated at once upon visible evidence of disease. Men would come to the island twice a week to hunt and bring supplies.

"I will have my men ferry you over tomorrow morning. Please gather your things and be ready by daylight. If there are a few things you need from the galley, check with Captain Williams." Lord Dunmore looked down at me and nodded.

"Yes, milord."

I told Sue and June I was leaving, and they could barely contain their glee. I said Lord Dunmore enjoyed their meal so much he wanted them to cook from now on, and he ordered me to the island to care for the sick men.

I rose in the morning before the sun peeked over the horizon, put my dress and one pair of boots in a cloth, and gathered a few supplies from the galley. Captain Williams allowed me to take one pot, and a few knives, some flour, tea, sugar, and salt.

As the sky turned from black to light grey, I mounted the ladder and met the men who would ferry me to the island. Captain Williams met me as I climbed over the side of the boat, down the rope ladder to the canoe.

"I wishes you the best. You doing a mighty fine service to the British, miss. I'll be over to see ye when I can."

"Thank you, Captain Williams."

"Take care of yourself—and that baby, too."

"You . . . how . . . oh . . . thank you, sir."

"Ha! You thought this old seadog wouldn't notice. Well, I sure did notice. Don't know why that baby's daddy ain't with you, why he'd leave such a fine one as ye, but tweren't none of my business. I wish ye well. And when we win—and we will—you'll be free. You and the babe."

I was overcome with emotion, and my foot missed a rung, I almost fell into the canoe. But Captain Williams grabbed my hand, and the British soldier in the boat steadied my foot. I smiled weakly up at Captain Williams and continued my descent. I looked back at the ship and saw Captain Williams salute, then looked ahead to my new abode, an island of death.

Over the next few weeks, I settled into a routine. Once my quarters had been constructed—a roughly hewn log shack—I had a semblance of shelter from storms. During my stay at Tucker's Point, I learned more about smallpox than a medical doctor. Men would be working, constructing barracks, hunting, fishing, then symptoms would suddenly show up. There would be little warning, and the first symptoms were not mild, but ravaging. I lost count off all the men I nursed after 100, and less than 30 survived. I remember Daniel best of all.

He was an excellent fisherman and brought me crabs and fish almost daily. He was Igbo, and I looked forward to his visits so we could converse in our language, which I had almost forgotten. He would always announce himself.

"Ndewo, Miss Olu. Come and see what I have brought you today. Twill heal the sick and raise the dead."

"Oga diri gi nma. What is it, Daniel?"

"Only a net full 'o them nice blue crabs you love."

"Ahhh. I do love them. And so do the men. Crab cakes for supper then."

"Can I ask you again?" Daniel tilted his head and looked at me.

"Ah, Daniel. Why do you go on so?"

"That ain't a 'no.' Marry me, Olu?" Daniel beseeched me, with his brown eyes wide open and pleading. He was grinning, hands joined as if in prayer. Now reader, Daniel was a fine, tall man, a good two hands taller than me. And when he smiled it became hard to turn him down.

"God has the perfect woman for you, Daniel."

"I'm lookin' at her."

"When you find . . ."

"I get it Miss Olu. Don' worry. I be asking again."

A few days later he didn't show up with a catch, and I worried about him. The sickest men on the island were in a rudely constructed barracks, with twenty cots lined up side by side. Their pustules were either clear or opaque, the red blisters ravaging their faces, hands, arms, and feet. Their stifled moans penetrated the air, filling the barracks with agony, the only sound other than scratching. After breakfast I came down to the barracks to check on the men. A British soldier always accompanied me, but never came into the barracks, unless to remove the dead. Invariably, a man or two had not survived the night. The soldiers dreaded the task of removing the dead even more than the physical labor involved in digging graves. After the first week, graves were no longer dug for each smallpox victim. Larger graves housed three to five men apiece.

The day dawned one waits for all winter long—high, strong sun nearly blinding in its brilliance, a few wispy clouds, and temperatures abnormally high. While the weather cheered me, I dreaded what—or rather who—I would encounter in the sick barracks.

I paused outside the entrance, the squat, rectangular building had only openings, no actual windows or doors. As I stepped out of the light and into the dark, my spirits sank as I saw Daniel in the first cot. His eyes were open, but glazed with pain, and I thought he was already dead. I knelt by his cot and pulled a cold compress out of my bag, pressing it gently on his forehead; heat permeated the cloth and warmed it instantly. Daniel's eyes focused on my face and he tried to smile. "My angel—come to lead me to heaven."

I offered an herbal broth and a cold compress, wishing I had an actual cure instead of scant alleviation of symptoms. As I talked to Daniel I felt his weak pulse, and assessed his strength, also weak.

Sunlight and fresh air aided in the healing process, so I tried to get the men who could stand and walk to come outside for a short walk, or even a short time of sitting outside in the sun. Daniel had a few flat, red spots which had not blistered up yet. I helped him sit up and rest for a few minutes before I assisted him to a standing position.

Taking his elbow, I let him lean into me as he stood, shaking a bit. He slipped his feet into his shoes, and I escorted him outdoors. The British soldier standing by the door almost fell backward in his attempt to get out of our way. Daniel blinked at the brightness of the sun and shielded his eyes with his hand. After a minute or two I could tell he was flagging, so we stopped and rested on a rock heated by the sun.

"You are my angel, Olu. Just wishing you were my wife, too." Daniel smiled weakly.

I smiled and helped him up. It took longer to walk back to the sick barracks, and the soldier had not resumed his position by the door, but stood far off, leaning against a tree, smoking a pipe. When Daniel reached his cot, he lay down and immediately fell asleep. I checked the other men—two had died during the night, ten were visibly worse, and four seemed to be the same; they probably survived the worst. Although their pustules looked ghastly, red pimples covering their faces, hands, arms, even feet, when I touched their brow, the fever had abated, and their eyes were clear. I can best tell sickness and health by the eyes.

The soldier was most unhappy to learn he had two dead men to bury, and unceremoniously wrapped them in old blankets, drug them out the door, and threw them in an open grave already containing two other bodies. I tried to distract the alert men.

The next day I brought goldenseal tea for the men—I had an extra portion for Daniel. I scouted around the island, to the dismay of the two soldiers sent to assist me, clambering over rocks and hills to see if there were any familiar herbs, awkward with my growing belly. I was thrilled to find goldenseal and shepherd's purse, though I couldn't find any lady's mantle or yarrow.

My soldier for the day set down the pot of boiling tea, and I checked on the men, beginning with Daniel. His blisters were larger, he looked lethargic, and he was hot to the touch. I didn't think he would survive the day. I first served tea to the men who were awake and alert enough to drink it—all six of them. Then I sat on the floor by Daniel's cot and applied a cold compress to his forehead, his neck, his cheeks—it warmed up instantly. He was burning up. I held his hand and prayed for him in Igbo.

Over the next few days, Daniel remained unchanged, he moved in and out of consciousness, and I spent more and more time by his side. I knew it was unwise to become attached, but it was too late. Daniel was so sweet to me, always joking, laughing, and proposing! One day I stayed by Daniel's cot for hours, neglecting my other duties. The soldier with me left for about an hour and returned with Captain Williams. I looked up, sensing trouble.

Captain Williams believed I was spending too much time with the sick and neglecting my cooking duties for the shipmates. I reminded him smallpox was a fierce enemy, maybe even worse than the Patriots, and it had stolen a lot of our men. Smallpox met its match in me, he said. He also brought a message from Lord Dunmore: while tending the sick, don't forget the living. The men onboard the ship hadn't gotten any soups or stews for a week, while I was busy tending to Daniel and the other sick men.

I promised to resume cooking for the shipmates on the morrow and asked Captain Williams to assure Lord Dunmore I had not forgotten my duties, nor my promise. Captain Williams tipped his cap to me and practically ran back to shore in his haste to leave the sick behind.

The next morning, I took my time preparing my breakfast, and checked on some herbs before I walked down. I was escorted by a very young, very skinny British soldier, whose freckles popped out on his cheeks and nose, and ears waved from the side of his head. We walked slowly, and arriving at the sick barracks I immediately noticed the quiet. Rain the night before had cleaned the air outside but did little to rid the shelter of the acrid stench of disease and death. Three more men had died, and the skinny, freckly soldier looked so confused and scared it would have been comical if it weren't so tragic. He went out and didn't return for at least an hour, so I poured tea for the recovering men myself, nudged each one to a sitting position, and assessed the progression or remission of the smallpox. Once the scabs fell off men either died quickly or began the slow process of recovery. After a few weeks I became adept at predicting who would live. It was all in the eyes. A yellowish tint meant death, while a clearing or opaque tint meant survival. Most of the time.

The soldier returned with another even younger soldier, heavier and taller than the first. They removed the three dead Africans, and I whispered a prayer as they went by. I had avoided Daniel's bed for as long as I could. I sat down on the edge of his cot. Daniel's eyes were closed; I took his wrist and felt his pulse—weak and irregular, but alive. I held his hand and placed my palm gently on his forehead, fingers reaching into his fuzzy hair, in a traditional Igbo blessing.

In Igbo I said, "God, here lies my friend, Daniel. Take him gently into your loving arms. Give him peace. Amen." I heard a very faint echo of "amen" from the cot. I remained at his bedside until he exhaled his last breath.

I didn't want to leave him, but I didn't want to stay. With no energy to cook, I wandered down to the beach, sat on a rock and looked out across the water. To my right, Dunmore's fleet sat anchored. There appeared to be fewer ships, but a new ship with a large British flag sat alongside Dunmore's ship.

Looking down toward Norfolk again, gazing at a flock of geese moving slowly in formation, a black triangular slash across the blue sky, spring-like weather contradicted my bleak mood. I noticed the trees had begun to bud, crocuses and wild irises peeked out through the thawed winter soil. And then I felt it. My baby, our baby, Teddy's and mine, moved. More like a whisper of wind against my belly, or an eyelash fluttering on my cheek—so subtle, yet so pronounced.

After my long reverie on the waterfront, I went back to the sick barracks and enlisted the help of a nearby soldier. He helped me wrap up Daniel's body in a sheet and bury it alone, in a shallow grave. I alone covered it with dirt and found a branch, from which I broke off twigs, so that it resembled a cross. I placed it atop Daniel's grave, stood next to it ... and cried.

When Captain Williams showed up to retrieve dinner for the men, I was not ready. The potatoes were not done roasting, and the duck was still stewing in the big pot over the open fire.

"Now see here, miss," Captain Williams sternly began, and I burst into tears.

"Ach, well ... oh, damn. Sorry. Hmmm."

# CHAPTER NINETEEN: OLU

I felt so sorry for him, and his discomfort was so comical, I burst out laughing.

"Well, I'll be miss. I do believe this here sick island is getting to ye."

He was right. The island, the sickness, the deaths, were all getting to me. I thought of Daniel, and the tears returned. I told Captain Williams Daniel died.

"Ah, poor soul. And what a fine fisherman he was. He'll be sorely missed I can tell ye that. No finer fisherman have I known."

I stirred the stew, tasted a spoonful, and poked a fork into a potato.

Captain Williams informed me Lord Dunmore wanted me back onboard ship. The doctor finally showed up with enough doses of smallpox vaccine to inoculate everyone and I was needed to help them through the reaction. If only he'd come sooner.

Unbeknownst to me, earlier that day an American warship captured the British sloop H.M.S. Edward, not far from where Lord Dunmore's fleet anchored. I imagined this rattled Lord Dunmore, and he was gathering everyone to him, possibly in preparation for battle.

I ran to Daniel's grave to say goodbye. When I got back to my room, it took less than ten minutes to put my few things in a sweet grass basket and join the three men at the boat. One of them asked, "It's Easter today, ain't it?"

"Yep, April 7th. Resurrection Day."

# CHAPTER TWENTY

## Joanna

### May 1821—Ely, Cambridgeshire

I sat in the morning room looking out the window at the view I never tired of—low, undulating hills, meadows, sheep, fields growing with wheat. I enjoyed visiting London but knew I would never want to live there for any length of time. The countryside was home—familiar, welcoming, calming, beautiful.

Uncle John strode into the room with a letter in his hand and an unreadable expression on his face. He asked me to guess who it was from. I had no idea and told him so.

"Hmm. Well, this letter which I hold in my hand is from none other than . . . the Reverend Henry Bromley."

"Oh!" I exclaimed, smiling.

"Oh, indeed. And what do you suppose he has written to me in this short missive?"

"Perhaps . . . possibly he has asked to . . . to call upon me?" I looked up at him.

"To call upon you? After one meeting years ago and a recent brief meeting? That seems rather unlikely, does it not?"

I suddenly sympathized with anyone in the courtroom under Uncle John's examination. I mentioned to Uncle John that Henry had performed the christening and we met afterwards and talked. After further interrogating me, he smiled and admitted his admiration for Henry.

"So shall I permit him to call upon you then?" Uncle John asked.

"Don't tease me so, Uncle John. Of course you should permit him!" I clasped my hands in front of me.

"That is your wish then?"

"Yes!"

"I'm happy to hear it. He will be dining with us this evening." Uncle John nodded to himself.

"Tonight?!?" I extended my hands in a question.

"Yes, tonight."

"I must get ready!" I leapt up and hastily left the room.

"Joanna, dear," Uncle John called after me, "It's not for hours yet. Not till six o'clock. How long does it take to get ready?" I had started upstairs and didn't answer.

By noon I had tried on and discarded eight different gowns, finally settling on one of my mother's gowns. A pale yellow, the gown's three-quarter length sleeves flared out ribbon-like to right below my elbow, a high stand-up collar in the back gave way to a modestly low neckline, showing the promise of, but not the actual cleavage. With a high waist, the dress widened out to the hem, so that when I walked, the gown swished about me. I wore a cameo around my neck given to me by Anne featuring a female slave with the inscription, "Am I not a woman and a sister," and pearl drop earrings given to me by Grandmamma. Short white gloves completed the outfit.

Annie had prepared my favourite dinner—roasted duck with apricot sauce, baby potatoes, spring peas, creamed spinach, and lima bean soup. Henry was scheduled to arrive at six o'clock, and at five o'clock, I had an unread book open in my lap, counting down the minutes. Uncle John came sauntering into the drawing room at five minutes before six o'clock.

The knocker on the door sounded, and Mr. Blake answered promptly, ushering Henry into the drawing room. Uncle John grasped his hand in a firm, affirming handshake. I rose and Henry took my hand in his, bowing over it and kissing it lightly, leaving my gloved hand tingling.

"How charming you look this evening, Joanna." Henry smiled in appreciation.

"Thank you," I replied, enjoying his admiring gaze.

"While you young people get reacquainted, I'll check in with the cook on dinner," Uncle John said, excusing himself.

I sat back down on the settee, and Henry took the chair beside me.

"That is a very becoming gown, Joanna."

"Thank you. It was my mama's. I received several gowns as part of my inheritance."

"It must be nice to have that reminder of her, to wear what she wore. Do you resemble her?"

"I have some of my papa's features and some of Mama's. I'm a bit mixed up!"

"Ah, but what a beautiful mix!" Henry's eyes lit up in approbation.

"Thank you, Rev. Bromley." I blushed.

"Please, call me Henry."

"Well, Henry, I find that most men don't know quite what to make of me, so they make no attempt to try."

"What do you mean?"

"I imagine they wonder—is she English, is she African? What is she?" I looked at Henry to gauge his reaction.

"Does it really matter all that much?" His head tilted to the right.

"Doesn't it?"

A beautiful mix, practically black, half-caste, or African English. I knew I wasn't all of one or the other, but a combination of colours and backgrounds. I had begun to embrace my heritage, and Henry's admiration helped the process. We discussed the importance placed on background and birth and Henry argued for those without a noble birth; they could work hard to achieve a place of respect in society. I pointed out that while some may respect a merchant, a barrister, or a successful farmer, they could never hope to gain the respect given to an earl, a baron, or a duke—who may be lazy and not work a day in his life.

Uncle John entered and added his thoughts. "Such a deeply philosophical discussion before dinner! Birth, nobility, race, such weighty matters. Let's retire to the dining room and find a more frivolous subject to discuss if you please. And did you reach any conclusions?" Uncle John asked.

"On a subject that has been assumed God-ordained for centuries, have we solved it in minutes?!" I asked.

"Two great minds, one a religious academic, the other a master tactician—beware Rev. Bromley, she may look sweet, but she's brutal in chess! Two such great minds should be able to solve this dilemma."

"I agree that birth is important, but it's not all important," Henry began. "Even in scripture, we see the importance of birth, Abraham, Isaac, Jacob—the lineage of Jesus through the House of David. But then Paul writes in Galatians, there is neither Jew nor Gentile, slave nor free, female nor male. In Christ, birth is not important."

"But in England it is!" Uncle John said, simply to keep the debate going.

"And it's important in Africa as well," I added. "Papa's father was an *embrenche*."

I explained Papa's father was a chief, kind of like a prince. Henry laughed and told me I argued for the commoner, but I was actually a princess. I had never thought of myself as a princess. I guess my aunt, Oluchukwu, would be a princess. She was the only daughter among seven sons.

We walked to the dining room, abandoning the discussion of birth and nobility, but ended up in another debate.

"St. John's College far surpasses Trinity College," Uncle John said, sparking the debate, drawing Henry into the fight.

"In what way, sir?" Henry asked, not yet taking the bait.

"Oh, in most every way. The scholarly excellence of the graduates, the success of the athletes, contributions to society."

"Ah, I see. You would argue that the contributions of Isaac Newton, Francis Bacon, and Lord Byron are not exemplary?"

"Touché. You have scored a punishing blow. But I shall try to recover. What of William Wilberforce, Thomas Clarkson, and William Wordsworth?"

Annie served dessert, clucking at the men and shaking her head, before any more points could be scored on either side. The plum pie fully consumed our minds and mouths for the remainder of the meal. After dinner, we retired to the drawing room. Uncle John asked, "Rev. Bromley, tell us a little bit about your family."

"My father made a living as a solicitor. He has always been involved in non-conformist churches. Even my grandfather attended a dissenting church—so that has been passed to me over generations. I admit I find a sense of comfort in the tradition, and what I might dare call the pageantry of the Church of England. But I much prefer the freedom of worship, of expression, of governance, in non-conformist churches."

Since the Act of Uniformity in 1662, all men who took holy orders or sought to teach at a university had to adhere to 'unfeigned assent and consent' to the Book of Common Prayer, continuing the Anglican ceremonies, and be ordained by a bishop. Those clergy who did not agree were considered dissenting, forfeiting their living (income), and acting against the laws of England, and this included Congregationalists, Baptists, Methodists, Unitarians, and others. They differed widely amongst themselves but had a disdain for the Anglican church in common.

Uncle John asked Henry if he had received a call to a church. Henry filled the pulpit at several churches in Cambridgeshire, and one in Devon, but no calls had yet come. I asked if there wasn't more uncertainty as a non-conformist minister.

"Only if one is trusting in man. I believe God will provide a church!" Henry replied.

"Well said, Rev. Bromley. But I do hear Joanna's point as well. The Church of England is well established, a parish in every town. Non-conformist churches are not as prevalent. They seem to spring up here and there. Some flourish and some fail," Uncle John noted.

"True. But that may be a positive factor. If a church is not growing, not meeting the needs of the community, if the minister is not teaching the Word of God, in those cases failing may be positive, not negative," Henry argued.

"You have a point," Uncle John admitted.

"I see we have reached another impasse this evening, gentlemen," I said. "What shall we tackle next?"

"How about a friendly game of chess, Joanna," Uncle John asked.

"I'd like nothing better."

It took about forty minutes, during which time the conversation was on food and weather, but I finally cornered Uncle John's king into checkmate. Henry came and sat opposite me. I smiled in encouragement, but Henry looked nervous.

"Now Uncle John, no coaching, coughing, or distractions please. I'm sure Henry will do well without your intervention."

"You wound me, Joanna. I wouldn't think of such a thing."

I gave him a stern look, and Uncle John attempted to look as innocent as possible. Henry made the first move, advancing a pawn, and I followed suit. We were both concentrating so hard, conversation came to a halt. Before Henry realized what had happened, I captured his queen, then a rook, and a few moves later I put him in checkmate.

"I hope you won't be offended, Joanna, but I've never seen one of the fairer sex play chess as well as you."

"How could I be offended at such a compliment?"

Uncle John had gone out to check on his appointments for the morrow, so we were alone again, though the door to the drawing room was open wide. We moved to sit by the fire and began to talk about parts of the country we had visited. Henry enjoyed Bath and the Lake District, which I had never seen. We reminisced about Gore House, the Wilberforces' lovely home. Henry talked about the narrow streets in Cambridge, the rarefied academic atmosphere, the River Cam, races in the courtyard, the camaraderie of the men, and the mediocre meals. I related stories about Mrs. Limebear's school, the other girls, especially Anne, and my friend Barbara Wilberforce.

When I expressed my worries about Barbara's health—a bad cough that didn't abate, Henry suggested she try leaving London as the air there is detrimental for lung complaints. I told him the Wilberforces were all in Surrey now, Marden Park, many miles down the road from Westminster Bridge.

"That should help. I'll remember her in my prayers," Henry promised.

"Thank you, Henry."

"I have an item for your prayer list."

"What is it?"

"The Independent Chapel in Appledore has expressed an interest in me," Henry said, a serious expression on his face.

"That's wonderful! Isn't it?"

"Yes. It's a fine community, and the church seems stable. It would be my first pastorate. But they have yet to issue a call, and I'm seeking God for guidance."

"I'll be happy to pray for your wisdom in this. It's an important decision."

"Yes, and one that may involve others," Henry agreed, looking intently at me.

I wondered, hoped, he might mean his decision would affect me, but that would be true only if we were to marry. If only I could interpret his gaze. For my part, I knew I was already halfway in love with this handsome, funny, sweet man.

## Summer 1821

Henry took me to Cambridge on two separate occasions—our courtship had begun. On the first visit, we walked up St. Andrew's Street, then down the narrow streets to King's and Trinity colleges, and down Silver

Street to his own college, Queens. I couldn't help gazing up at the ancient stone and brick halls, but my favourite was King's Chapel—the tallest and grandest of them all. Henry showed me the center courtyard, where races against the clock were held, which he loved to engage in, but never won. I felt a twinge of envy—how wonderful it would be to live in such beautiful surroundings, reading and studying, discussing finer philosophical and theological points with others of like interest. How lovely it would be to read to my heart's content.

Queens College bordered the River Cam, which we sat beside and admired on our first trip. On our second trip I knew what to expect and was excited to see the university again.

"We're almost there, Joanna," Henry said, looking out the windows of the coach.

"Cambridge is so close to where I grew up, but our last visit here was my first ever. Now I want to keep coming back. I adore the old buildings—there is an atmosphere of . . . I don't know . . . of greatness here!"

"Why thank you, Joanna," Henry said, grinning.

"Oh, I meant, you . . . of, of course."

"Not Sir Isaac Newton?"

"Him, too," I admitted.

We were accompanied by my maid Deirdre, who carried a wicker picnic basket. As we exited the coach, Deirdre stood beside us, gawking at the size and grandeur of the buildings. "If this don't remind me of our Trinity College in Dublin!" she exclaimed.

Our first stop was a chocolate shop where Henry and I enjoyed a cup of chocolate and a chocolate biscuit.

"You have discovered my vice," I admitted.

"If you have only one, you're better than I."

"My main one. Not my only one. I love chocolate." I crossed my wrists over my breasts and hugged myself.

"That's not a vice—more like a preference."

"More like a need. I've been known to become very unreasonable when there's no chocolate in the house."

"That's easily remedied. I will keep a copious supply on hand."

Did Henry mean in a home we lived in together as husband and wife?

"Now that I've told you mine, it's your turn." I looked over at Henry.

"Well, hmmm . . . I love horses. If I had a penchant for taking risks, I'm sure I'd be an inveterate gambler. But as it is, I'll probably own more horses than I need or could possibly use."

"I love horses, too! Uncle John believes I speak their language," I said, with a wry smile.

"What an unusual talent. I look forward to witnessing a conversation!" Henry said.

I thought about Seamus, the horse at Mrs. Limebear's School, and the beautiful palomino I befriended at Astleys. The more I learned about Henry, the more I liked him.

"So, horses and chocolate." I put one hand out, then the other.

"What a pair we make, Joanna," Henry smiled. "Oh, I have one addition to my list. Books."

"Books?"

"Yes. I can't seem to get enough. To read enough. I'll need a very large library."

"Okay, a library and a stable."

"Your needs are more easily met—chocolate takes up very little room!" Henry laughed.

Henry and I left the chocolate shop and walked, my arm tucked under Henry's, down to the River Cam, with Deirdre following behind. The sun had begun to peek through the clouds, and the temperature rose. Henry asked me to wait by a tall maple tree, while he went back to tell Deirdre something. Henry came back to me and gathered up my arm in his, carrying the basket with his left arm.

"Would you like to go punting on the River Cam?" Henry asked.

"I'd love to. It looks like such fun!"

"Perfect. Let's go down and rent a boat. We used to do this at university. It's great exercise for the arms. It looks deceptively easy to put the pole down into the riverbed and push the boat along, but it's not. I'm going to rent a boat and a punter so we can sit back and enjoy the ride."

"How delightful." Henry's sense of adventure intrigued me.

For the dear sum of fifty pence, Henry rented the boat and punter for two hours. I took it all in, wanting to remember every detail to tell Anne and Barbara. The small, red, flat-bottomed boat had two wooden benches—just boards really—and Henry helped me into the boat. I lifted my dress up to step over the side. The punter looked up at me admiringly as I lifted my skirt, and Henry didn't suppress a glare. I adjusted my bonnet, to shade my face from the now bright sunshine, and settled myself on the crude bench, shifting about and rocking the boat. Henry sat down beside me in an instant—taking neither the time nor the care I did—and placed the basket on the bottom of the boat under the other bench.

"Let's go down past Magdalene College," Henry instructed the young college student serving as punter.

"Yes, sir," he replied.

Many other boats punted down the river. I looked about me, smiling at a young couple with a baby, a group of four college students, and two older women, all enjoying the river on this early June day. Some of the older people we encountered on the river glanced at us, looked away, then turned back to stare. I wondered if my bonnet was askew or my dress amiss and hoped no more pernicious meaning lay behind their double-takes.

"Henry? Is there something wrong with my hat, or my dress?" I asked.

"No, darling. You look beautiful." Well! That was the first time Henry called me darling—or beautiful—and it came all in one sentence!

"I was wondering why those people were staring at me?"

"I don't think they're staring at you, my love. They're staring at us. We make a rather unusual couple." First, he calls me darling and beautiful; then he calls us a couple. I got a distinct impression his interest in me might match my interest in him.

"Does it . . . bother you?" I asked, not wanting to admit it was because I was a woman of colour, but that would explain the curious and even hostile glances.

"Not at all," Henry said. "Look, what is that bird on the tree hanging over the river?"

"You're trying to distract me." I put my right hand on my hip akimbo.

"Is it working?"

"Not really. Let me see." I gazed at the tree where Henry pointed. "It looks like a long-tailed bushtit."

"I don't know how you tell all the different birds apart."

"One simply needs to know what to look for. Every bird has distinctive features. Maybe a longer beak, or an extra stripe on the wing, or a different colour leg. Each one is unique and special."

"Just like us." Henry brought the conversation back to the point.

"Hmmm. Maybe. Although the male birds are always more colourful and attractive than their female counterparts."

"So, not like us, you are more attractive than I am! But I guess some folks aren't accustomed to the colour of your plumage!"

"Rather an odd way to put it, Henry. But you could be right."

"Or they aren't used to seeing a dark-skinned woman with a pale fellow like me. I think we complement each other rather nicely." Henry held my hand, looking at our interlocking fingers. I liked the zebra pattern of our entwined hands. I knew there were over 20,000 people of African descent in London, but other than my parents, I didn't know of any mixed marriages. It wasn't illegal, but it also wasn't common. I had few qualms about marrying a White man, but at the time I had no idea what opposition we might face.

We were silent for the next several minutes, absorbing the gentle rocking of the boat, hearing the swishing and popping of the pole dipping in the water and pushing the boat along, until the boat was alongside the shore. Henry helped me out, then he retrieved the picnic basket. He asked the punter to wait about an hour and led the way up the hill. Henry put the basket down, retrieved some bread and cheese, and ran back to give it to the appreciative student punter.

Henry knew the area, and he held my hand, bringing me to a spot shaded by trees with a perfect view of the river below, the university, and the town, with no one else in sight.

"This is lovely!"

"Yes. The view is amazing from right here." Henry looked only at me. I removed my hat, and tendrils of my long hair fell down my back.

Henry took the blanket out of the basket, and we each grabbed an end, pulling so it bellied in the air before settling on the lush grass.

"I'm famished!" I admitted.

"Well, I've got just the thing right here. Don't you worry." Henry started to pull out two plates, then an assortment of containers. "Ham, cheese, bread, cherries, grapes, turkey, more bread, pudding ... and wine. Oh, and chocolate! Happy now?"

"Delirious!" I laughed.

Henry and I served each other and ate until we were satisfied. I leaned back against a tree, and Henry sat across from me. He took out two wine glasses and poured us each a glass.

"To new beginnings," Henry toasted.

I smiled and clinked my glass against his.

"We haven't known each other long, Joanna," Henry began, "but I believe I know you very well."

"I feel the same way," I admitted.

"I've grown very fond of you, to the point, well . . . I can't imagine living without you. And I'll be leaving soon." Henry looked down at the river.

For some reason, I focused on his leaving rather than his statement he couldn't live without me. He couldn't live without me? Then why was he leaving?

"Leaving?" I asked.

"Yes . . . and . . . I'm not doing this very well, Joanna," Henry said, looking directly into my eyes and taking my hands in his. "What I'm trying to say is, I would be most honoured if you would consent to be my wife. Will you marry me?" Having said his piece, Henry slumped back a bit, still holding my hands in his, looking a bit more anxious now as he awaited my response.

"Yes." One softly spoken word changed his life . . . and mine. I believe we don't know how we really feel until a choice is offered, and we accept or decline. Henry's proposal confirmed my love for him. Saying 'yes' was not really a choice—my heart and mind propelled me to answer yes. I couldn't deny his love for me nor my love for him.

"Yes?" he asked, sitting upright, squeezing my hands tightly.

"Yes, Henry. I would love to marry you." Henry stood up quickly, drawing me with him, into his arms. As he held me, he caressed my hair, and sealed our promise with a quick kiss on the mouth, followed by a slightly longer kiss . . . His warm, searching lips met my tentative lips, but soon we were both fully engrossed in kissing, expressing our love wordlessly.

Flushed, happy, and newly engaged, we sat back down. Henry leaned against the tree, and I leaned against Henry. "I love you, Joanna. You're the most amazing woman I've ever known."

"I love you too, Henry. You . . . you said you were leaving. Where are you going? Where are we going, I should say!"

Henry told me the church in Appledore called him to be their minister. The ordination was scheduled for later this month, June 24th. We'd have to move to Appledore. I was excited about the marriage, and so happy for Henry to get this confirmation and a call to his first church. My elation was briefly tempered with a fear the church might object to me, but Henry reassured me. He didn't anticipate any problems, and said if there were any, if we were not accepted as a couple, he wouldn't want to minister there.

"Please don't say that Henry. I don't want to be a burden," I said.

"You are my greatest joy—never a burden. I'm not naïve. I know some may not be accepting of our marriage. But we will have each other, and God will help us." Henry put his arms around me and drew me back against him.

"We have so much to do, to decide," I said, turning my thoughts to the wedding. "When do you want to marry?"

"The sooner the better," Henry said, standing, pulling me into his arms again. He kissed me gently yet passionately, letting me sense his desire. "The sooner," another kiss, "...the better," he said again.

"Yes, I . . . hmmm . . . I see what you mean," I stammered, blushing.

I was flustered, having never been kissed, and now twice in one day. It was very pleasant. No, more than pleasant. It was downright pleasurable. I wondered what other pleasures lie ahead. Then I smiled, remembering Barbara's insistent question, "Did he kiss you?"

"Why are you smiling?" Henry asked.

"Other than because I'm so happy? I was remembering Barbara asking me if Fredrik kissed me."

"And did he?" Henry asked, suddenly looking very unhappy indeed.

"No, he didn't. But I could never see the purpose of kissing," I admitted.

"Do you now?" Henry peered at me.

"I'm beginning to."

Henry wanted to marry as soon as possible—and I did, too. We decided to set a date in August and marry in London. We discussed the church, who would officiate, and how many would be invited.

"We can decide all these things together. We'd best be getting back. Oh! I almost forgot!" Henry pulled a ring out of his pants pocket, a wide gold band with an emerald in the middle. He took my hand and slipped the ring on my finger. It fit perfectly.

"It's beautiful! Thank you, Henry," I said shyly, and kissed him on the cheek.

"It was my grandmother's. I'm glad you like it."

Since my parents both died when I was so little, and I had lived largely with Uncle John and my Grandmamma, both of whom were single, I hadn't been around happy marriages growing up. William and Barbara Wilberforce were my best example—they seemed very loving, happy, and compatible. I hoped my marriage to Henry would be as good as theirs. I believed we had all the ingredients to make a happy marriage . . . I was right.

Two months later, on August 29th, Henry and I were married in London, St. James Church, Clerkenwell. Only family and a few close friends were invited—there were less than twenty in attendance. Anne came, and Mr. and Mrs. Wilberforce with Barbara, and their son William; Uncle John, and Aunt Jane, her husband and sons; Henry's parents, his sister Catherine, and a few of his Cambridge friends. The wedding was held at ten o'clock, followed by breakfast. Henry took me by carriage to the Lake District where we stayed in a quaint little inn for four nights and went horseback riding every day. He bought a horse there, Bella, with whom I had a delightful conversation while he looked on in amazement. We got to know each other better and better—both inside and outside the bedroom!

The wedding and the wedding holiday were such happy occasions, but I was distracted with concern for Barbara who had been coughing, even during the ceremony, and she had lost colour, and wasn't . . . she wasn't her normally mischievous, vivacious self. I decided to visit Barbara in Bath that fall.

## Fall 1821

I arrived in Bath with conflicting emotions. Prepared to allow Bath to charm me, I also knew seeing Barbara ill would be heartbreaking. Mrs. Wilberforce greeted me at the front door.

"I'm so glad you've come! Barbara could use a bit of cheering up. Her illness seems to have robbed her of her natural cheerfulness, and she sits hour after hour gazing out the window. I can't even tempt her to leave her room."

I knocked softly, and barely heard Barbara's soft 'enter.' I hesitated slightly before opening the door. I'd seen Barbara at my wedding two months earlier, but I was shocked at the dramatic change in her appearance in that short period of time. Barbara's cheekbones jutted out of her face, and her normally rosy complexion had become wan and ashen. I could see Barbara's chest rise and fall with the effort to breathe. Barbara attempted to rise, but I rushed over and knelt beside her instead, holding her bony fingers gently.

"It's so good to see you, Barbara," I said.

## CHAPTER TWENTY: JOANNA

"Mrs. Bromley, I'm glad you came. But I don't think . . . your new husband will spare you . . . for very long," Barbara paused to breathe between each word.

"Henry is very understanding."

"Which is why you married him . . . I'm sure. I'm so happy for you, Joanna. So . . . happy. I do . . . like Rev. Bromley. You made . . . an excellent choice."

"He's a good man, Barbara. A wonderful husband."

"Yes, but is he . . . a good kisser?!?" Barbara attempted to smile.

"Still asking me about kissing, is it? Actually . . . he is!" I grinned.

"Ahhh! I will have to live vicariously . . . through you."

"Nonsense. Once you have recovered, I will introduce you to some fine young men and you will see for yourself."

"Tell me . . . what's it like? Being married?" Barbara leaned back and closed her eyes.

I regaled Barbara with stories about men's rituals—cleaning boots, shaving, and tying cravats, that sort of thing. I wasn't used to sharing a room, so not having privacy took some getting used to.

"So you share . . . a bedroom . . . hmmm?" Barbara opened her eyes.

"Yes, Barbara. You're incorrigible!"

"And what do you do . . . other than sleep . . . in that bedroom?"

"Barbara!" I was too embarrassed to divulge details.

"A girl can ask . . . can't she?" Barbara shrugged.

"All I will say is that Henry is a very passionate and considerate husband."

"No baby yet?"

"Barbara! We only got married two months ago," I reminded her.

"Right."

"How are you feeling, Barbara?"

"Trapped," she said, anger and defeat lacing her tone.

"Trapped?"

"My mind is active . . . but my body won't cooperate. I have no . . . energy. It takes . . . effort to breathe . . . and the medicines don't seem . . . to help the coughing." Barbara began to cough, unused to talking so much.

"Let me talk; you can rest," I assured her.

I told Barbara about our wedding trip to the Lake District; our attempt at canoeing together, which produced more laughter than movement; and the horse Henry bought. I entertained Barbara with stories about the parishioners at the Chapel, characters in the village, and our new cook, Bridgett. Barbara began to nod off, so I pressed her hand gently and said "Rest now. I'll come back and visit this evening."

I went downstairs to the drawing room, deep in thought. Mrs. Wilberforce was sitting in her chair, holding an untouched piece of needlework.

"How does she seem to you, dear? I know it must be somewhat of a shock to see your friend so ill. This consumption is dreadful." Mrs. Wilberforce looked up to me with shadowed eyes and a weary smile.

"She's lost so much weight. Yet she still has an active mind and a vibrant wit. It's almost as if her body has betrayed her."

"The doctor visits regularly but offers little hope. He says she may recover, but in such a way that we prepare for her leaving us. I pray God would . . . heal her or take her home."

"Has it come to that then?" Tears escaped down my cheek.

"I'm afraid so, dear."

I stayed a few more days. That was the last time I saw Barbara. She didn't recover and died 30 December. My best friend, my honready sister, my soulmate, was gone. I missed her dearly, and grieved not just for myself, but for her parents who missed her more than I did. Henry was a great solace to me, but my heart ached.

After Henry and I had returned from our wedding trip, we settled in the village of Appledore, a village north of Exeter and south of Swansea, near the coast. Five years sped by as we adjusted to pastoral life, village life, and married life. There were so many new things to do, learn, and see that it was all a bit overwhelming at times.

Henry felt the chapel was a good place to begin his ministry, but not somewhere he wanted to stay for his whole life. When Henry was asked to fill the pulpit in Clavering, I joined him for the church visit. We both loved the area, all the farms, rolling green hills, horses. That night we talked about how welcome we felt, what an exuberant congregation it was. Only then did we realize how discontented we were in Appledore. The congregation of mostly older women, few men, and even fewer young families, resisted Henry's idea for change and considered outreach unimportant. Henry felt stymied and unable to carry out the plans he so carefully prepared. When the call came from the Congregational Church in Clavering, inviting Henry to take over as minister, we didn't hesitate to make the move.

# CHAPTER TWENTY-ONE

## Olu

April 1776

THE MOVE BACK TO the ship felt odd. I had lost my sea legs after staying on the island and caring for the sick men for so many weeks. Lord Dunmore's exuberant welcome outweighed the lukewarm reception from Sue and June. Happily, they had gained confidence and skill, and men to keep them happy, so while they were not thrilled with my return, they accepted it.

Instead of a welcome, they informed me they did fine without me, the men liked their cooking. They wanted to know why I was back on the ship, what I would be doing. I sensed they didn't want to give up cooking. I'd be working with the doctor to inoculate everyone on board against smallpox, including them, I couldn't help adding.

My stomach growled as I walked down to the sick bay. There were five men on cots. Three Blacks had the pox, one White soldier appeared to be wounded, and a second White man appeared to be in the beginning stages of the pox.

I introduced myself as Olu.

"Another woman on board," one of the Blacks nudged his cot mate.

"A vision. She ain't real. I'm dreamin'," the other sick man replied.

"Are you real?" the third one asked.

"Yes, sir. Real as you," I replied.

"Where you been?" the first one asked.

I told them I had been on Tucker's Point, tending to the sick, but now I was here to take care of them, and help inoculate everyone on board the ship. The White soldier had recently been inoculated and used some choice words to describe the doctor. He questioned the wisdom of getting a person sick to cure him. I assured him the illness was much worse than the cure, wished them a pleasant evening and headed back to the galley. Sue and June were cleaning up, and I offered to help, hoping to eat the remnants of supper. I was leaning back, my hand rubbing my sore lower back, and noticed Sue and June whispering.

"You expectin'?" June asked.

"Yeah," I said. I wondered why they hadn't noticed my expanding waist earlier, but then they were usually absorbed in their own lives, and didn't notice me much at all, and I had been off the ship for weeks. They peppered me with questions, which I avoided as best I could. Sue and June transformed before my eyes! They sat me down on a barrel and ladled out the bits of stew left in the pot, plopped a mug of hot tea beside the bowl, and urged me to "eat for two." I fought back tears at their uncharacteristic sweetness and generosity.

## May/June 1776 Gywnn Island

For the next several weeks rain interspersed with sunshine, but most of the time I was below deck, assisting the doctor with inoculations. He trusted me to prepare the lancet with the powder, although he would administer the cut and sprinkle in the dosage. The men came from other ships, while we remained the lead ship. By the end of June almost all the men had been inoculated, but for many it came too late. Those unfortunate ones were shipped to Tucker's Point. When I asked Captain Williams who was caring for the men there since I had left, his noncommittal reply confirmed my worst nightmare. No one.

## 9 July 1776

I was so accustomed to living on an anchored ship lulling me to sleep and rocking gently throughout the day, I was unprepared for sudden movement. But on this day in July men raised the anchor, hoisted the sails, and the ship sailed. I became seasick within minutes, joining others on the deck who leaned over the railing to empty their insides. The wind blew strong and steady, and we climbed over the waves, only to fall back down on the other side. The waves splashed back up and washed the vomit from my face.

We now numbered almost 100 ships. By day's end we dropped anchor again—off St. George's Island. On our ship men were working, there was little sickness, and all appeared to be well. But one night I overheard Lord Dunmore and Captain Williams talking. They were debating the benefits of staying put or moving on. Captain Williams suggested we move on, as food and water were scarce and most of the other ships housed mostly sick men. Lord Dunmore decided to burn the contaminated ships, and his ship would sail off to parts north.

"Sir, my lord, it be for the best. There ain't nothing else to be done," Captain Williams said.

"Send a scouting party out. Ferry the sick to the island. Report to me which ships remain clean," Lord Dunmore ordered.

"What shall I tell the men who ask, what their fate will be on the island?" Captain Williams asked.

"Tell them . . . tell them . . . oh damn . . . tell them we'll send help as soon as we can." Lord Dunmore ran his fingers through his hair.

"And, my lord, will we?"

"Of course not," Lord Dunmore mumbled so softly, I could barely hear him.

The news I heard was grim. Many men had not yet been inoculated, and would die a painful, and lonely, death. I thought of volunteering to stay behind. Then my baby moved.

## 6 August 1776

I woke up to the stench of smoke and burning wood. When I came up to the deck, I couldn't believe my eyes. The sea was aflame. Even though I knew what Lord Dunmore had planned, to see all the ships ablaze shocked me. In three directions flames and smoke rose from the sea, obscuring the sun. I later learned that sixty-three ships burned that August morning.

Captain Williams approached me and said, "Well miss, I don't imagine I'll be seeing you again. You be off north with Lord Dunmore, whilst I be leading a small fleet south, taking Sue and June along with half the men."

"You've been most kind Captain Williams. I'll miss you." I leaned over to kiss his hairy cheek.

"Well, hmmm, most folks don't accuse me of that. Don't spread it about, miss!" Captain Williams put his finger to his lips.

"Your secret is safe with me."

"Take good care of that wee lad you be carrying." Captain Williams pointed at me and patted his own stomach.

"Lad or lassie, yes, I will. Godspeed, Captain Williams."

"Godspeed, Olu."

We sailed all day and night, leaving all that had become familiar behind—again. On the third day we set anchor. I had no idea where we were, or where we headed. It turns out we were off the coast of Cape May. We had to wait for a few of the slower ships to join us.

I was in the galley preparing breakfast—or trying to find enough edible food to assuage the men's hunger a bit. No oats, only a dozen or so eggs, no fruit. I decided to make potato pancakes, heavy on the potatoes and onions. The batter was finished, the pan was hot when I ladled in the first batch to fry. I heard muffled yelling coming from down the hallway and could only hear a word here and there. The only words I heard clearly were "Olu, Captain, demand." Could that be Teddy's voice? I thought I was imagining it. Frying pancakes, and general noise on the ship, made it nearly impossible to hear. I leaned out the doorway and heard Lord Dunmore's angry reply.

"Who are you?"

Then the other voice again—oops—almost burned the pancakes. This wouldn't do, there was too little food to waste any.

I clearly heard Teddy say, "Olu is my wife."

Oh, my Jesus! It was Teddy! How did he get here? How did he find me? Wife? His wife died. I was confused, elated, worried. I wanted to see Teddy, wanted nothing better than to hug and kiss him, let him feel our baby, and leave all the decisions up to him. But my mistrust of White men ran so deep, I was still skeptical about why he was here. I tried to focus on the pancakes and was torn between my desire to throw myself into Teddy's arms and wait to see why he had come. I didn't have to wait long.

Pounding footsteps preceded Teddy's appearance in the doorway. He joked, "I couldn't stay away from your griddle cakes, Olu."

I removed the potato pancakes, slowly and carefully, biding my time, and turned to face Teddy. He immediately looked down to my swollen belly, his eyes widened in shock, and he whispered, "mine?"

Before I could answer, Lord Dunmore showed up. "I will have this man removed immediately, Olu," he promised, in his most commanding voice.

"No need, my lord. He's an old friend."

"Friend?" both men echoed.

"He said you were his wife," Lord Dunmore growled.

"He did, hmmmm. Please, Lord Dunmore, allow me to finish breakfast and talk to Teddy, then you can . . . remove him."

"I have a soldier posted outside," Lord Dunmore affirmed.

"Thank you, my lord."

Left alone, neither of us spoke.

Then I said, "Yes, Teddy. The baby is yours. I have known no man but you."

He stepped closer, pulled me into his arms, and embraced me tightly.

"Olu, how I have searched for you. Why couldn't you wait? I told you I'd go with you. I've been frantic with worry. Look at you! You're even more beautiful than I remember. So lovely." He leaned forward to kiss me gently on my lips.

"Teddy, why have you come?"

"Why have I . . . ? Olu, what are you asking me? Don't you know?" He leaned back and looked at me, brows furrowed, lips pursed, arms crossed.

"Have you come to capture me?" I asked.

"Capture you? Capture you! That's right. I've come to capture you." He nodded.

For one long moment I gave in to my paranoia.

He put his finger under my chin, nudging my head up so I could meet his eyes.

"I've come to capture you. To capture your heart. To capture your love. To make you mine. To bind you to me. Olu . . . marry me?"

Teddy looked at me with such earnest love, I knew he meant it. And I knew I shouldn't have questioned him.

"I want to marry you, Olu. Before I knew you were carrying my child, I wanted to marry you. But now, even more so. Don't leave me again, Olu," Teddy pleaded.

Lord Dunmore's voice boomed down the hallway: "Is all well?"

"Yes, my lord," I nearly giggled. "Very well."

I returned to finishing breakfast and Teddy told me he had looked for me on over fifty ships, across seven states, and questioned every guide, Indian, and African who would talk to him. Not to return me to his undeserving brother, but to marry me.

"I love you, Oluchukwu, my Olu. When Lydia died . . . I thought I would never love again. Something died in me when she died, and our child. And then I loved you—and I felt, I thought, you loved me, too?"

"I do love you, Teddy." Love was never the issue.

"And then I left with Sam to examine some of his other property, amid all the rumours of war. And when I returned . . . you were gone. Why didn't you wait for me Olu?"

The pancakes were done, and I rang the bell for a soldier to retrieve the pan and deliver them to the hungry men. Teddy stepped back as the soldier appeared in the doorway, and looked at Teddy with a questioning, unfriendly glare, and said, "Mmm, potato pancakes. Thank 'ee, Olu. Got a new kitchen helper, do ye?"

"An old friend," I replied.

"Hmph," Teddy grumbled.

The soldier left and I began to clean up, while Teddy helped. I explained that once I found out I was pregnant, I felt I had no choice. I saw no way forward for us and wouldn't allow our baby to be born a slave. I reminded him I was his brother's slave. I saw no happy future. The time was right, so I left.

Teddy was happy when he found out I escaped, and Martha showed him my drawing—my clue left behind. Sam was furious, but Teddy persuaded him not to post a reward for me. So where did that leave us? I told Teddy I would not go back—his head jerked back as if I had hit him.

"Of course not, Olu. This ship is headed north—to New York, or New Jersey. We'll go. We'll make a new life."

"And your brother?"

"Needs to know nothing. I've tried to reason with him for years. I warned him to stay away from you—I know he's taken advantage of some slave women. He's my brother, so I love him, but I can't condone his behavior or his slaveholding. There's no contest, Olu. I choose you."

"But will you . . . tell him you've found me?" Somehow, even in our nascent reunion, I couldn't let it go. I needed to hear Teddy say it.

"No, Olu. He need not know. I'll write to him, on occasion. But he need not know of your whereabouts."

"Teddy." I fell back into his arms, dishes left uncleaned, and we held each other closely. Much later, a soldier appeared with an empty tray and ordered Teddy and me to report to Lord Dunmore on the deck.

## CHAPTER TWENTY-ONE: OLU

Teddy held my hand tightly as we climbed the circular, narrow stairs to the deck. It seemed unbelievable to me that he was here with me, he loved me, had been searching for me. The touch of his hand, his woodsy scent, his nearness, created in me a yearning, an immeasurable need.

Lord Dunmore called out, "You there, friend Teddy, come here." I winced at his description. We stood before Lord Dunmore, still holding hands.

"Sir, what is the nature of your relationship with Olu?" Lord Dunmore demanded.

"My lord, she is the woman I love," Teddy affirmed, in a loud voice.

"Yes, I see. The only one?"

Teddy was momentarily speechless. "Yes, my lord, the only one."

"Hmmm. And the child she carries . . .?

"Is mine, my lord. I take full responsibility." Teddy cut Lord Dunmore off in his rush to reply.

"As you should, I'm sure. And what were the circumstances of your meeting?"

"You see, my lord, she was the slave of my brother," Teddy said.

"Your brother's slave! And you impregnated her and helped her escape! Strange brotherly actions indeed!" Lord Dunmore exclaimed.

"No, my lord, I didn't help her escape. She neither asked for, nor needed any assistance. Olu is an able woman, confident and strong willed." Teddy corrected him.

"I agree with you. She has proved herself to be invaluable to me these past several months—nursing the sick, assisting the doctor, caring for the dying . . . and cooking. And what do you propose to do with this woman you love, your brother's ex-slave?"

I hated the fact that they were talking about me as if I weren't there.

"I propose to . . ." Teddy stopped talking and addressed me directly. "Olu" he said, looking in my eyes with tender compassion and love, "will you consent to be my wife?"

Without hesitation I replied. "I will." I remembered those few weeks we had together, how happy we were, and the years beforehand. Teddy was always on my side, always looking out for me. I loved him as my advocate and friend before I loved him as my lover. I didn't want to live without him.

Teddy turned back to Lord Dunmore. "I propose to marry her, my lord."

"Yes, I see. When?" Lord Dunmore inquired.

"How about right now?" Teddy said, with a gleam in his eye.

"Now?" Lord Dunmore and I asked.

"Yes, I assume as governor you have the authority to marry."

"Hmm, yes, this is true. I've only conducted one wedding, and I don't recall all the vows, but if the two of you are determined, as I can see you are, I will be pleased to perform the marriage rites."

"Oh, but . . ." Teddy began.

Was he backing out already? "What is it?" I softly asked.

"I don't have a ring for you," Teddy replied. Teddy looked around the deck, found a length of unused, braided rope, unbraided it, cut off a small piece with his pocketknife, and fashioned it into a ring—the most valuable, precious ring I would ever wear. When he replaced it with a gold band years later, I kept the small rope ring in the bottom of my jewelry box.

With no other impediments, we wed. I don't remember all the vows. I do remember I pledged to honor, cherish, and love. Other soldiers came up from below-decks, so over 100 men witnessed our vows, cheering when we kissed. Our babe wiggled around during the ceremony, pushing out a knee, or an elbow, on which I placed Teddy's hand.

Teddy had brought few belongings, some tools, some clothes, some money. Lord Dunmore found us a small private space, more like a big closet than a small room. That night after supper, when we retired to bed, on my narrow hard cot, Teddy was afraid to touch me.

"Thou . . . you are so large with child. Won't I harm the baby?"

"No, my love." We came together as if we had never been apart. Our lovemaking was gentle, yet passionate. Despite my large belly, we fit together perfectly.

Now let me pause reader and tell you how this memoir came about. Teddy insisted I do something with a few journals I had written, expand on my story, and have it published. He thought the story of my life might aid the abolitionist cause, though I knew my experience of slavery was far less harrowing than many. I have pieced together my journals, and added to them as memory permits, leaving gaps where time or energy or access to writing supplies limited the effort. My journals from the plantation covered early years, and I wrote the story of my escape while on the ship.

## CHAPTER TWENTY-ONE: OLU

### 9 August 1776

A few days later, the ship was moving. The wind must have picked up during the night, I could tell we were moving quickly. Teddy opened his eyes and smiled at me, as I dressed and prepared to make breakfast. My back was sore and I stretched up to try and ease the pain. He rose on an elbow and said, "I suppose I should rise and see how I can be useful."

"You could do that . . . or you could sleep in a bit," I said.

"Don't tempt me. I'm used to rising early; maybe I could help you in the galley?"

"Ah, well, I, uh, I'll be fine. If you're truly getting up, show up on the deck and he's sure to put you to work."

We separated and Teddy was indeed put to work immediately. Once Lord Dunmore learned Teddy was a trained carpenter, he had a long list of repairs on board. As I finished breakfast clean-up, my back began to hurt even more. I went back to the room for a quick nap, and that's where Teddy found me a few hours later.

"Olu," I heard, and felt someone gently shaking me.

My back still hurt, even more than earlier, and I felt nauseous and restless.

"Are you all right, my love" Teddy asked.

"I'm . . . okay. My back hurts."

"Only your back?" Teddy asked, looking concerned.

I put my hand on my back, and on my stomach. I looked at Teddy. "I think I'm in labor," I whispered.

A pain stretched across my belly like a belt constricting me from inside. That belt inside me squeezed tighter, then released, then squeezed tighter, and longer, and another wider belt was added, and the bands of pain expanded.

"What can I do? How can I help?"

I told him first labors generally took hours, or even a day. I would rest, walk around when I had the energy, and wait until I progressed. Teddy looked uncertain but agreed. He asked if he could get me anything to eat or drink.

"Just some tea, maybe a few crackers or a piece of bread, please."

Teddy left and I lay back on the bed, remembering all the babies I had helped Martha birth, and the babies I had caught myself. I tried to remember the good births, but the image of Martha pulling out a dead baby kept playing in my mind. I forced myself to picture the wiggling, screaming babies, healthy and full of life.

By evening the pains were coming every four or five minutes, I felt weaker and weaker, and wanted nothing more than to push the baby out. I have no idea how long the pains lasted, but I felt like the sheets Suraya and I used to twist hard, first to the right, then to the left, to wring out water. The pain emanated from my core and spread out to my extremities. Every time a contraction started, I tensed up to fight it, and remembered what I had told the enslaved women I helped through their birthing—relax, breathe, in and out. Good advice, but, ooh, so hard to follow. I kept breathing and forcing myself to ride the wave of pain until I felt an urgent need to push.

Teddy, bless him, stayed by my side through the whole ordeal, giving me tea, holding my hand, praying for me. I know he wanted to help, but there wasn't much he could do. My groans had alerted a passing soldier, who informed Lord Dunmore, who called on the doctor. Just as I pushed down with all my might, screaming at Teddy to catch the baby, the doctor appeared in the doorway. Then she was out. Teddy caught the slippery, bloody baby, looking very pleased with himself, which somehow really annoyed me, and the doctor was telling me to push again to expel the afterbirth. I did and it slid out, along with a tremendous amount of blood. The doctor looked concerned, Teddy looked terrified, and I instructed them to apply cold towels and make me shepherd's purse tea. The doctor cut the cord and laid my baby on my chest, after cleaning her up a bit; then he sent Teddy to soak towels in cold water and get the tea. I swooned as the baby latched on to my breast and sucked. I don't remember anything after that.

Teddy later told me that he and the doctor worked together to stop the bleeding while I was unconscious. I awoke to see the two of them standing over me, looking down on me, Teddy with loving concern, the doctor with anxiety.

The doctor said, "The afterbirth didn't come out cleanly. You lost a lot of blood. You'll need a nourishing diet, though how you'll get one on this ship without cooking it yourself, God only knows. And you need rest. The baby, your daughter, is well. She is perfectly healthy."

I closed my eyes in relief, and heard Teddy's concerned "Olu?"

With my eyes still shut I answered, "I'm fine, Teddy. She is Theodosia—Sadie for short."

"Theodosia? Oh, my love—what a perfect name."

"I'll leave the three of you. I'll check in on you and the baby later, Olu," the doctor said.

Teddy took Theodosia, held her, sang to her, and sat on the edge of our narrow bed.

"She's beautiful, Olu. What a lot of curly brown hair she has. And your perfect nose. Though I think her eyes resemble mine."

"It's been so hard to imagine. A future. I have lived one. Day. At a time. Thinking of you. Constantly. But not daring to imagine. I'd see you again." I was exhausted, and out of breath, but wanted to talk to Teddy.

"Then I heard. Your voice. Then I saw you. I couldn't. Trust you. Forgive me. Then you said. You wanted to marry me. Then, only then. I looked ahead. And I can't. I can't see clearly. What lies ahead."

"We will find our path together. Rest now, love."

That encouragement was all I needed. As I closed my eyes, trying to ignore the discomfort of my stretched womanly parts, the fatigue, I heard Teddy talking to the doctor outside the door.

"She should not have another pregnancy. It's too dangerous. She lost a lot of blood, and it's still uncertain if she'll fully recover."

"She's a strong woman, doctor. She'll recover," Teddy said.

When I awoke it was to the sound of a newborn's cry. I thought I was still pregnant, dreaming, but as I came fully awake, I remembered. Our daughter, Theodosia. I opened my eyes to see Teddy trying unsuccessfully to quieten the baby. I smiled weakly.

"She wants what only I can give." I reached out my arms, settled her on my breast, and breathed deeply as she sucked, my insides contracted, and my limited energy was sapped as Sadie sucked. Teddy had prepared tea, bread, and eggs, or someone had, and when I finished nursing, he took Theodosia, changed her, and urged me to eat. I felt famished and finished off the repast gratefully. Thankfully the bleeding had stopped completely.

The next few days were a blur of nursing, sleeping, and eating. Teddy worked on the ship while we slept, and suddenly appeared when she awoke. I had yet to change her.

The ship sailed as the winds picked up, and after a few days we stopped. When I had the strength to come up to the deck, what I saw astonished me. Hundreds of masts had amassed, rising like tall, stately trees out of the sea. These British ships prepared for a major attack on the New York harbor. I wanted to stay as far away from battle as possible. Within a few days we were off the ship, on land, in a burgeoning military encampment on a finger of land called Sandy Hook. Buildings, troops, noise all greeted us as we came ashore. We were provided the most luxurious lodging, which reminded me of my rough house on Tucker's Point. But I had Teddy, and Sadie, and we made do.

## 21 September 1776

My energy had not returned, and a few weeks after we had arrived at Sandy Hook, I heard the news. The British succeeded in driving out the Patriots and now occupied New York. A fire broke out today in New York City, and the flames and smoke could be seen and smelled from where we were on Sandy Hook. The British blamed the retreating rebels. Many of the British now planned to move into New York, and Teddy wanted to join them.

I had made so many decisions on my own, and still felt exhausted, so I didn't protest. We packed our few belongings, bundled our precious Sadie, and boarded a ship—again—bound for New York. I hoped this would be the last ship I'd ever sail on. Within an hour, we saw the land jutting out into the water, spotted with buildings, some standing tall, others charred, the spire of a church, the profile of large ship masts, people scurrying here and there—a proud city. In all my life I never imagined I would see such a sight.

The dock protruded out into the water, so we didn't have to take a canoe to reach the land. We got off the ship right onto the dock. As I held tight to Sadie, Teddy handed me over the ship's side, and I planted my feet on the dock, looking around at our new home.

I was too weary to think much of our future, still recovering from the trauma of Sadie's birth. But I allowed myself to harbor hope—hope that I would be free, hope for our marriage, hope for Sadie to grow up free to be and do whatever she desired. I hoped our new family could make a home in this strange, foreboding city.

Lord Dunmore and many others were on board the ship and as we disembarked, we all looked around in amazement. The street facing us, Broad Street, was indeed broad, three carriages could travel side-by-side. The houses were wooden, tall, and narrow. We stepped onto a street made of rough stones. As we walked up Broad Street, we could see burnt areas; the fire had burned a significant area and most of the damaged homes and buildings looked beyond repair. The people also amazed me,

Blacks and Whites, walking together, riding in carriages. What kind of city would this be? Could we belong here, Teddy and me?

After walking only a few blocks, I had to rest. Teddy found a bench for me to rest on and impressed a soldier to keep me company. I'm not sure what he feared more—my health, my capture, my virtue, or my safety. Those first few hours and days, I felt ill at ease in this noisy, crowded, hurried place called New York.

Teddy returned less than an hour later. He had found us lodging on the third floor of a house, next to Wesley Chapel. We walked down John Street, and I looked first at the charming church, then up at our new home.

# CHAPTER TWENTY-TWO

## Joanna

February 1827

THE VIEWS AS WE approached Clavering in our carriage included groves of trees, rolling hills, vast fields, and a castle. It appealed to me more than Appledore. When we arrived in Clavering, a small contingent of church members met us at the manse. They carried an assortment of dishes and held a gaggle of children in hand. Captain Welbourne stepped forward out of the small crowd assembled on the front porch of the manse, holding the hands of his East Indian wife Sushila, and son Harish.

"Welcome to Clavering, Rev. Bromley, Mrs. Bromley. We're delighted to see you. These are the Partridges, the Georges, and Mrs. Pinter," Captain Welbourne said, and Henry shook hands with each in turn, while I curtsied. I was pleasantly surprised when no one looked shocked to see the new vicar with a wife who was a woman of colour.

"And I am Captain Welbourne, my wife Sushila, and this is our son, Harish." Seeing Captain Welbourne with an Indian wife also somehow bolstered my confidence—she was as dark as me.

"We are indeed happy to be here. What a pleasant welcome! Thank you so much. Won't you please come in," Henry said, making his way to the front door and opening it wide.

"Please accept our gifts of food. I'm sure you and Mrs. Bromley will want to settle into the manse. I'll bring the men back in a few hours, if I may, to help you unload and unpack."

"Thank you. That is most appreciated," Henry smiled.

## CHAPTER TWENTY-TWO: JOANNA

Henry and I entered the manse and looked around. It was much smaller than the houses we were used to, but big enough for the two of us, and one or two servants. Through the entryway, on the left, one entered a drawing room which might comfortably accommodate ten to fifteen guests. The fireplace was clean, the mantle empty. I began walking about, examining the furniture and the rooms. Across from the drawing room I spotted a small morning room, with tall windows on two walls, and a view of the garden, replete with nascent crocuses, snowdrops, and hyacinth. I noticed a small room with a high ceiling and several bookshelves behind the morning room.

"Come, Henry. This is perfect for your study."

"Indeed. It may even hold all my books. Let's look over here." Henry led the way to a small formal dining room beyond the drawing room, with a table for eight. At the rear of the house was a kitchen, and a small bedroom for a servant. Upstairs, the four bedrooms varied widely in size. Two would perfectly each hold one guest, one boasted a larger canopied bed, and a large chest topped with an oval mirror set in an ornate oak frame, with a bowl and pitcher perched on top of an elaborate doily.

"Your parents can stay here when they visit us, Henry."

"Yes, this room will suit them well."

The master bedroom was the largest room upstairs, with two large dressing rooms, and a large high bed in the center of the room.

"This . . . this is our refuge, Joanna. Ours and ours alone."

"What a charming room. I would like to replace the curtains, though. The bed is nice and big."

"Shall we try it out?" Henry grinned.

"Henry! It's the middle of the day!"

"Yes . . . and?" Henry approached me.

"And we may have visitors," I continued.

"We already did. They left."

"But it's . . . it's not proper!"

"Are you my wife?" Henry asked, moving closer, and moving both of us closer to the bed.

"Of course."

"Am I your husband?"

"Yes, but . . . Henry!" I exclaimed as Henry put his hands around my waist and guided me to the bed.

An hour later Henry and I went downstairs to further inspect our new living quarters. I wandered outside, to a chicken coop in the back of the manse.

"Oh!" The sudden flapping of wings and squawking startled me. "Who do we have here?" I inquired aloud.

"Nobody," a small voice called out from the back of the coop. I hadn't seen anyone, so I was doubly surprised to receive an answer when I addressed the chickens.

"Who is nobody?" I asked.

"Abner," a young English boy replied, coming out from behind the coop.

"Hello, Abner. I'm Joanna Bromley."

"Ye the new pastor's wife?" Abner asked.

"Yes, I am. My husband is Rev. Henry Bromley."

"'ee brown like you?" Abner wanted to know.

"No, he's not."

"Why is ye brown then?"

"My papa was African."

"Was?" Abner didn't miss much.

"He died a long time ago."

"Just yer papa? Yer mammy weren't brown, too?" What a curious youngster, I thought.

"Right. Just my papa."

Abner came around to the front of the coop to get a closer look. He declared me to be "very pretty" and asked if I lived here. Abner informed me he checked on the hens every day, and one of them was sitting on two eggs. I asked if he would like one and he said yes, but he had to ask his mother. When I inquired if he had chickens, he said they did, but they got hungry and ate them.

"How many do I have?" I asked Abner

"You gots fourteen."

"I've always wanted chickens."

"Now ye got 'em," Abner said as if I were a bit dense.

Abner lived over the hill and down the field and across the creek. His father worked the farm before he died. Abner didn't miss his father—who liked the drink. I was drawn to this young boy and liked his forthright questions and honest answers.

"So I don' miss him, but mammy do." He motioned his head to the left, presumably in the direction of his house.

"Do you and your mother come to the Chapel."

"Nope." I realized Abner said only what was necessary.

"Well, I would love to see you on Sunday."

"Why?"

"You're the first friend I have here in Clavering."

"I'm your friend?" Abner's eyes widened.

"Yes, you are."

"I don' got no church clothes."

"That's no problem. Come in whatever you have."

Abner's pale face contrasted with his large, dark, plentiful freckles, and he had a dimple in the middle of his chin. Abner wore a tattered straw hat, pants cut off below the knee, and a button-up shirt missing the buttons, two sizes too small. He had no shoes.

During our conversation I ascertained Abner was ten, couldn't read, and didn't attend school. When I asked if he'd like to learn to read, Abner got right to the point.

"Why?"

"So you can read books, read the bible, read a sign."

Henry came outside at that moment, looking for me.

"A chicken coop! Brilliant! Eggs for breakfast every morning."

"Henry, this is my friend, Abner. Abner, this is Rev. Bromley."

"I'm pleased to meet you, Abner," Henry said formally.

"Yes sir. Gotta go," Abner ran up and over the hill, and out of sight.

"Was it something I said?" Henry asked.

"I don't think so. He may not be too fond of men. Come look at our chickens. And this one is sitting on eggs."

"That's good. Must be fertile air here in Clavering!"

I mentioned to Henry that Abner didn't attend school. I wondered out loud if we could start a school.

"Darling, we haven't even unpacked," Henry pointed out.

"I don't mean this very minute, but soon. Boys like Abner need an education. Maybe we can start with a Sunday School."

"Yes, they have run a Sunday School here. The previous pastor told me ten children were enrolled."

"Only ten? There must be dozens upon dozens of children in Clavering. Certainly, we can do better than ten children."

"I'm sure we shall, but maybe we can unpack first?"

Henry and I went back to the manse and sat down to eat some of the food so generously given by neighbors. Henry dug right into a shepherd's pie, while I tried an unfamiliar-looking dish of lamb cubes and rice in a reddish sauce. I tried it and it was delicious—a cornucopia of spices exploded in my mouth. It was the spiciest food I had ever eaten, and I loved it. I urged Henry to try some. Henry took a small bite from my plate, coughed, and drank some water.

"Take more rice with it dear, to balance the heat," I suggested, holding back a smile.

Henry gulped down some wine, then more rice, until his reddened face slowly returned to its natural pale colour. He sniffed and wiped a drop of perspiration from his brow. I barely suppressed laughter. "I guess I'll have this dish all to myself," I said.

"You certainly will. Enjoy it, darling."

"I am. The captain's wife must have made this. What was her name?"

"Sushila, I think."

"Ah yes, Sushila. You have such a good memory for names, Henry."

"Thank you, June," he said with a smirk.

"That's not funny!" I said, laughing.

"Oh, so sorry, Josie."

"Henry!"

"You're beautiful when you're exasperated . . . Joanna."

By the time we finished eating, the men had returned to help unload boxes and furniture. I directed them all, while Henry helped unload. Once everything sat in its proper place, I offered the men some food, which they ate greedily, after mild protests that it was all for the Bromleys.

"Captain, what's the name of that dish your wife brought?" I inquired.

"Curried lamb. Did you like it?"

"I did, very much. I've never had spices like that before."

"We English aren't known for our spices. She uses Indian spices, grows them herself in our yard. I met her when I was stationed over in Bombay."

"I'll have to ask her for the recipe."

"She mostly mixes in a little of this, and a little of that—don't believe it's written down anywhere," Captain Welbourne said.

"Well, please tell her it was very good, and thank her for me."

"She'll be happy to hear you enjoyed it." He bowed his head.

The men finished up and offered to come back on the morrow to help with any small repairs. Henry closed the door behind him and drew me into his arms. "Welcome home, darling" he murmured into my hair.

## CHAPTER TWENTY-TWO: JOANNA

I truly felt at home, both in Clavering and in Henry's arms. "I believe I'm going to like it here," I said.

The first Sunday after we arrived, the church filled to capacity. Normally, about 70–80 people attended, plus 10–15 children. But on the second Sunday in February 1827, over 150 walked or rode to the Congregational Chapel in Clavering. Some came out of curiosity, some for entertainment, others to encourage and welcome the new pastor. Henry preached on Luke 8, the Parable of the Sower, and ended by praying that the Lord would find good soil in Clavering.

Henry and I stood at the entrance greeting people and shaking hands. There were no visitors or members of African descent, and Sushila was the only other person of colour. By the time everyone had left, Henry and I held hands and walked home, which took only minutes.

"You preached well, honey. And the church was full."

"It will be interesting to see how many return next week, now that they've heard me and seen us."

"Seen us?"

"I'm not so naïve that I don't believe some won't come back because my wife is not an English maiden," Henry said.

"Oh, but I am an English maiden, with an African daddy!" I added.

"I know that, but do they? I am glad to see another couple here like us, the Captain and Sushila. They seem very much at home here."

"I hope to get to know Sushila better soon."

"Why don't you invite her over for tea one afternoon this week?" Henry suggested.

"That's a wonderful idea. I think I will."

As we reached home, I went into the kitchen to instruct Bridgett on lunch, and Henry retired to his study to set goals for the upcoming year. Sitting in his study, he drew out his fountain pen and listed ten goals:

1. Develop a preaching schedule and preach a series for every season.
2. Spend 8–10 hours a week on sermon preparation.
3. Identify and mentor 5 church leaders.
4. Identify and train new Sunday School teachers. Appoint Joanna as Sunday School Superintendent.
5. Grow the church by 50% in the first 2 years.
6. Get to know the parish vicar and other nearby pastors.

7. Determine feasibility of opening a school.//
8. Conduct a revival in the summer.
9. Take a Sabbath day every week—probably Monday.
10. Read one book every week.

Henry met his goals by December, except for 9 and 10, as he was too busy meeting goals 1–8.

## January 1828

Almost a year later, on a cold afternoon in January, Sushila came over to the manse for tea. We had developed a friendship over the previous year, and I'd come to rely on Sushila's companionship and counsel. She was born and raised in Bombay, a big city on the west coast of India. She met her husband when he was stationed in India, and though her parents had already arranged a marriage for her, they acquiesced when Sushila said she couldn't marry anyone but her *dear captain*. They thought living in England would open opportunities for their daughter and permitted the marriage to go ahead.

"I brought some rasmalai," Sushila said, pulling a small container out of her bag.

"Mmmm. My favourite. Now we'll have buttermilk scones and rasmalai. How's your campaign going to sell your spices at Mr. George's shop?" I asked.

"He's selling cardamom, coriander, and cumin, but he claims they don't sell well because the women don't know what to do with the spices."

"Maybe you should give them a lesson," I suggested.

"A lesson?" Sushila tilted her head.

"A cooking lesson."

"Hmm. A cooking lesson. That's a good idea. But where?"

We discussed the idea and agreed that her house or the manse would both be good locations. It could be a nice way to meet some of the other local women, from the parish church, and the Methodist church. We didn't often do things together. We decided on the manse, our home, and now all I had to do was convince Henry. The end of March was ideal, and we would put an announcement in the Clavering Recorder.

I asked Sushila how she was feeling; I knew she was expecting. Her sickness lingered throughout the day, as it had with Harish. I recommended Sadie as a great midwife. Then Sushila asked me a question.

"And you, Joanna. Any success yet?" Sushila asked.

"None." I was silent for a few moments. I wanted desperately to have a child, to make our family complete. "I've tried what you suggested, the herbs and the tea. Honestly Sushila, my monthlies have become so painful I dread that time of the month. Something's wrong, but the doctor either doesn't know or doesn't want to tell me."

"I'm so sorry, Joanna. I know how you long to have children." Sushila reached out and held my hand.

"Maybe I'm not meant to be a mother. And it's not for a lack of trying!"

"Joanna!" Sushila exclaimed, laughing.

I joined her laughter. "I know. A pastor's wife shouldn't say such things. But Henry is still . . . very amorous."

Sushila giggled. "Well, there's nothing wrong with that."

Sushila remembered aloud when she and the Captain met in India; she never dreamed he would propose and bring her to England. She still missed Bombay.

"What do you miss most?" I wondered.

"Two things—my family, and the weather. I can't get used to this cold, the constant, pervasive, damp cold weather."

"But isn't it unbearably hot in India?" I asked.

"Hot, but not unbearable."

"And your beautiful clothes are ill-designed for English weather."

"So true. My saree and my salwar kamis are too light. I need layers and layers here."

"But in the summer, they suit."

"You mean the two weeks in August when the temperature rises to normal?"

"I'm glad you're here Sushila in our lovely, cold England."

"Me, too." Sushila smiled.

Sushila and I finished the tea in the teapot, the scones on the saucer, and the rasmalai in the container. We talked about the plans for the school, and I was happy to relate that Henry received approval from the County and the Education Office. The church board would meet this week to confirm a location, and the salary for the teacher. Sushila had worked with her son Harish at home, teaching him to read, but he wanted to be with other children.

"I felt the same way at his age as an only child and was happy to go off to boarding school."

"But?" Sushila prodded.

"It wasn't what I expected. You've met Anne. She's a dear friend, but the only one I made at school."

"I'm surprised. You're so friendly. Didn't you mention the Methodist Minister's wife was a classmate?"

"Miranda. A classmate, but not a friend." I frowned.

"Oh! She looks so charming."

"She can be. To the right people at the right time. But remember the verse in Samuel, "I look not on outward appearances, but on the heart'?"

"I take it her heart is not so charming," Sushila said.

"Who knows, maybe she's changed." I hoped she had changed, but I dreaded seeing her again. She perfected the art of appearing to be what she was not. I didn't trust her then, and I don't trust her now.

## March 1828

By midday Sushila and I had prepped the food, laid out spices, lit the fire, and assembled the chairs in Sushila's kitchen. We decided the cooking lesson would work best at Sushila's large house, as she had everything she needed at hand, and her kitchen could accommodate more women.

The first guests arrived right on time—the vicar's wife, Mrs. Portnoy and the Methodist minister's wife, Miranda Bentley. Sushila and I welcomed them warmly and ushered them into the kitchen where the warmth from the fire was cooled by the March air flowing in through an open window. Miranda kissed me on the cheek and gushed over Sushila's home.

"What a lovely home you have. So large and comfortable," Miranda said, looking around.

"My husband likes his space, after being in cramped quarters on ships for years."

Miranda exclaimed over Sushila marrying a naval captain and asked where they met. Sushila told her they had met in Bombay, where she was born and raised.

"How very romantic. And he brought you back to England with him."

"Yes, after we married."

# CHAPTER TWENTY-TWO: JOANNA

"Of course." Miranda looked down.

Mrs. Portnoy turned to me, "It's nice to see you again. We live so close to each other and see each other so rarely."

"And I regret that. I'd love our churches to do a few things together during the year," I said.

"Don't forget us Methodists," Miranda piped in.

"Yes, all three of our churches," I corrected myself.

More women arrived, and about a half hour later, Sushila began the cooking lesson. She demonstrated, step by step, how to make dahl, curried lamb, poori, and saag paneer. She had all her spices in a row and showed which spices were used in which dishes—explaining which spices were hot, smoky, and mild. And she gave out cards with two of the recipes written out for the women to take home and try themselves or give to their cooks to make. Then it was time to eat.

Sushila and I dished up the food as the women sat down in the dining room. I asked Mrs. Portnoy to say grace, after which the meal began. At first it was mostly quiet, only the sounds of knives on plates or chewing could be heard. Of the eleven women who came, two seemed to really enjoy the food. Miranda looked uncomfortable, and her cheeks took on a reddish tint. She began mopping her brow with her napkin and coughing.

I whispered to Sushila, "Why do you think Miranda is reacting so?"

"She must be like your reverend," Sushila responded. But the gleam in Sushila's eyes caused me to ask, "Sushila, what did you serve Miranda?"

"Oh, her lamb may have a bit more chili," Sushila admitted.

"Sushila!" I said, more loudly than I intended, causing heads to turn in our direction.

"How are you all enjoying the food, ladies?" Sushila asked.

A few nodded their heads, while Miranda choked out, "It's a bit spicy, isn't it?"

"Here, let me get you some more dahl and poori. It might be the lamb." I spooned the milder dahl on Miranda's plate and poured her more tea, taking pity on her. "Thank you," Miranda said softly.

The rest of the meal passed uneventfully, until Sushila prepared to serve gulab jamun. Miranda excused herself and rushed out in a very unladylike manner to the privy. Dessert and tea were served. Miranda returned several minutes later, her flushed red face now an ashy grey.

"Would you like some dessert, Miranda?" I asked.

"Is it . . . spicy, too?"

Sushila almost laughed out loud, until I glared at her.

"No, it's very sweet and mild," I confirmed.

"I'd love some," Miranda said, relief brightening her complexion.

The dessert course was a unanimous success, and when the women left, Sushila knew at least four of them would be buying her spices at Mr. George's. Hopefully, word would spread.

## July 1828

Henry set the school fee at 3d (pence) a reasonable sum, but out of reach of poorer families. With advice from other non-conformist pastors who had opened day schools, Henry decided to start small—with eight boys. I wanted to start with four boys and four girls but stopped resisting when Henry promised to add eight girls after one year. The boys ranged between eight and ten years old. The curriculum would be rigorous in the hopes many of the boys would proceed on to university. An entrance exam didn't exclude any boys but acted as a benchmark to determine on what level each boy should be placed.

Henry had announced the opening of registration at church in May. Three boys immediately registered, including Harish Welbourne, and within a month four more boys from the congregation had registered. One spot remained.

"Henry, you know who I want to fill the last spot in the school," I said.

"I assume you mean Abner, Joanna," Henry said.

"He's a bright boy, and I know he'll do well."

"He may or may not. But I can think of at least two obstacles. And one is nearly insurmountable. Mrs. O'Neil can't afford tuition," Henry reminded me.

"We can find a donor, surely, Henry," I pleaded.

"But Abner's work on the farm provides her only income. Sending him to school would deprive her of the limited income she has," Henry argued.

I thought out loud there must be something we can do. Henry didn't see a way. While Mrs. O'Neil was poor, she was also proud. She wouldn't accept charity. And Abner may very well not want to go to school.

"I thought of that. He doesn't get along with other children well. But that's precisely why he *needs* to go to school."

"I think we should look elsewhere for our eighth pupil." Henry was adamant.

"Henry, I love you, but I don't agree with you."

## CHAPTER TWENTY-TWO: JOANNA

"If you can find a solution, let me know." Henry left and retired to his study.

A few days later I walked down to talk to Mrs. O'Neil, Abner's mother. I noticed Mrs. O'Neil had a new apron, with a charming bodice, appliqués sewn on. I also spied a new curtain in the window.

"What a pretty curtain, Mrs. O'Neil. Where did you get it, may I ask?"

"Ach, I made it. Mrs. Pavitt, she sells cloth, and when she has bits left over she gives 'em to me. I likes to sew."

"And it's so pretty. Just from the remnants. So nicely stitched. Did you make your apron as well?" I asked.

"Ay, it ain't much," Mrs. O'Neil said.

When I reached home, Henry was firmly ensconced in his study. I checked with Bridgett on dinner, mutton stew, roasted yams, greens, biscuits, vegetable soup. Good. Henry would be well fed and happy after dinner. After we finished the sumptuous dinner, as Henry sipped the rest of his wine, I said, "I paid a visit to Mrs. O'Neil today."

"Oh? How is the family?"

"Scraping by, as usual. But I may have found a way for her to allow Abner to come to school."

"How's that?" Henry asked.

"She sews very well. And I don't mean simply even stitches. She is an inventive seamstress, sewing on designs, making patterns. I think she could earn enough to more than replace Abner's wages and even possibly pay for his tuition."

"That's based on two assumptions: one, she will agree to your idea; and two, there will be enough of a market for her sewing," Henry said.

"True. I can help with the market, and I think she'd love to do gainful work. I think she has no idea of how skilled she is."

"Don't press her too hard, Joanna. She may come to resent you later," Henry warned.

"I . . . won't. but I may present this to her . . . as an option?" I asked.

"Yes. If she's as good as you say, I need new vestments."

"Her second customer! I'm the first."

I got up and kissed Henry on top of his head.

"You're a darling, Rev. Bromley."

"So are you, Joanna. So are you."

The next morning, I surveyed my home and realized I needed a new tea cozy, and a new apron. The pillowcases would have to be replaced, and the kitchen curtains, well, I simply needed new ones. I went into town in the gig and purchased enough fabric for the cozy, two aprons, four pillowcases, and two sets of kitchen curtains. I also bought ribbons and lace. Many of the women in church, and in the village, came to visit me and talk over a cup of tea. I would point out the curtains and the tea cozy to generate business for Mrs. O'Neil.

On my next walk to the O'Neil's, less than a week later, I carried the rather large parcel of fabric, lace, and ribbons wrapped in paper. Mrs. O'Neil was outside when I arrived, looking in at the chicken coop. One of the chicks I had given Abner had her own chick, and Mrs. O'Neil liked to check on her often.

"The chicks look well fed and happy, Mrs. O'Neil," I said, by way of a greeting.

"Aye, the Spencers gives Abner feed, so they's alays enough."

"I brought you some fabric."

"Ach, ye didna need to do that!"

"I want you to make some things for me. Can we go inside?"

Mrs. O'Neil led me into her small home with a thatched roof. The crude windows let in little light, so Mrs. O'Neil lit a lamp to see the fabric better.

"God in heav'n, oh, forgive me, ma'am, this is so pretty." She fingered the off-white lace, and various coloured ribbons gently. "Look 'ee here! What a lot of cloth you bought. What do ye want me to make?"

I pointed out what I wanted her to make with each cloth—the curtains and a tea cozy with the red checkered cloth, pillowcases out of a large piece of soft blue jersey, and two aprons with the last piece of cloth, with adorable appliqués like she had on hers.

Mrs. O'Neil looked over at her daughters, curled up together taking a nap, then back at me. "Yer a right kind lady, Mrs. Bromley," she stated.

I replied that she was an excellent seamstress. She let me know it might take more than a week, and she'd send Abner to let me know when everything was ready. I didn't want to press Mrs. O'Neil with my plan to allow Abner to go to school. I would wait until the job was finished, and I paid her.

One week later, Abner came by. He knocked on the door this time.

"Well, hello Abner. Here to see the missus?" Bridgett asked.

Abner stood awkwardly, twisting his straw hat around and around in his hands as he chewed on a stalk of wheat.

"Yes ma'am," he said.

"Come in, then."

"Please, just tell Mrs. Bromley..."

"Hello, Abner, it's nice to see you. Come on in," I interrupted.

"I just came to tell ye... "

"Come in and tell me, Abner," I insisted.

His discomfort grew, but he followed me to the morning room.

"Please bring us some tea, Bridgett, and some of those fresh raspberry scones," I instructed her. Abner was about to protest, but at the mention of raspberry scones his eyes opened wide, and his mouth stayed shut.

Bridgett came in shortly with the tea and scones, and cream and jam, Abner couldn't take his hungry eyes off the scones. I put two on a plate and handed it to Abner, ignoring his dirty hands. He mumbled 'thank 'ee' and immediately ate one, almost whole. As I poured the tea, Abner ate the second one. I didn't correct his eating habits—there would be time for that in school, I hoped. Instead, I handed him a cup of tea, generously laced with honey and milk, no sugar.

"Mmmmmm. This is great! I ain't never had a proper tea 'n scones before," Abner said, around bites of scone.

"I'm glad you like it. Bridgett is an excellent baker."

"Mmmmm hmmmm," Abner said, his mouth full of tea. "My ma says she done."

"Wonderful. Shall we walk down to your house together when we're done?"

"Yes, ma'am." Abner wiped his mouth with the back of his hand.

Abner ate three more scones. He would have had even more, if there were more to be had! I would have to explain to Henry why there were no scones to accompany his tea today. I donned my bonnet, and change purse, and we set off on the familiar route to his house. As always, Abner was a perfect gentleman crossing the creek, helping me cross. We arrived at the house and Mrs. O'Neil was cooking soup on the outside fire.

"There ye are Abner. You brought Mrs. Bromley! Stir this soup. Let me get 'er package."

Mrs. O'Neil rushed into the house and came back out with the completed work and a separate package of remnants. I took the pieces out one by one, exclaiming over how pretty the apron was, with a cross appliqué, the tea cozy would not only fit perfectly, but it would also keep the tea hot. The pillowcases were exactly what the reverend wanted, and the curtains were sure to attract more customers.

"Customers, ma'am?" Mrs. O'Neil asked.

"Yes, Mrs. O'Neil. I have an idea I'd like you to think about." I smiled.

"Aye?"

"You have a skilled hand with a needle and thread. And I think you could earn a fine income by sewing for others."

"Ach, it ain't nothin' so good as that ma'am." Mrs. O'Neil shook her head.

"But it is. What you've done for me here, I will pay you 10d for."

"Ten pence? That dear?" she said.

I explained that if she sewed for others, she could make enough so Abner could come out of the fields and come to our new school. I looked at her closely. She hesitated—Abner's money was steady and necessary. I tried to persuade her that she could make more than Abner by sewing and added there was only one spot left at the school. I wanted Abner to have it and there was a scholarship available so she wouldn't have school fees to pay.

"No fees? Ach, but he make so much during harvest time. With the girls to feed, I can't see how I'd do without."

"School is out in July and August, so he could still work then." I could see her leaning toward my proposition.

"Well, you do tempt me. I alays said Abner's smart, I did."

"And he is. I'm sure he would do well in school." I didn't want to press too hard.

"Only one spot you say?"

I could feel my persuasion working. She had a doubtful look on her face as she asked if we really wanted Abner. I assured her we did. Mrs. O'Neil agreed to allow Abner to attend, but if she didn't make enough, she would have to pull him out and put him back to work in the fields.

"When do it start?" she asked.

"School starts in one month."

"And how does I get those customers?"

"I'll send a few ladies over, and I'm sure word will spread. A lot of ladies come to my home, and I'll point out all you've made for me. I'll leave these remnants with you for embellishments."

I was thrilled—we were starting a school and Abner would attend. It felt like a big accomplishment.

## September 1828

When Sushila went into her confinement, I reminded her of Sadie.

"Remember, Sushila, I know of an excellent midwife. Not only does she deliver the baby, but she also stays with the mother for a week or more afterwards. She's wonderful."

"The captain insists on having a doctor do the delivery." But as it happened, the doctor had to go on an extended visit to care for his ill mother. So as Sushila's impending time of happiness approached, she convinced her husband to call upon Sadie.

I invited Sadie to stay with me until Sushila had the baby and we spent two days together. I showed Sadie around Clavering, we went to the castle, the lake, the school, and we even visited Mrs. O'Neil. Sadie put in an order for some baby blankets.

My friend Anne paid a visit on the third day. She was still somewhat in awe of Sadie as one of the forerunners in the ladies' anti-slavery society, and the two of them talked for hours about the progress of the campaign.

That night, Henry was out at a church board meeting and Sadie, Anne, and I had recently finished supper. Anne went into the drawing room, and I told her we'd join her in a bit.

"Sadie, I wonder if I might impose on you?" I began.

"Certainly, Joanna. What is it?"

"Could you . . . examine me?" I asked.

"Examine you? Are you expecting?" Sadie asked.

"I think I may be," I said.

Sadie proceeded to ask me some questions: how long we were married—seven years; how often were Henry and I intimate—four-five times a week when I'm well; when am I not well—before, during, and after my monthlies; do you bleed a lot—yes; are my monthlies regular—usually, but I haven't had one for months.

"I see. And have you felt any movement, like a light fluttering, or a shifting about within?" Sadie asked.

"No. No I haven't." I put my hand on my belly.

"Let's go into your bedroom, so I can examine you."

Sadie examined me, asked a few more questions. After several more minutes, I had already deduced the answer from the tenor of the questions and the look on Sadie's face.

"I'm . . . not expecting. Am I?"

"I'm afraid not. It's likely you have a uterine disease, but a doctor would need to give you a better diagnosis."

My next words rushed out in a torrent of tears. I was so hoping I was with child. Every month I thought "thank You Lord" I must be finally expecting. But still, I was afraid I might not be. As I spoke to Sadie I was crying, hiccupping, and coughing. It was hard to breathe and hard to talk. I told her I hadn't mentioned it to anyone. Not Henry, no one. But I so hoped.

"Oh, Sadie! What shall I do?"

"Sweet Joanna. Let it all out. Go ahead and cry, child."

Sadie rocked me in her arms and soothed me with words. As she held me, Sadie glimpsed a book on the nightstand. Once my sobbing subsided to a quite whimper, Sadie stood, walked around the bed, and picked up the book: *The Interesting Narrative of the life of Olaudah Equiano or Gustavus Vassa, The African, Written by Himself.*

Sadie fingered the book, looked at the portrait of Papa, and asked me, "This is your book?"

"Yes," I said, recovering, breathing slowly as Sadie had suggested. "My papa wrote it."

"Your papa???" Sadie asked, eyes wide with shock.

"Yes. Why?"

"I don't believe it." Now Sadie was crying. Quiet tears flowed down her face, as she smiled and shook her head.

"After all this time. And now she's gone." Sadie was lost in thought, a look of stunned disbelief, and yet wonder and joy spreading across her face. Her tears flowed and now I was perplexed.

"Your father, Olaudah, Ledu, is my mama's brother!" Sadie stated clearly, though the tears continued to flow.

"Your mama? My aunt? Oluchukwu??? My Lord! I can't believe it!"

"Olu's my mother. I never knew Ledu's slave name, Gustavus Vassa. If I'd known, I would have asked you the first time we met. I only knew him as Mama's brother Ledu. Her favorite brother, they were kidnapped together," Sadie said.

"Oh, sweet Jesus! I've been looking for her since I was eleven years old. And you're her daughter. I thought I had lost all hope of finding any of my father's family. And you're here! No wonder we look alike! We're cousins!"

We embraced as if seeing each other for the first time, which in a sense we were.

"Cousin Joanna," Sadie laughed with joy, as she cried, and we hugged again.

Sadie recounted the life of her mother as a slave, what Sadie had been told and seen in her mother's journals. She related the story of Olu's

## CHAPTER TWENTY-TWO: JOANNA

escape, her marriage to Teddy, life in New York City, then Nova Scotia where the British had given plots of land to Blacks who helped them in the American Revolution. Sadie said she left Nova Scotia when she was in her early twenties.

I confirmed that Papa had indeed been in Charles Town in 1766 and was cheated by a White plantation owner.

"So that was her brother. She was right downstairs, and just missed him." Sadie shook her head in regret and told me that her mama, my Aunt Olu, thought she heard a man who sounded like Ledu arguing with Mr. Cross over a sale. Aunt Olu went upstairs, but she missed the man, and Teddy's attempts to catch up to him failed.

"Oh, it's too hard. Your mama searched for my papa, and I searched for her. But at least, at last, we have found each other," I said.

"We have each other," Sadie agreed, holding my hands in her own, searching my face for familiar features.

"But, you have no children, and it seems . . . unlikely I will. The line ends with us."

"No, it doesn't."

"Oh Sadie, don't give me false hope of a pregnancy," I pleaded.

"That's not what I mean. My mama had another child, a boy. My dad was very worried she would not survive the birth because she bled a lot when I was born."

"Did she?" I asked, afraid to hear the answer.

"No. She died giving birth to Ledu. My brother. Your cousin."

"Another cousin. Named after Papa. There are three of us! Oh, where is he? Tell me he lives!" I begged.

"He's still in Nova Scotia."

"Oh, this is too much! I have lost a child, or the hope of a child, and gained two cousins. All in one afternoon!"

Sadie and I held hands and went into the drawing room to tell Anne.

"Anne," I called out. She looked up from her chair. "Meet my *cousin*, Sadie," I said, tears in my eyes.

"Oh, my goodness. That's brilliant! That's why you look alike!" Anne stood up quickly, came over and embraced both of us. I looked over Anne's shoulder to see Henry standing in the doorway of his study, a tender smile on his face. He winked at me and set free a tear, which slid down his face unchecked.

# EPILOGUE

# Joanna

### 30 July 1833

Yesterday William Wilberforce died. Three days earlier, the Slavery Abolition Act was read for the third time in Parliament and garnered enough votes to pass. The decades of work by all the champions of abolition, men and women, finally bore fruit. Slavery will soon be illegal in all the British colonies. I'm so glad Mr. Wilberforce lived to know the end was near and all his efforts had come to fruition.

Henry and I are very busy these days. Though we have not been able to have any children, I feel like I'm raising dozens of children as Superintendent of the Sunday School! Our day school now has over one hundred children enrolled, and Abner will be graduating soon. I recently taught him to play chess, and he's quite good! Somehow, he always manages to show up for a chess game right after Bridgett has removed fresh scones from the oven. I think he has a discerning nose! His mother has a thriving sewing business, and her daughters are also at the day school.

Since Sadie and I discovered we were cousins, she corresponded with her brother Ledu, and he and his wife and four children now live in England. Ledu serves in the British Navy and while he is at sea his wife and children often stay with us. I love having all the little ones underfoot. They help me with the chickens and the garden, and Abner takes them into the village for sweets. They're here now—I hear a commotion downstairs and I may need to put down my pen soon. Ledu met his American wife, who was a slave at the time, during the American War of 1812. But that's a story for another day.

# Fact or Fiction?

When reading historical fiction, readers often wonder what parts are "fact" and what parts are "fiction." Please see the outline below for the historical facts included in *Remnant*, and the authorial prerogative I took to "adjust" the facts and dates as needed for the story.

**Chapter 1**—Olaudah Equiano gives a detailed account of his kidnapping, by two men and one woman, with his (nameless) sister. They were separated, reunited, and separated again. He never mentions her again.

**Chapter 2**—William Wilberforce gave a speech after the passage of the Abolition of the Slave Trade, and there was a hanging and stampede earlier that morning.

**Chapter 9**—The description of the grounds is of Middleton Plantation, Charleston, South Carolina, and its stair-like lawn. The house at Cross Plantation is based on Drayton Hall, Charleston, South Carolina. Africans were expert rice growers and brought their knowledge with them to southern plantations.

**Chapter 12**—Details about Astley's Amphitheatre, Philip and Patty Astley's acts, and Pablo Fanque's acts are all historical. The women's anti-slavery societies were not active until the 1820s and 1830s. Anne Knight is a historical figure, her mother did not die, however, when Anne was young. Anne never married and was active in the Chelmsford Ladies' Anti-Slavery Society.

**Chapter 13**—Stamp Act details are historical and Olaudah Equiano was in Charles Town in 1766. The details about Equiano's "owners" and his purchase of his freedom are historically accurate.

**Chapter 15**—Thomas Jeremiah was hanged for his part in a rebellion. I included the words from Lord Dunmore's proclamation offering freedom to slaves who joined the British side. Details about Lord Dunmore's proclamation are historical.

CHAPTER 16—William Wilberforce, Wilby to his wife Barbara, loved to play with his kids and they did celebrate Twelfth Night. Blind Man's Buff was a favorite game of Wilberforce. Zachary Macauley did bring a group of African kids to England for education, and many of them died. He was also involved in the emigration of freed slaves to Sierra Leone.

CHAPTER 17—Rivers were used as a common escape route for slaves fleeing to the north or to Lord Dunmore.

CHAPTER 18—Joanna Vassa Bromley inherited £950 on her 21st birthday. There is a plaque commemorating Anna Maria Vassa on the outside wall of St. Andrew's Church in Chesterton, England.

CHAPTER 19—Many Native Americans helped slaves escape and guided them along their way. Many of the slaves who went to Lord Dunmore contracted smallpox, and many died. On April 7, 1776 an American warship captured the sloop H.M.S. Edward off the coast of Virginia.

CHAPTER 20—Joanna Vassa married Henry Bromley on August 29, 1821, and John Audley and Catherine Bromley attended the ceremony in London, St. James Church, Clerkenwell. Henry Bromley was a pastor in Appledore before he and Joanna moved to Clavering. Barbara Wilberforce (daughter of William and Barbara Wilberforce) died December 30, 1821. I do not know if Joanna and Barbara knew each other.

CHAPTER 21—August 6, 1776, Lord Dunmore burned 63 of his ships due to disease, and abandoned hundreds of ex-slaves on Gwynn Island. There was a great fire in Manhattan on September 20–21, 1776—there is a debate about whether the Patriots or the British started the fire.

CHAPTER 22—Joanna was very involved in the Congregational Chapel at Clavering and is listed as Superintendent of the Sunday School in church records. Joanna Vassa Bromley was diagnosed with uterine disease and there is no evidence she and Henry Bromley ever had any children.

# Author's Note

WHAT INSPIRED ME TO write this book? The principal inspiration was Olaudah Equiano's *Interesting Narrative*. My master's thesis was on "Constructing an African Identity" and Equiano's memoir was among the books I studied. His fascinating story captivated me, and as I learned more about his life, I wondered what had become of his daughter Joanna. Her life held so many aspects close to my heart: she was biracial, married to a pastor, lived in England—I am married to a pastor and my sons are biracial (and I love England!).

After I began writing my mind wandered to Equiano's sister. What had become of her? No one knows, but my imagination took over and I constructed her storyline, to eventually merge with Joanna's storyline.

# Acknowledgments

My village of assistants and scholars starts in America. I traveled to South Carolina to visit plantations, so my re-enactment of them in the novel would be as accurate as possible. My son Ben accompanied me by train to South Carolina, and trudged around three plantations, hearing lectures on slave life, which was not entirely thrilling for a 12-year-old boy. He did get to go fishing later in the week! We stayed with my sweet friend Katie Moore and her husband Michael, in Columbia, and got much needed advice from them. Jeff Neale answered all my questions at Middleton Plantation, and Stephanie Abdon Bray and Craig Tuminaro were very helpful at Drayton Hall, the house I used as the basis for the Cross Plantation house.

I needed to go to England to see where Joanna lived, and her burial site, and I had an awesome foursome, not the Beatles, to guide me. Arthur Torrington, the President of the Equiano Society in London, took a whole day to guide me around London to the spots where Equiano lived and wrote his memoir, and he took me to Joanna's grave, which was discovered a few years earlier by Vincent Carretta, buried under vines in Abney Park Cemetery. Standing with Arthur and looking at Joanna's gravestone the reality hit me—this is a real person I'm writing about. She lived, and breathed, and died—and is buried right here.

I had very much wanted to meet Angelina Osborne, and I had the privilege the next day. She has done the most extensive research on Joanna Vassa Bromley, and she answered all my questions over a delicious Indian lunch. Vanessa Salter, at the Wilberforce Museum, shared my passion for William Wilberforce, and gave me much-needed advice. And Stephen Wombwell was an unexpected gift! My husband and I took the train to Clavering, to visit the church where Joanna's husband served as pastor, and see the countryside, and Stephen, the organist at Clavering Christian Centre, was very gracious. He showed us the church where

Joanna and Henry ministered, treated us to lunch at a nearby pub, and tea and cake at his home, sharing with us his knowledge of the church and of the Bromleys. He also gave me a copy of Henry Bromley's history of the church. These newfound friends deepened my knowledge of Joanna and her life in England. Any factual errors are mine alone, but any factual truths are largely due to the guidance of my awesome foursome.

Jacqueline Cooper helped immensely with details on Clavering. Special thanks to Philippa Gregory for answering my email and encouraging me on my research and writing back in 2013. My earliest readers Jean Parms and Velma Mitchell offered much helpful advice, along with subsequent readers Kimberly Reeve, Patricia Jones-Lewis, and Frances Thompson-Gee. Thanks also to my fellow writers at the North Jersey Christian Writers' Group, and to Barbara Higby for her leadership. Jim Hart, my agent at Hartline Literary Agency, worked tirelessly to find a publisher for me in the early stages of the book.

Candyce Edelen supported me in many ways, including the use of her lovely home for a writing space. My good friend Doreen Herron has been an invaluable friend and cheerleader. Colin Watson created some beautiful art for my draft copies; Ruby Evangel and Juan Sena never neglected to ask me how my writing was going. Dr. Talia Schaffer, my favorite professor at Queen College CUNY, always believed I could write this book. Diana Birchall, a wonderful, resourceful fellow Janeite, helped me understand the Georgian era and boarding schools. Diane Stockwell at The Editorial Department, used her keen editorial prowess to enable me to revise *Remnant*, reducing the dialogue and increasing the tension.

My sister Caroline has been a great encouragement to me and also my marketing guru! She continues to remind me of the importance of marketing, and this book and its launch would not be the same without her work with me and on me behind the scenes. Immense thanks and love to my husband Bill—I appreciate your forbearance when I mention Equiano or *Remnant* to the uninitiated. Thank you for supporting me as I travel, write, revise, laugh, cry, and rejoice during the long road to publication. Finally, I thank my Lord God for giving me vision, creativity, and stamina to write *Remnant* and see it through to publication.

# Helpful Books

MANY AUTHORS HAVE RESEARCHED the time period and people in my book, and know much more than I do. The most useful book on Equiano and his family is *Equiano, The African*, by Dr. Vincent Carretta. Dr. Carretta also patiently answered some of my pressing questions and guided my research process.

Both non-fiction and fiction books aided my research:

*Equiano, The African*, Vincent Carretta
*Bury the Chains*, Adam Hochschild
*Rough Crossings*, Simon Schama
*Epic Journeys of Freedom*, Cassandra Pybus
*Africans in America*, Charles Johnson and Patricia Smith
*Death or Liberty—African Americans and Revolutionary America*, Douglas Egerton
*Staying Power: The History of Black People in Britain*, Peter Fryer
*William Wilberforce*, John Pollock
*Hero for Humanity: A Biography of William Wilberforce*, Kevin Belmonte
*William Wilberforce: The Life of the Great Anti-Slave Trade Campaigner*, William Hague
*The Negro in the American Revolution*, Benjamin Quarles
*The Forgotten Fifth*, Gary B. Nash
*Water From the Rock: Black Resistance in a Revolutionary Age*, Sylvia Frey
*Black Ivory: Slavery in the British Empire*, James Walvin
*South Carolina Rice Plantation*, J.H. Easterby
*Sacred Hunger*, Barry Unger
*New York Burning*, Jill Lepore
*A Respectable Trade*, Philippa Gregory
*Hornet's Nest*, Jimmy Carter
*Burning Bright*, Tracy Chevalier
*Chesapeake*, James Michener
*1776*, David McCullogh
*Someone Knows My Name*, Lawrence Hill

# Book Club Questions

1. *Remnant* opens with Ledu and Olu's kidnapping. What scenes were especially vivid in chapter one, helping you sense the terror they must have felt?

2. What is the role of William Wilberforce and the abolition movement in *Remnant*?

3. Sadie is an important character in the novel. At what point did you realize how she is related to Joanna? How important is her character to the plot of the novel?

4. Female characters drive the plot and are central to the action. Would you describe any of the female characters as feminists? Which character do you most admire, and why?

5. Olu's escape mirrors the experience of thousands of slaves in the late 18$^{th}$ century. Have you read any slave narratives with escape scenes? How do escape scenes shine a spotlight on the horrors of slavery?

6. What are the primary themes in *Remnant*? Which of these themes relate strongly to both storylines?

7. Have you read dual-storyline novels before? Did you find yourself gravitating more to one storyline than the other? Did that change as you continued to read?

8. How do the two storylines enhance and complement each other? At what points do they intersect?

9. Olu and Joanna are the primary characters, while Teddy and Henry are secondary characters. Which passages highlight this dichotomy?

10. Did the depiction of interracial marriages in the novel affect your views of those unions?

11. Several minor characters make brief appearances—Captain Williams, Abner, Phillip Astley, Cap'n Thomas, Lord Dunmore, Maisie, Miss Martha, Suraya, Ambrose, Sushila, and others. Who were your favorite minor characters, and why?

12. Which leading man, Teddy or Henry, do you find more appealing? Why?

13. Were you familiar with the lesser-known aspects of the American Revolution and the role of enslaved people covered in chapters 15, 17, and 19? See the book list to learn more about this time period.

14. What is the role of race, self-esteem, and self-image in *Remnant*? How do Joanna and Olu overcome racist attitudes and behaviors?